The Keeping

Nicky Charles

Edited by Jan Gordon
Line edits by Moody Edits

Cover Design by Jazer Designs
Cover images used under license from Shutterstock.com
Tree and sky image used with permission from Sydney H. Brown
Paw print and wolf logo Copyright © Doron Goldstein, Designer

ISBN: 978-0-9951879-6-2

Acknowledgements

Many thanks to Jan Gordon who acted as my editor and tirelessly read, reread, advised, poked and prodded until this project was complete. Also, thank you to Ermintrude for her invaluable advice on locations and journalism. Finally, thanks to all of the 'Gutter Girls' and my readers at FictionPress who have offered their feedback, encouragement and allowed me to practise my writing skills on them.

In addition to the above, I would also like to thank Sydney H. Brown for allowing the use of his photograph on the cover.

Foreword

This book is a sequel to The Mating, my first Lycan story. Many people became enamoured with the characters in that book and kept asking what happened to them. Ryne especially seemed to capture readers' imaginations and so, in response to those many requests, this tale was written. I hope you enjoy the story as much as I enjoyed writing it.

The Keeping

The keeping of our secret is a wolf's primary duty. Threats of exposure must be swiftly eradicated. Should more than two outsiders learn of our existence, dispersal of the young will begin immediately. Remaining members will obliterate all evidence of the pack's existence. Humanity is a disease covering the earth, a force that cannot be fought. Better that a few should die to stop the scourge, than to risk the perishment of all.

Source: The Book of the Law

Prologue

Chicago, Illinois, USA...

The room was silent, except for the ticking of the grandfather clock that stood majestically near the doorway and the faint sounds of the old man's breathing. To look at him, one might wonder if he was alive or only a wax figure; his eyes were unblinking and the rise and fall of his chest were barely perceptible. His gnarled hands rested lightly on the arms of the chair in which he sat, their occasional tightening the only real sign of the emotion he was feeling.

Pale winter sunlight, so typical of early January, was valiantly trying to brighten the large, cluttered room. Its weak rays crept past the heavy velvet curtains and cast a beam across the floor, creating a bright swatch in the otherwise gloomy interior. Small specks of dust drifted lazily on the faint air currents before settling on the laden surfaces of the tables and shelves.

Sculptures, figurines and books covered every flat surface of the room. Similarly, artwork filled the dark panelled walls, yet the gentleman in the chair deemed his collection to be paltry and inadequate. Or, at least he'd felt that way until now. Years of searching and gathering everything related to his favourite theme had finally paid off.

The faintest movement near the corners of his mouth would let an astute observer know he was pleased. Over the fireplace mantel hung his latest acquisition. Studying it with care, his gaze traced over the subject matter, analyzing and assessing. A quiet grunt and a slight movement of his head was the only acknowledgement he gave that here was what he had spent his whole life looking for.

"That will be all, Franklin." His voice was deep and strong despite his years, instantly commanding respect and obedience.

A man, dressed in the formal garb of a butler, stepped out of the shadows that clung to the edges of the room and bowed at the waist. "Yes, Mr. Greyson. If you need anything else, just ring." Silently, the servant picked up the step ladder he had used to hang the picture and left the room, quietly shutting the heavy mahogany door behind him.

As Franklin's footsteps faded into the distance, the older man stood and advanced towards the fireplace. His steps were sure, his stride long—no decrepit shuffling for him, despite his years and the aching of his joints. Clasping his hands behind his ramrod straight back, he stood in front of the framed photo.

Excitement was bubbling inside him, though his calm countenance gave no sign. This was what he'd been searching for. Everything else in the room was now worthless. His priceless statues, the expensive glossy books, paintings by renowned artists; they all paled in comparison to this one piece.

"Proof." He whispered the word to himself, his eyes alight with a fire that had been missing for years. "After all this time, I finally have proof." Reaching out his hand, he traced the name scrawled in the corner of the picture matte. "Whoever you are, Ryne Taylor, you've made me a very happy man."

After those few words, he fell silent again, contemplating the subject matter of the picture. He'd acquired it two months ago and had spent the intervening time examining it, studying angles, looking for shadows, measuring length and distance, pouring over minute details with a magnifying glass. There was no refuting what he'd found. Now the amber eyes in the photo glared at him, challenging and arrogant, almost as if they knew his plan and were daring him to try and execute it.

Eventually the man looked away, staring at the thick carpeting beneath his feet. A dry chuckle rumbled in his chest. "I can't hold your gaze. You're not even here, yet you manage to be dominant." Shaking his head, he made his way back to his chair and sat down heavily. Picking up the phone, he dialled a familiar number and then waited impatiently for someone to answer, drumming his fingers on the arm of the chair. When the call was finally answered, he wasted no time on pleasantries.

"Greyson here. I need to talk to you, Aldrich ... What about?" He gave a short bark of laughter while looking up at the picture again. "A wolf, of course."

Stump River, Ontario, Canada...

Ryne wiped his hands on a greasy rag and pulled down on the hood of the aging pickup truck. He sauntered to the far side of the garage and pitched the filthy rag in the garbage. "Filter's changed, Ben. Anything else?"

Ben Miller looked up from the service desk, where he was totalling the work orders. "Nope. That's it for the day. Thanks for coming in to help."

"No problem. I can use the extra cash. The money pit I bought wants new plumbing."

Ben rubbed the back of his neck as he contemplated the man before him. Not for the first time did he question why a young fellow like Ryne Taylor would choose to live in such a godforsaken place as

Stump River. Not that Ben didn't like his hometown, he was just aware of its limitations. No nightlife except for the local bar and Wednesday night bingo at the church. A two-hour drive to the next largest community. Young people *left* Stump River, they didn't move here.

Mind you, George and Mary Nelson were mighty happy Taylor was bucking the trend. He'd bought their crumbling house and the large parcel of land it sat on. There hadn't even been any quibbling over the cost; he'd paid the asking price without batting an eye. The sale had provided the town with a nice bit of gossip to help pass the winter, as well as allowing the elderly Nelsons to retire to Timmins, a larger urban centre, in relative luxury. Ben looked around his small business and smirked. Maybe Taylor would buy his place, too, should he ever decide to retire.

Watching Ryne get cleaned up at the nearby sink, Ben felt a touch of envy. The local ladies positively drooled whenever Ryne was in town. Even his own wife wasn't immune. Ben had unwillingly eavesdropped on her conversation with a friend last night and had started to feel inadequate after listening to them go on about his black hair, blue eyes and devilishly sexy smile. Their words, not his, of course. When they'd started to enumerate his physical attributes—broad shoulders, long legs, lean hips and a muscular body—he'd turned the TV on real loud to drown them out.

Ben shook his head. All he saw when he looked at Ryne was a hard-working, confident man who knew his way around an engine. That was enough in his books. Ryne helped him out at the garage a few days each week and Ben was grateful for the assistance.

"Got any plans for the weekend?" Ryne had dried off and walked over to where Ben was working. He leaned against the counter and chugged down a bottle of water.

"The wife and daughter want me to take them into Timmins shopping. We might go to a show while we're there, too."

"Sounds like fun." Ryne wiped his mouth on the back of his hand and threw the bottle into the recycling bin. "I'm going to be working on the house, as usual."

"It was a huge project you undertook when you bought the place."

"I know, but I like the area and it came with a lot of land. My friends and I like our privacy."

"To each their own." Ben shrugged and handed Ryne a paycheque. "Here. Don't spend it all in one place."

Ryne laughed while stuffing the cheque in his pocket. "Nah. I'll spread it around. Some at the hardware store, some at the lumber yard and some at the bar."

"Lucy will be happy to see you, I'm sure." Ben mocked good-naturedly as the man walked out the door. Ryne merely waved and continued on his way. Lucy worked at the local bar and had been real cozy with Ryne ever since he and his friends had moved to the area a few months back.

Watching Ryne cross the street, Ben wondered about the man and the two other fellows, Bryan and Daniel, who lived with him. They weren't related, looking nothing alike, but something bound them together. At first, there'd been rumours they were gay, but their behaviour at the bar on Friday nights soon dispelled that rumour. The local lovelies swarmed around them and they did little to discourage the attention, especially the younger two.

Ryne was more discriminating. Oh, he'd been involved with a few of the local girls before settling on Lucy, but for the most part he held his liquor and was usually the one dragging the other two home at closing time, provided they hadn't hooked up with some woman beforehand. Ben chuckled. Business at the bar was a lot brisker since those three had moved into the community.

A few residents thought the newcomers were strange, but except for the fact they all lived together in the middle of nowhere, no one had any real complaints against them. The men were polite and didn't bother anyone. Most likely, it was as Ryne said; they'd moved here for privacy and because they liked the area. Nothing strange or mysterious about that.   .

Chapter 1

Smythston, Oregon, USA...

Damn! A sick feeling settled in Mel's stomach as she lost control of the vehicle and it began to slide across the snow-slicked roads into the oncoming lane. A horn blared as she managed to avoid an oncoming pickup truck, but relief from the near-miss lasted but the blink of an eye. A telephone post loomed ahead and she clenched the steering wheel tighter, trying to steer into the skid while bracing herself for the impact that was sure to come. When it didn't, she sent up a brief prayer of thanks.

"Stupid, snow covered roads." Muttering to herself, she felt the car straighten out of the skid, wincing as the vehicle almost brushed a farmer's mailbox. Moving back into her own lane, she blew a puff of air up over her face causing her bangs to float up and then settle back on her forehead. Annoyingly, her lashes kept catching in the too-long fringe of hair and she reminded herself she really needed to make time for a cut. Not daring to take her hands off the wheel to push her hair out of the way, she blinked rapidly finally managing to free her lashes and clear her vision.

The forecast had called for light snow, but the weatherman was obviously an idiot and didn't know a high-pressure zone from a low. Heavy white flakes were falling on her windshield and the wipers were having a hard time keeping up. Twice now, she'd stopped and cleaned the accumulated white stuff from the blades.

In retrospect, she shouldn't have trusted the fellow at the rental agency. He'd said the car was fine despite its appearance. At ten o'clock at night, after a long flight squished between a large man and a frazzled mother with a crying baby, all she had wanted to do was get a car, escape the confines of the airport and find a room at the nearby motel. Now she wished she'd been more particular.

A road sign proclaimed her destination, Smythston, Oregon, was rapidly approaching and she breathed a sigh of relief. She'd had a late start, having been up half the night listening to planes land and take off, and now her two-hour trip had turned into four hours of white-knuckle driving. Hopefully the room she'd booked was still available. The Grey Goose Tea Room sounded quaint and boasted luxury rooms with home-cooked meals. A hot shower and dinner followed by a nap were exactly what she needed...if she survived the drive!

An oncoming transport trailer uncaringly doused her car in slush and she swore vigorously as her view of the road disappeared. Flicking the wipers onto high, she peered out of the streaked windshield and wondered once again at the sanity of taking on this particular job. It was an odd assignment but paid well, and since she was next thing to being broke, she couldn't be too choosy.

After years of working dead-end jobs, she'd finally gone back to school, enrolling in the journalism program at Northwestern University. Computers might have been a more practical course but she knew she'd never be able to sit in an office all day, every day. She had itchy feet like her mother, which was probably why she'd constantly drifted from one job to another. After the initial thrill of learning a new skill wore off, she soon lost interest and found herself searching the want ads for yet another position.

Once she was a journalist, an employer would pay for her to move around. It wouldn't be a great wage, but it would be something she enjoyed, and it might help lessen the restlessness within her. Talking to people, visiting new locations, researching backgrounds; each day would be different. Or at least that's what she hoped.

Right now, she was taking a year off, being halfway through the four-year program and completely out of funds. By juggling two waitressing jobs and writing a few freelance articles, she was hoping to make enough money to go back to school next year and finish the program. That was why this job was exactly what she needed. A lawyer named Leon Aldrich had contacted her on behalf of a client—a wealthy client, no less—to do some work as an investigative journalist.

He claimed a college instructor had suggested her and she'd hesitantly accepted the explanation while wondering who had put in the good word for her. The lawyer had merely smirked, saying she'd been chosen from a number of other candidates and it was best not to look a gift horse in the mouth. Not quite sure what to make of the man, she'd shrugged and listened to his offer.

The job was a lucrative one. In exchange for a ridiculously large sum of money, she was to research a photographer named Ryne Taylor and write a piece on his life. After thoroughly checking out the lawyer's references and those of his client, Anthony Greyson, she'd decided the job was legitimate and agreed to the man's terms.

It was pretty simple. Find the reclusive Mr. Taylor. Research his life, how he chose his subjects, where he took his pictures and who had purchased them. She was to give updates on each new development, write a final article and then submit it to the lawyer. All expenses were paid and there was a very loose deadline.

The job seemed almost too good to be true, but if life was going to hand her a golden egg on a silver platter, she wasn't going to turn her nose up at it. She frowned thinking she had certainly slaughtered the use of those clichés. It was a good thing her thoughts were her own and not subject to editorial criticism.

Taking note of her surroundings, she realized she was now inside the town proper and, after following the directions on the brochure, soon found herself in the entryway of the Grey Goose talking to a distinguished looking gentleman who had introduced himself as Edward Mancini.

"Yes, Ms. Greene, I took your reservation over the phone last night. I'm so glad the weather didn't delay your travel plans too much."

She smiled and brushed her hair out of her face for probably the fiftieth time that day; she really did need to get it cut. "It wasn't the most pleasant drive, but I made it."

"Well, we're glad you're here safe and sound. If you'll follow me, Ms. Greene, I'll show you to your room."

"Please, call me Melody." Using her most ingratiating smile, she looked up at the man and noted in response, a faint upturning at the corners of his mouth. Personally, she didn't care much for her name and usually went by Mel, but men seemed to like the more feminine version and as a wannabe hard-nosed journalist, she didn't hesitate to use the fact to her advantage.

"Melody, then. And you may call me Edward."

As she walked behind him, she gave herself a point. Getting on a first name basis with the people you were going to interview was a great way to encourage them to open up to you, or so her college instructors had told her. And, while she wasn't going to be interviewing this man, she was hoping to extract a few bits of information from him.

As he led her into her room, she noticed he was looking at her surreptitiously. She knew what he would see. At five foot four, she wasn't tall, but she balked against the label of short. Her figure was a little disproportionate, being rather too rounded up top and bit narrow in comparison around the hips. Her legs were slim and thankfully, due to that fact, looked longer than they actually were. Shoulder length, honey brown hair and deep brown eyes gave her a warm, friendly look as did her generous smile.

Her college professors had said her friendly, girl-next-door appearance would help her make contacts and win the confidence of those she interviewed. Personally, she wasn't so sure. She'd rather be a drop-dead gorgeous, sophisticated reporter, the kind who could wrap an interviewee around her finger with a mere bat of her eyelashes and some pithy repartee. Of course, that wasn't likely to happen and she really was too old to be wasting her time on fantasies. Projecting the image of a solid, competent reporter was a more realistic goal.

It was impossible for Mr. Mancini to know what she was thinking, but for some reason the man's lips twitched as he finished giving her a once-over. He made no comment however, merely nodding his head and exiting the room, softly pulling the door shut behind him.

As the locking mechanism clicked into place, she turned to examine her room only to catch sight of herself in the mirror. A mortified groan escaped her. No wonder Mr. Mancini had trouble keeping a straight face. Her hair was a mess, her coat was buttoned crooked and there was a smudge of chocolate from her make-shift lunch smeared across her chin.

Her shoulders sagged. So much for looking competent. Oh well, even if she looked a mess, Edward seemed to like her, and that meant he'd most likely be willing to talk to her when she started doing her research.

She shrugged off her coat then sat on the edge of the bed and removed her boots before flopping backwards on the mattress. As she stared at the ceiling, she ran over her mental checklist on 'how to be a journalist'. Establish contacts—check. Be friendly so the other person will open up and talk to you—check. Listen attentively— umm, not quite a check. That was always the hardest part for her. She was a bubbly, outgoing sort who loved to talk and kept forgetting she wasn't supposed to interrupt the interviewee with her own random thoughts. In her mind, she tattooed the words 'shut up, Mel' across her brain, while ruefully acknowledging it probably wouldn't help.

Last on her to-do list was reporting the real story, without personal bias creeping in. That earned her another partial check. According to her instructors, she needed to report the facts, not opinions. Unfortunately, she had lots of opinions about almost everything and found it hard not to air them. At least this assignment was a straightforward report on a person's life. The man took pictures of flowers and wildlife; he wasn't likely to be involved in anything controversial, right?

The final report wasn't due for several months, so once she'd tracked the fellow down and interviewed him, there'd be plenty of time to write his life story. Writing was what she did best and those were the courses where she'd received her highest marks. Words flowed through her mind and onto the page in an unending stream. In fact, writing too much tended to be her biggest failing. Luckily, this report didn't have to fit the confines of a newspaper column, so she'd be able to ramble as much as she wished, provided Mr. Taylor had anything in his life worth rambling about!

So far, she hadn't discovered much. He was a photographer of some minor renown specializing in nature photography. A few art galleries had shown his work with sales being modest. The picture which had sparked her benefactor's interest had been purchased at Bastian's Fine Art Gallery in Smythston, Oregon which was only a short drive from the man's last known address. The previous week, she'd phoned the gallery, but the call had produced very little information. Yes, they had sold a Ryne Taylor photograph to a Mr. Greyson. No, there was no information available to the public about the photographer himself.

She'd latched on to that last statement. The fact the information wasn't available to the public meant there *was* information, she just needed to get her hands on it. Unable to find an address or phone number for the mysterious Mr. Taylor, she was resorting to old fashioned legwork by travelling halfway across the country in the middle of February to this small nondescript town.

Stretching, she ran her hands through her hair and forced herself to sit up. While she would prefer to be investigating someone on a tropical island, her present location wasn't all bad. Giving a small bounce, she deemed the bed comfortable and then looked around the room, for the first time taking real note of her surroundings.

Decorated in turn-of-the-century elegance, the room had gleaming wood and rich hues throughout, creating a warm and welcoming atmosphere. Aside from the mirror that had revealed her less than perfect appearance, there was a small fireplace with a love seat in front of it, a breakfast table and two chairs, a bed, night tables and a dresser. A door to the side of the room appeared to lead to the bathroom, which reminded her she wanted a warm shower and a meal.

Calling the front desk, she ordered dinner and then headed for the shower, emerging fifteen minutes later wrapped in a white terrycloth robe and feeling considerably refreshed.

Her timing was perfect. A knock on the door signalled the arrival of her meal and her stomach rumbled in anticipation. Thanking the slight girl who wheeled the cart in, Melody spared her a glance. She had dark hair and green eyes; a pretty thing, only a bit younger than herself.

"If you need anything else, just call downstairs and ask for me. My name's Elise."

"Thanks." She lifted the lid off her plate and inhaled the delectable scent of steak cooked to perfection. "Have you worked here long?"

"About four months. I usually work in the tearoom but Mr. Mancini asked if I'd help out up here this weekend. There's a flu bug going around and he's short-handed."

She forced herself to ignore her meal in favour of cultivating yet another local contact. Four months was long enough for Elise to have possibly encountered the elusive photographer. "This seems like a lovely place. Do you get lots of business?"

"It's steady. Quite a few locals stop by downstairs for lunch and some rent rooms for weekend getaways or if they have company and need a place for guests to stay. And, of course, we get a few travellers such as yourself. Where are you headed?"

"Actually, I'm a freelance journalist and I'm researching local artists for an article." That was the story Mr. Aldrich, the lawyer, had told her to use. He didn't want anyone knowing who she was really working for. Mr. Greyson was very private.

Elise smiled at her. "Be sure to check out Bastian's Gallery, then. It's just down the road. They show quite a few of the local artists."

"Thanks. I'll put them at the top of my list." She noticed Elise was rubbing her stomach. Was the girl coming down with the flu, too? Or was she pregnant? She recalled a fellow waitress had always been rubbing her belly when she was expecting.

"I need to get back to work. I hope you enjoy your stay here." Elise headed towards the door.

"I'm sure I will. It's been nice talking to you, Elise." Just then, her stomach rumbled again and she pulled a self-deprecating face.

Elise laughed softly and pulled the door shut behind her.

With Elise on her way, Mel sat down to enjoy her dinner. As she'd suspected, the food was delicious and soon her plate was empty. Giving a satisfied sigh, she sat back and checked her watch. It was five-thirty. She could walk down to Bastian's Gallery and see what information she could dig up about Ryne Taylor, but she was tired and making subtle inquiries was too much of an effort at the moment. A nap was eminently more appealing.

She rummaged through her suitcase, finding an old t-shirt to sleep in and quickly changed into it. Her skin immediately raised into goose bumps as the cool cotton slid over her body. Shivering, she pushed back the duvet then climbed between the crisp sheets. As her body heat warmed the bed, she felt her muscles relaxing and with a sigh, she closed her eyes. She'd take a short nap and then.

.

Chapter 2

Sun streamed in through the lace curtains and fell upon the table situated in front of the window. It glinted off the highly polished wood surface and cast a cheery glow over the whole room. The brightness made Mel squint and grumble against the assault on her vision. Her little nap yesterday had been much longer than she'd intended. Despite sleeping for over twelve hours, or perhaps because of it, she felt exceptionally groggy that morning. Maybe it was due to the fact this was the first time in ages that she had actually been able to get a decent night's sleep. Whatever the reason, her body was reluctant to let go of the wonderful sensation of resting in a warm cloud of eiderdown and fresh linen.

Back home in Chicago, her little apartment had intermittent heating, a lumpy mattress and paper-thin walls. The latter provided her with the privilege of hearing the tenants on all sides of her arguing, watching TV or engaging in...er...physical relations, at all hours of the day and night. That, on top of working two jobs in an effort to try and save money for her education, meant she was chronically bleary-eyed and over-tired. Friends told her to move, but being situated by the El—elevated train tracks—meant the rent was cheap and, with the building located midway between her two jobs, she felt she could suffer through the inadequacies of her dwelling with the ultimate goal of being able to afford better someday.

Blinking sleepily, she propped her chin up with her hand while sipping her coffee. The substantial windfall her assignment was paying meant she could quit one of her jobs and go back to school earlier than planned. With any luck, today she'd find out where Ryne Taylor resided and tomorrow she'd be on her way to his home. A few days of talking to him and the preliminary work would be done. This job was going to be a piece of cake.

A smile passed over her lips as she thought of how excited Mr. Taylor would be when he discovered he was the focus of an article. Trying to make a name for yourself in the art world was no easy task. Perhaps Mr. Greyson wanted to become the photographer's patron and the article was destined to be published in some fancy high-end art magazine. It would help her own career along, too. Yes, she and Mr. Taylor might both end up benefitting from their encounter in ways neither could even imagine.

Feeling the caffeine finally activating the synapses of her brain, she began to take a more active interest in the happenings outside her window. The snowstorm had passed by overnight and the sun was causing the temperature to rise. Icicles dripped from the eaves and the fluffy white snow of yesterday was slowly melting into a miserable, soggy mess. Early morning commuters drove slowly along the narrow downtown streets, streams of slush spewing behind them. Piles of snow lined either side of the roadway and merchants were out shovelling sidewalks and spreading salt on icy patches.

A silver pickup truck pulled in near the curb in front of the Grey Goose and she watched the scene below her with increasing attentiveness. First, a tall dark-haired man climbed out. From the second storey vantage point, she could easily make out his features and her heart beat faster in appreciation of his male beauty. He circled the vehicle and opened the passenger-side door, reaching in and lifting a woman out and over the piles of snow onto the safety of the sidewalk.

She smiled; good-looking, strong *and* chivalrous. Observing the man tenderly kissing the woman and then lingering to watch her walk away, she sighed with envy, her romantic streak coming to the fore. The fellow was smitten.

The woman turned to wave at the man and Mel caught a brief glimpse of her face. It was Elise, the girl who had brought in her meal last night. Lucky girl, to have a man like that! And wasn't that just the way? The good ones were always taken.

On that depressing note, she stood up and began to dress. The local businesses would be open for customers soon and it was time she got to work. She'd stop by the art gallery and see if she could wheedle any information out of the sales associates. Then, if it was a dead end, she'd search out Edward Mancini and maybe even Elise. There was always the possibility the photographer had stopped by the tearoom for lunch when he was at the gallery making arrangements for the sale of his photographs.

She wished she had a picture of the man, or at least a description. It was easier for people to recall someone from a photo rather than from a verbal description, of which she had neither. Glumly, she acknowledged Mr. Aldrich hadn't given her much to go on, beyond the man's name and occupation. At least the town wasn't too big. It was probably the kind of place where everyone knew everybody else's business.

Taking a final sip of her coffee, she put on her coat and left the room, her spirits high in anticipation of a successful morning.

Three hours later, she was back at the Grey Goose sitting in the downstairs tearoom, determinedly crunching a breadstick and totally unaware of her elegant surroundings. The potted plants, the period furniture, the soft music in the background, were all lost on her as she wallowed in her own bad mood. Her morning optimism had been seriously dashed and was now replaced by the starkness of reality.

After oohing and aahing over dubious artwork and schmoozing with the people who worked at Bastian's, she was still no closer to learning anything about Ryne Taylor. The staff at the gallery had been friendly and admitted they had sold some of his work, but no one was willing to talk about the man himself. All she'd garnered was the whole topic had a black cloud hanging over it. A few sly hints were dropped about a former, now missing, sales associate having had an affair with Taylor and misdirecting the proceeds from the sale of his work into her own account, but that was all she could discover.

When she'd first heard that little tidbit, the journalist in her had perked up her ears. A missing person, a steamy affair, pilfered funds; it had all the right elements to be a mystery worth investigating. Yet when she'd tried to dig for more specifics, everyone had clammed up, their barely suppressed enjoyment over the titillating scandal disappearing behind shuttered expressions. What were they hiding? Finally, the gallery owner himself had come over and glared at his workers, who had taken one look at his disapproving face and scurried off to the far corners of the establishment. Once they were gone, he'd addressed her coolly, informing her in the politest of tones she was keeping his employees from their work. Unless she was intending to buy something, she should be on her way.

Realizing she'd been too pushy, too soon, she left, all the while mentally kicking herself for alienating what was presently her only source of information. She knew she wasn't supposed to brazenly pump people for information, but subtlety was so frustrating and pregnant pauses made her fidget. Those people had information she needed. Why wouldn't they share? Surely, Mr. Taylor would welcome the publicity, if he only knew it was available to him!

Grabbing another breadstick, she bit into it, spewing bread crumbs all over the table. Right now Mr. Bastian was probably grilling his employees about her and even instructing them not to talk to her gallery again. Bastian's was going to be a dead end.

She'd glossed over that fact when she'd called Mr. Aldrich half an hour ago to report her findings. He'd been peeved she hadn't checked in last night, claiming to have been concerned about her safety. Even as she'd explained about being tired and the poor driving conditions, she knew in her gut the real reason for his attitude. The lawyer expected her to abscond with the large cash advance she'd been given.

Mr. Aldrich had never seemed too keen on her, his expression decidedly sour whenever they met. He felt she was under-qualified for the job and all but said so when delivering the news Mr. Greyson had picked her out of all the other applicants. Maybe it was because she was spending his client's money on a project he felt was foolish. Or maybe it was because Mr. Greyson was ignoring his lawyer's recommendations

Whatever the case, she hated reporting to him. Not only did he have a way or making her feel guilty, but she always felt the need for a thorough wash afterwards in order to remove any traces of their interaction, even if it had only been over the phone. This morning was no different. She'd stated the facts as succinctly as possible and explained her next move was going to be checking the archives of the local paper. The lawyer had reluctantly agreed with her plan and she'd hung up, feeling his disapproval oozing down the phone line.

With the unpleasant task over, she was free to sit and brood about her morning, something she was doing with great success. When a shadow fell across the table, she gave a start, having forgotten she was in a public restaurant. Looking up, she saw Elise standing beside her.

"Hi! You look down. Having a bad morning?" Elise's concerned inquiry immediately made her feel better. Here, at least, was one friendly face.

"Yeah. I was at Bastian's Gallery all morning. There's one particular artist I'm trying to get some background on for my article, but I struck out."

"They didn't have any information for you?"

"They said they didn't, but I think they're holding out on me."

"That's strange. Wouldn't an artist welcome publicity?" Elise furrowed her brow.

"You would think so."

A bell tinged in the distance and Elise glanced over her shoulder. "Oops, my order for table three is ready. Here's the menu. The luncheon specials are listed on the front. I'll be back in a minute to take your order."

Mel watched Elise's retreating form, thinking she'd try asking ask her about Ryne Taylor. Determined not to be quite so eager for information this time, she purposely engaged Elise in casual conversation when the girl returned.

"I saw you getting out of a pickup this morning. Was that your husband?"

"Yes." Elise rolled her eyes, seeming to be exasperated. "Kane's so over-protective right now. He wouldn't even let me drive in by myself this morning because of the snow."

"You mean he's not always like that?"

The waitress blushed prettily. "A bit, but it's getting worse now. I just found out I'm pregnant, and I swear he'd have me sitting with my feet up for the next eight months if I didn't demand otherwise."

She grinned inwardly. She'd been right last night! "Eight months? So you really did just find out. Those home pregnancy tests are getting more and more accurate, aren't they?"

"Actually, Kane scented..." She stopped and looked flustered. "I mean, Kane sensed...um..." Someone called her name, and she hurried away, appearing relieved to have a reason to abandon the conversation.

Sipping her water, Mel pondered what Elise had been going to say. Kane sensed...what? And why had she used the word 'scented' first? Dogs scented things, and from the glimpse she'd had of the man, he was anything but a mutt. The journalist inside her would love to pursue that but Elise's husband, while gorgeous, was not her primary concern.

Eventually, Elise returned with the lasagna Mel had ordered. The girl appeared leery so, to reassure her, Mel commented idly on the weather, holding back a smile as Elise started to relax. Through the course of the meal, Mel kept the conversation light whenever the waitress stopped by her table offering more water or breadsticks. By the time the meal was finished, Elise was chatting easily to her once again. Deciding to make her move, Mel casually introduced the subject foremost in her mind.

"Well, I suppose I'd better hit the streets again and see if anyone is willing to talk to me about local artists."

"Which artists are you interested in?" Elise glanced up from the debit machine in which she was entering the cost of the meal.

"A local photographer named Ryne Taylor. He used to live around here, but no one seems to know where he went." If she hadn't been watching, she'd have missed Elise's fleeting flinch. "Do you know anything about him?"

"Ryne...Taylor did you say? No, I don't believe I do. Of course, I only moved here in October." Elise kept her eyes down.

"Oh. That's too bad. I guess, I'll ask around town then." She was sure Elise was lying, but after her experience at Bastian's, she wasn't going to press the issue in case she needed the young woman for something else in the future.

Elise handed her the debit machine. Mel entered her PIN while watching Elise out of the corner of her eye. The server shifted her weight and worried her lip before posing a question in an overly casual voice. "Why are you asking about this particular photographer? I've never heard of him, so his work can't be very good."

"Someone who bought one of Mr. Taylor's pictures raved about the quality of his work so I thought I'd better check him out."

"Oh." Elise traced an idle pattern on the tablecloth with her finger. "Um...do you know what the subject of the picture was? If it was displayed at Bastian's, I might have noticed it once when I was shopping in the mall."

"I believe it was a picture of a wolf."

Elise noticeably paled. "Sorry, I... I have to get back to work. I'll see you later." She took a few steps back and then turned on her heel and scurried away.

Mel narrowed her eyes as she watched Elise leave. The girl knew something; the question was what?

She spent the afternoon at the Smythston library, looking through back issues of the local paper for any mention of Ryne Taylor. He did have an exhibit a year ago, but the article didn't include a picture of the man, nor anything else useful. Leaning back in her chair, she rubbed her forehead in frustration. It would seem Mr. Taylor was very ordinary or there would have been some mention of him. On the other hand, if he was so ordinary, why were the gallery and Elise withholding information about him? It was a puzzle and she had to solve it or risk having nothing to report to Mr. Aldrich. Arching her back, she pulled out yet another edition of the paper and got back to work.

Several hours later, she stood on the steps of the library, muttering under her breath and contemplating her next move. There must be a way to find Taylor. She'd long ago dropped the honorific 'Mr.' when thinking of the man. Anyone who was causing her this much frustration wasn't deserving of the extra title.

Shoving her hands in her pockets, she tilted her face to the sky, wishing inspiration would descend upon her. A few snowflakes were drifting lazily down and catching on her lashes, causing her to blink rapidly. If she hadn't been feeling grumpy about her unproductive day, she might have appreciated the lacy white precipitation. As it was, she merely brushed the flakes from her face, stomped down the steps and along the sidewalk, morosely noting how her pant cuffs were becoming soaked from the slush.

She was heading for the post office now, in the vain hope of finding a lead there. Possibly some mail was being delivered to Ryne's Smythston address. The local postmaster would need to redirect it to his new location, so maybe there was information to be had from that sector. Privacy laws would likely prevent her from having access to what she needed to know, but at this point, anything was worth a try.

Pushing open the heavy metal and glass doors, she entered the buff coloured building and glanced around. The impersonal atmosphere that habitually permeated all government offices greeted her. Scuffed terrazzo flooring, a bedraggled, fake fig tree and bland paint were the extent of the decor in the cavernous space. Post office boxes lined two walls and several kiosks stood in the middle of the room, displaying posters and various government brochures. At the far end of the room, people stood in a trance-like state waiting for their turn while others huddled around a nearby table, writing addresses on packages or affixing stamps.

Deciding she'd have a greater chance of success if there wasn't a long line, she pretended to peruse the posters and pamphlets while keeping an eye on the number of individuals awaiting service. No one spared her a glance, everyone busy with their own agendas.

The outer door opened, letting in a rush of cold air, causing the various papers and brochures to rustle in the breeze before settling down again. She glanced towards the source of the mini disturbance and was surprised to see Elise entering with her hunky husband. They appeared to be having a heated discussion, and some inner voice told Mel to make herself scarce.

Positioning herself on the far side of the kiosk, she concentrated to hear what the two were saying, thankful she'd been blessed with uncommonly keen hearing. Despite their voices being low, she managed to catch most of the conversation.

"I said I'd never heard of him, but I don't know if she believed me or not." Elise whispered to her husband.

Mel frowned. What had Elise said his name was? Kyle...? Ken...? Kane! That was it.

A male voice rumbled in reply. "And you say she mentioned the wolf picture?"

"Uh huh. She said someone had told her about it and now she wants to write an article on him."

"Damn! I knew that picture was bad news. I've tried to get it back without letting anyone know why. Hell, I've even offered to buy it for an exorbitant amount, but the agent representing the buyer claims it's not for sale at any price. Whoever owns it must know its significance."

"Maybe not. We might be jumping to conclusions. It was a good picture so perhaps someone likes it for its artistic merit."

Something growled and Mel had to resist the urge to peek out from her hiding spot. Did they have a dog with them?

"Kane! Shh! You know better than to do that in public." Elise admonished.

Mel frowned. Apparently, the man had been doing the growling. What a strange habit.

"Sorry. This is my worst nightmare. Someone discovering—"

Elise interrupted her husband and Mel nearly started growling herself. Discover what? Silently, she urged Kane to continue, but of course he didn't. Elise spoke in soothing tones. "Even if the owner of the photograph is suspicious, there's no way they'll ever discover where the picture was taken. The land is private and you've never allowed outsiders into the territory unsupervised. Plus, we've covered Ryne's tracks carefully and after the debacle of the missing payments for Ryne's other work, Bastian's doesn't want to be sued, so they're bending over backwards to keep us happy. They won't say anything. And the rest of the pack has always kept a low profile. No one really knows much about Ryne, least of all where he moved to."

Kane muttered something indiscernible and the two moved out of hearing range.

Mel inhaled deeply and tried to quiet her pounding heart. These people knew where Ryne was! And not only that, there really *was* some form of mystery surrounding the man and his photograph. She wished she could have seen the picture in question, but Mr. Aldrich said his client didn't allow casual viewings. It must be something pretty special though, to warrant all the money being spent to find the photographer.

After what seemed like an interminable amount of time, Mel saw the line consisted of only Elise and Kane. Edging closer, she buried her head in a brochure and eavesdropped some more.

"Good afternoon, I'd like to mail this to Stump River, Ontario, Canada. How much will that cost?"

Mel hazarded a peek and saw Elise place a package wrapped in brown paper on the ledge. As the postal worker weighed the package, the girl smiled up at her husband. "Do you think Ryne will like the sweater I bought for his birthday?"

"He'd adore a potato sack if you sent it to him." Kane sounded disgruntled and Elise laughed.

"Kane, I can't believe you're still jealous of him. You must know there's nothing between us. I'm having your child and I love you."

He bent over and kissed her cheek. "I know and I love you, too. It's never been a question of your affections. It's Ryne's interest in you that bothers me."

"He was joking, Kane."

"Possibly, but like I always said, once he gets his own..."

The conversation stopped as the postal worker announced the cost of mailing the parcel. Kane paid for the postage and the package was set to the side, being too large to fit in a regular mail slot. Mel watched them leave curious what Kane had been referring to. His own what?

Shaking her head to clear it of the questions floating about in her active imagination, she approached the counter and smiled at the frazzled woman behind the counter. "Hi! I was wondering if you could help me..." She paused as her gaze fell upon the package sitting only a foot away, awaiting mailing. It had Ryne's address printed neatly on the front in large block letters. Cha-ching! Jackpot! Okay, now she just had to distract the woman in order to get a good look at the label.

"Yes? You were wondering...?" The worker raised her brows, prompting Mel to continue.

"Oh, sorry. Yes...um...I was wondering if anyone had turned in my car keys. I think I dropped them in here yesterday."

"I wasn't working yesterday, but I'll go check in the back." The postal employee gave her a distracted smile and turned away. Mel leaned forward, craning her neck in order to see the address on the package clearly.

RR#1, Stump River, Ontario, Canada.

Stump River? What kind of a name was that? And Canada?

Hearing the postal worker returning, she memorized the address and was leaning casually against the counter by time the woman returned.

"Sorry. There were no keys turned in yesterday. Are you sure you lost them here?"

"It could have been on the street, but with all this snow..." She shrugged. "That's okay. I have a spare set."

The woman eyed her suspiciously. "You're not from around here, are you?"

"No, I'm passing through. Thanks for your help, though." She quickly walked away before the woman could asking more questions.

As she made her way back to the Grey Goose, she began to plan her strategy. First, she'd call Mr. Aldrich with an update then head back to Chicago first thing in the morning. It would probably take her a week to research Stump River and look for any record of Ryne Taylor in Canada. There had to be a reason he moved so far north? Was he hiding something? Or hiding from someone?

Excitement bubbled up inside her. Originally the assignment had only appealed because of its monetary rewards. But now with an actual mystery being involved, it was much more interesting.

What might Taylor look like? If the fates were with her, he'd turn out to be attractive, like Elise's husband. Of course, guys like that didn't grow on trees. Knowing her luck, the photographer would be seventy years old, balding and pot-bellied.

Chapter 3

Two weeks later, in Stump River...

Ryne sat quietly, nursing his drink in the local pub called The Broken Antler. Its name came from the old weathered set of moose antlers that dangled precariously on a rusty chain over the entrance. At one time, there'd been an actual moose head adorning the front of the building and the pub had naturally acquired the name The Moose Head. But when decay finally set in, and the trophy tumbled to the ground during an exceptionally windy storm, only the antlers remained in one piece. Armand St. John, the owner of the dubious establishment and an eminently practical man, salvaged the almost intact, yellowing rack, hung it over the door and renamed the pub to suit.

A dry chuckle escaped Ryne's lips as he watched Armand working behind the bar, simultaneously serving beer, laughing at a customer's off-coloured jokes and keeping a watchful eye over the activity on the floor. The bartender's name really didn't suit him at all. Armand St. John sounded like some effete interior designer and the bartender was anything but. Closer to seven foot than six, his body structure was like a bear and his appearance was not far off either; curly black hair peeked out of the collar of his shirt and covered the top of his head as well as the lower half of his face, his acquaintance with a barber or scissors obviously but a distant memory. A genial sort, he ruled the pub with an iron fist, acting as bouncer when the locals got too rowdy and providing a listening and sympathetic ear when needed.

The establishment, like its owner, was rough around the edges. Basically a decent place, it was clean but not fancy. Wooden planks, scarred from years of use, covered the floor. The walls were decorated with plaques, a few dartboards and some questionable artwork ranging from movie posters and dogs playing poker, to a few poorly done oil paintings. Some whispered the pictures had been painted by Armand himself, though no one dared to ask.

It was Friday night and the usual crowd had swelled due to the hockey game playing on the big screen TV Armand had proudly installed a few months earlier. The favourite team was in danger of being out of the running for the playoffs and everyone had gathered to lend moral support. By some miracle, they were up three points and shouts of excitement rang out from all corners of the packed room. Waitresses scurried through the crowds, trays of beer, hotdogs and pretzels skilfully balanced over their heads. Miraculously, they avoided the erratic movements of the patrons and managed to complete their jobs without mishap.

The heat from dozens of bodies, the flickering lights from the TV screen and the sounds from a myriad of conversations bombarded Ryne's senses. He let it all wash over him as he sat in the far corner, content to hide in the relative peace and darkness it offered. His eyes were half-closed as he watched the activity around him, his breathing deep and even, his body appearing relaxed. He was in his own isolated bubble, detached from his surroundings, yet aware on some instinctual level, in case something occurred that required a quick reaction.

Hockey was a fine game, the company was good, but tonight he had no interest in either the sport or in socializing. It was only at the insistence of his friends,

Daniel and Bryan, that he'd conceded to leave the house. Lately, he'd been feeling out of sorts and he was sure they were trying to cheer him up, not only as part of their duty as friends, but because they were tired of dealing with his moods.

Maybe it was the fact it was his birthday, and he was another year older. He didn't feel older, despite what the calendar said. Tired, yes. Older, no. The renovations on his house were extensive and almost every waking hour was spent trying to repair the place. It was hard work, but he didn't mind it. Sitting and doing nothing all winter would have driven him insane. The work gave him a purpose, even if it wore him out. So yes, he *was* tired, but that wasn't the real problem.

Taking another sip of his beer, he thought about the package he'd received in the mail this morning. His sister-in-law, Elise, had sent him a sweater for his birthday and a collection of cards from other members of the pack. It had been nice to read their well-wishes, but now he was feeling melancholy, missing the family he'd left behind. It wasn't as easy as he'd thought it would be, striking out on his own. The hard work and lack of money weren't difficult to deal with; it was the absence of an extended family. He was used to being part of a large group and now there was only himself and his two friends. They got along fine, but sometimes the large house he'd purchased felt empty and cold. Lately, he'd find himself looking around and imagining what it would be like to have happy voices and friendly faces filling the place.

Shifting in his chair, he absentmindedly watched a leggy blonde walking by his table for the third time. She gave him a thorough once over and flashed a smile his way. Automatically, he grinned back and winked, even though he had no real interest in her. Years of carousing had ingrained the reaction.

Maybe the problem was he needed to find a permanent companion. It was spring, time for all healthy males to look for a mate. The only difficulty was no one appealed to him as much as his sister-in-law did. She was a sweet thing, usually quiet and trying to please everyone, but with a strong, feisty side that crept out in the right circumstances. He quirked his lips as he thought about how much he enjoyed provoking her, seeing her temper flare and her cheeks start to flush. Elise was lovely, with big green eyes and dark brown hair that fell about her shoulders in a glossy sheet. Her voice was soothing and her smile could brighten even the darkest of days.

Too bad she was madly in love with his half-brother, Kane. They made a great couple and Ryne knew he'd never have a chance with her, but some part of him longed for a partner like Elise.

He snorted ruefully and took another swig of beer, wiping his mouth on the back of his hand. It was all a pipe dream; someone like Elise would never put up with him. There were too many rough edges to his personality for a girl like that. His sense of humour was too off-beat, he was too impulsive and too quick to anger. Mind you, if he made a mistake, he owned up to it and faced the consequences. It was what any real man would do.

This made him think of last fall's debacle. His then girlfriend, Marla, had turned out to be a scheming bitch, intent on forcing Kane into selling his land to an oil company so she could get her hands on the proceeds through computerized bank fraud. The woman had even stooped to murder to get her own way, killing the man who had been like a father to both himself and Kane. She then pitted brother against brother, alienating them from each other to the point of a fight to the death. He still kicked himself for allowing her to manipulate him. A nasty piece of work, the woman had planted evidence so he was blamed for her misdeeds. Luckily, Elise had put two and two together and foiled Marla's plans.

Once things settled down, he'd left the area. There were no hard feelings between himself and Kane, but he wanted to make a fresh start and the ad for a large parcel of land in Stump River, had fit the bill. He'd purchased the place sight unseen.

He had no regrets, beyond missing his former pack. The place needed lots of work, but it was his and there was room for growth with the possibility of purchasing even more land in the future as the aging population moved to larger centres that supplied more services for seniors. Yep, it had been a good move.

He glanced toward the bar to see how Bryan and Daniel were fairing. The two could get rowdy, and he felt a certain responsibility towards them. More than once since coming to Stump River, he'd reminded them to toe the line. He was in charge of this grand undertaking and he wouldn't tolerate their stupidity messing up his plans.

The younger men had asked to come with him when he announced he was moving here. Both had been eager for a new life after circumstances in their own had turned sour. He was grateful for their help and companionship, even if they did irritate him at times.

Now, he watched them indulgently. They were behaving – for now. Each had an arm around the waist of some local beauty and he was sure he knew how their evenings would end. A lot of wild oats were sown around Stump River lately, and as long as the oats didn't start to grow and cause a population explosion, it was fine with him. As a preventative measure, he stared intently at the two men, and as one they sensed his attention and swivelled their heads to look his way. Meaningfully, he raised his eyebrows and nodded towards the girls. Daniel immediately dropped his gaze and nodded, indicating he'd follow the rules. Bryan smirked and raised his beer in a mock toast before tilting his head in acquiescence.

He couldn't help but grin at the fellow's impudence. He and Bryan hadn't known each other long, but the two had forged a good relationship. Bryan liked to push his buttons, but knew when to back off. He was also their small pack's Beta and could be depended on if the going got rough.

Armand looked up and caught his eye. He nodded in response to the implicit question. Soon another beer would be in front of him. He'd already had several and was planning on having several more, drowning his sorrows in the golden liquid. Tomorrow, he might regret the action, but for tonight, it seemed like a good idea.

The beverage appeared in front of him and he looked up to thank the server. An impressive cleavage met his eye with a nametag affixed to it, proclaiming the owner of the bosom to be Lucy. Interest stirred within him and he moved his gaze up higher. Lucy had full red lips and big, baby blue eyes that always made him feel he was being stripped naked. Unbidden, his body responded to her silent invitation.

His lips began to curve into a predatory grin and he snaked an arm around her waist pulling the woman down onto his lap. He and Lucy had become well acquainted since he'd moved to Stump River. Possibly she was the distraction he needed tonight. She giggled and ran her fingers through his hair, wiggling in his lap.

"Is it time for your break?" He rumbled into her ear.

She glanced towards the bar. Armand had his back turned, watching the game; their team was on a power play. Lucy leaned forward and nipped at his ear. "I don't think Armand will mind if I spend some time with a lonely customer."

Smirking, he stood up, quickly leading the girl down the dark hall towards the employees' washroom.

When they exited some time later, Lucy was flushed, her hair slightly dishevelled but a satisfied grin graced her face. She made a show of straightening the front of his shirt then kissed his jaw and whispered in his ear.

"Happy birthday, Ryne. Bryan and Daniel told me what day it was, so I thought I'd better give you something."

"Why thank you, Lucy. It was the perfect gift for the man who has everything." He responded with his trademark grin, patting her rear before sending her back to work.

As she sashayed back to the bar, he remained where he was, leaning against the wall of the darkened hallway, thinking about what had just happened. He wasn't sure if he should thank the other two men or hit their heads together for interfering in his life. They probably meant well and noticing he was sitting by himself in a dark corner, decided to cheer him up by sending Lucy over. Usually a romp with the waitress would have raised his spirits and he'd spend the rest of the evening enjoying her company. But not tonight.

Running his hands through his hair, he pondered what was wrong with him. Maybe it wasn't his birthday, or missing the family or the fact it was spring and he was alone. Maybe it was the phone call he'd received two weeks ago. It had been gnawing at him ever since Kane contacted him, letting him know some woman was in town asking about a man named Ryne Taylor.

At first, he'd laughed. Lots of girls asked about him and as long as she wasn't pregnant... Kane had cut through his laughter by announcing she was there because of the picture. His brother hadn't even had to say which picture. He knew just as surely as mention of it caused a cold hard ball to form in his belly.

He was a photographer and he had no qualms about admitting he was good. There'd been a few showings of his work and some minor critical acclaim bestowed upon him. Last fall, when he'd needed money, he'd instructed his then girlfriend, Marla, to sell all of his pictures with the exception of one. Even though their relationship had turned sour, he'd had faith Marla would be professional and do her job. The woman worked at an art gallery and he thought she'd be able to get a fair price for the photographs. Of course, like everything else touched by the bitch, it had all gone wrong. His pictures had sold, but Marla stole the proceeds. Worst of all, she'd sold the one picture he'd expressly said not to show to the public. Now the picture was out there somewhere, and everyone was waiting for the proverbial other shoe to drop.

He hadn't told Bryan and Daniel yet, but if someone was inquiring after him and mentioning the photo, it could only mean one thing. The secret was out and now he had to prepare for the fallout.

Chapter 4

It was the middle of March. Spring was making its presence known and the snow was finally starting to melt in Northern Ontario. Bits of green were poking out of the ground and buds were beginning to swell on tree branches. The air contained an indescribable quality of warmth and promise that the last of the wintery weather was past and fairer days were ahead. On the local radio station, the forecaster happily babbled away about seeing flocks of tundra swans overhead as the birds made their annual return migration north, while his co-host squealed with delight over the appearance of a robin in her backyard. Their positive mood should have been contagious, but Mel was too busy dodging potholes on the road to appreciate the wonders of the changing season.

Not for the first time did she curse Ryne Taylor and whatever demon had possessed him, for deciding to move north. Stump River was in the middle of nowhere, beyond decently paved roads, fast food restaurants and shopping malls. With the exception of a few small farm houses, she would have thought there was no one even living here. It was at least an hour since she'd passed through a town, if the small group of houses clustered around a gas station and a general store could even be called something that grand.

The gas station attendant had assured her Stump River was 'a nice sized place, just down the road a ways'. She had grave doubts about the man's idea of a *nice* size, especially as he'd also assured her the road was fine, only suffering some slight disrepair due to the spring thaw. As the car lurched and bounced through a successive series of craters, she swore. Her teeth were clicking together and her head was almost brushing the roof as she joggled up and down in the driver's seat. Yeah, right. The road was *perfectly* fine if you were looking to spend a ton of money getting your car repaired and then visiting a chiropractor to have your spine realigned. Thankfully, she was driving a rental. Her own vehicle, at its advanced age, would never have survived this rough treatment.

On the other hand, at least her car had decent seats. The rental did not. This fact pointedly came to her attention when a loose spring poked her in the rear for what felt like the hundredth time. That area of her anatomy would never forgive her for the treatment it was enduring. Shifting into a relatively more comfortable spot, she wondered if Taylor was actually a harbinger of bad luck rather than good fortune. Yes, she was being paid, but both of her trips to find him had resulted in her facing bad driving conditions to obscure towns in poorly maintained vehicles. Surely her luck was due to turn around soon.

Twenty minutes later, she pulled into a parking space along the main street of Stump River. She turned off the ignition and sighed with relief that the bone-rattling journey was finally over. Roughing it wasn't her forte; the lack of smooth roads and the absence of washrooms and coffee shops on every corner had her feeling like she'd fallen into some kind of time warp and was now trapped in the back of beyond.

Yes, she knew she was being melodramatic but her head ached and her body was stiff. What she wouldn't give for a soothing latte right now. Ruefully, she surveyed her surroundings and fought off despair. Small town—one point. Fancy coffee—zero. On the bright side, at least, it was larger than the last community she'd passed through.

From her vantage point, she checked out the street to the right, which was approximately two blocks in length. A small new-ish looking medical clinic was at the far end of the town. Next in line was a little diner simply called Ruth's. Red checked curtains hung in the windows and wooden planter boxes stood on either side of the door awaiting planting. A church with a modest spire and a small graveyard beside it came next, then a cenotaph and finally a barbershop followed by a few houses. Swivelling her head to the left, she noted she'd parked beside the local newspaper office. A sign in the window stated that publishing occurred every Wednesday and items must be submitted for inclusion by closing time on Monday.

A disreputable looking bar caught her attention next, and she quickly skimmed over it, having no intention of ever setting foot in such a place. Located beside it was a gas station that had one set of pumps and two bays for car repair. Several vehicles were parked to the side, some were in decent shape, while others appeared to be defying the odds by still being on the road despite advanced rust damage.

Through her rear-view mirror, she could see a general store, which seemed to be the main hub of activity; several people entered and exited even as she watched. It also had signs indicating it was the location of the post office and the catalogue order store as well. A hand-painted sign pointed to the rear and proclaimed unisex hair designs were available around the back.

Light traffic moved up and down the street, which sported the grand total of one traffic light. Chuckling, she noted a dog sitting patiently on the curb as if waiting for the light to change colour. Sure enough, when the signal turned green, the canine stood and went on its way. A few pedestrians were also crossing the road, though they were less law-abiding than the dog and unabashedly jaywalked across the town's main thoroughfare. At least one person slowed their pace and looked her way, apparently realizing her vehicle wasn't a local one and hence someone new must be in town.

Welcome to Stump River, she thought. A place where everybody knows your name. The idea of such a small community made her vaguely uncomfortable. On the other hand, it could help in her search for Taylor. If the man had lived here for more than a week, the locals probably knew his life history.

With this thought in mind, she climbed out of her car and headed towards the building beside her, the home of the Stump River Gazette. Hopefully, the local reporter would know exactly where Taylor lived and perhaps even help her locate a place to stay overnight. She crossed her fingers, praying there were rooms to rent locally, not looking forward to the idea of travelling the so-called road every day for the next week or so while she conducted her interviews.

A bell jingled merrily as she entered the Gazette, the scent of newsprint and old coffee hitting her as soon as she stepped inside. It was a stereotypical small-town newspaper with past articles pinned to the wall along with posters for free kittens and an upcoming fundraiser. Three wooden chairs sat waiting for someone to sit in them and a tired philodendron graced the corner near an ancient cast iron heater. Midway across the room, an old laminate counter divided the work area from the customer service zone. Behind it, a middle-aged woman sat frowning at a computer screen, the piece of technology rather at odds with its surroundings. A short distance from the computer station, a man of similar age was engaged in a conversation on the phone, occasionally jotting notes as he nodded at something the caller must have said. He glanced Mel's way and raised a finger, indicating he would be a minute.

She leaned against the counter and waited patiently for the man to finish his business. It was a short wait and soon he was strolling over to talk to her.

"Good morning, ma'am. How can I help you?"

"Hello. My name is Melody Greene. I'm looking for Ryne Taylor and I was wondering if you'd be able to tell me where to find him?"

"Ryne, eh?" The man rubbed his chin thoughtfully and she noted how the overhead lighting shone off his mostly balding head. "It's Saturday so he won't be in town today. His place is about ten miles away, on Stump Line. Are you familiar with the area?"

"No. It's my first visit to Stump River."

"I thought so, since I couldn't recall having seen you before. My name's Josh Kennedy, by the way." He reached across the counter and they shook hands. His grip was firm and friendly, a polite smile gracing his pleasant face.

"Pleased to meet you. Is Taylor's place hard to find?"

"Well, it's set back in the woods and the driveway is easy to miss if you aren't looking for it. Is he expecting you?"

"No, not really. It's a surprise." She felt it best to keep her cards close to her chest for the time being in case these people were as inclined to keep her away from her goal as Elise and her fellow townsfolk had been.

"Uh-huh." Josh looked her up and down as if he knew something.

She swore his eyes lingered on her waist and she felt herself blushing. He likely thought she was an abandoned girlfriend, possibly even a pregnant, abandoned girlfriend a fact which made her wonder about the photographer. Maybe Taylor wasn't seventy and pot-bellied, after all. Did the term 'playboy' better suit him instead?

"I can draw you a map, but I'll warn you. Ryne and his friends aren't overly fond of visitors to their house. They have no trespassing signs posted all over the place."

Friends? She'd viewed the photographer as a brooding recluse. Who were these friends and how many lived with him? Most likely a girlfriend, since Josh thought she was last season's rejected love interest.

While she wasn't pleased with the assumption she was a discarded lover, at least it let her know Taylor was probably under fifty and not totally unappealing to look at. The idea perked her spirits.

The woman had abandoned her computer, possibly thinking a newcomer was more interesting than whatever article she was writing. As she approached the counter, Mel decided she was a perfect match for her co-worker; both average height and weight with grey sprinkled throughout their hair. She had the same friendly, inquiring smile as the man did, too. "Who's this, Josh?"

"Melody Greene. She's looking for young Taylor."

"Ryne?" She laughed softly, shaking her head. "You and how many others?"

"Pardon?" Were other people trying to do research on him as well?

"Every unattached female below seventy and a few who aren't, have tried to catch Ryne's attention." She grinned mischievously. "He's a looker, I'll say that. And he knows how to charm the ladies."

"Beth." Josh gave the woman a warning glare and she responded by hitting him lightly on the arm.

"Josh, you know I'm still smitten with you even after twenty-five years. I only look at the man. It's strictly hands off." The two exchanged a look, and Josh pulled Beth into a one-armed hug.

Feeling uncomfortable, as if she was intruding on a private moment, she turned to study a poster on the wall, trying to ignore the emotions zinging through the air between the two.

Josh cleared his throat and she shifted her gaze back towards him. Beth, who must be his wife or at least a long-time companion, was returning to her desk. It was easy to see she had a light blush on her cheeks and her eyes sparkled.

Mel felt a twinge of envy over their relationship, but forced herself to focus on the matter at hand. "If you could draw me a map to his house, I'd really appreciate it."

"No problem, Ms. Greene. If you watch carefully for the names on the mailboxes, you should find Ryne's place without too much trouble." Josh pulled out a piece of paper and began to sketch a simple map, pointing out landmarks along the way. By the time he was done, she was sure she'd be able to find Ryne's house easily.

"Thanks." She folded the paper and carefully tucked it into her purse. "I was also wondering if anyone has rooms to rent. I'm planning on staying in the area for at least a week and was hoping I wouldn't have to do the two-hour commute from Timmins every day." Timmins was the nearest community of any size that offered much in the way of accommodation.

"Actually, we have a few cabins we rent out in the summer. They're not fancy, but since it's off-season we can give you a good deal." Josh looked over his shoulder and spoke to Beth. "We could open up a cabin for this girl, couldn't we?"

Beth looked up from her work. "Sure. I could take her out there right now. There's no rush on this article."

Pleased at her good fortune, she grinned. "I'd really appreciate it. Is there a grocery store where I could buy some supplies?"

"Brown's General Store probably has everything you need. I'll show you where it is on the way to the cabin." Beth grabbed her purse and coat, and soon they were on their way.

The Kennedys' cabins were about five miles outside of town, located at the back of their property, but secluded from view by a thick woodlot and backing onto a forest. There were three of them; each set a nice distance from the others. Made from logs, they sported a stone fireplace located in a cozy open-plan kitchen and living-room, a small bathroom and a bedroom.

"The fireplaces are safe to use and there's wood stacked beside the cabin. I'll turn on the electricity for you, but I'm afraid there's no phone service this time of year." Beth explained as she dug out a set of keys for her guest.

Mel peered into the small bath area, pleased to note a refurbished claw-foot tub, complete with a rainforest shower head. The kitchen had a microwave, stove and fridge and the bed appeared to be comfortable. "This will be perfect. Thank you so much."

"I should be thanking you. These cabins sit empty for a good part of the year. We get a few vacationers in the summer, some spring fishermen and some hunters in the fall, but that's about it. You're a bonus. Because of you, I might be able to convince Josh we can afford the new dishwasher I've been eyeing up in the catalogue."

Chuckling at the woman's practicality, Mel bid her goodbye and went back to the car to get her suitcase and laptop. It would be nice to have a temporary home base. She'd flown into Toronto two days ago, taken a smaller flight to Sudbury yesterday and had spent the day driving to Timmins as well as doing some sight-seeing.

The area really was beautiful with incredibly blue skies, a myriad of waterways and miles upon miles of forests.

Inhaling deeply, she appreciated the cool crisp air that seemed to contain more oxygen than her urbanized lungs had ever thought possible. Used to the staler air of city life, she found this to be almost intoxicating and eagerly looked forward to taking walks in the forest during her time here. Eyeing the heavily treed area situated behind the cabins, she wondered how safe it was. Were there many dangerous wild animals in area? She'd have to ask when she stopped in town to get groceries.

Glancing at her watch, she saw it was almost noon. Quickly, she finished emptying the car, locked the cabin door and drove back to town. The small diner she'd seen earlier would probably serve a good lunch and after that, she'd get some groceries and then drive out to Taylor's. She'd introduce herself to the man and maybe even arrange an interview schedule.

An hour later, Mel stood outside a locked gate, considering her options. While at the diner, she'd checked a phone book but found no listing for Ryne Taylor. Contacting him at his house was the next best solution, but it wasn't going to be as easy as she'd thought. 'No Trespassing' and 'No Hunting' signs hung in clear view, but so was the mailbox with the name Taylor printed on it. The man was somewhere behind that gate and she needed to get to him.

She approached the gate, giving it an experimental shake. It creaked slightly and the 'No Trespassing' sign slipped a bit to the side. Hmm.... What if the sign fell off the gate? If it was lying face down in the mud, then she couldn't see it and no one would be able to blame her if she went on the property, right? Her conscience pricked, but she firmly ignored it in favour of achieving her goal. Glancing up and down the road to ensure no one was about, she grabbed the sign in her hands and pulled.

It was resistant to its imminent removal, barely budging. She pulled even harder, leaning back and using her weight to aid her efforts. A screeching sound was the only hint the nails were giving way before she suddenly stumbled backwards, the sign clenched in her hands. Unable to regain her balance, she felt herself falling and scrunched her face in anticipation of the pain that would surely accompany her sudden stop and then… she was on her back, staring up at the sky, the sign clutched to her chest.

Surprisingly enough, the impact with the ground had been softer than she thought it would be, probably due to the fact she'd landed in one of the few remaining snow-banks heaped along the side of the road. Oh well, the sign was off the gate.

She stood up and assessed her injuries. Besides the tenderness of her backside and some bruising to her ego, she was unscathed. Checking again to make sure no one was around, she placed the sign face down on the ground. Part one of her plan was completed.

Her rental vehicle was pulled to the side of the road already, so she wouldn't be blocking traffic if she left it there for a while. Not that there was much chance of traffic in such an out of the way location; she hadn't passed a single house on her way here.

Slinging her purse onto her shoulder, she studied the gate. It was made of wood and almost a foot over her head. The fence extended from each side for about fifty feet in either direction after which she could see a large ditch filled with water from the melting snow. It was an impressive barrier and definitely suitable to keep people off Taylor's property. A small gap along the bottom of the gate caught her attention but she knew she'd never be able to wriggle underneath. Going over the barrier appeared to be the only option.

She jiggled the gate once more in the vain hope the lock would pop open. It didn't and she made a mental note to learn how to pick locks before taking on another such assignment.

Giving a resigned sigh, she grasped the top of the structure and pulled herself upwards while trying to swing her leg to the side to gain a foothold on the latch. After a good deal of huffing and puffing, she finally managed to reach the top of the gate and sat astride it, catching her breath and savouring the sweetness of success.

The feeling didn't last long, the top of the fence being decidedly uncomfortable. Cautiously, she swung her leg over and stared at the ground below. The distance had inexplicably increased now she was on top the fence and had to jump down. And she was recalling she wasn't overly fond of heights. Despite telling herself six feet wasn't that high, her stomach gave a funny little lurch as she contemplated her next move. Delaying wouldn't make things better though so she took a deep breath and jumped.

The landing was less than stellar and she wouldn't get any points for form or grace but at least she was on Taylor's property, albeit on her hands and knees in a muddy patch. Wincing, she got to her feet and brushed ineffectively at the mud on her pants. Her hands were filthy and her efforts at removing the mud were only making matters worse. Looking around, she decided to make use of the remaining snow and scooped up a handful to wash off the mud. It was cold and stung, but at least the filth was gone from her palms.

Drying her hands on her coat sleeve, she adjusted her purse on her shoulder and set off down the driveway. At least the hard part was over. Walking to the house and talking to Taylor should be a breeze in comparison.

Chapter 5

Twenty minutes later, Mel hobbled over to a fallen log and sat down, not even caring if the crumbling mossy surface stained her pants or not. Her optimistic spirits were seriously flagging. The fashionable knee-high boots, which had seemed eminently suitable in that they made her look taller, were not designed for long walks down an unpaved driveway. She couldn't even begin to count the number of times she had twisted and wobbled as her four-inch heels made contact with lumps of gravel.

She rubbed her sore ankle and wiggled her protesting toes while trying to peer down the drive but it vanished around yet another bend, obscuring her view of what might be ahead. Compressing her lips, she shook her head.

"No one in their right mind has a driveway this long." She spoke the words out loud, the sound of her voice echoing through the silence and it struck her how truly alone she was.

Trees surrounded her, their branches stretching and blending, partially blocking the view of the sky and shading the ground below. Because of this, the temperature felt much cooler than it had in the more open, sun-drenched space of the road. Now the cold was beginning to seep in, rising up from the cool surface of the log she was perched on, while the dampness of the air began to penetrate through her layers of clothing.

Rubbing her hands together briskly, she rose to her feet, idly noting animal footprints could be seen in the soft muddy ground. Nothing too large, she decided, based on the size of the tracks, probably a rabbit or a squirrel, which was good as she wasn't keen on meeting any wildlife face to face. And speaking of wildlife, she had to find that photographer!

She set off determined to find her quarry but less confident about the course of action she'd chosen. A feeling of unease was creeping over her; a certain prickling of her skin, an awareness the atmosphere of the forest had changed.

It felt like something was watching her every move, which was ridiculous because she was in the middle of nowhere. Nonetheless, she hurried her pace. Years of living in the city had ingrained in her the idea that walking alone in deserted parking lots or alleys was a bad idea. The concept probably transferred to forests as well.

The feeling of anxiety grew and she found herself unnaturally aware of her own breathing, the sound of her footsteps, the sheen of sweat forming on her skin. Wiping her palms on her pant legs, her gaze darted from side to side as she stumbled down the drive, no longer watching where she placed her feet. A noise to her left had her whirling around to face the source and her breath caught in her throat.

At first, all she was aware of was teeth. Large, shiny white teeth with pointy ends designed for puncturing and tearing flesh.

Then her focus widened as she noted black noses and gleaming eyes, pointy ears and thick fur covering sturdy bodies and long legs. A pair of very large guard dogs were staring at her and licking their chops as if she were the main selection on their dinner menu.

Instinct told her they weren't too pleased to see her. Or maybe they were; the thought that she'd be a change from a diet of dry kibble inanely came to mind as she stood frozen in place. Did guard dogs care about a varied menu selection? And, more to the point, why was she even thinking along that line?

A low rumbling sound came from one of the beasts, snapping her out of her statue-like state. They were holding their heads low and had raised the fur on their backs. She was sure she'd read somewhere that indicated an attack was imminent. Slowly, she started to back away, not wanting to lose eye-contact. The fact these might not be dogs was niggling at her mind but she shied away from examining the thought. Adding additional reasons to fear for her life would not be helpful at this point.

The beasts followed her, exactly matching her pace. Icy terror was working its way through her body despite the rapid beating of her heart. Surely, her blood should be rushing through her veins right now, oxygenating her muscles in preparation for flight? Where was the adrenaline rush everyone talked about? The super human strength that came out of nowhere when faced with horrible danger?

She blinked, realizing her vision was blurring, the world was darkening. Oh great. Passing out from fear. How lame was that? If only she'd had sufficient coffee fixes today, then she would have been better able to cope with the situation.

Shaking her head to clear her vision, she began to shoot glances from side to side, looking for a sturdy stick to grab and use as a weapon. It wouldn't be overly effective, but it was better than defending herself barehanded.

Just when she thought she saw a suitable branch, her heel came down on a large stone. Her foot twisted to the side and she lurched to the left, flaying her arms wildly as she tried to maintain her balance. Fear made her overcompensate and instead of righting herself, she made matters worse. As she stumbled against a tree trunk, the animals took exception to her sudden movement. They rushed towards her, barking and howling. She opened her mouth, inhaled deeply and resorted to the age-old solution of screaming for help at the top of her lungs.

Ryne groaned as the sound of howls and barks penetrated his alcohol-soaked brain, forcing him from his sleep. He was seriously hung over from last night and was contemplating the benefits of death over the way he was presently feeling. Dark thoughts ran through his mind as he determined the source of the noise that had dragged him from blessed oblivion.

Obviously, Bryan and Daniel were out acting like idiots and it was the last thing he needed today. If they wanted to go out hunting, it was fine with him, but keep it quiet. No rabbit or squirrel or whatever they'd cornered, warranted that much noise. He rolled over and winced as his head pounded. How many beers had he consumed last night, anyway? It was all sort of blurry. The favoured team had won the hockey game and everyone had started buying rounds and then...?

Gingerly, he opened one eye and squinted against the assaulting rays of light streaming in around the window shade. He swore and let his eyelid fall shut, raising his hand to his throbbing head. At least his stomach wasn't protesting the treatment he'd subjected it to.

The sounds from outside continued, and he was muttering under his breath when a scream pierced the air, drilling into his brain with unmerciful sharpness. He shot upright, ignoring his protesting body and swung his legs out of bed. Some corner of his mind noted he was dressed in last night's clothes and only needed to slip on his shoes. A second scream followed the first, and he was out the door before the sound even died out. What the hell were Bryan and Daniel doing? They were scheduled for patrol duty and shouldn't be fooling around. He muttered darkly about their demise as he ran down the front steps, moving with surprising ease for someone who, only minutes before, had felt like death warmed over. They knew better than to bring a woman here. And what were they doing to make her scream like that?

Both the howls and the screaming stopped abruptly before he was even at the end of the sidewalk. He froze and cocked his head to the side, trying to catch any sound that might indicate what was happening.

Footsteps approached. He crossed his arms and leaned against a nearby tree. There was no point in him rushing down the driveway when they were coming to him.

It didn't take long for the source of the footsteps to appear. Bryan and Daniel came into sight, glaring daggers at each other. They must have had one of their famous arguments about who was at fault for the most recent predicament they found themselves in.

Bryan was carrying something—no, make that some*one*—and, from the way the arms and legs hung limply, the person was unconscious. Narrowing his eyes, Ryne realized it was a woman and no doubt the origin of the screams that had woken him. Shit!

He pushed off from the tree he'd been leaning on and widened his stance. The two men looked up and noticed him, their pace immediately slowing as if trying to delay something unpleasant. He sneered. How right you are my friends. This *will* be unpleasant.

As soon as they were within hearing distance, he began. "What the fuck did you do this time?"

Daniel stared at the ground.

Bryan kept his head up, but averted his gaze. "We found her on the property."

"And you decided to what? Go hunting with her as the prey?" Ryne snorted derisively.

Bryan flushed, but didn't back down. "No. We thought we'd scare her off. You know, chase her a bit and she'd run back to wherever she came from."

"Your plan doesn't appear to have worked very well since she's now here at the house." Ryne folded his arms and jerked his chin towards the unconscious woman. "What happened?"

Daniel began to speak, shooting glances up at Ryne as he spoke. "We...um...we stalked her a while and she was backing up towards the road, but moving real slow."

"So we thought some noise might hurry her along," Bryan added. "But she tripped or something, just as the barking started and then she began screaming."

"And then it was the weirdest thing, like you'd see in a cartoon." Daniel jumped in, his wonder at the event he was describing apparently causing him to momentarily forget he was in trouble. "She turned to run and bang!" Clapping his hands together, he gestured to show what happened. "She ran right smack into a tree and then just sort of slid down the trunk." He shook his head. "I never thought that sort of thing happened in real life."

Ryne bit back the chuckle the mental picture evoked. "Is she all right?"

"I think so. There's a lump on her head and that's why we brought her here. We didn't think we should leave her lying on the ground." Bryan shifted the woman in his arms.

"Bring her inside and we'll check her out." Ryne tightened his lips as he turned and stalked back to the house. They couldn't have approached her like normal human beings and told her she was on private land, could they? Oh, no. That would make too much sense.

Once inside, Bryan laid the woman down on the sofa and Daniel disappeared, only to return with a damp washcloth and the first aid kit. Kneeling beside the sofa,

Ryne nodded his thanks. Daniel was a good kid; he just didn't think sometimes.

Gently, Ryne brushed the unconscious woman's hair from her forehead and probed the bump on her head. It wasn't too large, but the skin was broken, no doubt from contact with the rough bark on the tree. Her skin was warm and soft to the touch. Inhaling deeply, he took in her scent and stored it for later analysis before proceeding with the first aid treatment. He washed off the area and applied a bandage then leaned back to study his patient.

Her hair, spread out upon the cushions, was a shade between blond and brown. Incredibly long lashes lay against her cheeks while her mouth was wide and full. The faintest dusting of freckles showed across the bridge of her nose making her appear youthful. His gaze worked its way down her body and he concluded she probably wasn't as young as he initially thought; mid-twenties perhaps.

He looked back up at her face and studied it more carefully. She wasn't strikingly beautiful, nor blatantly sexy, but there was something appealing about her. Glancing at her mouth again, he wondered what her lips would feel like against his own, then frowned. He didn't go for the girl-next-door-type; real women who knew the score were more his style. Women like Lucy. Giving his head a shake, he decided his hangover must be muddling his thinking.

Something nudged his shoulder and he looked up to see Bryan gesturing towards their visitor. Her eyes were showing some movement behind her closed lids, indicating she was coming around. While he was relieved she didn't seem to show any signs of permanent damage from her experience, he now had to decide what he'd do with her, once she woke up.

If luck was on his side, she'd apologize for trespassing and leave. Worst case scenario, she'd start screaming 'sue' and threaten to call the police about the dangerous animals he kept. The thought had him clenching his fists. He stood and moved to the nearby kitchen, indicating the other two should come with him. Standing in the doorway, so he could still see the couch, he began to rip a strip off the other two men.

"That was the most stupidly, idiotic idea you two have had in ages. Why were you trying to scare her off? Why didn't you just say it was private property?"

"We didn't mean any harm." Daniel began.

"I'm sure you didn't, but look what happened anyway. This isn't like back home, you know. We don't have people in the right places to help brush things like this under the rug. It's us three against the rest of the community, and we have to blend in, not draw attention..." Ryne listened to himself talk. When had he suddenly become the heavy? Hell, he sounded like his foster-father used to after he and Kane had pulled some stunt or another. The thought brought him up short and he exhaled gustily. After a moment of silence, he rubbed his neck and glanced at the other two. They were waiting quietly, eyes downcast. "Just...don't do it again, okay?"

"We won't." They spoke in unison, looking up at him sheepishly.

He gave a dry chuckle and punched Bryan lightly in the arm. "I thought you were supposed to be the smart one."

Bryan shrugged. "Yeah. But she was kind of cute. I was sort of thinking once she was near the gate, I'd show up and 'save' her from Daniel. She might have been grateful, you know?" He winked and Daniel laughed.

Ryne did too, but inwardly he felt his hackles rise. Bryan's statement bothered him, though he didn't know exactly why. "Why don't you two go see if you can make something for us to eat? I'm starving." They nodded and headed towards the fridge. "Oh, and brew up a large pot of coffee. I'm still feeling hung over from last night."

With the other two busy, Ryne headed back into the living-room and sat in his recliner facing the sofa. The initial coolness of the leather felt good given his less than prime state of being. Not for the first time, did he wonder why he kept accepting all the drinks sent his way. He knew the locals were somewhat in awe of his capacity for alcohol, and he suspected there might be some bets going around about who would be the first to drink him under the table. It would never happen, but still, he should be more careful. Drawing undue attention to the ways in which he was physiologically different from his neighbours was not a good idea.

He leaned his head back and switched his attention to the girl lying unconscious on his sofa. Through half-closed eyes, he watched and waited while speculation ran through his mind. Why had she been on his land? She wasn't a local; they'd never go walking in boots like hers. Maybe somebody's relative, visiting for the weekend and out for a stroll? Possibly. After all, who else would have a reason to be roaming around Stump River?   .

Chapter 6

Mel opened her eyes and blinked, momentarily confused. Where was she? Her dumpy, little apartment in Chicago? No, that was last week. This week she was in Canada, looking for that photographer. She'd driven to Stump River and rented a cabin and then... Oh damn! She sat up quickly and immediately regretted it, clutching her head as it throbbed in protest.

"I wouldn't move so fast if I were you." A deep, sexy voice spoke to her left and she turned her head to see who owned it.

"Ow!" Her head protested again and she grasped it in her hands, propping her elbows on her knees.

"See? I told you not to do it." The voice laughed dryly and she was immediately annoyed this person, whoever he was, found her pain amusing. Squinting, she stared across the room trying to get a good look at the fellow. Unfortunately, the angle of the bright light entering through the window cast him in a shadow and she could only see his outline.

"I don't usually take advice from complete strangers." She didn't attempt to hide the sarcasm in her voice. The man must be a total jerk. She'd just survived an animal attack and was suffering from a head injury, for heaven's sake! Where was the sympathy she deserved?

"You don't talk to strangers? Aww. What a good little girl you are." He mocked her, then switched to a harder, more accusing form of speech. "Too bad you don't follow the rules when it comes to wandering onto someone's land, completely ignoring the 'No Trespassing' signs."

She didn't respond at first, recalling how she'd removed the sign so she could claim ignorance of its existence. Well, in for a penny… "I didn't see any sign. Where was it?"

"Right on the gate that blocked the driveway you walked down."

"Really? I didn't notice it. Maybe it fell off." She concentrated on brushing some dust from her pants to avoid looking in his direction.

"And maybe it had some help from you."

She gave a non-committal shrug.

"And of course, the six-foot-high *locked* gate, didn't give you any clue you should stay out."

"No, not really." She cast a saccharine sweet smile in his direction. "Though, of course, if there'd been a sign stating there were vicious dogs roaming free, I would have been more cautious."

"Dogs? Those weren't dogs. They were wolves and you're lucky they didn't rip you to shreds." He sounded quite pleased to deliver that piece of news.

She swallowed hard. She'd had a sneaking suspicion they weren't dogs, but thought she'd throw the idea out there, just in case. If the man owned out of control animals she could threaten to sue him if he got nasty about her trespassing. Now, with that small hope gone, she had to acknowledge how much danger she really had been in. Guilt and a ton of regret for her impulsive actions also came into the mix. She should have gone back to town and tried to make a proper appointment with Taylor, rather than sneaking up on him.

Sitting up straighter, she decided to try to smooth things over for the sake of the interview she hoped to get. But, before she could even open her mouth, everything started to turn dark and her vision blurred. Feeling the blood drain from her face, she clutched the cushion she sat on and closed her eyes until her equilibrium settled. Damn, nothing was going the way she planned. Like many of her ideas, it had seemed a good one at the time. She was supposed to be confidently walking up to Ryne Taylor's house, knocking on his door and coolly requesting an interview. Taylor's surprise at her unexpected presence would have had him immediately agreeing to her request.

Instead, she was stuck talking to this ill-mannered person. At least he wasn't Taylor. From the way everyone spoke, the photographer was a ladies' man and likely had smooth banter down to a science. Unlike someone else, she added, glaring towards the chair housing her tormentor.

He must be one of the people who lived with Taylor but how did the photographer put up with this fellow's sarcastic attitude? She'd known him for less than five minutes and already wanted to smack him. True, she shouldn't have trespassed, but he needn't be so nasty about it.

"Hey, are you all right?" The man leaned forward, possibly concerned over her sudden pallor.

"Yeah." She flicked a glance his way and stiffened in shock. His change in position had brought his face out of the shadows and he was visible for the first time. Her eyes must be playing tricks on her. Before her sat one of the most gorgeous men she'd ever seen. Messy black hair hung across his forehead, while the stubble darkening his jaw line gave him a dangerously sexy vibe. Deep blue eyes, a straight nose and a firm mouth completed the picture.

A second reason for her surprise was that he was almost a carbon copy of Kane, the husband of the waitress at the Grey Goose. The eyes were different, but otherwise the two men were very similar. They had to be brothers or at least first cousins. Narrowing her eyes, she began to connect the dots and an unnerving thought came to mind.

Was this man Ryne Taylor?

No, he couldn't be. Elise's name tag had declared her surname was Sinclair and she seemed like the type to assume her husband's last name; Kane Sinclair's brother would be a Sinclair as well, wouldn't he? But then again, there was always the possibility... She sighed heavily and decided she'd best find out. Starting the introductions, she stated her name.

"I'm Melody Greene."

He ignored the implicit social norm that would have him supplying his name in return and glowered at her. "And why, Melody Greene, were you traipsing all over this property?"

"I wasn't traipsing all over. I was walking down the driveway. And I'm here because I want to talk to Ryne Taylor."

A nod was the only response she got. Not even an eyelash flickered.

Under her breath, she cursed him. Was he, or wasn't he, Ryne Taylor? His reaction gave no clue either way.

"Why do you want to talk to him?"

She noted the use of the word 'him'. Ah-ha! So this person wasn't Taylor. She considered answering his question truthfully, but decided she didn't want to share anything with the man. He was too damn annoying. If he wasn't willing to even provide his name, then she wasn't going to give away any extra information either. For all she knew, he might try to sabotage her attempts to talk to the photographer out of pure spite.

"That's between the two of us." She added a hint of a mysterious smile and watched with satisfaction as the man's eyebrows rose. Make what you want of that, she thought to herself.

"It's time for you to go." Abruptly, he rose to his feet

"Pardon?"

"You need to leave. I trust you can make it back to your car by yourself?"

"Well, yes. But..."

He extended his arm towards the doorway.

"Fine." She snapped the word out, temper at his cavalier dismissal had heat flooding her face. Spying her purse lying near her feet, she snatched it and jumped up, only to stagger as her head once again protested the sudden change in elevation.

An exasperated sigh filled the room as the man caught her and steadied her on her feet. "Obviously you're in no shape to operate a vehicle. I suppose I'll have to drive you home." Unceremoniously, he scooped her up in his arms and walked out of the house.

She knew her mouth was opening and closing like a fish gasping for air, but she couldn't begin to formulate the words needed to sufficiently express her indignation. Finally, choosing the direct route, she issued a succinct command. "Put me down!"

"No." He didn't even look at her and continued to stride down the driveway, his long legs covering the ground at an astonishing pace.

"Let me go!" She struggled, pushing against his chest. He merely tightened his grip. Doubling her efforts, she began bucking and kicking her legs. It made her head throb, but at least he took notice and stopped walking.

"Are you trying to make me drop you?"

She froze as she noticed the distance to the ground. He really *was* tall. "No."

"You aren't steady enough on your feet to walk the length of the driveway at the speed I want you to go. Nor are your boots suitable for walking on gravel. Now stay still or I'll throw you over my shoulder. Hanging upside down won't do your head any good, but if that's what it takes..." He began to shift his grip on her and she had no doubt he'd make good on his threat.

"Fine." Crossing her arms, she pointedly stared straight ahead, gritting her teeth when she felt his chest quiver against her body. He was laughing at her!

The rest of the journey passed silently. When they finally arrived at the gate, he set her down, took a set of keys from his pocket, unlocked the gate and then relocked it after they'd passed through. Still not speaking, he looked at her rental car and then at her before giving a loud sigh and extending his hand, implicitly asking for the keys.

She rolled her eyes, but dug them out and handed them over, quite sure he would have no compunction about searching her purse if she refused.

With her chin in the air, she walked to the car, got into the passenger side, put on her seatbelt and folded her hands in her lap. The annoying man followed at a much slower pace, climbing in, adjusting the seat and mirror, before finally putting the key in the ignition.

"Where are you staying?"

"At the Kennedys'." She slid a glance his way. "I've rented a cabin from them. If you turn left and then—"

"I know where they live." He answered shortly, his lips pressed together, forming a tight line.

After that, the rest of the ride descended into uncomfortable silence again. When they finally arrived at her temporary home, Mel barely waited to get the keys from him before quickly exiting the vehicle. She grabbed the bag of groceries from the back seat and hurried towards the cabin, until a sudden thought had her stopping and reluctantly turning around. He was leaning against the car watching her, an enigmatic expression on his face.

"Umm... How are you getting home?"

"Don't worry about it. I can get a ride if I need one."

"Oh." As much as it irked her to do it, her mother had raised her with manners. "Thanks for driving me home."

"It was the easiest way to get rid of you."

His words erased her good intentions. "You have to be the rudest man I have ever had the misfortune to encounter."

He smirked and dipped his head in acknowledgement. "Thanks. I try my best."

"And you certainly succeed! I'm eternally grateful this is the last time I'll have to see you."

"Really? After tearing down that sign, climbing the gate, walking almost half a mile and facing a pair of wolves, you're giving up on me?"

"What do you mean?" She had a sinking feeling in her stomach.

"I'm Ryne Taylor, Melody Greene."

She felt her mouth drop open then she snapped it shut and quickly turned away fighting for composure. Why did these things always happen to her? Yes, the man was being purposely aggravating but she needed to work with him. She slowly shook her head in despair, wondering how she'd repair the damage. Pasting a conciliatory look on her face, she turned around prepared to offer apologies except... He was gone!

Looking around, she couldn't see a single trace of him. Nothing was in sight except what appeared to be a large black dog or maybe another wolf, running through the woods behind the cabin.

All too wary of canines after her recent experience, she hurried into the cabin. Taylor was on his own!

Ryne headed for home, loping through the woods and enjoying the chance for a run. The exercise was clearing the residual alcohol from his body and the cobwebs from his brain, though there weren't too many of those left after his encounter with Ms. Melody Greene. She was an impudent little thing; trespassing on his property and then insinuating he had vicious animals on his land, trying to twist events around so it became his fault she ran into a tree. No doubt, she'd probably threaten him with a lawsuit.

Why hadn't she asked who had rescued her from the wolves? Maybe the bump on her head had left her addled. At some point she'd probably start to question the point though and he had no idea how he'd respond. He should make Bryan and Daniel come up with the solution since the whole incident was their fault.

Grinning, he thought how insulted they'd be to learned she'd initially considered them to be dogs. The look on her face when he'd said *wolves* had been priceless. If he'd told her the whole truth and said werewolves or Lycans, she would probably have passed out again. It would almost be worth it, just to see her face. But the Keeping was one of their most fundamental laws and breaking it on a whim was a serious offence; even pups knew better.

From his earliest memory, he could recall his mother drilling the Keeping, as they commonly called the law, into his head. Non-Lycans could never know their true identities. Ensuring the pack's existence remained hidden from the human population was their first duty. Out of necessity, a few humans were aware of the truth, but selecting who to reveal the secret to was carefully considered by the Alpha and his council and had to be for the overall good.

Telling Ms. Greene she was in the Alpha den of a Lycan pack was definitely not in their best interests.

He slowed his pace, not tired but thirsty and paused by a stream for a drink, savouring the cold water as it cascaded down his dry throat. The spring thaw was on, causing the waterways to swell as the snow melted. Just last week, ice had covered most of this particular stream, with only the smallest trickle of free running water visible. Now it was a foot wide and by next week, he'd have to wade through it, rather than jump over it.

Bending to take another swallow, he absentmindedly noted his reflection; black fur, gleaming white teeth and bright blue eyes.

Ah, you are a looker, he mocked himself.

The female noticed it, too, his wolf murmured.

Indeed she had, which left him wondering why he'd felt the need to provoke her rather than charm her. He knew women found him attractive and had used it to his advantage in the past. Maybe it was being hung over that was to blame.

Finishing his drink, he licked the remaining water drops from his muzzle and continued running towards home, thinking about the young woman. Why did she want to see him? He'd certainly never met her before; he wouldn't forget someone like her. She wasn't his usual type but worth a second look, if he was interested in looking.

Which he wasn't.

Despite his drunken musings of the previous night, there was enough to do trying to establish his territory without having to worry about a female…at least not one as a mate.

Melody Greene was another story though. She was looking for him and he was pretty sure it wasn't for the pleasure of his company and a quick roll in the hay. Most likely, it was something to do with that damned picture. After all, what were the chances of two different strangers looking for him in the course of a month; one in

Smythston a few weeks back and now one in Stump River? She had to be the same person, but how had she found him? He and Kane had gone to great lengths to bury the trail that connected them. Ms. Greene must be one hell of an investigator and incredibly determined if she'd been able to ferret out his whereabouts.

His house came into view and he paused in the backyard, phasing back into his human form before walking to the building. The scent of frying chicken and fresh coffee drifted towards him causing his mouth to water. He inhaled deeply, savouring the smell, but then frowned as he realized Ms. Greene's scent lingered in the air too. Damn. Grimacing, he hoped he'd be able to get rid of her. He didn't need the type of complications she represented.

Chapter 7

Mel put off calling Mr. Aldrich as long as possible. She had nothing positive to report and was sure the lawyer saw through her attempts at evasion. During the job interview it had felt as if she were on trial and he'd been trying to delve into her brain to find every little secret she'd ever had. He'd ask questions nicely then moved on to a new topic, only to suddenly revert to the previous train of thought and re-ask the same question with slightly different wording and an accusing tone of voice. She had nothing to hide, but felt guilty and nervous nonetheless. At one point she'd almost confessed to stealing Timothy Hawthorne's chocolate bar in fourth grade! She'd controlled the urge, but was suspicious the lawyer already knew the truth anyway.

Despite being only average height and weight, Mr. Aldrich was an imposing man. His greying hair was too perfect; his eyes a pale ice blue while his face was impassive, only the faintest hint of a smile or frown gracing his thin lips. There was a cold, calculating vibe about him, and she hoped she'd never end up on his bad side.

She'd left the interview feeling she'd failed and had been delightfully shocked to receive a call weeks later saying she had the job. Her surprise was even greater when she discovered Aldrich worked for Mr. Anthony Greyson, head of Greyson Incorporated.

Anthony Greyson was a well-known business tycoon in the Chicago area. His name was synonymous with wealth and success, yet he led a life shrouded in mystery. Few people ever saw him and, even when he entertained, it was rumoured he only put in a perfunctory appearance before disappearing into the private depths of his mansion. Some said he was involved with the mob. Others claimed he led a double life and had homes all over the world where he assumed other identities. The tabloid stories about the man were even more ludicrous and not worth mentioning.

Whatever the truth about Greyson, the idea of working for him was both intriguing and intimidating and she hoped she'd complete the job to his satisfaction. If he was going to become a patron of the arts, maybe he would employ her again, asking her to do research on other up-and-coming artists.

With this in mind, she picked up her phone and dialled Aldrich's number, only to smile in relief when she discovered her phone couldn't pick up a signal. Problem solved, she decided, happily tucking the phone away. Who would ever have thought bad service could be a blessing? She'd have to call when she was in town tomorrow. Aldrich couldn't complain about her lack of contact, if there were no means of communication available to her, right?

Realizing she was hungry, she prepared dinner and then kept herself amused while eating by reliving her encounter with Ryne Taylor, adding pithy comments she wished she had been clever enough to say at the time.

In her mind, the man was soon overcome by her quick repartee and eagerly agreed to an exclusive interview with her. He was also careless with his comments and her clever questions soon had him revealing the reason why he appeared to be in hiding and why the wolf picture was so important.

She snorted at her imaginings. It wouldn't happen that way. Taylor was no pushover. Instead of trying to annihilate him with her scathing remarks, she should be thinking of ways to win him over with her pleasant personality so he'd be willing to talk to her. Usually she got along with everyone, but he seemed to bring out the worst in her which meant she'd have to try extra hard to get on his good side. Right now though, she didn't have any great hopes such a thing would occur in the near future.

Her meal over, she tidied the small kitchen then investigated the delights of the large claw-foot tub. It was big enough and deep enough she could completely submerge with only her head and neck above the water line. It was at times like these she actually enjoyed being a little on the short side. A lanky model would have her knees and shoulders sticking out over the top of the tub. Chuckling at the mental image that accompanied the thought, she leaned her head back and let the relaxing warmth creep into her body.

Steam rose about her, coating her face in dewy dampness. Her hair would be curling and frizzing soon but she didn't care. The heat was turning her skin pink and she stuck one foot up out of the water, wiggling her toes and observing their appearance. She needed to redo her polish, she thought lazily before letting her foot sink beneath the water line once again. Bubbles drifted by, gathering around her neck and clustering in little islands that floated here and there in response to the slight current she created whenever she moved.

By time the water had cooled, both her brain and her muscles felt like mush. She barely had the energy to get out of the tub and drag herself into the bedroom. Throwing on her traditional sleepwear of an old t-shirt and a pair of fuzzy socks, she crept into bed and curled up into a ball, quickly drifting off to sleep.

Unfortunately, the events of the day haunted her slumber. As was so often the case in bad dreams, she was trying to run, to escape, but her legs felt like they were stuck in quicksand. She pulled on her limbs, forcing each slow, plodding step, knowing the terror behind wasn't suffering from the same impediment. The air was cold and damp. Tree branches slapped against her face as she made her way through the dark woods. Whatever was chasing her, was getting closer; its heavy footsteps sounding louder and louder. She opened her mouth to scream but no sound came out.

Hot breath hit her neck. Long canines bit at her, tearing her clothing and piercing her flesh. Struggling to escape, she swung her arms wildly, gasping in surprise when her hand encountered something solid and warm. Now fingers clutched her upper arms, pulling at her, forcing her to turn around and face the horror that was attacking her. Heart pounding, she clenched her eyes shut. Like a young child, she hoped if she couldn't see it, it wasn't there.

"Look at me!" A strong voice commanded her and she was helpless to refuse. Of their own volition, her eyes opened and she looked up into the face of the wild beast tormenting her. Light gleamed off of its long teeth, their whiteness accentuated by the black fur covering its face. Her gaze travelled higher and then froze as it locked onto the creature's bright blue eyes. They stared at each other for what felt like ages and then the wolf's face began to shift and take on a human form.

His hazy features refused to come into focus, but his eyes remained clear and deep blue. He gazed at her, a low rumble emanating from his chest. She tried to inch away, still fearful, but her limbs refused to cooperate. The man leaned closer. She tried to say something, but he covered her mouth with his, kissing her softly.

Their location slowly morphed to the cabin and she was now in her bed. She knew she was dreaming, but everything seemed so real. The roughness of his hand touching her skin, the warmth of his breath, the softness of his lips. She felt herself relaxing and sighing as she sank into the kiss, clutching his shoulders. The nightmare had turned into an amazing dream and it promised to be one of the best ones she'd had in ages.

But, as dreams so often do, it faded just as things were getting interesting. The mystery man stood, the coolness of the cabin replacing his warmth. She shivered and whimpered in protest, reaching out, trying to draw him close again. Instead a blanket softly fell over her, a hand brushed her hair from her face. Smiling, she murmured her thanks and, wanting to see her benefactor, she forced her eyes open only to find the room empty. With a disappointed sigh, she fell back asleep.

Morning came much too soon, the sound of the alarm jerking her awake. She threw her arm out and groped wildly for the evil piece of technology, giving a grunt of pleasure when she silenced it. Still groggy from sleep, bits and pieces of her dream last night floated through her mind. The sensations had been so real. Too bad it had ended when it did.

Reluctantly, she left her bed, stumbled to the kitchen to turn on the coffee maker and then hit the shower, completing her morning ablutions with practised efficiency. Wrapped in a terry cloth robe, she went in search of her coffee. The wonderful smell of fresh caffeine was floating through the small cabin, perking up her senses and further activating her brain. Leaning against the counter, she contemplated her day.

She'd have to contact Aldrich and let him know she had found where Taylor lived, but hadn't yet made an appointment to interview him. It was the truth. Her contact with the man yesterday didn't need to be part of the report.

Mentally, she gave herself another kick for trying to sneak onto the man's property. It had been foolish and amateurish, more suited to a cheap spy novel than a journalist who had a paying client. Impulsivity had always been her downfall and she kept hoping with age she'd finally learn to control herself and avoid incidents like yesterday. So far, maturity wasn't helping.

Maybe she could blame her mother, she chuckled. The woman wasn't there to defend herself and she had been flighty in her day. Still was, if the truth be told. Mel loved her mother dearly, but the woman was in the habit of picking up and moving with no warning, simply because something had caught her fancy. Usually it was a man, but sometimes it was a charitable cause, something she'd seen on a travel show, or the need to undertake a new career like pottery or bee-keeping. While she'd been young, her mother had tried to curb her gypsy ways, but once Mel was grown, the restlessness had returned.

Currently her mother was living in Florida with a man named Fred and doing something with seashells. She didn't really understand the enterprise and knew better than to ask. The explanation would be long and complicated yet leave her with no clearer understanding for the telling.

Sometimes she wondered if her mother would have been more settled if her father had stayed around but the relationship had lasted only a week. He'd left without sharing his number or an address and probably didn't even know or care he had a daughter.

It didn't really matter to Mel though. Her mother had raised her by herself and they'd survived, just the two of them. There had been no grandparents to lend a hand, but friends had rallied around. They had become her honorary aunts and uncles celebrating holidays and sharing milestones with her. She'd been showered with love just as much as her friends who had blood relatives, perhaps even more so. Frowning, she realized she hadn't seen some of those people in almost a year. Maybe when this job finished, she'd make time for a visit.

Mulling the idea over in her head, she dressed and prepared to head into town in search of a phone so she could call Aldrich. Afterwards, she'd try to contact Taylor again, by more conventional means this time. Hopefully, he wasn't the kind to hold a grudge.

Chapter 8

Rather than heading straight to town, Mel found herself driving by Taylor's property. She'd been day-dreaming about nothing in particular and the car seemed to have a mind of its own. Once she realized where she was, she resolved to drive right on by, even as her foot was depressing the brake pedal and her hand was shifting the car into park.

She sat in the idling car, not at all sure why she was here. A repeat of yesterday was definitely not in the cards, so what would she gain by staring at the locked gate? Nothing really, but something drew her to this place. Could it be the fact Taylor was behind the gates? Possibly. There *was* an air of mystery surrounding him, and she'd always loved solving puzzles.

Why did Greyson want her to get information on him? Was it his photographs or was there something else? And why was Taylor so obsessive about his privacy? A padlocked gate, a half-mile long driveway, living in the middle of nowhere in a town few people had ever heard of. It seemed excessive to someone such as herself who'd lived most of her life in the city surrounded by people. Maybe, if she ever got to interview the man, she'd find out.

She moved her hand to the gearshift preparing to put the car into drive, when she noticed someone walking down the road. A stab of excitement shot through her. Striking up a friendly conversation with one of the neighbours might prove useful. Small towns where notorious for people knowing each others' business, right? Eagerly, she awaited the arrival of her potential informant.

The approaching figure was a man, tall, good-looking and around her age, with sandy blond hair and hazel eyes. His stride faltered when he saw she was waiting for him and she hoped he wouldn't turn and retreat.

After a brief hesitation, a wide grin spread across his face and he walked up to her jauntily.

She rolled down her window and called out a friendly greeting. "Hello. It's a lovely morning, isn't it?"

"Sure is." He stopped beside her car and looked down at her. "Can I help you? We don't get too many visitors around here."

"I imagine not, given how off-the-beaten-path it is. I'm interested in meeting Ryne Taylor. I've heard he lives here. Do you know him?"

The man seemed to be suppressing a chuckle and she quickly glanced at her face in the rear-view mirror, memories of Edward Mancini chuckling at her dishevelled appearance haunting her. Nope, all was clear. Maybe the guy was just the cheerful type.

"Yeah, I know Ryne. He's my Al...er...friend."

"So you live around here?" She felt her spirits perk.

"Uh-huh. I actually live with him. We've been together for about five months now."

"Really?" Hopefully, her shock didn't show in her tone. Taylor being gay had never crossed her mind. Darn, it was always the good-looking ones. She felt herself wanting to pout over the fact, not that she'd really been interested in the man, of course!

Something niggled in her brain. Taylor couldn't be batting for the other team. From the way everyone spoke, he was a ladies' man. A switch hitter? Or maybe this fellow meant something entirely different by the term than the popular vernacular implied. She continued to gently probe for information. "So it's just the two of you?"

"No, Daniel lives with us, too. I'm Bryan, by the way."

A threesome? She tried to keep her expression neutral as she shook the hand he extended towards her. Their living arrangements were their business, she reminded herself. Her only concern was getting an interview with Taylor and this person—Bryan—might be her way in. "I'm Melody Greene. I'd really like to meet Mr. Taylor. I've seen some of his pictures and he's an amazing photographer. Do you think he'd be willing to discuss his work with me?"

Bryan hesitated, then shrugged. "He's not much of a talker, so I wouldn't count on it, but you never know."

"Could you give me his phone number so I could call him?"

"No, it's private but I suppose I could ask him to call you. What's your number?"

She shook her head regretfully. "My cell is having trouble picking up a signal, and the cabin I'm at doesn't have a phone hooked up but he could leave a message for me with the Kennedys and I could get back to him." She hoped Beth wouldn't mind.

Bryan nodded. "The Kennedys? Sure. Everyone knows who they are."

"Thanks. It's been nice talking to you." She started the car, gave a cheery wave and drove off. Glancing back in her mirror as she went on her way, she was surprised there was no sign of Bryan. Apparently, he moved as fast as Taylor did!

Back in town, she made her way to the diner, recalling from yesterday there was an old-fashioned pay phone in the entranceway. She listened to the rings while twirling the cord around her finger and mentally rehearsing her report. Finally, the answering machine picked up. Aldrich wasn't in the office. Relieved, she left a message, thanking her lucky stars at being able to avoid talking to the man.

After hanging up, she turned to stare around the crowded diner. It was an L-shaped dining area with a row of small tables lining the windows that faced onto the main street. Next there was a row of stools by a counter, behind which you could get a glimpse into the kitchen through a serving window. Along the side, leading towards the back was a long narrow area with a row of booths on one side and various small tables on the other.

It was mid-morning but the place was busy, most of the seats taken and the waitresses scurried about delivering what appeared to be a Sunday brunch special. Hoping to pick up some local gossip about Taylor, she made her way to the counter and hopefully ordered a latte. The request was met with a blank stare so she settled for regular coffee and turned in her seat to take in the atmosphere of the diner.

A myriad of scents tantalized her nose; cinnamon, pancakes, bacon, frying onions. The sound of dishes clattering in the kitchen, the hiss of grease as it sizzled on a griddle; it was all comforting and familiar, reminding her of her own waitressing jobs back in Chicago. Nostalgically she thought of her fellow waitresses, the regular customers, Joe the cook, the long hours, the lousy tips, her sore feet. Yeah, maybe she wasn't feeling so nostalgic after all.

Pushing thoughts of the 'good old days' aside— because quite frankly, they weren't that good—she let the buzz of voices wash around her as she sipped her coffee and pondered how to pass the time while she waited for a response from Taylor. Absentmindedly, she began to follow the different threads of conversation.

"And then I said to him, if that's how you feel..."

"My back has been so much better since I got a new mattress..."

"If you really want your engine overhauled, I'd contact Ryne..."

"So then she had the nerve to..."

Wait! Back up. Had she just heard Taylor's name mentioned? She swivelled the stool she was perched on and scanned the crowd for the source of the conversation. Two women were talking at the first table. A group of elderly men sat by the next. At the far corner, a group of teens had congregated and on the far side of the counter, two men... Yes. It was them. Discreetly, she shifted over one spot and tilted her head in their direction, once again blessing her good hearing.

"Ryne's busy fixing up the old place he bought from the Nelsons. He doesn't have a lot of spare time, but I know he needs extra money to pay for repairs." The man talking was in his mid-fifties with a hint of grey at his temples.

She noted his hands showed signs of hard work, their strength and capability evident even as he cradled a cup of coffee in them. Despite the relatively new soft grey jacket he wore, she could tell this was definitely someone who knew about physical labour and from the faint traces of grease around his nails, she determined he was probably an auto mechanic. She gave herself a point for her deductive skills and then turned her attention to the second man, who she judged to be a farmer.

"Thanks, Ben. I love my old truck and it would be great to have it running again. If Ryne could work on it in his spare time that would be great. I don't care when it's done."

"He'll be in town tomorrow. He covers for me on Mondays, running the gas pumps and doing repairs, so I can catch up on the paper work from the previous week.

I'll talk to him and, if he's interested, he can stop by on his way home and look the old girl over, see what he thinks needs doing."

The two men tossed some change on the counter and walked out still talking. Through the window, she watched as they parted ways, one getting into a car and driving off, while the other—Ben—walked across the road towards the service station, pulling a key from his pocket and unlocking the door.

A dog came bounding out and she recognized it as the one she'd seen yesterday, waiting to cross the road. She smiled at the memory. How had Ben managed to train the dog to do a trick like that? To the best of her knowledge, dogs were colour-blind, so how did it know the difference between a red light and a green one?

In her mind, she could see the man squatting on the ground at the curb, talking to the dog and explaining the intricacies of safely crossing the road while the dog nodded solemnly, absorbing this new knowledge. Shaking her head, she watched as the animal in question bounced around, no doubt excited for some company.

The waitress came by to top up her coffee and must have noticed Mel was watching the man and his dog.

"That's Ben Miller and Harley." The woman gestured with the coffee pot towards the activity across the street.

"He's a nice-looking dog. A lab?"

"Yep. About three years old. He's supposed to be a guard dog, but he's too darn friendly and not overly smart. If anyone were to break into Ben's place, the only thing Harley would do is drown them in drool."

"I think he seems pretty clever. Yesterday, I noticed him waiting for the light to change before crossing the road."

"Yeah. He never used to do that, but about a month ago he ran across the road and almost got hit. Ryne—he's a guy who works for Ben—saw it and scooped up Harley, took him to the corner and in less than half an hour had him trained to use the light. Strangest thing we ever saw. The whole town was talking about it. Josh Kennedy—he owns the local paper—even ran an article about it, but Ryne didn't want any credit or to have his name mentioned. Said he didn't have time to talk to all the dogs in the area, but he'd tell Harley to spread the word." The waitress laughed. "That Ryne can be so funny sometimes."

As the woman wandered off to serve another customer, Mel sipped her coffee thoughtfully. So, Taylor worked on cars and was some sort of dog whisperer as well as being a reclusive photographer. It was an eclectic collection of skills. What else did he have hidden up his sleeve? And, did he only work on Mondays? If she knew his schedule, maybe she could corner him at service station.

Next time the server made her rounds, Mel worked the conversation around to Taylor again. "I was wondering if you could recommend someone who could look at my car tomorrow. It was making a funny noise when I started it up this morning."

The woman nodded her head towards the window. "Right across the road where you've been staring is where you want to go. Miller's Service Station, though we just call it Ben's. He does good work and his prices are fair."

"Great. It must keep him busy though, running the whole place himself."

"His son, Greg, helped him out until he headed off to college, but Ben was real lucky 'cause soon after the boy left, Ryne moved to town."

"Ryne?"

"Uh-huh. Ryne Taylor. He's the guy I was telling you about who trained Harley. Ben hired him to work part time. He moved here back in November and knows his way around an engine. And around a woman too, if you know what I mean." The woman winked and sighed dramatically. "The man is the stuff dreams are made of."

Mel's mind flitted back to her own dream last night. Was Taylor as talented as her imaginary lover? This woman seemed to think so. Was it because the waitress had personal experience with Taylor's sexual prowess? The idea made her frown which was ridiculous. Taylor was an assignment. What he did, and with whom, was no concern of hers. Getting a firm grip on her wandering mind, she finally replied. "Thanks for the information."

"You're welcome. Oh, and you'll see the oh-so-sexy Ryne tomorrow if you take your car in. He works Mondays, Wednesdays and sometimes on Fridays if Ben's real busy."

"You seem to know his schedule quite well." She sipped her coffee and eyed the woman speculatively.

"Yeah. Ryne and I are good friends. He comes in here a lot and to the bar, too. That's my second job, working at The Broken Antler."

"So he's your boyfriend?" A pang of jealousy shot through her.

"Sort of. I mean, we see each other, but Ryne's not the type to be tied down, you know?" The woman shrugged, tucking a stray lock of bleached blond hair behind her ear.

She made no comment, merely nodding.

Leaning her hip against the counter, the waitress appeared to be settling in for a long conversation. "You came to town yesterday, right? Melody's your name?"

"Melody Greene. But you can call me Mel."

"Mel it is, then. Beth Kennedy was in earlier today and told me how she'd rented a cabin to you. She was all excited because now she can order a new dishwasher and Josh can't—" Her train of thought was interrupted by a bell ringing, signalling someone wanted service at the cash register. The woman sighed. "Damn, that's for me. I hope you enjoy your stay."

She nodded. "I'm sure I will. Thanks for your help...er..." She checked the woman's name tag, before continuing. "Lucy."

.

Chapter 9

Mel headed back to the cabin, making a brief stop at the Kennedys' first. It was a modest brick rancher with a few shrubs in the yard and some spring bulbs beginning to poke their way up through the ground. She rounded to the back door, hoping the husband and wife team didn't think she was too presumptuous, assuming they'd take messages for her.

As it turned out, they didn't mind. In fact, Bryan had already called saying Taylor was considering her request and would let her know in a few days. Thanking her temporary landlords, she hid her disappointment at the vague response and headed back to her cabin all the while berating Taylor.

Consider it. Who did the man think he was? Rembrandt or something? This was a big break for him! If Greyson liked the article, Taylor could be famous. His face and his work might become recognized throughout the art world. There could be gallery displays and talk-show interviews. He could charge exorbitant prices for his photos. People might even commission him to take pictures. This interview could lead to great things. Why was he stalling? Most people would jump at the chance for free publicity!

Was it his experience with Bastian's Gallery that was holding him back? Perhaps they had promised him publicity and it had gone wrong. There was the hint of gossip she'd heard; something about an affair with a sales associate who had disappeared and missing money. Her eyes widened as a thought occurred to her. Had Ryne flown into a rage, murdered the woman and was now hiding out? It certainly would explain his reticence!

Forcing herself to rein in her imagination, she tried to consider her theory with calm logic. He wasn't eager for an interview, but that didn't make him a criminal. The woman was missing, but maybe she'd run off with the money to some tropical island. And Ryne was *considering* an interview not flat-out refusing. A murderer would have said no right away.

Relieved her wild imaginings were just that, she wandered over to the side of the cabin where she stared at the forest beyond. It was frustrating having to wait but grinding her teeth and getting in a stir would serve no purpose. Plus, there was no firm time limit for this assignment. Willing herself to relax, she inhaled deeply letting the crisp early spring air invade her lungs.

Leaning against the side of the cabin, she consoled herself there were worse places than Stump River to spend her time. It seemed a nice place, except for the lack of a decent latte. And no one was waiting for her in Chicago. She'd quit both of her waitressing jobs and paid her rent for the next month. She should look on her time here as a vacation.

Closing her eyes, she concentrated on the sensation of the warm sun beating down on her. After a long, snowy winter, it felt good to absorb the rays. By the time summer came, she'd be back in Chicago with waves of blistering heat bouncing off the pavement and everyone would be worrying about the UV levels. See? Here was something positive. For this moment in time, she could simply enjoy the sun.

Her other senses seemed heightened with her eyes closed; the solid wood of the cabin behind her, the light breeze causing her hair to brush against her cheek. In the distance, birds were twittering and an occasional squirrel chattered. Water steadily dripped off the edge of the roof and hit the ground in a dull rhythm as the remaining snow, trapped in the eaves' troughs, melted.

She could feel the coiled tension unwinding from her shoulders and jaw. Why had she allowed herself to get so upset over Taylor? It didn't really matter if he took his time making his decision. As long as he eventually agreed.

As a matter of fact, the longer he took the better. It meant more down time for her. She could do some writing; put some polish on articles she wanted to submit for publishing. Maybe she'd even get a repeat of last night's dream. Now *that* was something to look forward to.

Pushing off from the wall, she glanced down and noticed a few bits of green poking out of the ground. Crocus maybe? She bent down to take a closer look and then nearly fell back in surprise. Large paw prints were evident in the mud right under her bedroom window. Even more surprising were two sets of large human foot prints. Just two. One set was facing towards the cabin, and the other was facing away. She stood and studied the surrounding ground carefully. There were no human prints leading to her cabin, nor away. How could that be? The ground was soft and even her slight weight was leaving indentations in the soil.

Stepping back, she studied the roof line, the location of the porch, and the walls of the cabin. Could someone have come down off the roof? Possibly, but how did they get up there? It was quite high and she saw no sign of a ladder. Technically, she supposed a very determined person could have stood on the porch and then scrambled to the window without touching the ground. The cracks and crevices between the logs would provide toe and finger holds, but why would anyone go to all that trouble? And why were they outside her bedroom window?

A frisson of fear jolted through her as several unpalatable possibilities popped into her head. Regardless of how they got there, someone had been peering in her bedroom window. Had they watched her sleeping? Changing her clothes? How much screening did the thin curtains on the window provide? And she hadn't even checked if they were closed properly last night!

She shivered and took a deep, calming breath. Maybe the owner of the footprints had been here while she was out today. That was better, wasn't it? Unless the person was inside! Looking at the cabin with something akin to horror, she backed away until she was halfway across the yard, then turned and ran to the Kennedys', intent on calling the police.

"Beth? Josh? Open up!" She pounded on the Kennedys' door and almost immediately Beth appeared, a paint brush in her hand. The woman had been repainting the bedroom when she had stopped by earlier and was still engaged in the task from the looks of things.

"Melody? I'm surprised to see you again. Is something wrong?"

"Yes! I think... I mean, there's a possibility... You see, there were these footprints..." She paused and tried to collect her thoughts.

"Slow down; you're not making any sense." Beth opened the door wider. "Come on in and have a seat. We'll talk about whatever has you so upset once you catch your breath."

Mel gratefully collapsed onto the kitchen chair and pushed her tangled locks back from her face. Running definitely had a detrimental effect on her hair, which was why she avoided the activity whenever possible, she thought inanely. A bubble of hysterical laughter threatened to escape and she squelched it back down. Why was she worrying about her hair at a time

92

like this, yet alone laughing about it? Beth was already looking at her like she was half crazy. No need to add to her suspicions by giggling like some school girl.

Composing herself, she took a deep breath and explained what she had discovered in a relatively calm and collected manner. Beth frowned and called Josh into the room from the den where he'd been watching TV.

After hearing the details, Josh decided to take a look around himself. "No point in calling the police yet. This is a small town and we don't have our own police force. The OPP—the Ontario Provincial Police—are in charge, but it's a large area and it could take up to an hour for a patrol to get here depending where the nearest cruiser is. I'll check the cabin out and if someone really has broken in, then we'll call."

"But what if someone's in there?" Mel twisted her hands not wanting Josh to face an intruder by himself. What if the criminal was armed?

Josh had no such worries though. "Did you have anything valuable in there?"

"Not really." Mel shook her head. "Just my laptop."

"Well, then, he's probably long gone, if robbery was his motive. It wouldn't take long to search such a small cabin." Josh put on his coat and headed for the door.

Mel followed hoping he was right.

Josh made small talk on the way to the cabin, showing no signs of concern. "Did you manage to find Ryne's place yesterday?"

"Yes. The map you drew was very helpful." She didn't mention the little adventure she'd had afterwards. As it was, she was sure Josh thought she was over-anxious and worrying about nothing. There was no need to add to his dubious impression of her.

"I've been by his place a couple of times, but never up to the house. He bought the place from the Nelsons. They were an older couple who wanted to retire to Timmins. Everyone in town figured the place would be on the market for years so we were all surprised when Ryne bought the place practically the same day the sale sign went up."

That was interesting. She filed the information away for future reference.

When they arrived at her cabin. Josh went inside and looked around, while she waited outside. When he came back out, there was an I-told-you-so expression on his face.

"There's no one inside, Melody. And no sign anyone but yourself has been in there."

Breathing a sigh of relief some pervert hadn't been going through her underwear drawer, she led Josh to the side of the house, pointing out the mysterious footprints.

"See? There's one set facing each direction, like someone entered and then exited, but no other prints showing how the person came or left."

Josh rubbed his chin. "That is puzzling. Let me think about it." Just as she had, he stared at the ground, the roof, the walls and the porch." He got down and pressed his hand to the ground, observing the imprint it made in the soft mud. "Only explanation I can think of is the ground was frozen when this fellow came around. It still goes below freezing most nights, but the ground nearer the house would have been softer from the heat seeping out; these cabins aren't very energy efficient, you know. His prints would show here, but not farther away."

She nodded slowly. It made sense. "But why was someone here in the first place?"

Shrugging, Josh wiped his muddy hand on a handkerchief he'd pulled from his coat pocket. "Most likely a transient looking for a place to spend the night or wondering if there was anything worth stealing. I'm not a skilled tracker or anything, but these prints could be days old. See how the dog prints are on top of the man's? No telling exactly when any of these were made."

"Are you sure they're dog prints? Couldn't they be from a wolf?" She was thinking of the wolves she'd encountered on Ryne's property. Had they tracked her here?

"Wolves? I suppose. But they don't usually come near town unless the hunting is really bad, and the winter wasn't that harsh this year. These are most likely from a stray dog."

"Oh. Okay." She was relieved at the logical explanation. "I'm sorry to have bothered you."

"No problem. I know how skittish you ladies can get. Better to check it out, so you can rest easy." With a nod, Josh headed home.

After watching him leave, she went inside and looked around the bedroom. Everything was as she'd left it. Approaching the window, she pushed the curtain aside and stared at the casing. It was old, but in good repair though there didn't seem to be a locking mechanism. She'd heard rural areas could be pretty lax when it came to home security.

What would they think if they ever saw her apartment in Chicago? She had deadbolts, chains, a keypad, and a peep hole to check who was at the door. At times, she felt like she was in a prison, but crime rates were high. If you didn't want to become another statistic, you did what you had to.

Experimentally, she tried to open the window and was surprised when it slid upwards with hardly a sound. She pulled the glass back down again and studied it carefully. There were fingerprints on the pane. The first set must be her own, but who owned the others? Had

Josh tested the window? He might have, but she didn't think he'd mentioned it.

Biting her lip, she stepped back and jerked the curtain into place. Had someone been in her room last night watching her sleep? Touching her? Kissing her? The very thought made her skin crawl and bile rise in her throat. She rushed to the bathroom and leaned against the sink, willing the contents of her stomach to stay where they belonged.

When she finally regained control, she splashed cool water on her face and then grabbed a towel to absorb the droplets all the while scolding herself. No one had been there. Josh had said the footprints were probably old. Her imagination was simply working overtime.

A bit of trivia popped into her head and a smile began to form. She remembered hearing the weather report on the radio while driving back to the cabin. It said the temperatures had been above freezing the previous night. The ground would have been soft. Anybody out there would have left lots of footprints, not just one set. Josh was right. The prints were old. Feeling relieved, she stuck her tongue out at her reflection and then hung up the towel.

With a much lighter heart, she breezed into the sitting area and pulled out her laptop. She couldn't access the internet, but she could work on some articles she had started a while back. Humming to herself, she settled down to spend the rest of the day working, totally unaware of the controversy she was creating in various locales across the continent..

Chapter 10

Ryne glared at his Beta then abruptly turned away to stare out the window. Bryan was teasing him, but his comments were hitting too close to home.

"Aww come on, Ryne. If she's just a human female, then why are you letting her get under your skin?" Even with his back turned, Ryne knew Bryan was smirking.

"How many times do I have to tell you? She isn't getting under my skin."

"Of course not. I imagined the fact you kept Daniel and me away from her yesterday."

"The less she saw of the pack, the better." He answered in clipped tones.

"And naturally, you had to drive her home."

"She was dizzy. It wasn't safe for her to drive."

"What about going to see her last night?"

He turned, ready to deny the accusation, but Bryan shook his head and kept talking.

"You said you were going to see Lucy, but it wasn't her scent on you when you came home. And I talked to Lucy today at the diner. She didn't see you last night."

"All right." Ryne gave in to the other man's badgering. "I went to see the girl, but only because she had a head injury. I got to thinking that she was alone and could have a concussion. Someone had to check on her, to make sure she didn't fall into a coma."

"Yeah, right."

The two men stared at each other. Ryne felt his face darkening. Only the fact he was an Alpha kept him from looking away.

Bryan kept grinning wider and wider. "Face it, boss. She's caught your fancy. Why fight it? The way I see it, she's here for a week or two. Use the time to your advantage and get her out of your system."

The comment didn't sit well and he growled a warning.

Bryan raised his hands and backed out of the room. "Okay, I get the message. I'm dropping the subject for now. Don't go all Alpha on me."

As the door slammed shut, Ryne relaxed and slumped down on the sofa, rubbing his face with his hands. Bryan was right. Melody Greene was just a human female. She was cute, but irritating. Nothing special, really. So why was she running through his head?

He couldn't believe what he'd done last night. The idea of her alone with a head injury had bothered him all evening. After pacing restlessly and driving his friends crazy with his miserable attitude, he'd announced he was going into town to see Lucy. And he *had* planned on seeing her; a romp with Lucy usually left him feeling relaxed and mellow. He'd just gone to check on Ms. Greene first.

After parking the car down the road, he'd changed into his wolf form and silently padded up to her cabin. No one had noticed him sniffing around the building. When he had heard her ragged breathing, he transformed back to human and peered in the window. She was lying in bed, obviously distressed. Without thinking, he opened the window and climbed in.

She was apparently in the throes of a nightmare, thrashing about on the bed. He had gripped her shoulders and commanded her to look at him, thinking if she wasn't dreaming, she'd feel better. It was only later he realized how foolish he'd been. What if she'd completely woken up? Seeing him, uninvited in her bedroom in the middle of the night, would have had her screaming the house down. No amount of fast talking could have explained his way out of that one.

Thankfully, she'd only partially opened her eyes before closing them again, a blissful smile on her face as she relaxed. Then, without him even realizing it, his wolf slipped past his guard and took over. He found himself pressing a soft kiss to her lips and, when she kissed him back, reining in his wolf had taken an extreme effort.

When he'd started to leave, she'd murmured discontentedly, reaching out for him but he'd resisted. Instead, noticing she was shivering, he'd untwisted the blankets that had been tossed aside during her nightmare, and draped them over her. After tucking her in, he'd hesitated, then brushed her tangled hair from her face before hurrying from the cabin.

Once outside, he'd morphed back into a wolf and run through the woods until he could run no longer; the ache in his body replaced by exhaustion. He'd even considered visiting Lucy but going from one woman to another wasn't right. He had some scruples. Not many, but they were there.

And so he'd headed back home, entering as silently as possible. Daniel had been in bed. Too bad Bryan had been watching a movie. Ryne had known he must look a mess, his hair tangled, his breathing rough. Their gazes had locked and, even though he was Alpha, he had shifted uncomfortably under his Beta's gaze. Bryan hadn't said anything, merely sniffing the air, no doubt picking up Melody Greene's scent, and then turning back to his movie.

Inexplicably, Ryne had felt the need to explain and even opened his mouth to do so, only to shut it again.

How could he explain what he himself didn't even understand? Instead, he'd walked to his room, climbed into bed and stared at the ceiling most of the night.

Melody Greene was bad news. Not the girl herself, but what she represented. Her arrival couldn't be a coincidence. A few weeks ago, some woman had been in his old home town of Smythston asking about him. Now, a woman was in Stump River, also wanting to see him. In all the years he'd openly shown his photographs, no one had ever wanted to interview him, except for the local paper.

If he was vain enough, he might have thought his talent was finally drawing interest from the art world. It was more likely, however, the interest was because of one damned picture. He wished he'd never taken it, let alone had it enlarged and professionally mounted. Why hadn't he left it as a snapshot in a family album?

Sighing deeply, he pondered what he should do about the problem Melody Greene was about to create. He hadn't told Bryan, but minutes before his friend had come in, Ryne had called his brother, Kane, to double check some facts about the inquisitive person who'd been asking about him. He'd been hopeful it hadn't been Ms. Greene, but of course that would have made things too easy. Instead, Kane had confirmed it was the same person, and a very uncomfortable conversation about options had followed.

If he ignored her, would she go away? Not likely, given the fact she'd travelled all the way to Stump River. For some reason she was extremely interested in him, either due to her own curiosity or because someone was paying her. Most likely it was the latter. She'd been too shocked when he'd told her the supposed 'dogs' were wolves. There had been no 'ah-ha' moment passing over her face, no hint of prevarication. If she really knew what she was looking for, she would have figured it out then and there. While she might be quirky, she wasn't stupid. Her repartee with him proved that.

How to proceed? Did he grant her an interview and tell her a bunch of lies? No. Lies could trip you up too easily. He couldn't tell her the truth. It went against the Keeping and he didn't know if she could be trusted.

A generation ago, the solution would have been easy; kill her and dispose of the body. She'd simply become another statistic. A young woman travelling on her own mysteriously disappears in the wilderness. Her car is found abandoned by the side of the road. Years later, bones turn up and the verdict would be she'd left her car, possibly to take a picture and got lost or was attacked by wild animals. It was efficient, but in this day and age more likely to lead to complications, especially if she had a family who might come looking for her.

He grimaced. Death was still a possibility; neither he nor Kane had ruled it out. It was, however, a last resort. They'd both agreed on that before ending their conversation.

Leaning his head back, he studied the ceiling and hoped for inspiration. The Keeping was their most important law. It existed to protect the whole pack, even the whole race. Their safety took precedence over the individual every time. If Melody Greene became too nosey, if it appeared she was on the verge of discovering the truth, his hands would be tied.

Getting up, he walked over to the liquor cabinet and pulled out the whiskey. He took a swig, not bothering to dirty a glass. The golden liquid burned as it slid down his throat and joined the knot was forming in his stomach.

"Here's to you, Melody Greene." The sound of his mocking toast filled the silent room. "Why the hell did you have to come here and fuck everything up?"

Chicago, Illinois, USA...

Leon Aldrich sat stiffly in the burgundy plush chair. It was directly in front of a large, leather-topped desk. As per usual, the room was dimly lit and on the cool side, despite the fact there was money to pay for electricity and heating. Aldrich appeared to take no note of his surroundings; the shelf-lined walls filled with leather-bound books, the stone fireplace, the expensive Persian rug spread out over old oak flooring weren't given so much as a glance. Instead, the man stared straight ahead. His hands rested on the report in his lap, his finger beating an impatient tattoo on the manila cover.

Anthony Greyson watched his lawyer with grim amusement. The man never indicated his displeasure by word or expression, the tapping of his finger the only sign he wasn't happy with the situation. Finally tiring of waiting for the man to break—he never did—Greyson shifted in his chair and spoke. "So, is there anything else to report?"

"No, sir. Ms. Greene's file remains unchanged. She has a distant though cordial relationship with her mother. There are no close friends nor romantic interests enquiring about her."

"And her father?"

"Listed as unknown."

"Good. Just wanted to make sure she hadn't been lying on her application."

"If she had been, I would have discovered it before she got this far into her assignment."

Greyson snorted. Nothing got past Aldrich, which was why he'd hired the man in the first place. Sharp as a pin and as closemouthed as a clam. "And her assignment is progressing?"

"If you can call it that. She is in Stump River." The man seemed to want to sniff derisively at the name of the town. Greyson watched intently for an outward emotional response, but none came. After the briefest of pauses, Aldrich continued. "She has discovered where Taylor purportedly lives, but claims she has yet to make contact with the man."

"Claims?"

"There was something in her voice that made me wonder. However, since it was a message on the answering machine, it wasn't possible to question her."

Greyson nodded. "It's to be expected. All our research shows Taylor isn't interested in publicity. Hopefully, Greene can get under his natural radar."

"I hope you're right, sir."

"I know you do, Leon. You think I'm a crazy old fool to spend my time and money on this. But if I'm right, and I'm sure I am, the payoff will be well worth it."

Aldrich stood and set the manila file on the edge of Greyson's desk. "If that's all, sir, I'll be on my way."

"Yes. You're dismissed. Franklin will show you out." He moved to ring the bell.

"That won't be necessary. After all these years, I know the way."

Greyson barked in laughter as the lawyer left the room. That pathetic attempt at humour was the closest thing to a human response he'd forced out of Aldrich in months. He leaned forward and picked up the file, thumbing through the contents until he found the page he wanted. "Ah, Ms. Greene. Whatever will become of you before this is over?"

Smythston, Oregon, USA...

Kane put down the phone and pinched the bridge of his nose. It was happening. What he'd most feared for years, hoped against with every fibre of his being, was finally occurring. He clenched his fist, uncaring his nails were digging into his palms, tiny drops of blood appearing.

It was beyond his control now and he didn't like the feeling. He was Alpha. Sitting back and waiting went against his nature, yet he knew reacting could cause the cards to tumble even faster. All he could do was wait while playing out the various scenarios in his head.

The ball was in Ryne's court. He trusted his brother to make the right decision, to do whatever needed to be done. He hoped it wasn't the worst-case scenario.

The door to his office opened and he looked up. His mate, Elise slid in and locked the door.

"Am I disturbing anything?" The warmth of her voice washed over him, soothing his fears with her calm tone. It had always been like that, right from the first time he'd seen her. She'd been young and frightened by his sudden appearance in her life, but something had attracted them to each other.

"You disturb me, but in all the right ways."

She walked over to him and stood behind his chair. Her hands on his shoulders, she kissed the nape of his neck.

He smiled, twisting around so he could see her. "To what do I owe the honour of this visit?"

"I was lonely." She pouted up at him and blinked her eyes innocently.

"Lonely? Or lusty?" He raised his brow, knowing the hormonal changes from her pregnancy were sending her libido into overdrive.

"Both." She laughed and she circled around so she was in front of him.

He stood and kissed her thoroughly before easing back to rest his hands on her waist. His child was in there and he dropped to his knee to kiss the slightly rounded surface. Pressing his ear to Elise's belly, he listened intently. Sometimes, he was sure he could hear its heartbeat, despite the fact Nadia, their resident nurse-practitioner, said it was way too soon. He gently rubbed the skin and whispered "I love you" to the child within. Feeling Elise's fingers combing through his hair, he looked up and flushed, feeling embarrassed.

She smiled at him. "I love how much you love our baby already."

He moved to bring his face close to hers. "I love his mother just as much."

"I know." She barely managed to get the words out before he captured her mouth with his again....

Sometime later, he was seated in his chair again, except Elise was now cuddled in his lap.

She nuzzled his neck. "Why were you looking so worried when I came in?"

He hesitated to tell her, but knew she'd find out one way or another. It was better coming from him. "Someone has found Ryne and is asking about his pictures."

She stilled her movements and pulled away, looking up at him with solemn eyes. "The same person who was here?"

He nodded.

"It could be totally innocent. She said she was writing an article about artists."

"Would she travel all the way to Stump River, if that's all it was?"

"Perhaps." She looked at him, a silent plea for reassurance in her eyes. When he didn't give it, her shoulders slumped. "What are we going to do?"

"Nothing. Yet." He sighed heavily. "Hopefully, Ryne can deal with it and it stops there."

"But what if it doesn't? What if she's working with someone? What if they come here looking for us?"

He shifted uncomfortably, not wanting to say the words, but knowing he must. "The Keeping is our most important law. Not only for us, but for our people everywhere. It's kept our kind safe from persecution and allows us to live in peace. We can't ignore it simply because it's inconvenient."

"Inconvenient?" She pushed away from him and abruptly stood up, protectively clutching her belly and the unborn child within. "Our lives, the lives of the pack members, the life of our child..." She choked on the words. "Those are more than *inconveniences*, Kane!"

"I know." He got to his feet and wrapped her in his arms, rocking her gently back and forth. "I know. I don't want our way of life to end. I don't want to be responsible for ordering the deaths of our friends and family." He put his finger under her chin, forcing her to look at him. He offered what little reassurance there was. "If it comes to that, if it appears they'll find us, we'll send as many of the young away as possible. Other packs will take them in. Just enough of us will remain behind to make it look real. The humans will say it was another cult suicide, and whoever these people are who are searching for us will be left with no evidence." Elise whimpered and he hugged her even more closely. "The Keeping is law. Our existence remains secret, even if it means death."

Chapter 11

Mel parked her car on the main street and turned off the engine. It was Monday morning and traffic in Stump River was light. A few vehicles were parked in front of the various businesses and pedestrians strolled down the sidewalks at the kind of leisurely pace you'd never encounter in the hustle and bustle of Chicago. There were no exhaust fumes, no angry commuters gesturing rudely at each other, no screeching brakes, no high-rise office buildings blocking the view of the sky. Life here appeared so simple and quiet, almost a throwback to a different time.

She studied the scene for a minute before shifting her attention to the building directly across the street. Miller's Service Station. The low, brick building was painted white and had a red and blue sign mounted above the door proclaiming the name of the owner and hours of business. A front office with a large plate-glass window offered a view inside.

"No metal bars to prevent break-ins," she murmured to herself. "And someone's moving about inside." She squinted her eyes but the glare from the sun, prevented her from seeing who it might be. Taylor? Perhaps but what was she going to do about it?

There'd been no message from him this morning, so he must still be undecided about the interview. The question was, should she go over there and talk to him? If she did, maybe she could convince him to agree. On the other hand, maybe he'd think she was pushy and flat out refuse. She furrowed her brow, weighing her options.

When no clear answer came to mind, she struck the steering wheel in frustration and then yelped. She'd hit the horn by accident and it was honking. Continuously. She stared at the wheel in shock before her brain kicked in and she began frantically jiggling the annoying feature. By the time she stopped the noise, everyone in the entire two block expanse of downtown Stump River was looking her way. Even Josh and Beth Kennedy were standing in the doorway of the Gazette. Giving a shy wave at her temporary landlords, she sunk down in her seat knowing her face was flushing with mortification.

Hopefully, the incident didn't make the front page of the paper. Not much seemed to happen in a town of this size. A stuck horn on a car could be big news. As she hid from view, she pictured the headlines; Foreigner Wreaks Havoc in Downtown Core.

Damn, this never happened in a movie when the heroine hit the steering wheel. And, the actress never hurt her hand either! She rubbed her palm surprised how hard a steering wheel could be.

After several minutes of hiding out below the height of the dashboard, she slowly sat up and looked around. Everyone had gone about their business. Traffic was moving normally and no one was staring out of their windows wondering who the idiot in the blue car might be.

Relieved, she headed into the diner. There was no point in sitting outside when she could be inside drinking coffee and possibly eating a Danish. Food could be such a source of comfort, she mused. Besides, since she'd have a perfect view of the service station, she could put it on her tab as surveillance related expenses!

Five minutes later she was at a table, a cup of coffee in front of her and a sticky pastry in her hand. She licked some stray icing off of her finger while checking out her surroundings. The diner was bright and clean with white counters and red vinyl covered seats. Red checked curtains hung from the large plate glass window, tied back so as to not obstruct the view of the street. A white board had daily specials listed on it and a glass display case showed a variety of homemade baked goods.

It was only moderately busy inside the establishment, with just one waitress and the chef on duty. She discovered it was Lucy's day off but Ruth and Al, the waitress and the chef, were equally inclined to chat. They were co-owners of the business and pleased to give her the low-down on the locals.

By the time she was done with her Danish, she'd learned the citizens of Stump River liked Ryne, Bryan and Daniel. Ruth reported the local women actually drooled over them.

"All three are definite hunks and very talented lovers, if even half the rumours can be believed." Ruth told her in a stage whisper, the thin knob of hair on top of her head bobbing up and down as she nodded emphatically. The woman's cheeks were stained pink as if uttering the words alone were enough to turn her on and she was dramatically pressing her hand to her meagre bosom.

Al scoffed at Ruth's description. "Quit all that foolish talk, Ruth. They're all real men. Not like those sissies you watch on your soap operas." The chef rubbed his bristly chin and leaned back, his elbows propped on the counter. "Those three fellows are honest, hard-workers. I've seen them hauling supplies at the lumber yard and they barely break a sweat. More important, they know the value of silence and don't go around talking your ear off, like some folks do." He stared pointedly at Ruth as he made that last comment. She responded by hitting him on the shoulder and shooing him into the kitchen to start heating the soup for lunch. He complied but not before pinching Ruth's bottom.

Mel laughed softly to herself as she listened to the banter between the husband and wife team. It was a relationship of opposites. Al was short, well-rounded and a man of few words while Ruth was tall, thin and loved a good gossip. They might bicker, but she could tell by the looks they exchanged, they cared deeply for each other. Stump River seemed to be the place to find solid marriages. Josh and Beth, Al and Ruth. She wondered how many other such couples were in town. Ryne and Lucy? Were they close to tying the knot? And why had that idea popped into her head?

Probably because the man in question was right across the street from her. He was putting gas in a car for a little old lady. From her vantage point in the diner, she watched him chatting away to the customer while providing basic service to her vehicle.

It was hard to miss how his black t-shirt clung to his torso, giving an excellent view of his muscles as he moved his arm back and forth while cleaning the windshield. When he bent over to check the oil, Mel saw how his tight rear-end filled out his low-slung jeans; no plumber's crack there.

He stood up and laughed at something the woman said. The whiteness of his teeth was apparent even from across the street and she was sure she could see a twinkle in his amazingly blue eyes. An unexpected wave of desire hit her and she blinked, realizing she was actually leaning forward, as if trying to get closer to the man. Possibly sensing someone was watching him, he looked up, staring straight across the street at her.

She drew back and snatched up the menu from the table, pretending rapt interest in its contents. Surely, he hadn't seen her ogling him? She peeked over the edge of the menu and then hid again. He was still looking her way! Mortified at being caught acting like a schoolgirl with a secret crush, she scolded herself for being so intent on checking out his physical attributes. Yes, he was good looking, but she was here to do a job, and it didn't include lusting over the man. Perhaps it was all hormonal. It had been a while since she'd been with someone, so of course, a hot-looking guy would seem even more appealing than usual, regardless of his personality.

Glancing across the road, she was both relieved and disappointed the customer had left, and Taylor was no longer outside. Darn! She'd wanted one more peek. Fanning herself with the menu, she reminded herself getting involved with him could skew her perception during their interview. Besides, Taylor was Lucy's and she didn't poach on another woman's territory.

A little voice felt it was important to point out the waitress had left her with the impression the two had a rather loose relationship; more a friends with benefits type of thing. She frowned, wishing she hadn't thought of that. The sexy, bad-ass draw of the man was hard enough to resist as it was.

Annoyed with her own thoughts, she drained her cup and checked the time. The diner was starting to fill with the lunch crowd. She probably should leave so there would be room for other customers.

Getting to her feet, she picked up her purse and then stepped outside. It was another beautiful spring day and, having nothing better to do with her time, she decided to go for a walk. The main street was only two blocks long, but there were a few side streets as well. With a smile, she set off to explore the little town.

Forty-five minutes later, she found herself standing in front of Miller's Service Station having discovered almost all of what the little town had to offer. Now, she faced the same dilemma with which she'd started the day; did she go in and talk to Taylor or leave him alone? Nibbling her lip, she weighed the pros and cons of each course of action.

"Adding stalker to your list of crimes now?"

Mel screamed at the sound of the deep, male voice so close to her ear and turned quickly. Unfortunately, she lost her balance and started to fall backwards, tipping off the curb and stumbling onto the street.

Simultaneously, several things happened. A horn blared, the owner of the voice grabbed her pulling her flush against his body and a truck whizzed by. It all happened so quickly, all she could do was gape up at the man.

"Suicidal, too?" Ryne Taylor was staring down at her, his expression somewhere between anger and exasperation.

Mesmerized by the intense blue of his eyes, she only slowly became aware of the way their bodies fit together. Her eyes were level with his throat, her hands pressed to his chest and his hips snugly cradled her stomach. She could see his throat move as he swallowed, feel the strong beating of his heart and smell the very male scent of him wrapping itself around her. Unthinkingly, she allowed her fingers to spread out over the hard planes of his chest, while her gaze focused on his lips. They were firm, the lower one slightly fuller and curved into a...a smirk?

Belatedly recognizing the situation she was in, she jerked her gaze back to his eyes. He was laughing at her! Oh, not out loud, but she could see his inner mirth. She struggled to step away, but he merely locked his arms more tightly around her.

"Let me go!"

"That's all you ever say to me." He sighed and pretended to pout.

"That's because you're always grabbing me!"

"And you'd rather I let you fall into the street and be hit by a delivery van?" He tilted his head.

She stopped struggling as the gravity of what had almost happened hit her. "No. I suppose I should thank you."

He nodded and looked at her expectantly.

"What?" She frowned and then realized what he wanted. She huffed, thoroughly put out by the man, even if he did save her life. "Okay. Fine. Thank you, Ryne Taylor, for pulling me to safety. Now let me go."

"Is that all?"

"All?"

"Just a thank you? Saving your life surely deserves something more...personal...tangible...than a mere 'thank you'. Actions speak louder than words, you know." He winked at her and gave an evil grin.

Closing her eyes, she counted to ten knowing exactly what he wanted. All right. She'd kiss him and then, if he didn't let her go, she'd knee him in the groin. Opening her eyes, she stood on tiptoe and placed a chaste kiss on his lips. At least it was supposed to be a chaste kiss. No sooner had their lips touched than he immediately took control.

Using one of his hands to cradle the back of her head, he angled their mouths, pressing his lips to hers and, shockingly, she found herself responding, her entire body tingling. She leaned closer, wanting even more contact with him and then suddenly she found herself standing a foot away.

She blinked in surprise. "What?"

He smirked, seemingly cool and unaffected by their encounter. "Okay, so you're a trespasser, a stalker, have suicidal tendencies, and you're a sex maniac."

"Sex maniac!"

"You're the one who kissed me."

"But you said..." She sputtered, unable to finish the sentence.

"I said something tangible would be nice to go with the thank you. It could have been a cup of coffee or a handshake. You assumed it was a kiss."

She narrowed her eyes and glared.

"You also disturbed the peace this morning." He folded his arms and gave her a look that was reminiscent of the one given her by the police last time she'd been caught speeding. "That was your horn, wasn't it?"

"Ooh!" Not even realizing what she was doing, she stamped her foot in frustration and Taylor burst out laughing. She gave him a drop-dead look and turned to leave only to find herself jerked back when he grabbed her arm.

"Hey! Where do you think you're going?" He'd stopped laughing, but was still smiling.

She tugged on her arm and spoke through clenched teeth. "I'm leaving before I do something I'll regret."

"Really? So you don't regret anything you've done up to this point, like trespassing, stalking or kissing me?"

It took a minute to figure out he was implying she'd enjoyed kissing him. She considered denying it, but he'd find a way to twist that around, too. Instead, she switched to one of his other accusations. "I'm not stalking you."

"No? You scaled my gate on Saturday. You parked outside my place on Sunday; my friend, Bryan, told me about that one. Today you've sat in the diner across from where I work and watched every move I made. Sorry, honey. That's stalking."

"I was not watching every move you made."

"Correction. You couldn't see inside the building but every time I stepped out, I could feel you watching me."

"You were only out once." She folded her arms and affected a pout, staring blindly at the building behind him, rather than looking at his irritating, but oh-so-handsome face. After a beat, she winced, realizing she'd given herself away. If she hadn't been watching him, how would she have known he'd only been out once? Damn! If he was paying attention, and she was sure he was, he'd have the goods on her.

"Stalker." He taunted her again. She glanced at him out of the corner of her eye. His hands were casually tucked in his back pockets and he had a look of infinite patience on his face, as if he'd wait forever until she conceded.

Sighing, she ran her hands through her hair, pushing it away from her warm face. "All right. I was sort of...stalking you."

He grinned. "See? That wasn't so hard to admit. You know," he paused, a considering look coming over his face, "I've never had a stalker before."

"Really?" How could someone with his amazingly good looks have never been followed around by a woman?

"Nope." He headed inside the service station and she hurried after him, intrigued. "Most women take one look at me and openly throw themselves at my feet."

She snorted and rolled her eyes. "Not conceited much, are you?"

Now inside the building, he turned to face her and leaned back against a workbench. "I prefer to call it having a healthy self-esteem." When she raised a brow, he laughed. "So, Melody Greene, aka stalker girl, I hear you want to interview me." His expression turned serious and it took her a moment to switch gears and organize her thoughts.

"Um...yeah. I mean, yes." She stood up straighter and looked him in the eye. "I want to interview you."

"Why?"

A coldness crept into his voice and the blue of his eyes turned icy, sending a shiver down her spine. Where had the man she'd just been talking to gone? Eyes like these could belong to a murderer. A thought flit through her head; maybe he *was* responsible for the missing sales clerk!

No, she'd already decided that wasn't a plausible theory. She licked her lips and gave a carefully worded answer. "I'm trying to write a paper on up-and-coming artists and I've seen some of your work and thought it was good. Really good."

Taylor didn't say anything. He just gave her a considering look, as if trying to decide whether or not he believed her. Abruptly, he pushed off from the bench he'd been leaning on, his movement bringing him into her personal space. She stepped back and swallowed. Something about him seemed threatening, over-powering, and she found herself staring at the ground, unable to meet his eyes. What sounded like a rather satisfied rumble came from his chest and she dared to glance up at him. He was still staring at her, but it wasn't so scary now. It was more a look of interest, as if he found her puzzling, but fascinating.

She cleared her throat. "I...I think the interview would be beneficial to your career."

"You'll need to convince me of that."

"Well—"

He interrupted, reaching around her to grab his coat, which was on a hook beside her.

She jumped back as his arm brushed against her breast and electricity tingled through her.

Taylor didn't seem to notice and talked as if there'd been no contact between them. "I'm done here; I only work until noon on Mondays. Meet me for supper at The Broken Antler at six-thirty. You can convince me then."

His sudden change of topic once again had her floundering. She hurried after him as he walked out of the building. "The Broken Antler?"

"Uh-huh. It's the bar next door. They have great burgers, hotdogs, chilli, chicken fingers; that sort of stuff."

Not sure what else to do but agree, she nodded. "All right. Six-thirty."

Taylor didn't respond. He simply walked across the parking lot, got in a black pickup truck and drove away.

Chapter 12

Ryne headed for home, mulling about his encounter with Melody Greene. He hadn't meant to approach her or to interact as he had, but seeing her standing mere yards away, he suddenly found himself walking towards her and starting a conversation. Damn his inner wolf!

She was a funny little thing and not inclined to back down from him either. Chuckling, he thought of how easy it was to tease her. Mind you, she'd held her own, dishing out some good comebacks. Sparring with her had been fun, invigorating even. He liked a woman who kept him on his toes and she certainly did that. There was a fire within her.

A grin spread across his face as he recalled how her cheeks turned pink and her brown eyes flashed with temper. She definitely appealed to him physically, too. He'd sensed his wolf humming in approval when he'd carried her from his house the other day. And today, when she'd kissed him...

He replayed the feel of her pressed against him, her mouth moving under his, her soft sighs tickling his ears. Good thing he'd had enough will-power to back off. He had no business messing around with her.

The girl claimed she wanted to interview him because she'd liked his work as a photographer, but he'd sensed deception on her part. Between Lycans, lies were hard to detect, but humans were less adept at hiding their true selves. The dilation of her pupils, the tilt of her head, a certain quality of voice and breathing patterns, all led him to believe Ms. Greene had told him a part truth, but not the whole truth. How had she tracked him down? What was she hiding? And what was her real agenda?

He stopped the truck as he reached the gated edge of his territory. Climbing out, he dealt with the lock, drove the truck through and then secured the gate again, pausing for a moment to enjoy the scenery. Tall pines rose up on either side of the driveway, acting like sentinels guarding the privacy of his home. Unlike much of the surrounding area, this forest was untouched and unharvested. Decaying logs, the remains of ancient trees, were scattered on the ground amongst young saplings and strong maturing conifers. Patches of snow were still visible, but he knew in another month ferns, wild flowers and other forms of natural vegetation would carpet the forest floor. Already, signs of animal life were increasing as the temperatures warmed. Tracks from a myriad of creatures tattooed the muddy ground while birds chirped and twittered overhead. This would be his first spring on his own land and he was anxious to explore his domain without a concealing blanket of snow.

A wolf needed to become one with his territory, knowing every wrinkle in the land, the placement of each plant. Like a lover, he would watch it breathe and grow, sensing its moods, caring for it, guarding it against those who dared to trespass. He inhaled deeply, taking in the earthy, woodsy scents.

Mine, both he and his wolf declared.

He knew some of the locals wondered about his obsessive need for privacy, the large gate, the plethora of warning signs, but no one was pressing for answers. That was one nice thing about Stump River. The people were friendly, but not too nosey, seeming to be content to leave each other alone. Maybe it was all part of their Canadian heritage. When researching the country, he'd read about their concept of being a cultural mosaic where individuality was encouraged. It was one of the reasons he'd chosen to move here. With any luck, people would leave him alone and his pack would flourish alongside the other citizens.

Provided someone, such as Melody Greene, didn't mess it up.

Frowning, he climbed back in his truck and drove towards the house. Which pictures of his had she seen? He didn't care about the sunsets or the birds or the wildflowers. It was one particular picture featuring his brother Kane in his wolf form that worried him. Anyone studying the picture—at least anyone who knew anything about wolves—would immediately see the animal in the photo was unique, a brand-new species, in fact. Well, technically not a *new* species given Lycans had existed since the beginning of time; they were just adept at keeping their existence hidden. Of course, there were rumours and supposed sightings, but most of those were attributed to hysteria and folklore.

It wasn't hysteria, though.

He *did* exist. He, and his family and friends, his whole *species* existed and flourished alongside humanity, but only due to carefully guarding their secret from the rest of the world.

It hadn't always been that way. Long ago, Lycans had been hunted to the very brink of extinction, forced to hide in the depths of the forest, living in constant fear. That was when the Book of the Law had emerged; the product of his people's desperation. The few remaining packs had banded together, creating a set of laws, which, if followed, would safeguard their existence.

And since that time, it had worked. True, in the beginning there had been terrible sacrifices. The complete relocation of every pack in order to make a fresh start. Whole packs needing to be destroyed when the careless or defiant actions of a few led to their discovery. Pack wars erupting when one group refused to bend to the law.   Those difficulties, however, had merely created greater determination in those who remained. Eventually, the universal good had outweighed the losses.   Their existence faded from human memory until only a few whispered rumours remained.

For the most part, his people had lived undetected over the past couple of centuries.   Alliances between packs had strengthened their common bond, the need to be careful, to avoid excessive attention, became ingrained into their way of life. Peace and prosperity were enjoyed by all; the dangers of the past now but a distant memory for most.   Who would have thought a simple snapshot might undo centuries of progress?

Ryne recalled the day as clearly as if it were yesterday.   He'd been out taking pictures and had come across his brother in his wolf form.   On a whim, he'd snapped a picture of Kane, and when he'd seen how well the picture turned out, he'd enlarged it and had it mounted.   It was supposed to be for the family, not publicly shown, but his ex-girlfriend had taken it and then sold it and now... Well, the severity of the fallout was yet to be determined.

According to Kane's report, Melody Greene had told Elise she'd heard of his wolf photograph, but hadn't actually seen it. But was that the truth? Did she know the significance? Had she realized, or had someone told her, it was probably the only picture of a real live Lycan in existence today? And if she knew, what did she plan on doing about it? Or was she really just interested in his work for its artistic merit? It was a possibility, but he was too much of a cynic to hope for that.   The worst-case scenario was she would figure out where the picture was taken and use the information to find Kane and his pack.

He clenched his hands around the steering wheel. That couldn't be allowed to happen.   The idea of his entire family entering into a suicide pact in order to preserve the safety of their race was unthinkable. He'd do whatever he had to do in order to save them. If need be, the secret of their location would die here in Stump River.

Mel checked her watch. It was exactly six-thirty. She stood outside The Broken Antler and nervously wiped her sweaty palms on the legs of her jeans. Hopefully what she was wearing was appropriate. Meeting with someone for an interview would usually call for more professional attire, but considering the location Ryne had chosen, that hadn't seemed too suitable. Instead, she'd settled on dark jeans and a pretty t-shirt with some chunky jewellery as an accent.

Clothes weren't really important to her, but knowing you looked good and were dressed appropriately did provide a boost of confidence. And confidence was what she needed right now. She didn't usually go into bars by herself; at least not ones as seedy-looking as this one. Hopefully, the interior was in better repair than the exterior. Taking in the faded paint, cracked cement and the burnt out lights in the sign, she decided the location matched Ryne's personality; very rough around the edges.

How she'd ever manage to interview the rude, sarcastic man without doing him bodily harm, she wasn't sure. If it wasn't for the large sum of money already in her bank account, and the promise of more to come, she might actually back out. However, she'd made a deal with Aldrich and his client, and she wasn't a quitter. Though, as she eyed a boarded-up window and the shards of glass on the ground below it, perhaps now was the time to start? Had the window been broken because someone was thrown through it? She gulped at the very idea.

A breeze swept down the street and she shivered; her denim jacket providing little protection against the cool evening wind. Taking a deep breath, she grabbed the handle and yanked open the heavy wooden door while eyeing the antlers hanging drunkenly overhead and hoping they wouldn't fall on her. Luckily, they only swayed slightly and she quickly scooted inside, not wanting to tempt gravity, nor the old rusty chain suspending them.

The interior of the bar was better than she'd hoped. It appeared clean, though the smell of beer and fried food overwhelmed any scent of cleaning fluid that might have confirmed the fact. For the most part the decor was unremarkable and could have been located anywhere on the continent. The lighting was dim, the air stale and pedestal tables with worn chairs were scattered about the large room. One wall contained a big screen TV, another had racks of pool cues and dart boards, while a bar occupied the third wall. Rows of glasses and bottles of liquor lined shelves backed by an old mirror that had seen better days. In front of the spirits, a large, dark-haired man, who closely resembled a bear in a plaid flannel shirt, stood lazily drying glasses. He was talking to the patrons who sat around the scarred wooden structure of the bar. A quick perusal revealed none of the men there were Ryne.

She shifted her gaze from the room's decor and began to examine each table. Was Ryne here or had she arrived before him? Seeing no sign of him, she twisted the strap of her purse in her hands, considering her options; sit at a table or at the bar? A few patrons were glancing her way with mild curiosity, but most ignored her. Even so, she felt conspicuous and moved towards the bar, eyeing a seat near the wall with a good view of the door. She'd sit there and wait for Ryne to arrive.

Settling onto a bar stool, she smiled politely at the man beside her and then fixed her gaze on the door. Minutes ticked by and she shifted uncomfortably. What if he stood her up? No, this had been his idea. He'd be here. Wouldn't he?

Unexpectedly, a large hand attached to a very hairy arm appeared in her peripheral vision and she jerked away, spinning around to see who it belonged to.

"What can I get you, little lady?" The bear in the flannel shirt was the owner of the arm and his deep gravelly voice had a hint of a French accent.

"Nothing, thank you. I'm waiting for someone." She smiled politely and made to turn away when he spoke again.

"And who would that be?" When she hesitated, he smiled at her revealing a mouthful of large teeth that appeared all the whiter for the black facial hair growing profusely on his chin. It was a friendly smile and helped make up for the fact he loomed over her. "I know everyone who lives here."

"Er...Ryne Taylor."

"Ryne, you say?" He chuckled and she had a feeling from the look on his face a lot of women had sat in this very spot waiting for Ryne. "You won't have to wait long."

"Really?" Again, she tried to turn towards the door but the bartender, whose name tag said Armand, gently took her by the shoulders and spun her bar stool to face the far corner of the room. A movement in that area caught her attention and, as her eyes adjusted to the dim lighting, she realized it was caused by the man she was looking for. He was leaning back casually in his chair, drinking beer and studying her with an impassive expression. As she made eye contact, he nodded and took another swig.

"Thank you." She gave the bartender a tight smile and hopped off the stool.

How long would Taylor have left her cooling her heels before coming to get her? The man really was insufferable. She wove her way between the partially filled tables and, when she finally reached her destination, she was sure the anger inside her would have steam rising from her collar. She opened her mouth to speak, but he beat her to it.

"Sit."

Frowning at the command—she wasn't a dog, after all—she pulled out a chair and plunked herself down, all the while wondering why she was complying rather than defiantly remaining on her feet. Her temper rose even further when she noted the smirk on the man's face. Well, she'd deal with that right now!

"And a good evening to you, too. Why thank you. Yes, I'd love to have a seat. What a gentleman you were, to come and meet me at the bar. Oh, it's lovely to see you again, too. What's that? The rest of my day? It was fine, thanks for asking." She held a mocking conversation with herself.

Ryne blinked and raised his eyebrows.

"That, you insufferable jerk, is how most people start an evening. It's called polite conversation." She was *not* about to put up with his rude behaviour.

Slowly, he took another swig of beer before responding. "You seem to know how it's done all on your own, so why should I bother?"

"Because..." She stopped herself and snapped her mouth shut. He was doing it again. Getting her all worked up with his little games. She wouldn't get caught again. Tonight, she was a professional. "Never mind." Settling back in her seat, she forced a polite smile on to her face and said nothing.

Minutes ticked by and silence reigned over the table. Ryne sipped his beer and Mel stared at the TV trying to appear as if the newscast held her riveted. She kept her hands tightly clasped in her lap and fought the urge to fidget. Finally, relief came. With her peripheral vision, she saw Ryne signal the server. When the woman approached the table, Mel turned ready to greet her as a long lost relative.

It wasn't a long lost relative, but at that point, she was sure the woman was the next best thing.

"Hey, it's Mel!" The server grinned and Mel grinned back, pleased to see a friendly face. It was Lucy, the waitress at the diner from the previous day.

"Mel?" Ryne looked at her incredulously. "That's the name of a guy who comes to fix your toilet."

"No it's not. It's a perfectly respectable nickname for Melody." She defended her name hotly while Lucy lightly hit him on the head with the menus she was holding.

"Ouch! Cut that out, Lucy." Ryne grabbed the woman's wrist and took the menus from her. "That's no way to treat a customer. You keep that up and I'll complain to Armand."

"Armand won't do anything; I have him wrapped around my little finger. You just be nice to my friend here." Lucy didn't seem in the least worried by Ryne's threat. She pulled her wrist out of his hand, planted a quick kiss on his cheek and sashayed away, calling over her shoulder. "If he gives you any trouble, you come see me, Mel."

"Thanks, I will." She felt considerably better after the exchange and turned to face Ryne. This time she was the one smirking. Knowing she had an ally in the building gave her more confidence. He was staring at her again, but his expression was friendlier now than it had when she arrived.

"Mel." He seemed to be trying the name out as he looked at her. Finally, he shook his head. "Nope. You don't look like a Mel. To me, you're a Melody."

"You and my mother." She sighed.

"Your mother?"

"Yeah. My mother's sort of a free-spirited, hippie type. She was going through a song writing stage when I was born and decided to call me Melody."

"I like it."

She blinked, surprised by the sincerity of his comment. "Well...that's good, I guess." She giggled as a thought struck her. "I suppose I should be thankful Mom wasn't in her sewing and quilting stage at the time or I might have been called bobbin or thimble."

Ryne's rich chuckle ran over her like a warm breeze and his countenance suddenly seemed less imposing. The tension eased in her shoulders and she smiled as she looked at him. Here was the man Beth and Ruth had been talking about; the sexy, charming heartthrob who had the female population of Stump River in a stir. His eyes were twinkling and his grin showed off white teeth, which contrasted wonderfully with the stubbly shadow appearing on his lower face. It was enough to melt the coldest of hearts; she felt her own give an extra thump her mouth went dry.

Thankfully, Lucy returned with cutlery and glasses of water. As the waitress took their orders, Mel had a chance to compose herself. Ryne might be hot, but he was also arrogant and she wouldn't feed his already inflated ego. Having managed to get herself under control and with the ice broken between them, they settled down to some friendly banter as they watched TV and ate. She made her pitch as to the benefits of an interview and Ryne asked friendly questions about her life. By the time they had finished eating, she decided Ryne could be reasonably polite if he put his mind to it. Maybe interviewing him wouldn't be quite the ordeal she'd imagined it would be.

When he excused himself from the table, she watched him cross the room, her chin propped in her hand. He really did have a nice tight rear, she thought to herself.

"Mighty fine butt, eh?" Lucy nudged her, shaking her out of her trance. The waitress had come to clear the table and must have noticed the direction of Mel's gaze.

"What? Oh. Yeah. Sorry."

"Sorry for what?" Lucy glanced up from gathering their dirty dishes onto a large tray and wiping down the table.

"You know." She shrugged. "I mean you and Ryne..."

Lucy chuckled and sat down in Ryne's seat, propping her feet up on an empty chair from the next table. "Listen, Mel, Ryne is a good-looking man. If you didn't notice, I'd have to wonder about you."

She relaxed, happy Lucy didn't think she was trespassing. "Thanks for understanding. Have you known him long?"

"Ever since he moved here back in November." She reached out and stole some popcorn from the complimentary basket on the table. "I remember the day he and his two friends, Bryan and Daniel, walked in. Everybody in the whole place sort of froze and stared, women and men alike. Ryne stood looking around the room; I swear he made eye-contact with every person there. And then he ordered three beers, walked over here and sat down like he'd always lived in Stump River. After a few minutes, everything returned to normal. It was weird, you know?" She shrugged and crunched more popcorn.

"I agree. That was sort of strange, wasn't it? I mean, I walked in here and no one noticed."

"Yeah, I don't know what it is about those guys, but they command attention, especially Ryne. Bryan too, but in a different sort of a way. Daniel's young, though he gets his fair share of respect as well."

"Daniel? I haven't met him yet."

"He's a real sweetie. Kind of quiet, but really nice. He looks to be around eighteen, I'd say. Works part time at the lumber yard. So does Bryan, for that matter."

"And Ryne? How old is he?"

"That I do know!" She winked knowingly. "We celebrated together a few weeks ago. He just turned twenty-seven. I'm not sure how old Bryan is."

"I met him the other day outside Ryne's place. He seemed friendly."

"He is and he has a good left hook on him, too."

"Left hook?"

"Yep." Lucy picked up Ryne's glass and took a sip. She glanced at Mel and winked. "Ryne won't mind sharing."

She was anxious to hear more about Bryan fighting. If she was going to be interviewing Ryne, she'd be around his friends and if they were violent, she'd like to know. "So, Bryan fights a lot?"

"No, not really. It was just that one time, but it was mighty spectacular. They'd been here about two weeks and it was a really busy night. A group of bikers had stopped in and were hanging around the pool table, giving all of us girls a hard time. One of them wouldn't leave this one girl, Annie, alone, so I went over there to try to help her. The guy shoved me away and his friends grabbed me. I called out for Armand, only Ryne and Bryan were suddenly there. Bryan slugged him and sent him through the window; that's why it's boarded up now."

Mel was sure her eyes were the size of saucers. The pool table was at least six feet from the window. She could imagine how hard Bryan must have swung to move a man such a distance. Lucy must've been exaggerating. Most likely the fellow was standing in front of the window to begin with. Still, she was curious to hear about the rest of the. "And what about Ryne?"

"Somehow he managed to take out the two who were holding me. It all happened so fast no one could figure out what happened, exactly. One minute those creeps were grabbing at me and the next they were flat out on the ground. Ryne didn't even have a scratch on him." Lucy shook her head, obviously still in wonder at the occurrence. "Anyway, the other bikers were frozen, like they were really scared. Then they backed out of the room and drove off, leaving their friends behind. Ryne and Bryan helped clean up the mess, dragged the two guys who were on the floor outside and made sure Annie and I were okay. Armand let us leave early. Bryan drove Annie home, and Ryne walked me home." Lucy grinned. "I gave him a big thank you once we got to my place, if you know what I mean."

Mel knew what she was referring to. But why did the idea bother her? She struggled to explain it, but came up empty.

Chapter 13

Ryne stood in the darkened hallway that led to the bar's washrooms. He had a perfect view of Melody or 'Mel' as she called herself. He snorted. It was a ridiculous name for a female and she definitely was one.

His plan for the evening was completely off track. He'd intended to be as rude and sarcastic as possible, goading her into getting mad and stomping out or at least rethinking wanting to interview him. But when Lucy had come over and he'd heard the name 'Mel' he'd been caught off guard. Plus, she was proving to be pleasant company and seemed genuine in all she said. There was no hint of deception about her tonight. Maybe he'd been wrong this afternoon.

Right now, Lucy was talking to her. He strained his ears, trying to make out what they were saying over the blare of the TV and the laughter of the crowd at the bar. Unfortunately, there was too much background noise. Narrowing his eyes, he considered his next move.

The possible implications of her being in Stump River concerned him, but a voice inside his head hinted sending her away so quickly wasn't in his best interests. There was truth in the adage about knowing your enemy. He'd managed to learn some facts about her, grilling her without her being aware. At face value, there was nothing remarkable about her or her background, however, he'd examine the information further once he was back at the house.

Lucy was leaving the table now. He'd have to return soon or Melody would think he'd run out on her.

Running wasn't what he planned on doing, though. No, he'd decided to grant her an interview; an edited version of course. His reasoning was, if she was in Stump River, he could keep an eye on her, learn more about her and, if need be, reach her quickly should something need to be done. The idea of carrying out the Keeping was no more palatable now, than it had been earlier, but as Alpha he had to face the possibility.

Pushing off from the wall, he sauntered across the room and sat down. "I see Lucy was keeping you company."

"She was telling me all your dirty little secrets."

He stiffened in his chair, suddenly wary. "Such as...?"

She looked at him strangely. "Nothing bad. It's just a figure of speech."

He tried to cover his mistake. "Well, with Lucy you never know."

"Relax. She was actually quite complimentary. Apparently, you and your friend Bryan saved her and another girl from the clutches of some big, bad bikers."

Slouching back in his chair, relief washed over him. Of course, Lucy didn't know his secret. This whole damned situation had him on edge. He cast an easy smile at Melody, keeping his lids lowered so she'd have no glimpse of his inner turmoil and raised his hand towards the bar. Armand nodded, catching his request for more beer. He was always amazed at how the man could catch the smallest flick of a finger when it involved the ordering of liquid refreshments, but could turn a completely blind eye to some of the other, more dubious goings on that occurred at the establishment.

"So," Melody prodded him. "Are you going to tell me about the bikers?"

"There's nothing to tell. They were a bunch of losers. We took care of them. End of story."

"Ah, you're modest." She tilted her head and there was a mocking edge to her voice.

"Of course." Smirking, he picked up the beer that had silently arrived in front of him.

She leaned back and appeared to be studying him. He remained calm under her scrutiny, watching her, noting the expressions flitting across her face. He could see he puzzled her. She didn't know what to make of him. Staring at her pupils, he tuned into her breathing and inhaled her scent. She was attracted to him. Was she aware of the fact? Possibly, on some level. What would she do, if he pushed the limits? Weighing the benefits and consequences, he decided if the opportunity presented itself, he'd conduct a test.

Finally, Melody seemed to have come to a decision about him. "You know, what? You're very unstable."

"Really?" He raised his brows. "And how did you reach that stunning conclusion?"

"Well, first of all you live behind locked gates in the middle of nowhere, with a private phone number and, quite frankly, it was almost impossible to verify your existence. So on one hand, you're an obsessive recluse."

He gave a half shrug. She was partially correct.

"But then, when I finally meet you, you have this nasty attitude, you're rude, and you keep goading me with your comments, so that makes you a sort of bad-ass character."

"Would that be a *sexy*, bad-ass character?" He wiggled his eyebrows at her and then leaned forward into her personal space, leering.

"There! That's what I mean." She pushed him back, looking exasperated. "Yet, you can actually be nice at times. Like at dinner tonight, and when you saved Lucy. And, I suppose, you were even being nice when you drove me back to the cabin the other day."

"And don't forget I didn't press charges for trespassing. That was nice of me, too."

She rolled her eyes and ignored his comment. "So, you can see what I mean. You're unstable."

"I prefer to think of it as interesting." He sipped his beer while attempting to look thoughtful.

Throwing up her hands in despair, Melody exhaled loudly. "Whatever. The point is, you're very confusing. It's going to make interviewing you and presenting an accurate portrayal very challenging."

"And do you like challenges?"

"Yes. If things are too easy, it gets boring."

"Then I guess I won't bore you."

She sat up straight and smiled at him. "So you'll let me interview you and write an article on your work?"

He hesitated before speaking, not wanting to appear too eager, which he wasn't anyway. It would be better if she thought she was wringing the information out of him. "Probably. I'll let you know for sure in a few days."

"Oh, that's great!" She beamed initially and then frowned. "A few days? Exactly how many? Two? Three?"

"Something like that. Maybe more." He held back a smile as he watched her struggle to maintain her composure. Eventually, she exhaled slowly and nodded. Satisfied with himself for having the last word, he drained his beer, checked his watch and stood up. "I need to get going. There's a kitchen waiting for me to start renovating it in the morning."

Pulling on her jacket and grabbing her purse, Melody stood too. "I should be going too. Where do we pay?"

"Never mind. Lucy put everything on my tab."

"Oh, but I can cover the cost. I'm the one who wanted to talk to you."

He shook his head. "No. I pay. Add that to my list of character traits. I'm old fashioned. When I eat out with a lady, I pay." He noticed she was taken aback and was pleased to have once again thrown her off balance. "Come on, I'll walk you to your car."

"You don't have to. I'm just parked..." Her voice trailed off as he stared at her, silently willing her to follow his commands. Not surprisingly, she caved in, giving him a quick, tentative smile, as if she wasn't sure what to make of him. "All right, you can walk me to my car."

Pleased she'd obeyed, he put his hand in the small of her back and guided her out. She was certainly a tiny thing. He'd sensed that when he carried her from the house the other day. Now, as she walked beside him, he noted her head barely reached his chin. Recalling their earlier kiss and how her body had fit snugly against his, he decided it was the perfect height for him.

All was quiet in downtown Stump River, most of the residents contentedly relaxing in their houses while the various businesses presented darkened windows and locked doors to any individuals still moving about. One lone car was waiting patiently for the town's only stop light to change to green before continuing on its way. As the car drove away, its wheels made a faint hissing sound that eventually faded into nothingness as it disappeared from sight.

With the car's departure, they became the lone individuals on the otherwise deserted street. The faint clicking of her heels on the damp sidewalk was the only sound to break the silence. Overhead, the sky was clear of clouds. A crescent moon was hanging low over the silent town and a few stars were starting to make their existence known.

Melody shivered in the cool night air; it was early enough in the spring for the evening temperatures to drop close to freezing after sundown. Ryne noticed she was chilled and wrapped his arm around her shoulders, sharing his body heat. At first, she resisted but eventually relaxed into him. He speculated as to whether she was feeling more at ease around him or if her need for warmth was outweighing her desire for independence. Either way, he didn't mind.

Adjusting his stride to match her shorter one, he relished the way their thighs occasionally brushed together. Her arms were folded in front of her and, as he glanced down, he noted with a distinctly male appreciation, she was unconsciously causing her top to gape at the neck, allowing him a satisfying glimpse of her cleavage. He found himself inclining his head towards hers. The scent of her shampoo tickled his nose and he inhaled deeply trying to place it. Green apples, possibly? Whatever it was, it mixed nicely with her own natural scent as it drifted upwards and wrapped around him.

Her car was, in fact, parked just a block down the road from The Broken Antler and they reached it sooner than he would have liked. As she turned to face him, he leaned in close until her back was up against the vehicle.

"Ryne?" She looked up at him as if uncertain of his intentions.

He'd thought earlier on he'd like to run a test to see how attracted she was to him. This was his opportunity. He cupped her face and ran his thumb over her bottom lip, noting how her eyes started to darken. Pressing closer, her breathing hitched and he could see the pulse at the base of her throat quicken. Yes, he definitely affected Melody. He should stop now he had his answer, but once again his wolf had other ideas.

Slowly, he lowered his head, gauging her response. When their lips were almost touching, he paused and waited. She made an indistinct little sound and stretched her neck the tiny amount needed to bring their mouths into contact. Gently, he brushed his lips back and forth across hers, savouring the sweetness of her breath as she exhaled, the softness of the plump surface, and the tingle of awareness that bounced between them.

He withdrew and let his eyes lock onto hers. They gazed at each other, questions and uncertainty quivering between them. Overriding it all was a desire for more. Of one accord they kissed again. Ryne wrapped his arms around her, felt her moving her hands up to clasp his shoulders. She worked her body even closer to him and he widened his stance, experimentally brushing against her. At first, she seemed to be responding, but then abruptly froze before starting to struggle. Now she was pushing him away, ducking her head to avoid his attempts at nuzzling. It took a minute for his brain to register her withdrawal. Dropping his hands to his side, he stepped back and took a deep, calming breath, forcing the animal within back down. Silence stretched between them. Clearing his throat, Ryne attempted to speak.

"No?"

She brushed her hair from her face, looking everywhere but at him. "I...I just met you and I don't hop into bed with a guy the first time I meet him."

"Technically this is the third time we've met. Once at my house, at noon today and now for supper." He quirked a smile at her, hopefully hiding how much the encounter had affected him.

"Nice try, Taylor." She shook her head and slid a glance his way.

He shrugged and shoved his hands in his pockets, responding in an indifferent tone. "I didn't think it would work, but figured I'd give it a shot."

She cocked her head to the side and then gestured between the two of them. "My getting to interview you wasn't contingent on the outcome of this, was it?"

He snorted, feeling offended. "Do I look like I need to blackmail women into sleeping with me?"

An embarrassed flush crept over her face, but she continued on. "No, but in some of the journalism courses I took, they warned us about getting involved with interviewees. Anyway," she took a deep breath, "thanks again for the meal. I'll be waiting to hear your answer in the morning."

"In the morning." He nodded and opened the door for her. She slid inside and he pushed the door shut. With a final puzzled look in his direction, she drove off. He stood there until her tail lights disappeared, before starting towards his own vehicle.

It would be a great night for a run, but turning into a wolf in the middle of Main Street, even if no one appeared to be about, was definitely courting trouble. Instead he climbed into his truck and drove home, mulling over the events of the night.

Chapter 14

Mel was having trouble sleeping. The bed was comfortable, the temperature correct and there was no noise outside to bother her. She wasn't thirsty, nor did she need to go to the bathroom. Even her feet were warm, due to the presence of her favourite fuzzy socks. So, if everything was perfect, then why did her mind refuse to turn off?

She flopped over for probably the twentieth time and firmly closed her eyes only to pop them open again as thoughts of Ryne filled her head. Her mind had switched from referring to him as 'Taylor' to calling him by his first name now he was no longer an anonymous research project.

Ryne found her attractive—their encounter had left her with no doubt about that fact—the question was why? She knew she wasn't ugly, but neither was she drop dead gorgeous. In her opinion, there was nothing about her that should attract someone as hot and sexy as Ryne.

Perhaps he went after any woman who crossed his path. She'd often suspected her father was that way, though she never mentioned it to her mother. Her father was the only taboo topic between them and even to this day, Mel had only the sketchiest information about him. Not that it mattered; it was just sometimes she was curious. With a shake of her head, she dismissed her father and returned to the more interesting topic of Ryne Taylor.

The man was definitely attractive but she couldn't act on it. At least not until after the interview. And even then, it wouldn't be a smart move. Burying her head under the pillow, she tried to erase Ryne from her mind by humming a popular tune only to realize it was a romance, then tried counting sheep that annoyingly morphed into wolves. Exasperated, she threw back the covers and stomped into the kitchen. Damn that man for interfering with her sleep!

She got a drink of cold water and stood in front of the window, pressing her warm cheek to the cool, smooth pane. The night here was much blacker than it was in Chicago. With no street lights or neon signs to hold back the night, it shrouded the world in complete inky darkness. It was calming, but also frightening to think, except for the Kennedys, there was no one around for miles. And without a phone, she had no way of summoning help.

A shiver passed over her as she realized how truly alone she was. Just herself, the darkness and whatever animal life existed in the forest behind the cabin. She set the glass down on the counter and walked to her bedroom, intent on climbing back into bed and hiding under the covers, but for some reason, found herself peeking out the bedroom curtains instead.

The view from the kitchen had been the woodlot, but this room faced the actual forest. She recalled the footprints she'd found the other day and searched the murky darkness for any sign of life. The moonlight was dimmer now than it had been when Ryne had walked her to her car; clouds were starting to roll in as the forecast had called for rain. As her eyes adjusted, she could make out the shadowy shapes of tree trunks and a few low-slung bushes.

For a minute, she thought she detected something moving. It was just a sense of the shadows shifting near the base of a tree and maybe a glint of something shining, but then it was gone. Her grip tightened on the curtain and for long moments, she waited and stared, but saw nothing. Eventually, she let the curtain fall back into place. There was nothing dangerous out there, it was just her imagination.

Ignoring the niggling worry in the back of her mind, she climbed into bed and with determination shut her eyes and concentrated on reciting the soliloquies from Shakespeare she'd had to learn in school. As usual, she only made it partway through the first one before sleep overtook her.

The next few days were interview limbo. That's what Mel dubbed them as she waited for Ryne to make his final decision. It irked her but she sensed this was some sort of test. If she pushed too hard, he'd refuse, just to put her in her place. And so, with unaccustomed patience, she waited, her days falling into a lazy pattern. She'd sleep in, drive to town and spend the morning at the Gazette where Josh and Beth were allowing her to hook up her laptop to their internet connection. Then it was on to the part of the day she dreaded the most. Calling Aldrich.

The communications followed a predictable path. He'd ask about her progress. She'd report she was waiting. The lawyer would make some condescending comment, and the conversation would be over. Though it lasted barely five minutes the experience felt much longer and left her deflated.

In happy contrast, once she'd done her duty, she rewarded herself by having coffee and conversation with Ruth, Al and Lucy. A running joke had developed between them. Every day she'd ask for a different type of coffee and they'd hand her a cup of plain black. Purposely, she made her requests more outlandish each day, enjoying their expressions as she explained the intricacies of each variety. Today's lesson was on one of her favourites, a caramel macchiato venti.

"So you see Al, then you take freshly steamed milk, vanilla-flavoured syrup, a double shot of espresso and top it with caramel sauce. Oh, and of course the key is to *slowly* pour in the milk to create layers of different coloured liquid."

The chef rubbed his stubbly chin and nodded slowly. "Yeah. Right." As per usual, he was leaning against the counter, his stained apron stretched over his rounded stomach. He reached back and flipped on the coffee maker. "One black coffee, coming up."

She giggled, loving his deadpan expression.

Ruth shook her head, taking a cup down off the shelf and placing it beside the brewing beverage, ready to be filled when the time came. "It beats me how you city folk have nothing better to do with your time than finding ways to mess up a perfectly good cup of java."

"Ah, Ruth," She teased. "You haven't lived until you experience drinking coffee properly prepared by a barista."

Straightening her uniform on her boney frame, Ruth sniffed and then patted Mel's shoulder. "I'll survive just fine, girly, don't you worry. The men on my soap operas give me a better jolt than caffeine any day."

Lucy wandered over and Mel settled into her favourite seat for a bit of gossip with the friendly waitress, all the while keeping a watchful eye on Miller's service station in case Ryne should emerge. He did occasionally, to fill gas tanks, wash windshields and check oil, but never to come across the street and agree to an interview.

She was positive he knew she was there. A couple of times, she even thought she caught him glancing her way, but he always went back inside, leaving her fuming and irritably drumming her fingers on the countertop.

The time spent at the diner wasn't a total waste, however. Ruth and Al enjoyed regaling her with tales of small-town life. She was actually writing some of the amusing anecdotes down, toying with the idea of composing a series of articles about the place.

Lucy was all for the idea when she heard about it. She'd lean against the counter, a pot of coffee in one hand to give the impression she was working, while conspiratorially whispering tidbits of scandalous yet amusing information on the various patrons of Ruth's Diner and The Broken Antler. It was surprising how much actually took place in the outwardly sleepy little town.

However, despite her enjoyment of the coffee, company and conversation, by the end of the week Mel was fed up waiting for Ryne. It was Friday and she'd made absolutely no progress with regards to her real mission.

"If he doesn't come over and talk to me today, I'm going to march across the street and strangle him," she confided to Lucy.

"I'll cheer while you do it." Lucy agreed.

"You two have a spat or something?" She looked at her new friend with concern.

"Nah, we don't have that type of relationship. There's nothing to really argue over when it's just about good sex." She poured more coffee into Mel's cup. "Nope, the problem is he hasn't been around to see me since his birthday and he promised me a month ago, he'd fix the leaky faucet in my kitchen."

"Not the reliable sort then?"

"What man is?" Philosophically, Lucy shrugged and then pointed out the window. "Hey, there goes Harley. I love watching him cross the street." The two women paused their conversation to watch the dog wait and cross at the light. Once he was on the other side, he turned and walked up to the diner and pawed at the door.

"What's he doing?" Mel queried.

"Beats me. This is a new one." Lucy walked to the door and opened it. "What do you want, Harley?"

Harley walked inside as if it was part of his daily routine, came right up to Mel and dropped a piece of paper in her lap. The paper was wrinkled and sticky with drool.

Gingerly, she picked it up, avoiding the worst of the slobber. There was a message addressed to her and, despite the ink smearing from the dog's saliva, it was quite readable. "It's from Ryne! He says he wants to talk to me about terms. I should be at his house at noon tomorrow. The gate will be open and he'll provide lunch." She happily clenched the soggy note in her hand. Finally, something was happening. "This is great news. Thanks, Harley!"

The dog woofed and sauntered out of the diner, heading back towards the traffic light. A glance across the street showed Ryne was standing by the door of the Service Station, his arms folded. Despite the distance, they managed to make eye-contact. He nodded and went back inside, ruffling Harley's fur as the dog returned from his mission.

"That's good news for you, isn't it, Mel?" Lucy grinned at her. "And when you see him, remind him about my leaking faucet, okay?"

Mel nodded, rereading the note. What might the terms entail? It was a straightforward interview about his life. Did he want a cut if she sold it to a magazine? That could be tricky, since Mr. Greyson was paying her. She'd have to ask Aldrich about that one.

Finishing her coffee, she thanked her friends and headed back towards the Gazette. She was going to e-mail Aldrich about this latest development and ask his advice about Ryne's possible terms. She knew the lawyer would be peeved about the e-mail, having made it plain he preferred phone conversations, probably so he could 'read' the speaker's tone of voice. Oh, well. Too bad for him. She'd already suffered through talking to him once today. Twice would be just too much.

Noon the next day found Mel driving down the road leading to Ryne's house. She'd stopped in town to call Aldrich. He'd emailed her back yesterday, his message terse and simple; call me. And so she did. While he'd tried to hide it, she was sure Aldrich hadn't been expecting her to get an interview with Ryne and it pleased her to no end to prove the man wrong. When she'd mentioned Ryne setting terms, Aldrich was adamant no mention of his client should occur.

Aldrich was a clever sort, she had to admit. He suggested if Ryne questioned to which publication she was submitting the article, she could claim it was a school assignment she was completing for extra marks and only a professor would be reading it. She agreed the story was a good one, but felt guilty she couldn't be upfront with the photographer.

She squashed her misgivings as she approached Ryne's property. As promised, the gate was open. Slowing down, she made the turn.

The drive from the main road to his house was eerie, due not only to the dark clouds rolling across the sky threatening rain, but also from the memories of her earlier visit and the wolves that had chased her. Obsessively, she peered into the woods but there was no sign of the creatures. Only acre upon acre of forest so thick it blocked the sky and made the dreary day even darker. As she rounded yet another turn and then trundled over a small bridge, she even began to wonder if she was lost. Surely, she hadn't crossed over a stream the other day?

Debating the wisdom of turning back, she slowed her pace to steer around a pot hole and that was when she saw it. Through a thinning in the trees, a house could be seen!

Too bad, the sight of the place made her stomach twist with dread.

Chapter 15

Mel sat in her car and stared at the house. The sidewalk was cracked and grass was poking up between the broken cement slabs. Stalks of dead weeds covered what should have been the front lawn, and the remnants of flower beds could barely be discerned among a tangle of old vines and leaves. A lone tree stood to the right of the building, its branches stretching out like greedy hands while a hole in the trunk reminded her of a gaping mouth.

"Perfect for Halloween," she muttered.

Averting her gaze from the creepy tree, she began to study the actual house. It was massive and stood out like something from a horror flick, complete with a dark stormy sky and a spooky forest in the background. Two storeys high, not including the attic, its wooden siding was a weathered grey where it wasn't hidden by ivy vines that seemed to be trying to slowly choke the entire building.

Over the front porch was a rickety balcony, access being provided by a set of French doors complete with cracked glass. Extending from either side of the main part of the house were two large wings of rooms, each with eight windows staring bleakly back at her. She couldn't even begin to speculate how many rooms the house might contain.

The slate roof looked new and sported a widow's walk along the top surrounded by a wrought iron railing. She could almost picture some tragic heroine pacing back and forth, wringing her hands in despair before throwing herself to the ground in a suicide attempt.

The style was...well... She wasn't sure. It appeared as if some architect had taken bits and pieces from several designs and centuries and then thrown them all together. It wasn't a pretty house; the best that could be said was it was uniquely interesting, and in definite need of repair. Ryne and his friends might be working hard to fix the place up, but there was still a long way to go.

Stepping out of her car, she stared at the structure, craning her head back as she walked towards the front door. On her previous visit she'd been disoriented and hadn't paid much attention to her surroundings. Now she was taking in every single feature. Long thin windows flanked the front door and she was surprised to see a stained-glass panel over the top of the entrance. The steps were new and the door had been refinished. She took a moment to admire the carved surface before raising her hand to knock.

Just as she was bringing her fist down, the door swung open and she suddenly found her hand held firmly in Ryne's.

"Trying to hit me already?" He quirked an eyebrow at her.

"No, that comes later, after the fifth time you annoy me. Right now, I'm knocking on your door. If you insist on opening it when my fist is up, I can't be held responsible now, can I?" She smiled with fake sweetness, while trying to retrieve her hand from his grip.

He didn't let go, instead, using his hold to pull her inside.

"Good. I thought we'd save the rough stuff until later, once we're better acquainted." He leered at her.

She bit back the retort that sprang to her lips, reminding herself she was here for an interview and needed to be professional, regardless of his behaviour. "I was pleased to get your message and I'm sure, whatever your terms might be, we can come to a satisfactory arrangement."

He dropped her hand, his face suddenly serious. "I hope so. I don't like interviews. I prefer my privacy, but with you, I think the easiest way to regain my peaceful lifestyle is to give you what you want."

She stared at him. Ryne was not a happy camper. In fact, she sensed he actively disliked her. Hoping to get on a positive footing, she tried to smooth things over with a smile and a conciliatory tone.

"I promise this will be painless. A few questions, some background information, and then I'll leave you alone."

He grunted and she wasn't sure whether he was agreeing or scoffing. Before she could decide, he turned and indicated she should follow him.

They walked down the hallway and she noted her surroundings. Wooden wainscoting covered the bottom of the walls while the upper half showed remnants of old flocked wallpaper. Looking up, she noted the embossed tin ceiling. Even with its layers of peeling and bubbling paint, she could make out the fine workmanship. Decorative mouldings framed the ceilings and surrounded the doorways and windows. It had been an elegant home in its day, but years of decay and neglect had taken their toll. Ryne had a big project ahead of him, if he intended to restore the home to its former glory.

And speaking of restoring.... They entered a room that was completely redone. Not in a vintage style but in homey comfort. From the flat screen TV, to the fireplace, bookshelves, leather couch and reclining chairs, the room could have been in any house across the continent.

"This is nice." She looked around taking in the bold, dark brown wall and white window mouldings. There were no blinds or curtains on the window, but Mel supposed being in the middle of nowhere, there was no need to block the neighbours out.

"Thanks. It's where we relax." He nodded towards the sofa. "Have a seat."

She sat down on the overstuffed piece of furniture and immediately felt herself sinking into its depths. It was soft and comfortable; in fact, she wasn't sure how she was going to get back up again without assistance. Adjusting herself as best as she could, she looked over at Ryne. He hadn't sat down yet and was pacing back and forth in front of the windows.

"So..." She began slowly. "What are these terms you were thinking about?"

He stopped and studied her for a long moment.

She forced herself not to squirm under his gaze

Finally, he spoke. "I have complete control over what you write. I want to see a list of questions ahead of time. Once I've read them over, I'll decide which ones I want to answer."

She opened her mouth to protest but he continued speaking.

"You are not allowed to ask my friends questions about me and, at any time, I can veto the entire article and you will leave Stump River immediately. If you don't like the terms, you know where the door is."

She snapped her mouth shut and considered the situation but she really had no choice. "All right. I'll make up a list of questions and have it to you by tomorrow. Would one day be long enough for you to read them over and have some answers ready?"

"It should be sufficient. If not, I'll let you know." He noticeably relaxed. "Okay. Business is out of the way. Want the grand tour?"

Pleased to feel the tension between them lessen, she agreed. When she struggled to stand, Ryne grabbed her arm, pulling her to her feet. The heat from his hand burned through the thin material of her light sweater and she was sure if she looked, there would be a mark on her skin from the contact. Sneaking a peek at his face, she wondered if he had felt anything unusual, but he was already letting go and was heading towards the door. She hurried after him.

"We put a new roof on as soon as we got here and then had an electrician rewire the place. The plumbing in the kitchen, my bathroom downstairs and one of the upstairs baths has been redone, but not the laundry room." He called the information over his shoulder as he headed towards the back of the house. "Right now, I'm working on the kitchen."

She found herself in a large spacious room. The floors were worn beige linoleum and the walls were a hideous shade of pea green. She couldn't help but wrinkle her nose at the decor.

He laughed. "Yeah. That's how I feel too. I've removed the cupboards and new ones should be arriving later today or tomorrow. New appliances are coming as well. After that, I'll add a backsplash and paint the walls."

"What about the floor?"

"I was going to go with tile, but then someone told me it can be cold and hard on your feet, so instead I'm going with hardwood."

She nodded in approval. "It'll match the rest of the house." She wandered towards the window and looked out back. The yard was massive, but overgrown. "A bit of a jungle out there, isn't it?"

"The previous owner, Edith Nelson, was an avid gardener in her day, but apparently the last few years she didn't feel up to taking care of it anymore so it really got out of hand." Ryne rubbed the back of his neck. "I don't know much about gardens and I have no idea when I'll find the time to do anything out there. For the now, it will have to stay a jungle."

"If I lived around here, I'd love to try my hand at that. My garden in Chicago consists of some sickly weeds growing between the cracks in the cement. This would be an interesting challenge."

"And you like challenges, do you?"

"I think you asked me something like that before, and the answer is still yes."

He gave her a half smile before leading her out of the kitchen to the next room. A fireplace, an arm chair and a sofa made up the sparse furnishings. "This is technically considered the dining room, but I'm using it as a living room right now, since the real one currently has drafty windows and broken floorboards."

She looked around the room with a sense of familiarity. This was where she'd woken up during her initial attempt to meet him. "Will you turn it back into a dining room some day? It's an awfully large space."

"I hope to have lots of relatives visiting eventually." Abruptly, he moved towards the doorway and she had to hurry after him.

By time they stopped to discuss different features and his vision for the renovations, it took almost an hour to go through the whole house. If he ever got everything done, it would be an impressive home, provided he was still young enough to enjoy the fruits of his labours. To her inexperienced eye, the task seemed monumental. Mind you, he *had* achieved an impressive amount in the five months he'd lived here. From the sound of it, only the wiring and plumbing had been hired out. He and his two friends were planning on doing everything else by themselves.

Now back in the kitchen, she sat at the table while he rummaged in the fridge. "Lunch isn't fancy. Soup, sandwiches and a salad are the best I can do with the kitchen torn up like this."

"That's fine. You didn't have to feed me, though. I could have eaten something at the diner in town."

"You could have, but this is more private. We can talk without half of the town knowing our conversation."

"It *is* a rather small place. I suppose not much happens, so even the smallest event is big news."

Ryne agreed as he stood at the stove heating some soup. "Uh-huh. If you sneeze in Ruth's diner, the nurse at the clinic is waiting with a thermometer by the time you step outside."

"I'm surprised you moved here if you like your privacy so much."

"Ruth's and the Broken Antler are fair game for gossip but beyond that people leave you pretty much alone if you're at home and for the most part, if you don't want to talk, they respect that. They're friendly and concerned, but not maliciously nosey."

Had there been a pointed barb in his last comment? He didn't expand on the point and she decided to let it slide hoping to eat her meal without getting indigestion from constant verbal sparring.

Thankfully that was exactly what happened. They discussed movies, books and food. She offered ideas for decorating the house while he casually asked about her schooling and upbringing.

She was feeling pleasantly relaxed as she accepted her host's offer and helped herself to a cup of freshly brewed coffee. The steam rose from the pot, the aroma bringing a smile to her lips. Just as she paused to take an appreciative sniff, a loud crashing sound filled the room. Her hand jerked and the hot liquid spilled onto her clothes. With a yelp, she dropped the carafe and pulled the material away from her skin. Ryne was immediately at her side, yanking at the sweater and pulling it over her head.

"What the hell do you think you're doing?" She sputtered, ineffectually trying to pull the top back down. It was no use. He had the clothing over her head before she could even finish the question. She crossed her arms protectively across her chest.

"I'm keeping you from getting seriously scalded. You can't leave hot material on your skin." He was working at the button on her jeans and she batted at his hand away.

"There's only a spot or two on my pants and if you touch me again, I'll kick you in the balls."

"Relax. I have no designs on your body." His gaze skimmed over her ample cleavage before he muttered. "At least not right now."

Feeling her face flush, she shifted her arms in a vain attempt to cover more of herself, but knew it was useless. There was just too much to hide. At least she was wearing a decent bra. She snatched a nearby tea towel and wrapped it around herself.

Ryne had already moved to the sink and was soaking a cloth. Once it was wet, he approached her and, flicking up the towel, pressed the wet cloth to the hot pink skin of her stomach. The cloth was ice cold and she gave a startled cry while trying to step back but he held her in place.

Pre-empting any comment from her, he spoke sternly. "Be still. It's important to cool a burn immediately. Hold this cloth while I stick your sweater in water so it doesn't stain." He grabbed her hand and pressed it to her stomach so she could keep the cloth in place.

"Oh." It was a small comment, but the only one came to mind. The cool rag *did* feel good and apparently, he had nothing else in mind but tending her burn. She watched him fill a large bowl with water and plunge her top into it. "How do you know how to do that? Treat a stain, I mean?"

He glanced over his shoulder. "I've been doing my own laundry for quite a while now."

She nodded. "What was that noise?"

He jerked his chin towards the window. Rain was pouring down and it was almost pitch dark out. "The wind has really picked up. I wouldn't be surprised if one of the older trees in the forest came down."

She giggled. "So if a tree falls in the forest and nobody is there, it really does make a noise?"

He chuckled back. "How's your burn?"

She took the cloth away. Her skin wasn't nearly as pink now. "I think it's better."

"Good. I'll wet the cloth again and you can hold it on for a while longer. You need to cool a burn for ten minutes."

"First aid training?"

"Something like that. I've lived in places where it pays to know how to take care of simple injuries." He fixed the cloth for her. "Wait here. I'll find a shirt for you to wear. As enticing as the tea towel is, I assume you don't want to drive home in it."

"Yeah, that would definitely give the people of Stump River something to talk about."

Ryne left and she moved to stand by the window, staring out at the pouring rain. It was coming down heavier by the minute and she could hardly even see across the yard. Something flashed by the window and for one startled instant she thought it was a pair of wolves. But why would wolves be running around the house in the rain? Surely, they'd hole up in a cave or a burrow or wherever they made their home.

A door slammed, the noise coming from the back entryway off the kitchen. She could hear male voices laughing and then two very damp, scantily clad men entered the room. When they saw her, they came up short and fell silent.

Speechless, all she could think of was that, while good-looking men might not grow on trees, Stump River.

Chapter 16

Mel studied the amazing specimens before her, taking in their tall, lean bodies and well-defined muscles. Little rivers of water were cascading down their bare chests, then rippling over their washboard abs. Some drops were lost in the indent of their navels, while other luckier ones travelled even lower, disappearing below the waist band of their shorts. Said shorts were sopping wet and clinging to their bodies, hinting at the interesting anatomy hidden beneath.

Tearing her gaze upwards, she felt her face flush and hoped they hadn't noticed the direction of her eyes. Unfortunately, from the smirks on their faces, she strongly suspected they had.

One of them stepped forward, his hand extended. "Hi! I'm Bryan. We met on the road out front the other day."

Forcing herself to stop ogling them, she accepted his hand. "Sorry, I didn't recognize you at first, with you being so wet and nearly naked..." She let her voice trail off, feeling her cheeks growing even hotter as he laughed lightly.

"That's okay; it's always nice to be appreciated. You're Melody Greene, right?"

She nodded. "You can call me Mel."

"Mel is good with me." He gave her a friendly smile and she lost some of her initial embarrassment. Giving his head a nod to the side, Bryan introduced his companion. "This is Daniel."

The man in question waved lightly. "Nice to meet you."

She noticed he had the most amazing eyes. They were a deep liquid brown, the kind that made her think of rich cafe mocha with pools of melted chocolate on top. He seemed like he'd be the quiet sort, a deep thinker with something unexpected lurking below his calm exterior.

Bryan cleared his throat and she brought her attention back to him. "I see you and Ryne have had an interesting afternoon."

"Interesting? Well, we talked and he showed me the house."

"Uh-huh. I always like a game of *show and tell* myself." Bryan gestured towards her with his hand.

Mel frowned, not getting his meaning at all.

He chuckled. Reaching forward, he flicked the edge of her makeshift shirt, also known as a tea towel. She gasped having forgotten she was shirtless and barely covered. Crossing her arms protectively over her chest, she struggled to not blush, yet again. Good heavens, her blood pressure had never had this much of a workout before!

"Hey! No need to be embarrassed." Bryan grinned. "I—"

"Bryan!" A low growl followed the utterance of his name and Bryan underwent a complete transformation. The grin disappeared as did his cocky stance. He turned to face the speaker, tipping his head down.

"Ryne, I was just—"

"I know what you were just doing. Keep your hands to yourself. Both of you get upstairs and dry off. And don't forget to clean up the puddles you left all over the floor."

Both men almost slunk out of the room, leaving Mel gaping at Ryne who stood in the doorway holding a shirt. His stance, his expression, the way his hand was fisted, all screamed aggression. He kept his eyes fixed on the other two until they were out of sight.

She shifted uncomfortably. "They were just introducing themselves. Neither one did or said anything wrong." She tried to placate Ryne while wondering why the other two put up with him bossing them around. Even if he owned the place, it was no way to speak to grown men.

"They know better. I told them to keep their distance."

"From me? Why?"

"I have my reasons." He abruptly changed the topic. "Here's a t-shirt to wear."

She took the offered clothing and turning her back, managed to shimmy into it without losing the towel. Once she was decently covered, she pulled the towel from underneath the shirt and hung it over the back of a chair. By the time she'd finished, Ryne was calmer but she was anxious to get away from him. He was too unpredictable for her to feel comfortable around him.

"I suppose I'd better go. I'll type up a list of questions and drop them in your mailbox tomorrow. That way you won't have to leave the gate unlocked."

"Actually, I'm in town tomorrow. I work at Miller's on Wednesdays."

"All right. I'll drop it off there." She found her purse and started to head towards the front door, keeping the conversation light for fear of setting him off again. "Thanks for lunch and the tour of the house. It really is an interesting home. When I first saw it from the outside, it was sort of spooky, but now I can see it has potential."

"Thanks." He spoke cordially enough now, and she felt herself relaxing. Her hand was on the door knob ready to open it when Bryan walked down the stairs, rubbing his hair dry with a towel.

He was whistling unconcernedly, not seeming to bear a grudge for the way Ryne had spoken to him. "I wouldn't go out there if I were you. It's raining so hard, I doubt if you could see to drive. And there's a large tree down across the driveway about halfway to the road. There's no way you can get a car around it."

"You mean I'm stuck here?" She couldn't keep the squeak of surprise out of her voice.

"I'm afraid so." Bryan turned to Ryne. "Daniel and I looked at it, but it will take all three of us and a chainsaw, to move it out of the way." He shrugged and wandered on his way.

Mel turned to Ryne, all thoughts of his earlier bad temper pushed to the side by a sudden pressing need to leave. She was his guest and he had certain obligations towards her. Rocking back and forth on her heels, she looked at him expectantly. "Well?"

"Well, what?"

"Well, do something." She fluttered her hands at him, as if shooing him on his way.

Instead of moving, he put his hands in his back pockets and shrugged. "If the driveway is blocked, it's blocked. Those trees are massive. You heard what Bryan said."

"I know what he said. What I mean is, why aren't you getting your coat and umbrella and whatever else you need to get to work?"

Ryne looked at her as if she was crazy. "Because it's pouring rain and there's a good chance of thunder and lightning. You can do what you want, but I'm not standing outside playing with power tools in the middle of a storm."

She processed his words and their implications. When it all made sense, she slumped back against the door and closed her eyes. "So I'm stuck here?"

"Yep. Probably until morning." Ryne glanced at his watch. "It's almost four now. By the time the rain stops, it will be getting dark and too late to do anything."

She whimpered and opened her eyes. "As I recall from the tour of the house, you don't have any spare rooms, do you?"

"Technically there are lots of rooms, but as you saw, they're sealed off because the windows aren't air tight and there's no furniture in them either. The couch is pretty comfortable though." He grinned cheekily. "And if you change your mind, my bedroom is right next door."

She didn't find his comment amusing. "Thanks, but I'm sure I'll be fine all on my own."

"You never know; you could have a bad dream."

She scowled and he laughed then headed back to the kitchen. Resigned to her fate, she followed him.

Dinner was pasta and, determined to use this as an opportunity to get on Ryne's good side, she helped cook and clean up afterward. She even volunteered to make the popcorn when they decided to spend the evening watching a movie.

After putting the movie into the DVD player, Ryne sat on the couch beside her while the other two settled in the recliners. She noticed while they spoke to her, they also kept their distance and never looked at her directly. Ryne must have warned them off for fear she'd ask them questions. He really was way too caught up in this privacy thing.

Thoughtfully, she munched on some popcorn and recalled the conversation she'd overheard between Kane and Elise. Kane had been worried about the discovery of something and it had to do with one of Ryne's pictures. Was it the one Mr. Greyson had? But what could be so special about a picture of a wolf?

Whatever it was, Ryne didn't want her finding out about it. And Daniel and Bryan must be aware the secret too, otherwise why would Ryne want to keep her away from them? She'd have to set up her questions for Ryne carefully if she wanted to unravel the mystery.

Speaking of mysteries, she glanced back at the TV screen and then hurriedly looked away again. The men had picked the movie and, of course, had chosen a horror flick complete with mass murder, blood, guts, undead monsters and a hapless female who spent a lot of time screaming and wandering into places she'd be better off staying away from, all in the middle of a storm. What woman would be that clueless?

Another blood chilling scream came from the speakers and even without looking, she was aware of the mutilated body parts on the TV screen. Ugh. What was wrong with a nice romantic comedy? A little hugging, a little kissing, a few misunderstandings and then a happy ending!

Beside her, Ryne shifted on the couch and she tried to imagine him watching a chic-flick. There'd be a girl snuggled up beside him, her head on his shoulder while he gently played with her hair. Frowning, she realized the girl was herself and quickly erased the image.

Why did her subconscious find him so appealing? Could it be the fact his dark hair looked thick and soft and had a slight curl to it where it brushed his collar? How would it actually feel if she were to run her fingers through it? Or—she studied him out of the corner or her eye—maybe it was the stubble gracing his jaw or the fine laugh lines at the corner of his eyes and the strong brow above. Just in time, she caught herself reaching up to trace the feature with her fingers.

Clasping her hands together to prevent any further slips, she inhaled deeply, ignoring the tingling in her hands while chanting 'don't touch, don't touch' over and over to herself. Her deep inhalation made her more aware of his scent, a combination of spice and woods and maleness. With him sitting so near, she could feel the heat coming off him and fought the urge to snuggle up close, just as she had in her fantasy moments before.

What was the matter with her? So what if he was the sexiest man she'd seen in ages. Getting all hot and bothered over him was not part of the game plan, no matter how much her body might wish otherwise. She snuck another look his way and noticed the corner of his mouth twitching. Quickly averting her eyes, she stared blindly at the screen.

Ryne leaned towards her. Out of the corner of his mouth, he whispered to her. "See anything you like?" Her audible gasp caused him to chuckle.

Crossing her arms, she compressed her lips and studiously ignored him. Thankfully, the closing musical score was now playing. The camera zoomed in on a particularly gruesome corpse as a background for the credits and she shuddered in distaste. Sensing Ryne looking her way, she pasted a nonchalant expression on her face. There was no way she'd let him know the contents of the movie bothered her; she'd never hear the end of it.

The other two stood and between yawns, carried on a discussion about the special effects they'd seen.

"Oh man, when that body ripped open, wasn't it great? Have you ever seen such realistic looking organs?" Bryan enthused as he gathered the empty popcorn bowls.

"Yeah and the zombie was awesome. The makeup was so real. I wonder how they got the rotting flesh to hang like that." Daniel followed Bryan's lead, gathering the empty drink cans and then heading into the kitchen.

She gulped, forcing herself to *not* think about rotting flesh and realistic organs. She got to her feet and hesitated as to what to say.

Ryne was placing the DVD back in its case. He looked over his shoulder at her. "You okay?"

"Sure. Never better." She put on her perkiest attitude and snatched up the pillow he'd set out for her earlier. "Can't wait to go to bed and get a good night's sleep."

She was sure she saw a smirk pass over his face before he nodded. "Right. If you need anything, you know where I am."

She hugged the pillow and waggled her fingers at him. With one more assessing look her way, he left the room.

Sometime during the night, she woke with a start, her heart pounding. She lay there, trying to separate dream from reality, to convince herself she was awake and no longer running through the woods being chased by a pack of wolves. What was it with wolves lately? They'd never figured prominently in her life before. Now they were in pictures, walking around her cabin, cornering her in the woods and even chasing her in her sleep.

She withdrew her arm from under the blanket and brushed her hair from her sweaty forehead, noting her hand was shaking with leftover fear. Pushing herself upright, she hugged her knees to her chest and pulled the blanket closer to block the chill of the room. Ryne's t-shirt was long enough to cover her adequately, but not overly warm.

The house was still; everyone apparently asleep, except for herself. Rain beat down outside, tapping on the windows while the occasional flash of light and the distant rumbling of thunder let her know Ryne had been right. A storm had rolled in.

As it got closer, lightning flashes briefly illuminate the room, casting weird shadows on the walls. She shivered again, but this time due to nerves. There was nothing in the room with her, she knew that, but she'd never liked shadows. They always took on ominous shapes, turning harmless daytime bits of furniture into scary creatures of the night.

A tapping sound began to make itself noticed and she stiffened, trying to locate its source. It seemed to be coming from the window. Carefully, and oh so slowly, she moved her head in that direction. She couldn't see anything there, yet the tapping continued. Her overactive imagination began to kick-in and she sought to suppress it with the weight of logic.

The house was quite old. It probably shifted and groaned all the time, the noises actually becoming comforting to those who dwelled within. She speculated how many people had lived in the house over the years. Had they been happy? Or had tragedy touched their lives? She amused herself for a while, populating the house with servants and children, husbands and wives. Did the spirits of the people remain, watching over the next generation?

She was never really sure what she believed when it came to spirits and ghosts. Logically, she knew they didn't exist, but sometimes she'd read something and wonder. And right now, she was wondering. It was a perfect night for that line of thought. Storms and ghosts seemed to go together. In fact, this was very similar to the movie they'd watched tonight.

The tapping was growing louder, forcing itself into her awareness again. What was making it? Her fertile mind began to come up with answers. Possibly there was some mystery surrounding the house; a long ago resident out in a storm and locked outside, shivering as the rain soaked their clothing. They had gone from window to window, tapping away, trying to gain someone's attention so they could come in out of the cold and wet.

Her palms were damp with sweat now and she surreptitiously wiped them on the blanket covering her. She was trying to be as quiet and as still as possible. No point in drawing attention to herself just in case. Nervously nibbling on her lower lip, she noted the wind was picking up as the storm got closer. It howled about the house, the sound rising and falling like the cry of a wolf. Were there wolves outside the house, even now? She gulped. Maybe wolves had always plagued this house! The new idea took root in her mind.

What if the person tapping at the window never made it safely inside? What if they had been purposely locked out as a punishment? And maybe, while they were outside, a band of hungry wolves had come by and attacked! The person would have screamed for help, but no one came to save them. In fact, the occupant of the house might have sat in this very room, listening to the pleas for help, laughing insanely as the dastardly plan came to fruition. Outside, the ill-fated victim would have known all this and with their dying breath, placed a curse on everyone inside. Now, every time it stormed, the horrible scene replayed and the victim came back, seeking revenge on whoever was inside refusing to let them enter...

The storm was almost over the house now. Lightning flashed, repeatedly illuminating the room then plunging it back into darkness, while thunder shook the whole building. The tapping was a frantic staccato now and her heart was trying to match the pace. Clutching the blanket tightly in her hands, she darted her gaze about the room, expecting some evil entity to leap out at her at any minute.

Closing her eyes, she took a deep breath. This was ridiculous; she was a grown woman. What she needed to do was to get up and investigate. She gathered her courage and tried to throw back the covers, but her hand refused to cooperate and merely grasped the blanket more tightly.

Scowling, she admitted the truth. Yes, she was afraid but there were options open to her. She could stay where she was, getting increasingly more scared or she could go find Ryne.

Except he'd tease her about it unmercifully.

Hmm... Neither idea was overly appealing.

Another flash of lightning illuminated the room, and she spied the fireplace. Ah-ha! If memory served her correctly, a set of fireplace tools were by its side. The poker could be used as a weapon!

Not giving herself time to chicken out, she leapt off the sofa and dashed towards the fireplace, her only goal being to grab the poker before something grabbed her. With more speed than grace, she made her way across the room, stumbling into an end table and causing the lamp on top of it to wobble dangerously.

"Damn!" She tried to grab the lamp, but only succeeded in stubbing her toe on something. Abandoning the lamp in favour of her throbbing foot, the fixture smashed into pieces on the ground. She hopped up and down whimpering in pain while simultaneously glancing over her shoulder towards the window. A burst of light filled the room and she was sure she saw the shadowy shape of a person by the window. Through the noise of the storm, the sound of footsteps reached her ears. It was coming to get her.

A scream ripped from her throat and she whirled around to grab the poker, only to crash into something hard. Hands grabbed at her and she screamed again, hitting and kicking in an attempt to elude whoever was holding her. Arms tightened around her as she lurched to the side, the suddenness of her movement knocking her opponent off balance. Together they landed on the floor, and she found herself pinned under a heavy body, her assailant's fingers pressed tightly over her mouth. Luckily, one of her arms was free and she swung it with all her might towards her attacker.

As her fist connected with a solid wall of muscle, pain shot through her hand and both she and the person she'd hit, emitted a shocked *oomph*. The only difference was, while she stopped her assault to focus on the throbbing in her hand, the other individual merely flinched and grabbed her arm, effectively immobilizing her.

"Are you crazy, woman?" A deep voice rasped in her ear.

She froze. Even through her fear, she recognized it was Ryne on top of her. Ceasing her struggles, she blinked up at him, relieved to see a friendly face. Well, friendly compared to the undead creature she'd been imagining.

"You're not going to scream again, are you?" He removed his hand from her mouth but kept it hovering near, ready to muffle her should the need arise.

She shook her head.

"Good, because my ears are sensitive to high pitches. I'll probably be deaf for the next few days." He shifted so his body no longer pressed flush against hers. Instead, he was straddling her. "Okay, explain what got you so worked up you started screeching and wrecking my entertainment room?"

"I..." Her mouth suddenly went dry. Now she was no longer staring at his face, she got a good look at the rest of him. Oh. My. Gosh. Ryne was on top of her. A nearly *naked* Ryne was on top of her! The flashes of lightning illuminated his body in amazing detail. Starting at his broad shoulders, her gaze ran over his muscular chest, noting the flat brown nipples, the faint trace of hair, the well-defined abdominals and lean hips. Black boxer shorts covered his lower half, but hung low enough she could see the beginning of an interesting 'v' that disappeared below his waist band. Under the cover of the boxers...well...a certain something pressed against sensitive portions of her anatomy.

She gulped and forced her eyes back up to his face only to discover he was glaring down at her impatiently. Oh, right. He'd asked her a question. Now she was no longer alone, the danger her imagination had conjured up had faded into obscurity. She blushed, feeling rather foolish and looked away, biting her lip.

Unfortunately, Ryne didn't relent despite her discomfort.

Realizing he wasn't about to give in to her silent plea, she replied. "I...er...heard something."

"Such as?"

"I know you'll think this is silly, but...it sounded like someone was tapping at the window."

"And your imagination took over?" He quirked an eyebrow at her and she felt herself flush even more. At least it was dark so he couldn't see—

The thought wasn't even completely formed when the lights went on, exposing her to Ryne's gaze. She winced at the sudden brightness. Couldn't anything ever go her way?

"Hey, what's going on down here?" Looking up in the direction of the voice, she saw Bryan standing in the doorway, his hand on the light switch. Muscles rippled across his bare chest and his pyjama pants hung low on his hips. Her heart gave a lurch as she realized nearly naked hunks surrounded her. Unfortunately, none of the hunks seemed as impressed by her, as she was by them. This latest one appeared to be laughing as he took in the scene.

"Nothing. Go back to bed." Ryne didn't move from on top of her and she squirmed, trying to give him the hint he really should move.

"Doesn't look like nothing to me." Bryan continued. "More like the two of you are about to get it on."

"Sorry to disappoint you, my friend, but it was nothing interesting. Melody thought she heard a noise at the window." Ryne completely ignored her efforts to dislodge him.

Mel stopped struggling, instead twisting her neck so she could better see Bryan. "Yeah, something was tapping at the window and I was getting up to investigate."

A grin started to spread over Ryne's face, as he called her on the veracity of her story. "Really? The window's the other way. It looks more like you were coming to get me to save you."

"No, I wasn't. I was going to get a poker from the fireplace and take it with me for protection." She lifted her chin, daring him to doubt her.

Ryne tossed her a disbelieving look while Bryan crossed the room to check the window. "Well, you did hear something Mel. The window is leaking and there's a steady drip landing on the floor. I'll get a bucket to catch the water."

As Bryan went to get a bucket, Ryne leaned forward, a teasing glint in his eye. He spoke in a voice that was menacingly slow and creepy. "I've heard evil drops of water often stalk fair young maidens in the middle of the night."

"Not funny." She pushed ineffectually at Ryne, trying to move him. "Will you get off me?"

"No, I don't think so. I'm comfortable here."

"I'm not. Now get off!"

Bryan walked in carrying a bucket just as she spoke. He chuckled. "Mel, would you mind waiting until I'm gone? I'd rather not be here to see Ryne *getting off.*

We're good friends and all, but there's some stuff I just don't need to see."

She was sure her face was as red as a tomato by now. "That's not what I meant, and you know it!"

Bryan said nothing else, merely setting the bucket in place and walking out of the room snickering.

.

Chapter 17

Mel awoke wrapped in a cocoon of warmth. She sighed contentedly and snuggled in closer to the source of the heat. Now this was the way to wake up. Funny, she'd never realized how comfortable her body pillow was before. It smelled good, too, spicy and masculine.

Wait. That wasn't right. Her pillowcase smelled like the lemon-fresh scent of her laundry soap. She moved her fingers, exploring the surface beneath her. Uh-oh. Last time she checked, her body pillow didn't have a rib cage. This was not good.

Cautiously she opened one eye and saw a muscular pectoral inches from her face. Oh crap, what had she done now? She pushed hard against the body pressed to hers, twisting away with the intent of creating as much space, as fast as possible, between herself and the person beside her.

As escape attempts went, it was highly unsuccessful. She barely made a quarter turn before strong hands caught her, pulling her back.

"Not so fast, sweetheart." Ryne's voice was rough with sleep.

Yep. Just as she suspected. She was in Ryne Taylor's bed and he was in it as well. Damn. Finding herself effectively trapped, she looked up at him and scowled. After last night's incident, he'd refused to let her stay alone, claiming she'd most likely have more bad dreams and he didn't want his sleep disturbed any more than it already was. Before she could even utter a protest, the annoying man had slung her over his shoulder, walked to his room and dropped her onto the mattress!

Without a word, he'd turned off the lights and climbed in beside her, punched his pillow into shape and closed his eyes.

She'd gaped at him in shock before clamping her mouth shut and flinging back the covers intent on leaving.

"If you make me get up again, I'll hog tie you to the bed post," he'd muttered not even looking at her.

She'd stilled, not entirely sure he was joking, and then slowly pulled the covers back up around her. Lying stiffly at his side, she'd planned on sneaking out as soon as he fell asleep but she must have dozed off first. Now it was morning and she was trapped beside him!

"Seems you aren't a morning person." Ryne rose up on his elbow beside her. His dark hair hung messily about his face and the morning stubble on his chin made him appear more handsome than ever.

How dare he look so sexy first thing in the morning, she thought thinking her own morning appearance was probably less than appealing. It really wasn't fair.

"Tsk, tsk. I can't have a grumpy woman in my bed. I have a reputation to uphold, you know." A crooked grin appeared on his face and his eyes twinkled with devilment. "I definitely have to do something about this." Without another word, he tilted her chin up and kissed her.

In shock, she gasped which provided him the perfect opportunity to slip his tongue into her mouth and, before she even realized it, her lips were moving against his, returning the kiss.

Ryne lifted his head and grinned down at her. "Ah, no more scowl, but not quite the look I was hoping for. Maybe..." And then, he kissed her again.

This time it was slow and gentle, his lips tender on hers before trailing lightly over her jaw to her ear. Taking his time, he feathered kisses on her forehead, down her nose, across her cheeks before finally settling on her mouth once again. His hand skimmed over her shoulder, fingers barely touching her flesh before moving to her collar bone, tracing the neckline of her t-shirt but never going lower. Her body clamoured for more, every nerve ending he teased tingling to life as something inside her instinctively responded to him.

Unable to resist, she pulled him closer, urging him on as all reason evaporated and only need remained. He teased her, pleasured her, drove her to the very edge until she was begging for more.

"Ryne…" She breathed his name, not hiding the desperation in her voice, looking up at him with longing as she ran her fingers through his hair, down to cheek.

His gaze locked on hers and then… He stopped.

A look flashed across his face, too quick for her passion-hazed mind to grasp but his next words certainly caught her attention.

"Now that's a better morning expression." He smugly ran his hand down her body then delivered a smack to her rear. "Up and at 'em."

She let out a yelp and gaped at him in shock.

Chuckling, he rolled out of bed and crossed the room, the muscles in his back and thighs rippling.

"What? But we were…?"

He paused in front of the dresser and she could see his arched a brow as he looked at her in the mirror. "We were what?"

"Umm…" Her brain was befuddled as she struggled to sit up while gathering the sheets to shield her.

When she didn't continue, he shrugged and headed to the bathroom. "I've got to grab a shower and then go see about clearing the driveway. If you think of what you want to say, you know where to find me."

As he disappeared from sight, her brain tried to process what had happened. He'd done that on purpose. He'd got her all hot and bothered and naked and then he'd just left her hanging. And he'd slapped her butt. Well, she'd like to give him a slap too, but there was no way she'd join him in the shower now!

The sound of water running filled the room and the scent of his soap teased her nose. In her current needy state, it was easy to imagine a picture of him... No! She quickly erased it from her mind and began listing his faults. Annoying? Yes. Egotistical? Yes. Smug? Cocky? A pain in the ass? Yes to all of the above! His numerous failings helped to cool her ardour and, realizing it wouldn't be long before he returned, she scrambled out of bed and rushed to gather her clothes.

By the time she was dressed and in the TV room, he was walking down the hall, his low-slung jeans clinging to lean hips and a t-shirt in his hand.

"You can use the shower now if you want." His glaze flicked over her from head to toe no doubt noticing her fully-clothed figure. "Or not. Up to you."

Her gaze was caught on a stray droplet of water that had dripped from his damp hair and was now making its way down his neck, over his shoulder and proceeding to his defined pecs. Despite his behaviour, there was no denying he was a magnificent specimen.

"Melody?"

"Yes?" She heard her voice crack and winced.

"I said to help yourself to coffee and whatever you can find to eat in the kitchen." He pulled his shirt on as he spoke but she was sure he was smirking, damn him!

Regardless, she cleared her throat and gathered her courage to speak. "About this morning..."

"What about it?"

178

"Well..." She stared up into his handsome face. His blue eyes were intense yet there was a shadow to them as well. What was it? Caution? Regret?

"Still can't remember what you want to say?" He shook his head. "Look, this morning was fun, but that's all it was. Don't get clingy. It's not pretty." He flicked a lock of her hair as he walked by. "I'm going to get the guys and move that tree from the driveway. We'll probably be back in an hour."

She watched him leave, her mouth hanging open, only one thought in her head.

Jerk!

She relented and took a shower after all—she hated starting the day without one—then made some toast and coffee while mulling over Ryne's comments. It was like he was trying to make her angry. Maybe it was normal for him, his idea of caveman charm? If so, she was surprised some woman hadn't killed him yet! Whatever the case, she wasn't going to make the same mistake again. Ryne Taylor would never have another chance to get under her guard again!

Trying to distract herself, she wandered around the house, checking the view from various windows and before deciding to investigate the book shelves. Books could tell a lot about a person, she mused as she began to scan the titles. Horrors, mysteries, war stories, ancient history. Which ones were Ryne's and which ones belonged to the other two?

She pulled out several old leather-bound books, the titles barely readable due to age and sat down to look through them. One was entitled Mythology and Cryptozoology, while another was on Lycanthropy.

"Lycanthropy? What's that?" She flipped through the book and decided Lycan was a more politically correct term for werewolf. Go figure. The book was the most worn of the collection and someone had made notes in the margins, underlining certain passages. The penmanship was bold and written in black ink. Could it be Ryne's? The topic didn't seem like one he'd pursue.

Studying the comments, she chuckled. Words such as 'idiots' and 'as if' were written near some of the illustrations of werewolves. Oops, Lycans. She mentally corrected herself and then continued reading. 'Almost got it right' was penned near a passage about the effects of the full moon and the words 'allergic but not deadly' were beside a paragraph about silver bullets. It almost appeared as if the owner of the book took the topic seriously. She raised her eyebrows at the thought of any intelligent person believing such stuff.

"Get a life," she muttered.

Still, it was interesting that people would devote so much time to create such a realistic myth. Having nothing better to do, she started to read.

It proved to be quite fascinating, so much so she was surprised to hear the sound of voices approaching the house. She shoved the books back on the shelf and grabbed her coffee cup. Intent on heading to the door to check on their progress, she took a sip from her cup and grimaced. It was cold. Changing direction, she went towards the kitchen instead. The guys could let themselves in. She needed fresh coffee.

Ryne entered the house and ran his hands through his windswept hair. Typical spring. After an unseasonably warm two weeks, last night's storm had blown in a cold front. A northerly wind whipped over the land causing the tree branches to sway and the remains of last year's leaves, still wet from the rain, to blow about; their damp, clammy surface hitting against his legs and face more than once.

Removing the tree hadn't been hard but he was still glad to get back inside. Cold weather didn't bother him, but he hated the wind. It swirled a myriad of scents in the air, confusing him as to the direction of their source while the distorted sounds and flying debris left him jumpy and irritable.

Now inside, he could relax. Well almost. The scent of fresh coffee and Melody teased his nostrils. His inner wolf rumbled approval at her presence even though he'd told the animal that getting involved with a nosey journalist was the last thing they should be doing. Having the woman here was too dangerous; one slip on his part, or by Bryan or Daniel and their cover would be blown. And if that happened, he knew what he had to do and being involved with the girl would make the task all the harder.

His wolf disapproved of his line of thinking. The beast had enjoyed having the female in bed. He had as well, if he was truthful. Waking up to see her beside him had lowered his guard and he'd kissed her. In theory it was supposed to have been a bit of teasing, only once he'd started he hadn't wanted to stop. It had taken considerable will power to walk away and he'd kept his back to her so she wouldn't see the evidence of how much their encounter had affected him.

Self-retribution had followed once he was in the shower and he'd turn the tap to cold. It had helped douse his desire and clear his head. 'Bad move, Taylor,' he'd scolded himself. She could very possibly be the enemy and his plan of giving her a quick and highly abridged interview didn't include having sex. He was supposed to be acting like an ass; offensive and uncooperative so that she'd hurry on her way. With this in mind, he'd purposely been a jerk towards her this morning, brushing off the encounter with none of the tender words a woman usually wanted to hear. Hurt and confusion had been

181

evident in her eyes and, while he wasn't the most sensitive of guys, he usually didn't treat his women that way. However, he'd steeled himself to do what was necessary and left her thinking the worst of him, despite the fact that his wolf was moving restlessly within him.

Maybe he should have just told her to go away in the first place, but from what he'd observed thus far, Melody wouldn't give up that easily. At least this way he knew what she was doing and could dole out measured bits of information; enough to make it seem real, but never anything important. Yes, it was the best plan. He just had to keep his mind focused on the possible threat she could pose, rather than her other interesting qualities.

Setting his jaw, he went off to find his unwanted guest.

Chapter 18

After leaving Ryne's house, Mel went home and concentrated on a list of questions to ask him. He was a reluctant participant, so she didn't want to put him on the defensive with the very first question, so where to start? Tapping her pen against her lips, she considered the problem, then settled on the tried and true; basic background. There was nothing threatening about that. Date and place of birth seemed pretty safe, followed by where he grew up and what schools he attended. Then she could move on to his work, inquiring how he had started in photography and did he have any formal training. What else?

She tried to imagine herself as someone interested in nature pictures. What would she want to know? Why was he interested in nature photography rather than people or buildings? How did he choose his subjects? What kind of cameras did he use? Were there special techniques that differed from other forms of photography? Any special considerations? Oh yes and the locations. How did he select them and where had he taken pictures previously? Aldrich had conveyed Greyson was particularly interested in the locations of the pictures. Personally, she didn't think it was important, but she wasn't the one paying for the article, was she?

The story of the missing sales associate and the pilfered money would be interesting to include, but she scratched them from her list. If she asked, Ryne would know she'd been talking to the people at Bastian's

Gallery in Smythston and she felt it prudent to not let him know she'd been there.

Setting her papers aside, she contemplated the rest of her day. It had been noon by the time she'd left Ryne's, declining the offer of lunch which had been enthusiastically delivered by Bryan and Daniel and only grudgingly acknowledged by Ryne. The asshole hadn't pressed her to stay, nor had he acted as if anything had happened between them earlier in the day. Well, she could be as blasé about it as he was.

Determined to not think about him, she picked up the romance novel she'd been reading, but after a few pages, set it down. After her early morning encounter, the sex in the story wasn't interesting. She stared out the window at the woods. The wind had died down and the sun shone brightly. Maybe she could take a walk.

Without further thought, she grabbed her coat and stepped outside. The temperature was cool, but not so cold as to prevent her from enjoying the day. After spending most of her life in the city, the idea of having nature right outside her door was rather exciting. Mindful of the possibility of wolves, she decided not to walk too far, keeping the cabin in sight.

As she tromped along, she tried to view the land as Ryne might, from a photographer's point of view. Light and shadows, angles and background, unusual subject matter. It was amazing that, when she actually looked, there were a lot of things to see in the forest. Kneeling, she peered at some moss growing on the side of a tree.

Up close, it was actually rather interesting; tiny little fronds of bright green clinging to the rough grey bark. And the bark itself was so textured and varying in shades. She ran her hand over the moss and then the trunk, marvelling at the contrasting feel of each. With an eye out for minute details, she continued exploring the edge of the forest, pausing every few feet to examine some new wonder she'd never noticed before.

By the time she finished, an hour had passed and she was full of enthusiasm for nature photography. In fact, she was itching to try some herself. How much would an inexpensive digital camera set her back? She'd have to ask Ryne when she saw him next. That is, provided he wasn't being a sarcastic ass. There were times she actually liked him, and others when all she wanted to do was give him a good swift kick. Note to self - ask him about the camera *before* she kicked him!

Her stomach rumbled and she realized, aside from some toast and several cups of coffee, she hadn't eaten yet. Time to head to town and see what Al was preparing at Ruth's.

When she arrived at the diner, she hesitated, guilt filling her as she recalled she'd spent the night with Lucy's man. Of course, nothing had happened. Well, not exactly *nothing* but still, she had a tender conscience when it came to things like this. And, now that she'd thought about it, Ryne had kissed her by her car when they'd left the Broken Antler the other night. That made it twice she'd broken the unwritten law regarding keeping your hands—and lips—off another girl's man!

Through the window, she could see Lucy laughing at something one of the customers said, while skilfully balancing a heavy tray of food in one hand and pouring coffee with the other. Lucy really was something. Once you got past the slightly ungrammatical speech, layers of makeup, bleached blond hair and too-tight tops, there was a warm, generous person underneath. A person who willingly offered friendship to a newcomer and she'd betrayed her. Ryne was Lucy's property, despite what the waitress might have said. Lucy had seen him first and so it should have been hands off. Damn, why hadn't she thought of that sooner? And what should she do about it now? If she told Lucy, the woman would be hurt. Yet if she didn't tell her, someone else might.

Ryne didn't seem like the kiss and tell type but what about Daniel and Bryan? They both suspected something had gone on this morning, if their knowing grins were any indication. But would they mention it to Lucy? No, the only way Lucy would find out, would be if Mel told her and she certainly wouldn't do that, would she? But if she didn't, it was lying by omission and she didn't like to lie to her friends. Yet the truth might hurt more than the lie.

Minutes passed as Mel wavered back and forth. Finally, she huffed in exasperation, got out of the car and went inside, deciding to gently broach the subject of having lunch with Ryne yesterday and gauge Lucy's reaction.

She slid onto her usual chair, picked up the menu and studied it, all the while watching for Lucy out of the corner of her eye. It was busy in the diner which was good as Lucy would have less time to spend chatting. Stiffening her spine, Mel made a selection and waited for the waitress to arrive.

"Hey, Mel! You don't usually come this late. Did you have a busy day?" Lucy bustled up; a blond curl bobbing up and down beside her ear being the only evidence the woman had been working hard. She leaned her hip against the tabletop as if she planned to stay for a few minutes.

"Umm, yeah. I was busy working on questions for my article."

"The one with Ryne? How did your meeting go with him?" Lucy's eyes sparkled with interest.

"Meeting?" Mel could feel heat creeping up her neck. The meeting was what had started the whole mess.

"The one Harley delivered the message for? Or did the big storm keep you from going? I heard there were trees down across the roads and some power lines too." Lucy tucked the wayward curl behind her ear.

Mel swallowed, but forced herself to answer calmly. "No, the storm didn't stop me from going to Ryne's house." It only kept me from leaving, she added in her head.

"Great. I've never been to his place... Oh damn! Table six wants more coffee. I've got to go. Do you know what you want? The chicken parmesan is real tasty."

"That sounds good." Mel agreed thankful Lucy had to leave before she asked any more questions.

"Great. I'll be back in a minute." As she walked away, Lucy yelled her order into the kitchen and the cook grunted in reply.

Mel nibbled on her thumbnail and when she realized what she was doing, clutched her hands together in her lap. She hardly ever chewed her nails anymore, which went to prove how guilty she was feeling over Ryne. Hopefully all the customers in the diner would be very demanding and leave Lucy no time for idle chatter. Squeezing her eyes shut, she sent up a little prayer to that effect and then slowly opened her eyes to check the results of her missive.

As per usual, it had the exact opposite effect she'd hoped for. A table of eight diners were standing up preparing to leave and two smaller parties were also showing signs of finishing their meal.

"Here you go, Mel. Enjoy. I'll be back later to chat." Lucy breezed by and set a plate of food in front of her.

With little appetite left, Mel placed her napkin in her lap and picked up her utensils. Half-heartedly she began to cut the chicken into small pieces, but only pushed them about her plate, making a show of actually caring about what was in front of her. Damn, damn, damn. Why had she given in to Ryne this morning?

"How's that dinner?" Al called out to her from the serving window between the kitchen and dining area, causing her to start in surprise. She looked at her plate. The food was now in small enough pieces even a baby could eat it.

"Delicious." She answered Al's question, pasting a smile on her face and popping a piece of food into her mouth. She chewed with feigned enthusiasm. It probably tasted wonderful, but at the moment she was sure sawdust would have been just as palatable. Taking a sip of water, she washed the chicken down then stared unseeing at the food in front of her again. To tell Lucy or not to tell Lucy, that was the question. If only she knew the answer.

She ran through the imaginary conversation in her head. Hey, Lucy. I have something to tell you. I'm really sorry but I ended up in Ryne's bed last night and this morning, well, we didn't actually have sex—

"What was that, Mel?"

She blinked and realized Lucy was standing in front of her. Oh no! Had she really spoken those words out loud? Surely not.

"You had sex this morning? With who?" Lucy slid into the empty seat opposite her and leaned in close, resting her elbows on the tabletop, eager for a juicy bit of gossip.

"Er...no one."

"You had sex with no one? You mean you were...um...self-servicing?"

"No!" She felt face grow warm at the assumption and slunk down in her seat, hoping no one could overhear the conversation.

"Then who? And don't give me any of that 'no one' business. I can see a love bite on your neck."

Mel clapped her hand to her neck. She didn't remember Ryne doing that!

Lucy giggled, sounding immensely pleased with herself. "Gotcha! Relax, there's nothing there. I was just tricking you into revealing the truth. You did have sex with someone, now give me the details. Which local stud got lucky?"

Now completely flustered by Lucy's teasing, she began to stumble through her explanation of what had happened. "You know I went to see Ryne yesterday. Well, because of the storm, I had to stay the night and—I hate to have to be the bearer of bad news and I promise this isn't as bad as it sounds—but I ended up in his bed." She stopped and frowned realizing that had come out all wrong.

"So...? What's the bad news?"

"Sorry. I didn't mean I was in bed with him... Well, technically I was but—"

"You're kidding me, right? In a bed or on a table, sex with Ryne is never bad." Lucy leaned back in her seat and frowned.

With her explanation completely twisted around, Mel explained again. "The sex wasn't bad. There was no sex. But I was kissing and...er....stuff with Ryne. *Your* Ryne."

Lucy blinked. "Well of course it would be with my Ryne. He's the only Ryne around here... Oh!" She gave an amused snort. "Did you think I was going to be upset? Mel, I already told you we don't have that kind of relationship."

"I know what you said, but I thought maybe you were just saying that."

"Mel, Ryne and I are friends with benefits. He's a nice guy, but he's not the one for me. Hell, he might not be the one for anyone; he's too much of a player." Lucy shook her head and smiled reminiscently. "When I first met him, I wondered if maybe he was the right guy, but he isn't. Ryne's a good man, but I want someone who'll take me away from all this." She flourished her order pad and gestured around the room. "Not some guy who's planning on spending the rest of his life in Stump River."

"You don't like it here?"

"Oh, I like it fine, but I also want to make a new start. Here, I'm just good old Lucy. All the guys know me, if you get my drift, but none of them really want to settle down with me." The server's eyes suddenly seemed lonely and wistful.

Mel reached across and grabbed Lucy's hand, sensing behind her happy, carefree facade Lucy had more than a few scars on her heart. "Lucy, you're a wonderful person. Any man would—"

Shaking her head, Lucy interrupted her attempt at offering comfort. "No, Mel, not *any* man. At least not here in Stump River. But someday, when I save enough money, I'm going to move to a big city like Toronto or Montreal and make a new start for myself. Find some guy who thinks I'm more than a roll in the hay." She gave a determined smile. "Don't get me wrong. The people here are good to me, but I want more. I *deserve* more."

Mel looked at her friend, taking in the tilt of her chin and her narrowed eyes. Her heart swelled with pride in the woman. Lucy *was* more than people thought she was. "You're right, Lucy. You do deserve more and if I can help, I will." She wasn't sure exactly what she could do, but was willing to offer her services. The two women's eyes met and Lucy nodded, obviously understanding the sentiment.

Lucy patted Mel's hand. "Now enough about me. It's you I'm worried about. If you want Ryne, you go for it. Just don't be expecting a lot more than getting your teeth rattled. He wouldn't purposely break your heart, but he's not into long-term commitments. Keep that in mind."

Mel brushed Lucy's concerns away. "It was a one-time thing. I'm here to interview him. It's a job, that's all."

"Nothing saying you can't enjoy your work." Lucy stood up and winked.

"Maybe. But I doubt it. All we've done so far is argue with the exception of this morning. Besides, I'm pretty sure I'm not his type."

Lucy gave her a once over. "I don't know. I've noticed him watching you on and off this past week, when you weren't looking. He's had his eye on you."

"Really?" Mel felt a ridiculous gush of happiness at the idea of Ryne taking notice of her.

"Uh-huh. If you play your cards right, you might get lucky." With another wink, Lucy went on her way.

Mel watched her leave and mulled over the conversation. Lucy had basically told her to go after Ryne and that Ryne might be interested in her. Her logical self told her to not even consider it. However, there was no harm in a little fantasy now and then, was there? Her appetite back, she began to eat with gusto. Al really did make good chicken parmesan, she thought as she happily munched away.

Chapter 19

Ryne arrived late at Miller's Service Station on Monday morning. The kitchen cabinets he'd ordered had arrived at the house just as he was leaving and he'd stayed to double check the order was correct. Ben wouldn't care, but Ryne hated being late.

"Hey, Harley." He greeted the black lab that wiggled with joy at his appearance, ruffling his fur and giving a quick scratch behind his ears before sending him to tell Ben of his arrival. Harley was a good dog and Ryne enjoyed the happy-go-lucky beast. When they'd first met, Harley had whimpered and hidden whenever he came around, but once the dog understood Ryne was a benevolent Alpha, they'd gotten along just fine. Not that he could truly 'talk' to the dog, as the locals were fond of saying, but he understood and used some universal canine body language to communicate.

Sending the dog on his way, Ryne headed for the office to check the day's work orders. Pulling out the buff coloured pages from his mail slot, a white envelope tumbled to the ground. He picked it up and turned it over in his hands. Only his name appeared on the front. Even as he tore the flap open, he had a sneaking suspicion as to what lay inside.

Yep. True to her word, Melody—he would never be able to think of her as Mel—had left him a list of interview questions. It had been too much to hope that she'd forget the whole thing. As he scanned over the outline, his face grew grim. Where was he born? Where did he grow up? Where did he go to school? How many people were in his family? All those questions had to be vetoed. He couldn't take a chance she'd associate him with Kane's pack. How he chose his subjects? That was okay. Camera techniques? Yep, he'd discuss those. Where he took his pictures? No way. No one could ever discover the wolf picture had been taken just outside Smythston, Oregon.

Rubbing, his forehead, he tried to ease the headache he could already feel building. This wasn't going to be easy. He'd have to come up with some cock-and-bull story as to why he wouldn't answer what were basically simple questions.

Ben Miller sauntered in, Harley leading the way and wagging his tail, pleased to have completed his mission. "Hey, Ryne, you look worried. What's up?"

"Nothing much, Ben." He folded the list and stuffed it in his pocket, then bent to pat Harley as a reward for following orders.

Ben nodded towards Ryne's pocket. "That letter you were reading, it was from the new girl in town. Mel, I think her name is. Anyway, she was here bright and early wanting to give it to you so I said I'd make sure you read it."

"Thanks, Ben." He turned to go.

"So, is she your new girl?"

Ryne rolled his eyes, but turned to face his boss. Ben didn't usually indulge in idle gossip so maybe there was some point to this conversation. "No. Melody isn't my new girl. She wants to interview me about some pictures I took a while back."

Ben nodded. "That's what I heard. I also heard someone say you were planning on leaving with her and heading back to the States because you're really a famous photographer."

"Famous? Hardly. Would I be working here, if I was?"

"Now don't be putting down this fine establishment of mine." Ben unsuccessfully tried to look affronted. "But I suppose you're right. If you were famous, you wouldn't have started fixing up the old Nelson place or be getting your hands dirty, changing oil for me. I just wanted to check to make sure you weren't planning on suddenly taking off with that girl and leaving me high and dry."

"Rest assured, Ben, I have no plans of taking off with Melody. Stump River is where I'm staying."

"Good to know. Now quit standing around here yakking and get to work." Ben headed back towards his office.

Ryne shook his head. Nothing ever happened in Stump River, so Melody's presence was a big event and lent itself to the production of rumours. He hoped the attention died down when she left. Attention was the last thing a Lycan pack wanted.

By the time noon rolled around, Ryne had a few ideas for avoiding some of Melody's questions. Hopefully, she'd accept what he said at face value and not press too hard for more details. He'd keep things simple and not too friendly!

As if on cue, Melody wandered into the service bay. She was wearing a denim jacket, tight jeans and a loose red top that was gathered at the base of her throat by a tie and then flowed over her full breasts to her waist where it swirled gently every time she moved. Ryne considered what would happen if he undid the bow at the neck. Would the top fall from her shoulders and puddle at her feet leaving her bare? He felt a grin spread over his face at the idea and shoved his hands in his pockets to resist the temptation of seeing if his theory was right.

Unaware of his thoughts, Melody absent-mindedly played with the string that held her top in place, drawing his attention to the rise and fall of her breasts. "Hi! Did you get the list of questions I left? They're pretty simple, so I was wondering if you were ready to start on them today."

It took Ryne a moment to realize she was waiting for an answer and forced his gaze away from the interesting activity of her fingers. "Today?" He pondered the question. There was no reason to delay any longer. He'd done that all last week for the perverse joy of annoying her. But now the time for games was over. "All right. Today's fine. I'm almost done with work for the day; I just have to put my tools away."

"Great!"

"You can wait over there." He pointed towards a group of chairs by a set of vending machines then grabbed a rag and began wiping down the wrenches to remove the dirt and excess grease, before arranging them in the proper drawers of the tool cabinet.

A sound behind him drew his attention and he saw Melody was buying a chocolate bar. The look of happiness on her face as she peeled back the wrapper made him smile. From what he'd seen of her so far, she was seldom without coffee in her hand. Apparently, when coffee was unavailable, she moved on to chocolate. She was a funny little thing.

Concentrating on finishing his job, he locked the toolbox and put the keys away. Moving to the sink, he turned on the water, poured some hand cleaner on his palms and began to work the industrial strength soap into his hands. Soon the layers of grease and grime were washed away and he dried off.

Melody had just finished her treat when he walked over to her.

"Ready?"

She nodded in agreement. "Do you want to talk at the diner or...?"

He hesitated. At the diner, everyone would be eavesdropping and the chance of his neighbours interrupting with questions of their own was highly likely. "No. There's a nice little place near the cenotaph with a couple of benches. We can sit there."

Giving a quick nod, Melody stood and picked up her purse. He ushered her out, calling a goodbye to Ben who was working in the office. The older man grunted in acknowledgement and Harley gave a woof before settling down to finish one of his many naps.

They walked in companionable silence down Main Street. A few people called a greeting or waved from their vehicle as they drove past. Ryne nodded in response thinking within half an hour everyone would be talking about him and the 'new girl' in town.

Sitting down on the bench, Melody pulled out her steno pad and a pen. Ryne braced himself, hoping his answers would be sufficiently convincing to keep her from probing too deeply.

"Ryne, we're going to start with some simple background information, like date of birth, where you grew up, what your childhood was like, that sort of thing. It will give readers a more rounded picture of you; make you more real to them."

"No."

"No?"

"No."

"Oh." Melody blinked at him. "Why?"

Ryne assumed his most arrogant expression. "Because I didn't truly *exist* before photography."

"I beg your pardon?"

"You heard me." He shifted uncomfortably, feeling like an ass. It was such a dumb answer but he hadn't been able to think of anything else.

"Yes, I did, but what does that mean?"

"That my life before I started taking pictures was of no importance; it was a vast wasteland of ill-spent years trying to find my real passion, my real reason for existence."

"Are you pulling my leg?" She set her pad and pencil down in her lap and gave him a look that was half laughing disbelief and half fear he wasn't joking.

"No. I'm not. Next question." He stared at her, allowing his wolf to show in his eyes, demanding she accept his word as law. There was a flicker of something in her eyes, an acknowledgement, or recognition of his position and then she dropped her gaze, even going so far as to slightly tilt her head as if offering her throat. It was curious behaviour. Most humans looked away or cowered. Brushing the little idiosyncrasy aside, he relaxed the force of his will.

Melody gave a sigh as if she were relieved to be released and cleared her throat. "All right. So no background information. Um...do you have any formal training in photography?"

"No. One day I was out running in the woods and when I stopped to rest, I just really started to look closely at my surroundings. The intricacies of nature's designs, the variety of hues; they all captured my imagination. The next day I brought a camera with me and started taking pictures."

"Really?" She sat up straight, excitement washing over her face. "The same thing happened to me yesterday afternoon. I was out walking around the cabin and trying to see the forest the way you might and it hit me. I really wished I had a camera so I could try some different shots."

The enthusiasm in her voice caught his attention. He noted how her eyes were sparkling and her cheeks glowed. Before he realized it, he heard himself not only offering to lend her one of his digital cameras, but to take her on a hike and show her some photography techniques.

"Oh, that would be awesome. When?"

"How about now?"

"Sure, though..." She paused and looked down at her feet.

He stifled his laughter. Her boots were the same four-inch heels she'd worn sneaking onto his property that first day. "Definitely not the proper footwear. Tell you what. I'll go home and get a couple of cameras and meet you at your cabin in an hour. You can change into some hiking clothes." He flicked the tie on her top and watched how the bow relaxed revealing an inch more skin. A low growl rumbled in his throat.

"How do you do that?"

He quirked a brow. "Do what?"

"That rumbly thing with your throat. I've never heard a man do that before."

He inwardly cursed while trying to casually pass it off. "Just one of those weird habits people have. Some guys give a wolf whistle when they see a pretty girl. I...er...growl."

"Oh." She paused then brightened. "So you think I'm pretty?"

He smiled, noting how nicely she blushed. It wasn't an all over red, more a stain of pink along her cheek bones. "Yeah. I do." Leaning forward, he gave her a gentle kiss and then abruptly stood up. "I'll go get those cameras."

"Sure. I'll see you in a while."

As he strode away, he glanced back. Melody was sitting there with her fingers pressed to her lips. Damn! He'd done it again. What the hell was wrong with him?

Back at the cabin, Mel pulled on a heavy sweater, traded the fashionable boots for sneakers and extra thick socks and then headed out to wait for Ryne.

She was excited to try some nature photography and, if she was honest, to see Ryne again. Part of her hoped he saw her as more than a casual lay, but logically she knew she shouldn't hold her breath. Her main focus, as Aldrich pointed out repeatedly during her daily report, was to get this article done.

At least now she could tell the lawyer she'd started even though Ryne's answers had been less than satisfactory. That whole 'I didn't exist before photography' bit was just too corny. Yet, even though she knew it was ridiculous, something in the way he looked at her, the tone of his voice, the angle of his head, had compelled her to obey, to not question. It was weird. Even now, she couldn't imagine asking him again. Hopefully, she'd be able to get enough information with her other questions that no one would notice a lack of background detail.

Ryne's truck pulled up to the cabin and she walked over to greet him. He gave her apparel a once over and then nodded in approval.

"Much better. Here's a camera you can use. It's an older model I have as a back-up, but it takes a decent picture." He took some time to show her how to use the zoom, flash and shutter speed adjustments. "The megapixels aren't high, but it's sufficient for a starter like yourself."

"Pixels?"

"It's how precise or clear your picture will be. Usually, the more pixels, the sharper the image. The term comes from combining the words 'picture element'. You know how pointillist artists, like Seurat or Van Gogh used a bunch of little splotches of paint to create a whole picture? Well, millions of pixels combine to create an image."

As they walked through the woods, he continued giving explanations and pointers about focal points, shadows and a myriad of other small details she'd never considered before. By the time they headed back to the cabin, she had a much greater appreciation for the art of photography.

"I hope you know you've ruined me. I'll never be able to point and shoot again." She laughed up at him as they stood by his truck, their shoulders lightly touching.

"You won't be the first woman I've ruined." He quirked a smile at her, yet she felt her happy mood suddenly sour at the mention of his womanizing ways.

She stepped back and stuck out her hand. "Thank you for your time. Maybe we can continue the interview tomorrow."

He looked puzzled. "What's the matter, Melody?"

"Nothing's the matter, and my name is Mel."

"No. To me, you're a Melody." He ignored her outstretched hand and, much to her surprise, pulled her into his arms. Once she was pressed flush against him, he questioned her again. "Now what's wrong? One minute we're laughing and enjoying ourselves and the next, you're the ice queen."

She compressed her lips tightly, reluctant to explain herself, yet feeling compelled to bow to his wishes. It was annoying, this effect he had on her. Against her will, she found herself explaining. "You mentioned all the women you've...er...ruined. And it reminded me I'm only here for a while and I have a job to do. Getting too friendly with you is a bad idea."

Ryne's arms tightened around her briefly before letting her go. This time he was the one to step back. She immediately missed the contact with him.

"You're right. Our getting involved the other morning wasn't the best idea, but..." He paused, appearing conflicted, almost as if he didn't want to utter the next idea. "That doesn't mean we can't at least enjoy each other's company, right? There'd be no harm in that. Sitting around a table asking and answering questions won't be a lot of fun." He gave her a half smile and winked.

No harm. She repeated the words inside her head, not sure if she believed them or not. She would never use the word harmless to describe him. But she did need to finish the interview and it *was* much more pleasant to have a friendly conversation.

She made a face. "You're right. I was over-reacting. Our...encounter yesterday morning threw me off." Feeling herself flush, she forced herself to continue. "It's not the sort of thing I usually do."

"Really?" Ryne reached out and tucked a lock of hair behind her ear. His fingers felt cool against her warm cheek. "I'd never have known. You seem to have a natural talent in the area."

She blinked at him unsure if she should feel honoured or insulted.

He gave a short laugh, obviously pleased at having confounded her yet again and chucked her under the chin before getting into his truck. Once inside, he rolled down the window. "You can keep the camera while you're here. Play around with the different settings and see what you can do. There's a cable in the case so you can download pictures onto your laptop."

"But won't you need it?"

"No. Like I said, it's my back-up. I hardly ever use it. The batteries are rechargeable, but I put a fresh set in before coming over, so you should be good for a while."

"Thanks. I appreciate this." She tucked the camera in the case. "Can we get together again?" Seeing the evil twinkle in his eye, she quickly clarified. "For another interview session, that is?"

"Sure... If I can ask you a question."

"What?"

"How did you find me? Here in Stump River, that is. I've kept a pretty low profile."

She swallowed hard not wanting to admit she'd been watching Kane and Elise at the post office in Smythston and then snooped through the mail. Falling back on a tried and true answer, she smiled nervously. "Reporters never reveal their sources."

His face darkened. "What kind of an answer is that?"

"It came from the same shelf as 'I didn't exist before photography', Mr. Smart-ass."

"Pure bullshit to avoid answering, in other words."

"Worked for you." She raised her brows and folded her arms.

He grunted then gave a reluctant grin. "I'll be in town on Wednesday. I work until four. We'll have dinner at The Broken Antler and talk then."

She nodded and with a wave of his hand, he drove off.

Chapter 20

Ryne pulled up in front of the house and turned off the engine. He made no move to get out; his mind occupied with Melody Greene and why, when he was around her, the real reason he was spending time with her kept slipping from his mind. For an Alpha, it was unacceptable behaviour.

He rubbed his chin. The afternoon had been fun. Melody was an enthusiastic companion and eager to learn about her new found interest. He chuckled, thinking of how she'd furrowed her brow and bit her lip while absorbing what he told her. Then when she'd snapped a picture and the image appeared on the screen, her delight had lit up her whole face. She had a natural artistic streak, too. When she set up a picture, she seemed to know how to frame the shot and take the best advantage of the light and angles.

Her affinity to nature was surprising in someone who had purportedly grown up almost exclusively in a big city. Yet, the wonder in her eyes when she'd crouched beside him, examining the pattern on leaves and the path of an early ladybug, was real. More than once, he'd caught himself reaching out to grasp her hand as they walked along in companionable silence, soaking in the world around them. He'd actually enjoyed spending time with her and sharing his passion.

And speaking of passion, her nearness had stirred him more often than he really cared to admit. Her scent had filled his mind, making it hard to concentrate on taking pictures and explaining photographic theory. In reality, all he wanted to do was throw her down on the ground and taste her sweet lips one more time. The sex between them had been great and, even though he knew any involvement with her was dangerous, he was eager to experience her again.

Maybe it was the element of danger that was drawing him to her. She was like a forbidden fruit and he'd never been one to toe the line any more than he had to. But, as Alpha, the needs of the pack came first. He knew the law and what was at stake. The actions he might have to take were spelled out clearly.

Yet despite this knowledge, his wolf kept urging him towards the woman, pushing all other concerns into the background. Did his wolf know something he didn't? They were usually of one accord, but now a dichotomy was developing within him. It was something he had never experienced before and didn't know how to handle, yet handle it he must. The situation was too crucial. Who knew how many lives were depending on the decisions he would make over the next few days? Having his mind clouded with lust was unacceptable.

He clenched the steering wheel and tightened his jaw. When he set out on his own, he knew he wanted to create his own pack, to be Alpha, to use the power within him. Now he had his wish and he'd live up to his obligations, no matter what his personal inclinations might be. And so he'd continue to see Melody, answer her questions as slyly as possible, maybe even bedding her again if he thought it was needed to keep her distracted from what was under her very nose. Then, when he was sure she'd bought his story, he'd send her on her way.

But what if she doesn't buy your story? What if she keeps poking around? The wolf inside questioned him angrily. *What will you do then?*

"Whatever it takes," he answered back. "I'll do whatever it takes."

He climbed out of the truck and slammed the door. Bryan and Daniel were inside supposedly installing the newly arrived cabinets. He'd better see how they were doing. They meant well, but enthusiasm didn't always translate to solid construction.

He spent the rest of the day and most of the next, helping with the installation of the cabinets followed by new countertops and a sink. By the time the job was finished, the kitchen looked considerably improved. The tempers of the three men, however, were not. The walls of the old house were less than plumb and there had been considerable trimming and shimming required, a tedious and frustrating process at the best of times.

Standing in the room surrounded by the scent of new wood and the gleam of granite countertops, he knew it had been worth it though. This was a kitchen suitable for his vision of the future. He could see it filled with pack members; some lounging at the breakfast bar, others busy at the stove. It would be loud and friendly and—

"Hey, Ryne! Bryan and I are heading up to The Broken Antler for dinner and some fun. Armand has a pool tournament arranged. Want to come along?" Daniel popped his head through the doorway, buttoning his shirt, his hair damp from a shower.

Glancing down at himself, Ryne recognized his own need to clean up. Bits of sawdust clung to his pants and pricked his skin where it stuck in the sweat of his chest and arms. "Nah. I have to get cleaned up and then I want to go for a run." He shrugged his shoulders and stretched his arms, feeling the tightness of his muscles. The work in the house was taxing, but still not enough to ease the tension within him.

"Suit yourself. If you change your mind, you know where to find us."

"I might, but if I don't, behave."

Daniel rolled his eyes and laughed. "Don't we always?"

"No."

"True, but it's more fun that way."

Ryne faked a growl back at him, then shook his head as the boy turned on his heels and hurried out. It was good to see the kid loosen up once in a while. Daniel was far more serious than Ryne had ever been at that age.

Scratching his chest, he grabbed a broom and began the mundane task of cleaning up sawdust, discarded nails, scraps of lumber and bits of packing material. The other two would have helped if he'd asked, but he didn't mind the time alone. Besides, they'd worked hard the past two days and deserved a break.

He heard the door slam as his companions left, laughing about their plans for the night. Soon the sound of a vehicle starting floated inside followed by the crunch of gravel as it began to move down the driveway. Pausing his sweeping, he listened until the sound faded into the distance, then resumed his task. The house echoed with silence now, the faint scrape of the broom against the floor the only sound. It was both calming and lonely, if such a combination actually existed.

For a moment he regretted turning down their offer, but other thoughts weighed too heavily on his mind to make him a suitable companion for the night. He still hadn't told Bryan and Daniel about his concerns over Melody. They viewed her as a delightful little pest and had given him no end of teasing about her while working on the cupboards. Good naturedly, he'd gone along with them. There was no use giving them cause to worry when nothing might come of it. If the need arose, then he'd inform them.

Giving the kitchen a last glance, he propped the broom and dustpan in the corner, then headed for the shower. He'd get cleaned up, then take a run around the perimeter of the property to check for signs of intruders. If he planned his route properly, he'd end up a mile or so from Melody's cabin. Not that he intended to stop by. After spending the previous night tossing and turning, he'd come to the conclusion his association with the woman had to be short and sweet. It was the safest course of action for all involved.

Mel sat in her cabin staring blankly at the computer screen, waiting for it to download the pictures she'd taken with Ryne the previous day. Why was it taking so long? There were a lot more pictures in the file than she thought there should be. Idly she wiped a bit of dust from the screen with her finger, contemplating the fact she really should buy one of those little laptop cleaning kits when she got back to Chicago. Maybe she'd check out Brown's General store when she was in town tomorrow. For such a backwoods type of location, it had quite a varied product line. Adding that to her mental to-do list, she glanced at the screen and sat up straight, a look of anticipation spreading across her face. The pictures were done downloading.

Disconnecting the camera from the laptop, she put the cable away and tucked the camera back in its carrying case, mindful of the fact it was a loan. Then, turning back to the computer, she found her picture file and began to scroll through, looking for her nature shots, anxious to see how they'd turned out. Scanning down the menu, she found the proper folder and opened it up. A bubble of happiness grew within her as she examined the fruits of her labours. Darn, but the pictures weren't half bad!

After going through the photos twice, she gave herself a congratulatory pat on the back. For a beginner, she felt she'd done pretty well and was eager to show Ryne how they'd turned out. Maybe she'd even take a few more on her own and surprise him with how well she'd remembered what he taught her. Glancing at her watch, she saw it was only four o'clock. There was plenty of time to go for a walk, snap a few pictures and be back home before dark.

Closing the folder with her pictures, she noticed another folder above it. Now what had she put in that one? She really did need to organize her hard drive with proper labels. Quickly clicking the folder open, she scanned the contents. That was odd. She hadn't taken any of these pictures. Who were these people?

As her finger hovered on the mouse, she realized these must be pictures Ryne had taken but never erased from the chip. She'd accidentally downloaded them with her own. Well, she'd delete them later, she decided, pushing away from the table without further thought. She wanted to get outside while the light was still good. Grabbing the camera and her coat, she headed outside. There was a stream not far away; it might provide some interesting subjects.

Half an hour later, she sat crouched beside the stream, tired from her hike but pleased with what she was seeing. Recent rain had swelled the small lazy stream into a swiftly moving waterway that provided a number of interesting possibilities. She spent some time trying to capture images of water drops splashing upwards around rocks and partially submerged pieces of log. Occasionally a leaf or bit of grass would float by, twirling in the current and bobbing up and down.

Feeling adventuresome, she carefully picked her way along a set of makeshift stepping stones that led to the middle of the stream. The water and mud had washed up onto them making them slippery, but she was confident in her ability to keep her balance. If she could walk on four-inch heels, this should be a piece of cake.

Placing each foot carefully on a relatively flat surface, she bent forward, intent on taking a picture of an old, weathered log. The water was lapping gently at the edges of it, the light dancing off the surface and shimmering like diamonds. It would make a lovely shot.

Slowly she bent her knees to get the proper angle, then she framed the shot in the view finder. Yep, that was it. She snapped a few pictures before shifting the camera ninety degrees to get a different angle. Even better. Zooming in, she focused on a leaf that was momentarily caught on the edge of the log and, when it finally worked its way free, she stood to watch its progress down stream.

A movement to the right had her swinging her head to the side. There, at the base of a pine tree, sat the largest wolf she'd ever seen. It was as black as the night except for intense blue eyes staring right through her.

"Oh my gosh!" She gave a startled cry and instinctively stepped backwards, remembering too late there was nothing to step back onto. The stomach lurching sensation of falling filled her as she tipped backwards barely having time to utter a cry before her head submerged. Icy coldness wrapped itself around her, her clothing quickly becoming saturated and heavy, tugging her down towards the bottom of the stream. At the last second, she thought to keep her hand up in the air attempting to save the camera from a watery grave.

The soft, silt of the river bottom cradled her body for but a second then something grabbed at her arm and hauled her upward. Her head broke the surface and she gasped, coughing and sputtering as her lungs sought to simultaneously inhale oxygen and expel water.

Stunned, she found herself set on her feet, hard hands gripping her upper arms. For a moment she simply stood dripping and gaping, too surprised to even push her wet hair from her face. Thankfully, someone else did it for her. Blinking, she realized she was staring at Ryne. He did not appear happy.

"What the hell were you doing?"

"Huh?" Why was he yelling at her?

"What kind of an idiot stands in the middle of a swollen stream in the height of run-off season? Don't you know how dangerous that is?"

"Idiot? I'm not an idiot! I was perfectly fine until that wolf... Oh damn!" She looked desperately side to side, trying to locate the beast. "We have to get out of here. There's a wolf somewhere nearby." She took a step and then froze, unsure of which way to go. The cabin was to the right, but so was the wolf...

"Wolf? What wolf?" Ryne sounded puzzled.

"The wolf that was right over there!" Pointing towards the trees, she glanced at Ryne to see if he was looking where she was pointing. He wasn't. Instead, he was frowning at her.

"Melody, there was no wolf here unless... Did you see Harley? He was out walking with me."

"No. It wasn't Harley. It was a wolf. Really. I saw it." She faltered under his disbelieving gaze. "Well, it looked like a wolf." She crossed her arms and pouted.

"I suppose, if you were really intent on taking a picture, you might make that mistake." He appeared as if he was about to pat her on the head like she was a foolish child.

Compressing her lips, she sloshed over to the edge of the stream, shivers starting to wrack her body. "Where's Harley now?"

"He probably ran off when you started to yell. He's very sensitive, you know."

"Yell? I didn't yell. At least not much." She was now shaking so hard she could hardly get the words out.

Ryne shook his head, pulled off his jacket and wrapped it around her.

"You don't have to do that." She protested and tried to hand him back the piece of clothing. "You're wet, too."

He ignored her and shoved her arms into the sleeves and zipped it up. "Don't worry about me. It's only my pant legs and besides, I hardly feel the cold. Come on, let's get you home." He moved to pick her up, but she put out her arms, shaking her head.

"Uh-uh. I can get home perfectly well by myself." She set off for the cabin at as quick of a pace as her soggy shoes would allow. Behind her, she could hear Ryne huff in exasperation before following.

By the time they reached the cabin, the brisk walk had warmed her, but she longed to get out of her wet clothes and into a warm shower. Ryne apparently had the same idea, for he walked right in and headed towards the bathroom and turned the shower on. Exiting, he looked around the room, spied her robe and threw it at her. "Here, get out of those wet clothes and take a shower while I make you a cup of tea."

"Coffee."

He stopped mid-stride. "What?"

"Make it coffee. Nice and strong."

He rolled his eyes, but gave a huff of laughter and she scooted into the bathroom, a warm feeling filling her despite her chilled skin.

By the time the hot water had run out, she felt considerably better. She pulled on her terrycloth robe and exited the bathroom, sniffing appreciatively as the smell of fresh coffee greeted her. Automatically, she turned towards the kitchen, but a sound behind her, drew her attention. It was Ryne, propped up in her bed.

His upper half was naked, his lower extremities hidden by the covers. He was sipping a cup of coffee and appeared to have made himself quite at home.

She folded her arms and frowned at him. "Why are you in my bed?"

"My clothes were wet and none of your clothes fit me. I didn't think you'd appreciate me wandering around in the nude. Besides, it's warmer under these blankets."

"Oh." It made sense.

"I started a fire and spread my clothes in front of the fireplace. They'll dry eventually."

"Wouldn't you warm up faster if you were in front of the fire too?"

"My clothes are draped all over the chairs. There's nowhere to sit and the floor is hard."

Nodding, she stood undecided about what to do. Should she go stand in the living room and leave him alone? It seemed rude, but standing here while he lay in her bed didn't seem right either. She also needed to get dressed, but wasn't going to do that in front of him.

Ryne patted the space on the bed beside him. "Why don't you keep me company?" When she hesitated, he pulled out the big guns. "I have a cup of coffee here for you." He gestured to the bedside table and she zeroed in on the steaming cup. In mere seconds, she was sitting beside him, sipping the dark liquid and sighing appreciatively.

Chapter 21

Mel leaned back against the headboard and stretched her legs out in front of her. Searching deep inside, she silently repeated her mantra while looking for inner peace and tranquility. Well not really, but she thought it sounded better than 'trying to ignore the hottie beside her'. She purposely kept her eyes fixed firmly forward. With studied nonchalance, she sipped her coffee and wiggled her toes, noting she still needed to redo the polish.

"Hey, I'm over here." Ryne waved his hand in front of her face. She tilted her head so she could see around it. "What are you doing?"

"I'm ignoring your presence in my bed."

"Oh." He considered the fact and then frowned. "And why would you want to do that?"

"Because, yesterday we decided this," she slid a glance his way and gestured between the two of them, "isn't a good idea. I'm only here for a few more days. We need to maintain a professional relationship." She crossed her ankles, inhaled deeply through her mouth and then slowly exhaled through her nose. Or was it supposed to be in through the nose and out through the mouth? Darn. She could never get those relaxation techniques right! Grimacing, she realized trying to relax the *correct* way made her feel more tense.

"Huh." Ryne nodded and looked away, sipping his coffee. "So you're going to act like I'm not even here?" His tone was casual, conversational even, as if it really meant nothing to him at all.

"Yep." She nodded emphatically and sipped her coffee again, savouring the taste. The man *did* brew a good cup of caffeinated bliss.

"Bet you can't do it."

"Bet I can." She sensed him watching her and lifted her chin in determination.

"Nope. You can't." His voice was irritatingly smug.

"I can so."

"Can't."

"Can."

"Okay."

She turned her head fractionally and looked at him. He had given up much too easily. There was something akin to an impish gleam in his eye. Then he smiled blandly at her and shifted so he was staring at the wall, seeming to be content to lie there. She slowly turned away and stared at the wall as well.

Silence stretched between them, only broken by the faint crackling coming from the fireplace in the other room. She amused herself by imagining she was the heroine in the romance novel she was reading. The front cover showed the woman lying on a fur rug in front of a fire, a devilishly handsome man leaning over her. Hmm... What if that man was Ryne? And what if she was the woman? She felt herself growing warm at her musings and slid a peek sideways to check out what the man beside her was doing. Shockingly, she discovered he was staring right at her, a wicked grin on his face, as if he knew the direction her thoughts had taken.

She jerked her eyes away and stared straight ahead. Licking her suddenly dry lips, she forced her mind to abandon that oh-so-interesting train of thought. It wasn't prudent when they were lying half naked in bed together. She wiggled her toes again, trying to focus on mundane matters and not on the man beside her. A lock of hair was falling in her eyes and she brushed it away, then began twirling the hair around her finger. Hair. That was a safe, distracting topic. She'd trimmed the bangs herself a few weeks ago, but it was getting way too shaggy. A good cut was what she needed, maybe even a new style. Highlights? Or a totally different colour? Shifting so she could see Ryne better, she sought his opinion. "What do you think I should do with my hair?"

"Your what?"

"My hair. It's really getting long and there's no style left. Do you think I should get new layers put in it or go for a complete change? I could dye it red or even black. Maybe cut it really short and make it spiky on top? I don't want anything that requires too much work, though. It needs to be something simple so I can just wash, add a bit of product, dry and go." She knew she was babbling, but the silence between them was too hard to handle. Setting her cup down, she shimmied around so she was sitting cross-legged, facing him.

"Um...I think it looks fine."

She noted he had a sort of dazed look about him. Hairstyles probably weren't his cup of tea, but since he was a man, she'd figured his opinion was worth exploring. "I've done it all, you know; short, curly, straight, streaked, long. I've always heard men prefer longer hair, though I don't know why. What's your opinion?"

He stared at her, his lips twitching. "It's sexier."

"Really? How so?"

He set his coffee cup down and turned so he too was facing her, a mischievous grin on his face. "Because, you can run your hands through it." He demonstrated. "And use it to pull a woman closer." Which he did and then leaned in close to whisper against her lips. "And, when you're in bed, the feel of her hair brushing softly against your skin drives you wild."

"Oh!" She squeaked out a response as Ryne gently brushed his lips back and forth over hers. He'd buried his fingers in her hair and was now leaning back and using her long tresses to slowly pull her down on top of him. Once he was on his back and she was leaning over him, he deepened the kiss. Vaguely, she noted how her hair provided a curtain around them, blocking out the rest of the world. Mmm... Long hair did have its advantages she thought as she slid her hands over his chest.

"I won." He whispered against her lips.

"Won what?" She traced his lower lip with the tip of her tongue.

"The bet." He nuzzled the curve of her neck, inhaling deeply.

"Bet?" She guided his face back up.

"That you couldn't ignore me." He cupped her face and stared into her eyes, a teasing twinkle apparent.

"Oooh!" She sat back, furious she'd fallen for more of his games. Eyes narrowed, she gave him her deadliest look.

He grinned. "You should see your eyes. That look would do a she-wolf proud." Abruptly, he stopped speaking and a frown appeared on his face.

His comment touched her sense of humour and she chuckled, leaning back on her haunches. "Is that a polite way of calling me a bitch?"

Ryne stared up at her then he shook his head. The wild look faded. "No." Grasping her by the hips, he lifted her off and sat her down beside him. Then he swung his legs over the side and sat with his back to her. He rubbed his face roughly with his hands. "You're not a bitch. Far from it. But I'm definitely a bastard. I only meant to tease you but things got out of control. Again." There was a pause and then he forced out one final word, as if he wasn't accustomed to uttering it. "Sorry."

She watched in confusion as he stood and walked towards the door, the sight of his taut rear-end and muscular thighs doing unspeakable things to her insides. "Where are you going?"

"To see if my clothes are dry. I should head home."

Blinking slowly, she processed his message. He was leaving. Right in the middle of everything. With an exasperated huff, she pushed her hair from her face and clambered off the bed. She tightened the belt on her robe, straightened the covers then picked up the empty coffee cups.

Teasing her! Ha! She was getting tired of his *jokes*. Intent on informing him of just that, she marched into the living area only to freeze when she saw him, still naked, leaning over her laptop. It was one of her little quirks, but she didn't like people messing with her electronics.

"What are you doing with my computer?"

Ryne ignored her question and countered with one of his own. "Where did you get these pictures?" He gestured towards the screen; his tone was sharp and angry.

She walked to the table and peered over his shoulder. It was the file of pictures she accidentally downloaded from the camera and explained as much to him.

"Did you look at these?"

"No, not really. What are they? Part of the next Ryne Taylor exhibit?" Her attempt at lightening the mood fell flat.

He glowered at her, his lips pressed flat.

Sighing, she started to explain. "I opened the file, wondering what it was. I skimmed over a few, and when I realized they must be yours, so I stopped. End of story."

He searched her face then gave a grunt before turning back to the computer and deleting the file.

She held back her indignant reply that he had no right to delete things from her computer. They *were* his pictures and she should have erased them right away. Seeking to keep the peace, in the spirit of ensuring a future interview, she apologized.

"I'm sorry. I didn't mean to snoop. I was downloading the pictures I took and I didn't think to see if there were other photos there. Your pictures are still on the camera, though; I didn't erase the card." She looked around, grabbed the camera from the table where she'd set it upon returning home and handed it back to him. "Here, you can have it back."

Taking the camera from her outstretched hand, Ryne appeared about to say something, but then thought better of it. Instead, he turned and headed towards the door.

"Umm... Didn't you forget something?" Despite the tense mood filling the room, she couldn't keep the amusement from her voice.

"What?" He had his hand on the door knob, his back to her.

"Clothes?" A snicker escaped her lips, despite her best efforts to keep it back.

His whole body went rigid and he turned, shooting her a filthy look before grabbing his clothing from in front of the fire. "I'll get dressed outside." And then he left, carrying his clothes in his arms.

Well! That had been an...interesting...encounter. At least there were no neighbours nearby to question why a naked man was getting dressed in front of her cabin. She giggled again. It sure beat the traditional gnomes and pink flamingos as far as lawn ornaments went!

Her mood sobered though as she returned to her computer. Why hadn't Ryne wanted her to see his pictures? It couldn't be because they were bad shots, he didn't strike her as having a perfectionist streak in him, and the few she'd seen had been perfectly fine.

Furrowing her brow, she tried to recall the images on the screen. The one he'd seen, the one she'd left open on the computer, had been of a lake. Before that, there was a house, an older couple, a woman by a lake, a group of people, and a butterfly on a flower. That was all she could recall. It seemed pretty innocuous. There was no reason for him to get all bent out of shape. Sure, he was heavily into maintaining his privacy, but she hadn't purposely gone snooping and the pictures didn't really show anything.

Or did they?

Had she missed something significant? Or were there important photos she hadn't viewed yet? Too bad he'd erased the file. For curiosity's sake, she'd love to have another look. It would certainly make Aldrich happy if she could come up with something specific about the man.

She winced, thinking of his disparaging comments when she'd reported Ryne's 'I didn't exist before photography' answer. He'd been even less impressed than she was, insisting she needed to be pushier when delving into Ryne's background. His cold accusing voice echoed in her head.

"Excuse me if I'm mistaken, Ms. Greene, but isn't an investigative reporter supposed to actually *investigate*? Not wait around for the subject to hand over the information. From where I sit, all you've done is tiptoe around the man. Hardly earning your keep now, are you? Especially considering how many zeros were on that cheque. If things continue as they are, don't be surprised to find Mr. Greyson initiating legal proceedings with the aim of obtaining a full refund of all monies paid, up to and including this date. Unfortunately, you'll be out of pocket any expenses you've incurred thus far, but that's what happens when you don't deliver what you promise."

He'd hung up then, leaving her madly calculating how she'd cover the cost of the plane tickets, the car and cabin rental and her meals. She'd been living hand to mouth before getting this job and used her small savings to pay her apartment rent a month in advance. If Ryne didn't want to talk, what was she supposed to do?

She stared at the computer screen and her hand manoeuvred the mouse across the screen even as an ethical battle raged inside her. Ryne didn't want her to see those pictures, was obviously worried they'd reveal some personal information, but... Her teeth raked her lower lip as she double clicked on the recycle bin icon and stared at the deleted, but not yet erased file.

Ryne, unabashedly naked, headed across the open space that served as the front lawn for Melody's cabin. His clothes were damp and the idea of putting on wet denim was repugnant so he shoved the clothes under a nearby bush, pulling some leaves up to cover them. Satisfied no one would notice the clothing until he returned to collect it another day, he headed into the woods and once concealed behind the trees, closed his eyes and brought his wolf forward.

Even with his eyes shut, he could sense the air shimmering around him, knew if he opened his eyes, the images he saw would be distorted as if looking through a cascade of glitter in a snow globe. It was only a momentary phenomenon and then the world righted itself. Giving himself a shake to adjust his fur, he stretched his front quarters and then his hind before picking up the camera in his mouth and heading for home.

Luckily the boys would be out at the bar and not see him return home naked. Oh, the teasing he'd get if caught. It was a source of pride that pure-blooded Lycans could change and magick back whatever they'd been wearing when they shifted. Only the teenagers, during their first few changes, forgot that crucial step. Of course, those who were the products of mixed matings weren't as lucky. Human genes, no matter how many generations back, interfered with the transfer of magical abilities, one of the first to be lost being the ability to shift forms while clothed.

Other tricks, such as sensing auras and mind-reading between mates varied considerably depending on the purity of the blood line. A few of the aristocracy had supposedly even been able to appear and disappear, though he had yet to encounter anyone who had actually seen the phenomenon occur.

Ryne knew his mother was pure-blooded. As for his father, he hadn't seen the man since he was two and had little knowledge of that side of his heritage. His mother had never spoken of what happened there between herself and his sire and he'd never asked. His relationship with his mother had never been close; his bastard of a step-father had seen to that, dragging them all over the country from pack to pack, either neglecting them or flying into fits of rage.

His mother, in a moment of clarity, had finally left Kane and himself with her home pack in Smythston before heading off with her unstable mate. Ryne never knew what she saw in the man, but she'd given up her children rather than leave him. The only good thing Ryne could say about his step-father was that he'd sired Kane, his half-brother.

Kane... Damn, Ryne hoped there wasn't a picture of his brother on the camera. How could he have been so careless as to not erase the memory card before lending it? Melody claimed she hadn't really looked at the pictures and he'd sensed no deception on her part but the incident reinforced the foolishness of his plan to keep her close so he could watch her. She needed to leave now before she stumbled on to something she shouldn't.

Chapter 22

Greyson stared at the wolf picture, making a show of being lost in thought. He knew Aldrich was waiting for an answer, but he wasn't inclined to hurry. The damned man could wait. It didn't matter that time was money. Money was the least of his worries; he had too much of the filthy stuff as it was. Aldrich would get paid for his time and if he had other clients waiting at his stuffy downtown office, too bad. The man shouldn't have scheduled them for the same day. The lawyer knew all other clients took a back seat to the needs of Greyson Incorporated.

He listened to the faint sound of creaking leather. Good. Aldrich was shifting in his seat. The man was getting impatient, but didn't dare say so. Suppressing a chuckle, Greyson kept his back turned. Aldrich was becoming too full of himself. It was time to show him who was really in charge. Another minute or two and maybe he'd put the man out of his misery.

In the meantime, Greyson amused himself studying his picture. The animal held its head regally, challenging the onlooker. Its amber eyes conveyed an intelligence no normal wolf could possibly possess. And that was the whole point. It was no normal wolf. He knew it and now, he suspected, so did Mr. Taylor. It was no longer a case of an unwitting photographer snapping a one in a million picture. Taylor's reticence to be interviewed and his evasive answers, pointed to one thing. He *knew*.

Suddenly swivelling his chair around, he caught the lawyer off guard, surprising a sour look on the man's face. A perverse thrill filled him.

"Ha! I caught you, Leon. You were sneering at me behind my back!"

He had to give Aldrich credit; the man's features were now as bland as oatmeal. "Of course not, sir. A slight case of allergies. I was merely attempting to discreetly sniffle."

"Good try, Aldrich, but I know you think I'm an arrogant bastard. And you're right. I am. So sneer if you want and I'll keep you waiting as long as *I* want."

Aldrich merely inclining his head.

Greyson chuckled, pleased to have yet again proven he had the upper hand. "So, Taylor's giving cock-and-bull stories to avoid answering questions, is he?"

"Those are the words Ms. Greene employed." Aldrich shuddered slightly at the inelegant phrasing.

"And Ms. Greene?"

"She seems to be *trying,* in her own inimitable way, to conduct an interview with the man. Her success rate, however, is deplorable. A more seasoned reporter—"

Greyson cut the other man off. "A more seasoned reporter would ask too many questions, both of us *and* Taylor. No. Ms. Greene's perfect for the job, in more ways than one."

"If you'd inform me of her *unique qualifications,* as I believe you called them, then I might feel more comfortable with her completing the job."

Narrowing his eyes, Greyson slowly rose to his feet; the sound of his chair scraping against the floor was ominous. He leaned over the desk towards Aldrich, the solid oak creaking as he rested his weight on his fingertips. It was a look and stance that had turned many captains of industry into quivering idiots. Greyson knew the effect and used it indiscriminately. Intimidation was one of his favourite tools. "Your *comfort* is of no concern to me, Leon. I will tell you what I wish to tell you. Nothing more."

To give the man his due, Aldrich didn't flinch. His fingers tightened on the arms of the chair and he blinked twice in rapid succession, but that was all.

Damn, the man was good, Greyson acknowledged begrudgingly. Of course, if he hadn't been good, the lawyer would never have made it this close to his inner circle.

Curving his lips into the barest semblance of a smile, Aldrich answered, his voice as calm and steady as ever. "But of course, sir. Foolish of me to forget."

Greyson slowly sank back into his chair and turned to face the picture again. "Foolish indeed, Leon. Foolish indeed."

Wednesday dawned with Mel's feelings in a distinct muddle. She lay in bed, tired after a night of dreaming about a certain nude photographer prancing around her yard taking pictures of pink flamingos that were being chased by gnomes riding on black wolves. In between each photoshoot he'd pull her close and kiss her senseless, only to walk away because she wasn't a she-wolf.

When she wasn't having weird dreams, she had been awake thinking what to do about the pictures on her computer. In the end she hadn't looked at them, but wasn't sure she wouldn't eventually give in to temptation. She supposed it all depended on how reticent Ryne was during their interview. She had to have something to report and the photos might be her only source of information.

Maybe she should demand he sit down and answer her questions. Even as she considered the idea, her gut told her Ryne didn't respond to demands. If she pushed too much, he'd push back even harder. He'd only agreed to a very restricted interview because...well, why *had* he agreed? Possibly he'd been feeling benevolent towards her at the time? If that was the case, the status of today's interview would be up in the air given he'd left in a snit last night.

Crawling out of bed, she turned on the coffee maker and prepared for the day, her thoughts constantly drifting back to Ryne. Sarcastic, broody, sexy...she never knew what to expect from him. He was beyond frustrating. He was...well...she wasn't sure what. By the time she was showered, dressed and had her hair back in a clip, she still hadn't found the perfect word to describe him.

Dressed in jeans and her favourite red top, she grabbed her laptop and purse, filled her travel mug with coffee and headed out the door, determined not to think about the annoying man until their interview that night.

The bell tinkled softly as she pushed open the door of the Stump River Gazette. Beth looked up and smiled with considerably more enthusiasm than she usually did and hurried across the room.

"Mel, I'm so glad you're here! Can you do me a favour? Josh broke a tooth last night and had to go into Timmins to get it taken care of and it's Wednesday. The weekly paper has to be delivered and I was hoping you could man the office while I do the rounds?" She paused for breath and looked at Mel with hopeful expectation.

Only momentarily taken aback by the rush of information, Mel agreed. "Sure, I'd be happy to help out. You've been letting me use your internet every day for free. This is the least I can do."

"Oh thank you! I was thinking I'd have to lock up the office. It's not like we get a ton of business, but I hate not to be open, just in case." Beth beamed and looked like the weight of the world had been lifted from her shoulders.

"Just tell me what I have to do." Mel placed her things on a table at the back the Kennedys had set up as her temporary office and then returned to the front counter.

"It's pretty simple. A few people might come in to buy a copy of the paper. It's a dollar. There's the possibility a few advertisers might stop in. If they feel there was a problem with the layout of their ads, or if they want to buy more space, get their name. Make a note of what the issue is and say I'll get back to them. Umm..." She looked around for a minute obviously trying to think if there were any other jobs. "Answer the phone and take any messages and, of course, if a big story happens, grab a camera from my desk drawer and go take a picture of it." Beth laughed. "We seldom have any real news, but you never know!"

"I'm sure I can handle it," Mel assured.

Beth gave her a quick hug, gathered up a bundle of papers and left.

Shoving her hands in her pockets, Mel looked about the office. So. She was in charge. Surveying her domain, she rocked back and forth on her heels, wondering what to do. Since there was nothing to keep her busy, she headed to her own table to set up her laptop. From what she'd observed over the past week, life was pretty calm at the paper. She could easily do her work while simultaneously watching the front counter.

In no time at all, she had the outline of her article on Ryne before her. Her fingers hovered over the keys. What to type? She knew so little about the man. Wracking her brain, she decided she could include something about how he was renovating a big old house. Mentally she formed a picture of the place and began to record some ideas.

By mid-morning, she had answered the phone four times and sold about a dozen papers and made note of a concern about a misspelled name in one of the articles. She'd also exhausted her meagre knowledge of Ryne's home renovations and had even listed the names of some of the books she'd found on his library shelf.

The book on Lycanthropy she'd found on his shelves had caught her fancy for some reason so, to help pass the time, she searched the internet for the topic and was soon immersed in the subject. It was hard to believe anyone would spend so much time creating a mythical world inhabited by people who turned into animals. It was utterly ridiculous and yet oddly fascinating at the same time. There were even sites you had to apply to before they'd allow you access to the data in certain sections, as if it were top secret or something!

She shook her head as she examined the application form. They wanted your family tree so they could verify your lycan blood line. As if! Still, it was a cute gimmick. Did anyone ever actually apply? And if they did, then what happened? On a whim, she completed the form. If nothing else, it would give the webmaster a chuckle that someone had actually tried.

She'd just pressed send, when Beth returned. She plopped down beside Mel with a happy satisfied look on her face. "Hi! How'd you make out?"

"Run off my feet." She winked. "Did you get all your deliveries made?"

"Yep. No problem, though I did have a few people standing by their mailboxes wondering why I was late. The delivery of the Gazette is the high point of the week, you know!" Beth laughed and then leaned forward to look at the computer screen. "Lycans? You're interested in shape shifters?"

"Not really. Mostly, I'm fooling around, seeing what's out there on the topic. I saw a book on it and thought I'd check it out. This site—Lycan Link—is the most realistic I've found yet. Not only does it list all these great fictional stories featuring Lycans, but there's a 'myths and facts' area and an FAQ." She snorted as she pointed out parts of the menu. "Look here. This is where you'd go to help Lycans find jobs, immigration assistance, find physicians; you name it. Of course, I can't access most of these areas because my application hasn't been approved yet."

Beth examined the page and frowned. "You didn't really tell them all about yourself, did you?"

She snorted. "No. They just wanted to know my family tree. I had to 'prove' I was a Lycan but since I don't know my father, it was pretty sparse." When Beth raised her eyebrows, she hastened to reassure her. "And no, I don't think I'm a Lycan. I was curious about what would happen. You know, does anyone ever respond to this type of thing? What kind of reply will I get back, if any? It's harmless fictional stuff."

Nodding, Beth still looked concerned. "I suppose there's no harm in it."

"Beth, don't worry. I only had to fill in a bit of information. No phone number, no street address, or anything else. I haven't opened myself up to an attack by a cyber weirdo. Besides, I bet nothing will even come of it. There are tons of sites like this, created by avid fans of paranormal stories. It's all for fun. No one really believes it."

With Beth no longer needing help, Mel went for a walk around town. As she passed by Miller's Service Station, she tried to see if Ryne was working so she could ask about tonight. Unfortunately, there no sign of him. However, Harley came out to greet her and she crouched down, spending some time telling him what a good boy he was, even if he had scared her the other day.

231

"Yes, Harley. You scared me, yes you did. You scared me down by the river yesterday." She baby talked to him while scratching his silky ears. He half closed his eyes, his tongue lolling out to one side, showing how pleased he was with all the attention.

"What's this about Harley being down by the river?" A deep male voice spoke beside her and she looked up to see Ben Miller watching her. She explained her comments to the dog.

"So you see, when I looked up and saw Harley, I thought he was a wolf. It scared me and I slipped into the water." She bent over and rubbed the dog's chin. "But you didn't mean to surprise me, so I forgive you, Harley."

Harley thumped his tail as if he understood what she was saying.

She straightened and smiled at Ben. "I'm glad he made it back home by himself. That's quite a distance for him to travel."

Ben rubbed his neck. "I don't know exactly what you saw, Ms. Greene, but it wasn't Harley. He was with me all day yesterday. I took him to the clinic for his annual rabies shot and then kept him inside afterwards."

She felt her jaw slacken. "You mean that might have been a real wolf?"

"Could be. Or a large stray dog. All I know is, it wasn't Harley."

"But Ryne said..." Her voice trailed off. Had Ryne really said it was Harley? Yes, she was pretty sure he had. But why would he lie? And what animal had she seen? Knowing she wouldn't be satisfied until she had some answers, she decided to query the man's whereabouts.

"Ryne said what?" Ben looked at her curiously.

"Er...nothing. Is he working today? I need to talk to him about something."

"No. He called in early this morning and asked to switch his day to Thursday; said there were some things he had to take care of today."

"All right. Thanks for the information." With a final pat on Harley's head and a nod to Ben, she slowly crossed the street, heading towards the diner. This definitely deserved some thinking and a very large, very strong cup of coffee.

Chapter 23

Mel sat in the diner, only providing absentminded answers when Ruth and Al spoke to her. Thankfully, the two were in a heated debate about possible changes to the diner's menu and only looked to her for an occasional grunt or nod.

"We need to diversify, Al! We've been serving the same thing for the last ten years. Tastes change. People want fancier food with sauces and exotic names; isn't that right, Mel?"

"Uh-huh." She nodded. Why would Ryne pretend there wasn't a wolf, or at least a wild dog present, when there really was?

"Our customers are the same ones we've always had, Ruth. They like the food, they know what we have to offer and that's why they keep coming back. You like what we serve, don't you, Mel?"

"Yep." She gave Al a smile and then returned to her musings. Had Ryne arranged something that looked like a wolf and set it there to scare her? But why? And what had he used? And how had he known she'd be there? She rubbed her forehead, trying to massage away the beginnings of a headache, while ignoring the great menu debate going on around her.

Thankfully, Ruth and Al finally moved their argument into the kitchen and she no longer had to feign interest in what they were saying. Unfortunately, Lucy arrived to take their place. Apparently, the waitress was more observant than her employers for she plunked down beside Mel and looked at her earnestly.

"So what's wrong with you, hon? You look like you're miles away. Not still brooding over me and Ryne, are you? Because if you are, there's no need."

"No. At least not much." She glanced up at Lucy. "Even though you say you don't care, I feel sort of weird about it."

Lucy scrunched her forehead as if thinking hard. Then her face cleared and she smiled. "Have you ever found a pair of jeans or shoes you really liked?"

"Yes." Mel answered slowly, not at sure where this was going.

"Well, you like them and try them on, only they're a bit tight, but you like them so much you buy them anyways. Then, when you get home, what do you do with them?"

"Um...I put them in the closet."

"And?"

"Sometimes I try them on at home, just to see if, by some miracle, they finally fit." Mel gave a self-deprecating laugh. "Of course, they never do, so I stick them in the back of the closet again."

"So, what happens eventually?"

Mel thought of her jam-packed closet and the annual purge she always performed. Items that were too worn were discarded or put in the rag bag while clothes she didn't like or didn't fit were given to friends or charities. "Eventually, I admit they'll never fit and give them away to someone."

"Exactly!" Lucy leaned back in her seat, folded her arms and smiled.

Blinking, Mel pondered what her friend had said, but finally admitted defeat. "Lucy, I have absolutely no idea what my bad shopping habits have to do with you and Ryne, or me feeling guilty."

An exasperated look passed over Lucy's face. "Don't you see? Ryne is my pair of shoes that don't fit!

He's gorgeous and I like having him, but he's not really made for me. So rather than hanging on, I'm giving him to a friend so she can see if he's right for her or not. Understand?"

Mel stared at the other woman and then chuckled. "You know Lucy, that's a very good analogy."

Lucy made a show of buffing her nails against her chest with her nose in the air, attempting to look superior. "I thought so."

Gently nudging the waitress with her shoulder, Mel smiled at her. "Thanks for trying to make me feel better."

"Did it work?"

She forced a smile, not wanting Lucy to think her efforts were wasted. "Yeah, I guess I feel better."

"You feel better, but not great. So, what else is bugging you? Maybe I can help with that, too."

Mel traced a pattern on the tabletop with her finger, hesitant to speak her concerns, but really wanting another opinion. "Do you think Ryne is honest? I mean, honest as in telling the truth."

"Ryne? I suppose I consider him honest. He's always been upfront about relationships; never promising me, or any of the other local girls, anything beyond great sex as far as I know. Why? Do you think he's stringing you along?" Lucy frowned at her.

"No. It's nothing like that. I mean honest as in making up stories."

"As far as I know he's never told me an outright lie. Well, except about coming to fix my leaky faucet, but that's more him being busy and forgetful than lying. What's going on?"

Mel took a sip of her coffee before answering. "I'm not sure. The other day he told me something and I'm pretty sure he knew it wasn't true."

"Was it to, you know, protect your feelings? Like when a guy says you don't look fat in a sweater, but you know you do?"

Mel snorted, but considered the situation. Would lying about Harley being there have protected her feelings in any way? No, not really. She shook her head at Lucy and the other woman continued.

"Was it a lie of omission? Like he didn't say anything or he left something out? I know Ryne's real private and he's great at avoiding questions and changing the topic, when he doesn't want to answer you."

"Maybe. I don't know. It wasn't really that kind of a situation..." She let her voice trail off, reluctant to explain the whole incident. "I think it's something I'll have to work through in my head."

Lucy got to her feet. "All right, but if I can do anything for you, let me know; besides more coffee, that is." She tagged on the last bit because Mel raised her cup hopefully. While pouring her a refill, Lucy added one last point. "I don't know what's going on between you two, but I do know my gut tells me Ryne's a good man and I'd trust him with almost anything."

"Thanks. I'll keep that in mind." Mel took a sip of the warm brew and nodded appreciatively at her friend. "Good as always, even if it isn't a—"

"Cafe mocha, whipped cream, with shaved chocolate curls and a cinnamon stick." Lucy cut in and finished Mel's thought, looking rather pleased with herself.

Mel knew her face must reflect her surprise because the waitress giggled.

"I've been reading up on all those fancy coffees you keep talking about. When I finally move to the big city, I'll need to be able to handle complicated orders like that so I figured I should start practising now." Lucy gave a wink and walked away to see to the other customers.

Left to her own devices again, Mel tossed the Harley-wolf incident round and round in her mind. The only possible reason she could think of why Ryne would lie about the wolf was he hadn't wanted to frighten her. But, when she'd first met him, after nearly being attacked by wolves on his property, he'd relished telling her about the vicious beasts and the damage they could have inflicted. And why had he shown no concern over the presence wolves on his property? Plus, how had he saved her from those very same wolves? Just before she'd knocked herself out, they'd been howling and snarling, yet Ryne never mentioned chasing them away.

Draining her cup of coffee, she decided to head back to the Gazette ad do some more work on her laptop. Maybe she'd compile a list of everything wolf related and see if any pattern appeared. There probably wouldn't be one, but it was a way to spend some time before heading over to The Broken Antler. She hoped he'd show up. And if he did, she'd have some very pointed questions for him.

Ryne sat in the small donut shop and studied the man across the table from him. The fellow's story was solid and there was no scent of deception. Just the usual amount of nervousness and fear any wolf would feel when meeting an Alpha for the first time. His gaze shifted to the far side of the seating area, where, at another table, two young women and an infant sat awaiting his decision. Both females kept their eyes downcast, one quietly humming to the child cradled in her arms while the other, possibly sixteen or seventeen years of age, nervously tore a napkin into pieces.

"So, tell your story again." Ryne shifted his attention back to the male before him.

The man replied quietly and respectfully. "As I said, there was a change in leadership. The Alpha and I did not agree on the mating of my younger sister. He saw her and desired her, but such a union was not pleasing to her and she was too young. As a result, we had a falling out."

Ryne nodded. It was commendable the man wasn't bad-mouthing his old Alpha, even if the leader sounded like a bastard. "So you moved to Canada from Spain. Was there no pack in another part of Europe?" He sipped his coffee and observed the man over the rim of his cup.

"My previous Alpha has much influence with the European packs. We thought it best to make a completely new start."

"And you chose my pack, how?"

"The registry, of course. We thought, as a developing pack, you might be more willing to accept us. We wouldn't represent a drain on your resources or space."

Ryne nodded in understanding. The more established packs were often reluctant to accept outsiders, especially when there was little opportunity to expand the territory on which they lived. Wolves might be social animals, but they also needed room to roam. His pack—all three of them, he inwardly chuckled—didn't face such problems. Stats would show there was considerable space around Stump River and he'd listed the pack as being open to accepting new members. Many packs were harder to join than the most exclusive human country clubs, birth, or bonding being the only possible avenues in.

"What was your position in your old pack?"

"I was a scout." The man lifted his chin slightly, obviously proud of his job which entailed constantly patrolling the territory, keeping tabs on neighbouring packs and warning the rest if there were intruders.

"Good. We can use help in that area." He smiled at the man for the first time. "How are you at construction work? Ever done any carpentry?"

"A little. Does this mean, you accept us?" His tone was cautious, but Ryne noted a flush of excitement showing under the man's swarthy skin.

"Yes. Welcome to my pack, Marco Lobero." They shook hands across the table and Ryne stood, gesturing towards Marco's family. "Come and introduce me to your mate and sister."

It was five o'clock. Mel sat at the bar in The Broken Antler, morosely sipping her beer. She didn't like beer and wasn't sure why she'd ordered it except, when Armand approached her, she'd been too in awe of the giant man to think.

"Bear." It was the first word that had popped into her mind and out of her mouth, when looking at the man. Trying to cover up her faux-pas, she'd quickly coughed and then said, "I mean beer."

Armand had smirked and she had a sneaking suspicion he'd known exactly what she'd said and found it highly amusing. He hadn't commented though, merely placing a glass in front of her.

Nervous at being alone in the bar, she drank the first glass much faster than intended. It had given her something to do and kept her hands occupied, as she continuously scanned the room for any sign of Ryne. When the first glass was gone, another had miraculously appeared in front of her. She'd been going to protest but the firm look Armand gave her had her quietly accepting the offering.

That had been two beers ago. Ryne still wasn't here and she'd given up looking expectantly at the door every time it opened. She knew she should leave, but some small part of her held onto the hope the he'd been delayed.

She took a swig of her beer while wondering why she was masochistic enough to wait for a man who didn't have the decency to tell her he'd be late or unable to come at all. Not only that, but he'd lied to her about the wolf by the stream, and she strongly suspected there was something fishy about the wolf attack on her first day in Stump River. On top of those sins, there was the fact he had given a ridiculous answer to a very basic and harmless question about his background.

'Didn't exist before photography' indeed! He'd been mocking her, just as he'd done so many times before. And why had he been all in a snit about those stupid pictures she'd accidentally downloaded? Walking away, right when things were getting interesting between them was another mark against him. How dare he get all naked and hunky in her bed if he didn't intend to follow through? She felt herself getting aroused at the memory and shifted on the bar stool.

"You okay, little lady?" The bear was back, leaning against the bar and staring down at her from his incredible height.

"Sure, I've never been better." She tried to put on a happy face and lifted her glass to take another sip, only to find it empty. She set it down and pouted. Darn, it was all gone, just when she was starting to actually like the stuff. Without her even asking, the bartender placed yet another beer in front of her.

She smiled up at him. What a nice man, even if he did look like a bear. She told him so and he laughed. It was a booming sound that filled the whole room, causing several patrons to turn and look their way.

"*Merci.* So, if I'm a nice man, do you want to tell me all your troubles? I am a good listener."

She considered the idea while eyeing him up and down. He was big and hairy, but in a friendly, overgrown teddy bear kind of a way. "Well, you see—"

"Mel!" A friendly voice spoke behind her and an arm encircled her shoulders. She looked up to see Bryan grinning down at her.

"Hey, Bryan!" She peered around him, spotted Daniel and waggled her fingers at him.

Bryan slid into a seat beside her. "What are you doing here all by yourself?"

She felt her mouth droop. She didn't want to bad-mouth his friend, so just shrugged.

"That is what I want to know." Armand added. "She has been sitting here for over an hour, alone and drowning her sorrows."

"An hour? You mean you didn't read Ryne's message?" Bryan stared at her quizzically.

"Message?"

"Yeah. I left it at the Gazette for you when I went to pick up a copy of the paper. Beth said you weren't in yet, so I..." His voice trailed off and he got a funny look on his face. "Oh man, I'm in deep trouble now."

"Why? What's wrong?" Mel, Daniel and Armand spoke simultaneously as they watched Bryan dig frantically in his pocket, finally pulling out a crumpled piece of paper.

He handed the paper to Mel, then folded his arms on the bar and buried his head in them. "I am *so* dead."

She opened the note and blinked at it. The scrawl that passed for writing was hard to read given the dim lighting and the wrinkled state of the paper. Nor was the legibility improved by the way her eyes kept going in and out of focus as the effects of the beer she'd drank took further hold.

Armand plucked the note from her hand and read it out loud. "Melody, I have to go out of town. Meet me at six."

"Oh, that explains it." She glanced at the clock on the wall and frowned. It was a typical round-faced time piece except for the fact all the numbers were fives rather than the accepted one to twelve. Underneath there was a caption 'This bar opens at five.'. Huh. She supposed it was funny. Right now, however, it was annoying, because it really was five, or at least she thought so. Scrunching her face, she studied the clock carefully; the big hand was at the twelve...

Noticing her confusion, Daniel reached over and patted her shoulder. "Yes, it really is five o'clock, so Ryne won't be here for another hour."

"Great. I've sat here for a whole hour for no reason and now I have to wait an hour more." She growled in frustration and lightly smacked Bryan on the back of the head.

"Hey, that's not nice." He lifted his head and glared at her.

"Neither was forgetting to tell me." She propped her chin on her hand.

"We'll make it up to you, won't we, Daniel?" Bryan sat up straighter and glanced at his friend.

"Sure, but remember when Ryne shows up, none of this was my fault." Daniel held up his hands, indicating an abdication of responsibility.

Bryan scowled. "Glad I have your support."

"Any time." Daniel grinned and then guided her off the bar stool. "Come on, Mel. Let's go wear off some of that beer and play some pool. Armand, can we have some food to help soak up the alcohol in her system?"

.

Chapter 24

Ryne hummed under his breath as he approached The Broken Antler. Damn, but it had been a good day. New pack members, what more could he want? They seemed like a nice family and were staying in Timmins until temporary housing could be found in Stump River. Marco's mate, Olivia, had expressed her thanks several times while joggling the baby, Angelo, on her hip. Tessa, Marco's sister had been quiet, nervousness emanating from her. He supposed given the fact the last Alpha had been trying to force a union, it was understandable. The girl had no worries on that front, of course but it would take time to gain her confidence.

At first, Marco had wanted to come back with Ryne, but there weren't enough rooms prepared in the house yet. Also, to keep people from wondering too much about the new arrivals, Ryne had decided they should appear to not really know each other at first and then gradually develop a friendship.

"Otherwise, the townsfolk might become suspicious as to why I'm suddenly importing families to Stump River and housing them at my place," he'd explained. After ensuring the family had all they needed, he'd given Marco the job of contacting the registry. Soon the underground Lycan network would be in motion, working on the necessary documentation to smooth over immigration laws. No one would ever be able to question the family's sudden appearance in a new country.

Ryne spotted a familiar pickup truck parked near The Broken Antler. The boys were in town. He grinned, thinking Bryan and Daniel would be pleased with his news. He hadn't told them why he was going to Timmins, though he suspected Bryan had a good idea. The boy might enjoy a good time, but he was no dummy, able to read his Alpha's mood with a high degree of accuracy. Ryne appreciated that quality. It saved time, not always having to explain himself.

Approaching the bar, he went over his plan, if you could call something so simple a plan. He was going to tell Melody he'd changed his mind and the interview was cancelled. She'd protest, but he was sure he'd be able to get her to comply. For some reason, she bowed to his Alpha will almost instantaneously.

He regretted cutting off their relationship so abruptly, but it was for the best. With more pack members to watch out for, the need to remain out of the limelight had intensified.

As he contemplated Melody leaving, anger filled him, strong enough that he stopped in his tracks. What the...?

Giving his head a shake, he leaned against a nearby building and rubbed his hands over his face in frustration; this was happening too often. His wolf was forgetting its place, fighting for dominance, affecting his moods, leading him into actions he would normally think twice about, such as bedding Melody even though he knew she was a potential threat.

He pressed his back into the brick wall, welcoming the rough texture of the wall digging into his back and the distraction it provided. Keeping his senses busy meant his wolf was also busy so his human self could regain control.

Slowly, he felt himself calming and relaxed his tightly coiled muscles. If he didn't know better, he'd think his wolf was love-sick; all moody emotions and more randy than ever. But Mel wasn't a Lycan, so that explanation fell short. To be sure, weres and humans occasionally met and fell in love, but it followed a slower, mushy, 'human' pace, or so he'd been led to believe.

A car passed by and honked its horn. Automatically, he raised a hand and waved, not really knowing who he was waving at, but Stump River was friendly that way. The noise brought him out of his reverie and he pushing off from the wall and headed to the bar, sternly reminding his wolf the girl was off limits no matter how much growling and protesting went on.

As he entered the bar, the usual scents and sounds swirled around him. Sweat and beer and oil for frying. The room was dimly lit, the glow from the big screen TV casting a bluish hue over the people and furniture near it. It was a typical Wednesday night crowd, not packed, but enough bodies that it took a few minutes to find whoever you were looking for.

He narrowed his eyes, scanning the crowd and searching the scents. Was Melody here yet? He was a few minutes late and she'd been prompt last time. Ah-ha! She was by the pool table with Bryan and Daniel.

As he made his way towards them, he could hear Melody's excited voice accompanied by Bryan's laughter and the guffaws of other males. What was going on? Quickly covering the last few yards, he shoved between the shoulders of the gathered crowd and stopped short.

Melody was playing pool.

By itself, it wasn't so shocking, but her appearance certainly was. Her face was flushed, her eyes unfocused. She was giggling, as if there had never been anything funnier than leaning on a pool cue and wobbling back and forth with a distinct lack of balance.

Before he could move, Melody leaned over the pool table to take a shot and the crowd erupted in approving catcalls. She looked up at her fans and smiled, batting her long lashes and giving her ass a little wiggle, which elicited even more cheers. Then, frowning in concentration, she stuck the tip of her tongue out of the corner of her mouth and lined up her shot. Ryne took in the angle and arrangement of the balls. It would be difficult, but a skilled player could feasibly clear the board. He doubted Melody fell into that category. Ignoring the game, he looked at her instead.

Her hair was pulled up on top of her head in some form of knot though quite a few strands had escaped and fell about her face in interesting little ringlets. She exhaled, arranging her mouth so the poof of air went upwards and lifted the curls for a moment before they settled back in place. He noted she wet her lips as her arm drew back, ready to strike the ball with the cue. She was wearing that red top he'd admired the other day, the one with the draw string around the neck.

He shifted his gaze to the neckline and stiffened. The tie was undone and the top was gaping open, giving everyone assembled an unrestricted view of her bountiful assets. Little wonder they were cheering. A rumble rose in his throat. No one should be looking at her, except him!

Stepping forward, intent on hiding her from prying eyes, he didn't even notice she'd made her move and the balls were rocketing across the pool table before tumbling into the pockets.

The crowded cheered and Melody stood up grinning, raising her arms in victory.

"Way to go, Mel!" Bryan whooped in delight. "All right everybody, time to pay up!" He pulled a piece of paper and pencil from his pocket and looked expectantly at a disgruntled group of men.

Daniel grabbed Melody by the waist, gave her a congratulatory peck on the cheek and then spun her around. "I knew you could do it, Mel! Three games in a row!"

"Daniel!" Ryne's voice cut through the general air of jubilation like a knife, his fury a tangible thing.

Despite the noise of the crowd, Daniel had no difficulty hearing his Alpha's voice; his response was immediate. The boy froze and unceremoniously let go of Melody who stumbled at the sudden lack of support.

"Ryne! You're here." Daniel winced even as he spoke and took a step back, his expression wary.

"And not a moment too soon. Did you forget my instructions?" Ryne snarled and flashed his eyes towards Melody before staring at his packmate again. Daniel gulped and nudged Bryan who was busily collecting money from one of the patrons, not having noticed the general stillness that fell around the pool table. Bryan looked up, paled and backed away.

Good. Get away from the girl. His wolf growled.

Ryne nodded in a brief acknowledgement of their obedience before focusing his attention on Melody. She was tipsy, but none the less smiling happily at the group of men gathered around her. One was shaking her hand while another congratulated her, patting her on the back. Someone pressed a kiss to her cheek. No! The thought erupted from him.

They have no right to touch her, kiss her!

Without caring what the crowd might think, he reached out and grabbed her by the arm, yanking her to his side. Then, despite the protests of those gathered, he strode across the bar hustling Melody along with him.

He moved swiftly down the long dark hallway that led to the employees' washroom, but when he reached the door his hand hovered over the handle. No, not here. Moving farther along, he opened another door and stepped inside. The sign proclaimed it to be Armand's office, but he didn't care. Kicking the door shut, he flicked the lock and turned with a growl to face the surprised woman by his side.

"What the *hell* do you think you are doing?"

Melody blinked at him owlishly and then frowned. "Are you angry with me?"

"Angry? I'm..." He clamped his mouth shut unable to put into words the multitude of emotions he was feeling. She'd put herself on display, let other men touch her. And she'd been drinking and who knows what might have happened with her inhibitions all...un-inhibited! Breathing heavily, he fought to remain in control.

"Ryne? Don't be upset. I didn't lose any money. I won all the games." She was sliding her hand up his chest while staring up at him earnestly.

He closed his eyes as delicious little frissons of electricity erupted along the pathway her hand had travelled.

"What's wrong? I was just waiting for you." A hiccup escaped her lips and she giggled.

Ryne wrinkled his nose at the smell of beer on her breath. "You've been drinking."

"Uh-huh. Armand gave me beer. Lots and lots of beer because you didn't come at four like you said and I was waiting and waiting and waiting." She shook her head disapprovingly and made tsking noises before ruining the whole effect by giggling again.

Letting go of her arm, he ran his hands through his hair while trying to remember he was angry with her. She was adorable when she was drunk. Ringlets swished back and forth as she shook her head and he longed to wrap them around his fingers. He forced himself to remain stern.

"I left you a note, saying I'd be late. It's your own fault if you arrived too early."

Her lips formed into a pout. "No, it's not. Bryan never gave me the note. Oops!" She clamped her hands over her mouth and stared up at him wide-eyed. Whispering between her fingers, she continued. "I wasn't supposed to say that, 'cause we don't want you to be angry. You won't yell at him, will you?"

Suppressing a growl, Ryne agreed. "No, I won't yell at him." Kick him in the ass maybe; put him on the night watch for a month, possibly. But yell at him? No.

"That's good." She grinned at him, happy once again. "See? You can be nice when you want. You're not always an ass-hole."

"Oh really?" He folded his arms and stared down at her. If she wasn't acting so cute, he'd have ripped a strip off her for that comment, even if there was a grain of truth to it. "And how have I been an ass-hole?"

"You won't talk to me about your work, and when you do, you give stupid answers. Then you lied about Harley and you keep getting me all worked up by being nice and sexy and then, poof, you're cold and sarcastic. And you left me sitting in the bar by myself for hours and hours and hours..." Melody's happy mood seemed to have faded and now she was scowling at him. She ended her statement by shoving against his chest and turning to leave.

"Oh, no you don't." Ryne grabbed her arm and hauled her back. "You're not leaving yet. We have to talk."

"We have talked. Now I remember why I was mad at you and I want to go." She huffed and blew a strand of hair out of her eyes.

"No!" His wolf was stirring restlessly again. The female was defying him, trying to leave. He pulled her closer to him so their bodies were touching.

Melody squirmed in his arms and he chuckled at her feeble attempts to escape him. The sound apparently pissed her off because next thing he knew, she'd kicked him in the shins.

"Hey!" Instinctively, he moved back and she kicked at him yet again. Ryne lost his balance and fell backwards, somehow pulling her down with him. They landed on an old couch that creaked in protest at the sudden application of weight.

"Oomph!"

For a moment they stared at each other in shock and then they were in each other's arms, the heat of anger having morphed into passion, the flames of need scorching their self-control. And as the desperate desire drove all reason from their minds, the wolf rose to the foreground, ready to claim its mate.

Chapter 25

Ryne stared down at his companion. Melody had her eyes closed, a happy smile curving her lips. He felt his own mouth forming a similar expression. Contentment filled him and his wolf.

This is how it will be from now on, the animal inside murmured. *No more talk of sending her away.*

No sooner had the thought passed through his mind, than he swore. Damn! He had no business smiling at the likes of Melody Greene. Whether innocent or not, he'd come here with the express intention of severing all connections. Instead he'd ended up having sex. What the hell was wrong with him?

Melody stirred and of its own volition, his hand reached out to gently brush damp curls from her forehead. Slowly she opened her eyes and stared up at him. He bit back a gasp at the tender emotions evident in her eyes. She smiled, then mimicked his movement, brushing his hair from his forehead before curving her hand to cup his cheek. He leaned into her caress thought better of it, and pulled away.

She opened her mouth as if to speak, then froze. The happiness drained from her expression and her hand fell to her side.

He knew he was the cause yet couldn't bring himself to remove the scowl from his face. This was all wrong; himself and Melody, his wolf, the Keeping, new pack members. There was no equation that could make them work.

"Oh crap! You're doing it again." With surprising speed, she slid away from him, half falling onto the floor before catching herself and stumbling to her feet. She looked around and snatched up her clothes, turning her back to him while she quickly dressed, all the while hurling accusations over her shoulder.

"What is *wrong* with you? What kind of a man glares at someone he's just had sex with?"

Ryne stood as well, saying nothing to defend himself, nor offering a kind word to ease her emotions. It was better this way.

Once she was dressed, she turned to face him, arms crossed in a defensive gesture. "What are you? Some kind of Jekyll and Hyde?" She gave a brief, dark laugh. "Do you enjoy messing with my mind this way? One minute you're so nice and the next it's like I'm a mass murderer or something. Which is it, Ryne?" When he didn't answer, her eyes started to cloud with tears. "Do you even care one iota about me or am I just convenient lay?"

Guilt washed over him at the hurt in her eyes. He didn't enjoy treating women this way. Hell, he *never* treated them this way. He loved women; the way they looked and talked, the quirky way their brains worked, the scent and feel of them. Sure, he wasn't a roses and pretty words kind of guy, but he had his own code of chivalry towards the fairer sex and it didn't include blowing hot and cold.

"Melody, I—" He stopped. How could he tell her his inner wolf lusted after her, but because she might be the catalyst that brings about the destruction of his pack, he had to push her away? Thankfully, she didn't notice his hesitation.

"Never mind. Whatever you have to say, I wouldn't believe anyway. After all, you can't even give me an honest answer about a dog!"

"What are you talking about?"

"It doesn't matter. I'm leaving. I'll...I'll talk to you later about the damn interview." She turned on her heel and grabbed the door handle to throw the wooden panel open. At least that's what it looked like she'd planned on doing. Unfortunately, she hadn't noticed the door was locked and merely succeeded in wrenching her arm by pulling on the unyielding handle. Muttering under her breath, she dealt with the lock and stormed out of the room.

Wait! She can't leave... His wolf whimpered in protest.

"She just did, so deal with it," he snarled. Pulling his shirt over his head, he dropped onto the couch and leaned back, exhaling loudly. Damn, but he'd screwed up big time. How had his plan to send Melody packing gone so wrong? They'd had sex. He hadn't even used a condom. What was he? Some dumb-ass teenager?

Staring at the ceiling of Armand's office, he noted a spider web in one corner and a few stained ceiling tiles. There must be a leak in the roof, he thought idly. Maybe he'd offer to fix it as payment for using the man's couch without asking. Not that Armand probably cared. No doubt the bartender had used the couch for similar purposes a time or two.

He sighed. The ambiance of the office wasn't going to improve his mood. He took in the dark panelling, over-filled filing cabinets and truly bad paintings on the wall. Armand might have the soul of an artist, but his talent was better suited to serving beer.

Heaving himself to his feet, he went in search of a drink.

As Ryne leaned against the bar, the cracked mirror backing the liquor shelves showed his face appeared to be set in stone, cold and unfeeling. It was a suitable mask to present to the world. Alphas did not show weakness.

Armand set a beer in front of him and quirked an eyebrow. "What gives, my friend? You came in looking happy enough and in less than five minutes you were taking the little lady out back. Now you are in a dark mood. Was she not cooperative?"

He gave a dry laugh. "She cooperated. We had a...falling out afterwards."

"Ah, clingy was she? She didn't listen to your warnings beforehand." Armand nodded wisely. The barkeeper and he had shared numerous conversations about women, so the man knew Ryne's policy. It wasn't the case this time, but Ryne wasn't about to correct him.

"Something like that." Glumly, he took a swig of beer and turned to face the room. Near the pool table, Bryan and Daniel were racking the balls, preparing to play another game. They were showing no ill effects from his earlier growling. In the far corner, a few men were playing darts while half-watching a rerun of last week's hockey game. There was nothing to hold his interest, so he returned to brooding. Was Melody still here? He needed to tell her the interview was off.

He closed his eyes and discreetly sniffed the air. Her scent lingered, indicating she was probably somewhere in the building. Good, he could say his piece here rather than driving out to her cabin. Scanning the length of the bar, he searched for signs of her.

Armand gave him a nudge. "The little lady is at the far end of the bar, if that's who you are looking for."

Nodding his thanks, Ryne started to get to his feet, but Armand placed a restraining hand on him. "What?"

"It would be wise if you gave her some time to cool down. She was angry when she came back from your encounter and I do not believe her mood has improved substantially. In my experience, a woman in such a mood is not to be taken lightly."

"Normally, I'd agree with you, but the sooner I make this break, the better." He glanced at the barkeeper then looked away. Armand was studying him with a puzzled expression.

"You are brushing her off so quickly? Why?"

Sighing heavily, Ryne tried to avoid the question. "Maybe I'll be able to explain later, but not now. It's too damned complicated."

"It is your choice. It is wrong, but it is your choice." The large man shrugged, grabbed a bottle of whiskey and went to serve another customer.

Well, Armand had certainly made his feelings known!

Ryne turned his attention back to Melody. She was tracing rings in the spots of water on the bar, occasionally nodding in agreement to the men who stood around her chatting. Obviously, her success at the pool table had made her the newest local celebrity. Ironically, getting tipsy had probably improved her game.

A light was almost directly over her head and the beam illuminated the gold in her hair. It seemed to glow as did her skin, giving her an almost ethereal quality. With his keen sight, he was able to detect how her lashes swept down over her cheeks. They appeared darker and spikier than normal as if tears had recently pooled in her eyes. The sight caused an ache in the region of his heart.

Something one of her groupies said had her to looking up and Ryne could see the sadness in her eyes. Oh, she was trying to hide it, laughing politely at the man's comment, but it was there and he was the cause. And now, he was going to add to her misery. With reluctance, he pushed off from the bar.

Walking over to where she sat, he shouldered his way in beside her, ignoring the protests of the men gathered there.

"Melody—"

"Hey, man. You can't barge in here. Me and the boys were talking to her." A rough voice spoke to him and someone pulled at his arm.

Ryne didn't even turn around, merely shrugging the hand off. He tried again. "Melody—"

"Go away, Ryne. "She didn't even look his way. "I have nothing to say to you."

He leaned his elbow on the bar, bending in an attempt to see her face more clearly. "I need to talk to you."

"Too bad." There was both anger and hurt in her voice.

He reached towards her instinctively, but she leaned away avoiding his touch. Her rejection cut deeply, even if it was what he deserved.

"See? She doesn't want to talk to you. Now get away from her." A burly man sidled up, placing his arm around Melody's shoulders and glaring at Ryne.

A look of discomfort passed over her face and she shrugged out of the man's grasp.

"I don't think she's too keen on you, either." Ryne pointedly stared at the man's arm that now lay limp at his side.

"Will both of you leave me alone!" Melody's cheeks were flushed and there was a hint of tears in her voice.

Armand began to move down behind the bar towards where a small crowd had started to gather. The possibility of a fight always spread like wildfire through the establishment. Tonight was no different.

Seeking to avoid a confrontation, Ryne curled his lip at the man, biting back a growl, before shifting his focus back towards Melody. He'd say his piece and then leave before things got out of hand.

Unfortunately, the other man wasn't following the same script. "Don't turn your back on me. I'm not through with you yet!"

Irritated, Ryne faced the fellow. The events of the night had shortened his temper considerably.

How dare this person interfere? His wolf wasn't too pleased, either.

Ryne tried to rein in his temper. "Listen, buddy..."

He barely had the words out of his mouth when the other man swung his meaty fist. Only years of practice enabled Ryne to shift enough so the punch hit his shoulder and not his face. Unfortunately, he didn't have time to brace himself and as a result spun around from the force of the blow. The momentum propelled him towards Melody who, somehow sensing impending danger, raised her arms defensively in front of her face. As his body impacted with hers, they both fell to the ground, the bar stool collapsing under the sudden force. Ryne landed on top of her, her elbow shoved up into his face. A sickening crunching sound filled his ears accompanied by a wave of pain as his nose broke. Blood gushed, running into his mouth and down his throat. Melody gave a cry. Shouts erupted around them. Chairs scraped across the floor and soon several people were reaching down, grabbing at the two of them.

Giving his head a shake, Ryne pushed the helping hands away and surged to his feet. His mouth tasted of copper and he spat the bloody liquid onto the floor. Using his arm, he wiped the blood from his face, his gaze sweeping the crowd for his attacker. He'd only seen the man briefly, but it was enough; the image and scent were imbedded in his mind. In a flash, he located his target.

A rage such as he hadn't experienced in years came over him and, with a roar, he swung at his attacker, sending the fellow spiralling across the room. Without even thinking of his audience, Ryne rushed after the man.

Who did this person think he was, to not only strike an Alpha, but touch his female as well? The punishment must be swift and heavy. His wolf growled menacingly. *I will be satisfied with nothing less.*

Yet even as he grabbed the man's throat, he was attacked from behind. Turning to face his latest adversary, he met a set of glowing eyes. Strong hands held his shoulders while another, equally powerful pair grabbed at his arms, trying to drag him away. His rage grew, his muscles bunched.

Who are these seeking to keep us from our rightful revenge?

He snarled a warning and prepared to strike, then a noise caught his attention. A cry!

It is the female!

A glance in Mel's direction reassured him she was being helped up, not hurt. There was blood on her arm; her face was pale.

"Ryne! Come on, man. Snap out of it."

An urgent voice penetrated the wildness consuming his brain and he jerked his eyes towards the speaker. Bryan?

"That's it. Look at me. Get control of yourself."

Ryne blinked and shook his head, the rage subsiding. At his feet lay the man who had attacked him, completely unconscious. Across the room, Lucy appeared from somewhere and was guiding Melody to safety, cradling her arm in a towel while expertly weaving a path through the various brawls that had erupted around the room.

"We need to go before anyone sees you up close. Your fangs are showing." Bryan gave him a push towards the door. "I'll stay here and take care of things.

Daniel, take our wildman home before he does any more damage."

Daniel answered in the affirmative and Ryne suddenly found himself outside the bar, heading towards the pickup. He dug in his heels and stood still.

"No. I need to make sure Melody is all right."

Daniel, in his usual calm manner, gently tugged at Ryne's arm. "She's fine, Ryne. Lucy is taking care of her. You can talk to her in the morning. It's more important we get you home."

Shrugging off the boy's hand, Ryne rubbed his hands through his hair in frustration, not wanting to listen to the logic of the argument, but knowing he was right. He'd been in fights before, but he'd never lost control like that in public. The sooner he was out of sight, the sooner people would begin to forget. Bryan would stay behind fulfilling his Beta role by helping Armand break up the brawl. And, knowing Bryan, he'd probably use a liberal application of free liquor and some carefully worded suggestions, to lead the bar patrons into doubting what they had seen. With any luck, by morning the story would be that of a usual fight over a woman. No one would recall the ultra-human speed with which he'd crossed the room, nor the distance he'd thrown the man. And his broken nose...well, it would heal by morning and everyone would assume it had just been a bleed.

Finally nodding agreement, he followed his packmate to the truck and headed home.

Chapter 26

Melody winced as she dressed the next morning, her injured arm stiffly responding to her commands. Her back wasn't happy either, telling her in no uncertain terms it didn't appreciate how she'd landed on the floor last night with a large man on top of her. Neither was her rear-end overly pleased with its part in acting as the initial point of impact. She had a headache from too much beer, her eyes were gritty and her mouth tasted like...well, she didn't even want to think about that.

A hot shower and the liberal use of both mouthwash and toothpaste helped alleviate some of her woes, but the gash on her arm wasn't being as cooperative as the rest of her anatomy. Her arm throbbed from the cut she'd received the previous night. As she nursed a cup of coffee, she relived the events of the previous night.

When Ryne had crashed into her, they'd both fallen to the floor and the bar stool she'd been sitting on had shattered. A sharp piece of wood must have cut her arm, though she didn't recall exactly how it had happened. At first, she'd thought the blood had all been Ryne's. Her elbow had ended up in his face and she was sure she'd broken his nose, given the amount of blood that had been present.

Initially, she'd been stunned, lying on the floor and dimly aware of a roaring noise and a rush of movement. When she'd managed to sit up and look around, Ryne had already been across the room seeming intent on giving payback for the punch he'd received. Meanwhile, fights were breaking out all over the room.

Having never been in the middle of a brawl, it had held a sort of macabre fascination.

Fists were flying; furniture was being knocked over and thrown about. Grunts and shouts; blood and saliva, spilt drinks. The sights and sounds had been overwhelming and she'd done her best to scuttle backwards towards the relative safety of the bar. Searching the sea of angry faces, she'd spotted Bryan and Daniel. They were making their way over to Ryne, probably planning on restraining him. She'd lost sight of them when Armand had stepped in front of her.

The bartender pushed the crowd away from her, effortlessly lifting her to sit safely on top of the bar before wading into the various skirmishes, yanking the participants apart by the scruffs of their necks. She had been so engrossed with what was going on around her it had taken a few minutes before she noticed the nerve endings in her arm were starting to protest. Glancing down, she saw her arm was covered in fresh blood, much of it hers, not just Ryne's. By the time Lucy arrived, the cut had begun to throb and burn painfully

Unperturbed by the brawl, Lucy had grabbed a towel to help stem the bleeding and then led the way to a relatively quiet area near the back.

"Fights don't usually start this early," Lucy had muttered as she cleaned the cut and applied bandages. "Do you want a ride home?"

"No, I'll be fine." She'd declined the offer, not feeling up to answering the slew of questions that were probably percolating in the waitress's mind. "I'll just rest here a few minutes and then be on my way."

Most of the fights had wound down by the time she made her way to the door. Many of the participants were helping to tidy up, merely avoiding the few who were still pushing and shoving each other. Surprisingly, there had been laughter coming from various locations, as if it had all been in good fun. Even Armand had chuckled once or twice, though his expression soured when he spotted the cracked frame on one of his paintings.

Bryan approached Armand and placed what appeared to be a consoling arm on his shoulders, while talking quietly. Armand nodded and took the painting down, tenderly cradling it in his arms. As he headed towards the bar, he'd called out a crowd-pleasing statement. "A free drink for everyone. Bryan is buying!"

The patrons had cheered and gathered around the young man, thumping him on the back. Bryan smiled in return, giving high fives and looking thoroughly at home being in the thick of things. There was no sign of Ryne or Daniel, but decided they must be all right or Bryan wouldn't be buying drinks. Besides, she was disgusted with Ryne and he didn't deserve her interest.

Finished reminiscing about the previous night's escapade, she rinsed out her coffee cup then headed towards the car with a determined stride. Her list of questions for Ryne was tucked in her purse and today was the day he was going to answer those questions whether he liked it or not. And, after the interview, she'd pack her bags and head back to Chicago.

Aldrich might not be pleased it wasn't as in-depth an interview as his employer wanted, but if Ryne was going to be difficult, there was no way she could force him to talk. If Greyson was unhappy, she'd give him some of the money back. It had been a healthy sum and even if she returned a couple of thousand, there would be sufficient left for her needs.

She parked in front of the Gazette, planning to check her e-mails and see what flights were available. At noon, she would call Aldrich to tell him she'd be back in a few days. The man would press for a specific date and time, but she wasn't feeling inclined to tell him since he'd probably demand she visit his office the minute she stepped off the plane. Too bad for him because it wasn't going to happen.

She grinned, pleased with the no-nonsense attitude she was developing. It would serve her well when she hunted down Ryne. No more Ms. Nice Guy.

Beth looked up from her computer when Mel entered. She stood up and began talking like a circus ringmaster. "And here she is; the star of last night's brawl and the Queen of the Pool Table... Mel Greene!"

Mel winced, feeling the heat of embarrassment flood her cheeks. "I guess you heard about what happened at The Broken Antler?"

Beth walked over to the counter and propped her chin in her hand. "Nope. Don't know a darn thing about it." The comment was followed by a wink.

Rolling her eyes, Mel plopped down in one of the chairs near the front of the office, absentmindedly wiping dust from the leaves of the neglected philodendron on the table beside her. "I suppose the rumour mill has been working overtime since last night. Tell me the worst, Beth. What are they saying about me?"

"Only that you were roaring drunk, turned into some form of hot, sexy pool shark and won a wad of cash by beating some of the best pool players Stump River has to offer."

"What?" She sat up straighter, abandoning the plant and focusing her attention on Beth. "I was *not* roaring drunk. Tipsy, maybe, but I still had complete control over my faculties. And I'm *not* a pool shark, it was simply luck. And the 'wad of cash' was loose change, for heaven's sake!"

Beth affected a pout, but then brightened. "You didn't deny the hot and sexy part, though!"

A vague memory of wiggling her tush before taking a shot during the impromptu pool tournament flashed through Mel's mind. And there was something about being too warm and loosening the tie on the front of her shirt. She clapped a hand to her cleavage. How much had she been showing off? Feeling her face flush, she fought for composure while secretly dying inside. Of course, then there was what happened with Ryne afterward! It certainly eclipsed a little hip wiggling and cleavage display.

"Er...I might have been less inhibited last night, but I did nothing inappropriate in public." Strictly speaking, it was the truth. No one needed to know about Armand's office. Being screwed and scorned by Ryne was her own personal humiliation and heartache.

"I suppose the story about Ryne and Billy Watson fighting over you and wrecking one of Armand's paintings is false, too."

She nodded emphatically. "I don't know if the fellow was named Billy or not, but he and Ryne weren't fighting over me, I'm sure. They probably have some sort of history or it was one of those guy things. Ryne doesn't care enough to fight over me and I'd never met the other man before. As for Armand's picture, there might be the grain of truth in that. He was looking at a broken picture frame when I left."

"But what about your arm?" Beth gestured towards the large bandage on Mel's forearm. "Something must have happened for you to end up with an injury."

"I think I cut it on the bar stool. Some of the wood probably splintered when it broke." She rubbed the area around the wound. "It stings, but it's not serious. It should be healed in a few days."

The other woman gave a disappointed sigh. "I guess I'll have to delete most of what I wrote this morning. Such a shame. You could have been front page news."

Narrowing her eyes, Mel studied the other woman. Was she joking or not? Given this was Stump River, where nothing ever happened, there was a strong possibility she wasn't. Just to be sure, Mel clarified the matter. "I'm sure something else exciting will happen before next week's edition."

Beth shrugged and then straightened from where she'd been leaning on the counter. "You never know." Wandering over to the coffee maker, she filled two mugs with the freshly brewed beverage and handed one to Mel, who had moved to join her at the back of the office. "So, what are your plans for today? The usual web surfing, walk about town and then coffee at Ruth's?"

Mel accepted the mug before sitting down at her work station and powering up her computer. "Not exactly. I've made up my mind Ryne's giving me a full interview today whether he likes it or not. He's been stringing me along ever since I arrived and I'm putting my foot down. No more delays."

"Maybe he's been dragging his feet, so you'd stick around longer." Beth gave her a speculative look over the rim of her cup.

"No." She let her shoulders slump as she admitted the truth. "I half hoped that was the case, but last night..." She shook her head. "Let's say I found out otherwise."

"Are you sure? I don't know Ryne well, but he seems to be paying you a lot of attention. You've had dinner together, been out to his house, people have seen you sitting together at the cenotaph." Beth numbered off the interactions on her fingers.

"What is this? Am I under twenty-four-hour surveillance or something?"

"No, just staying in a small town." Beth chuckled and pulled out a box of cookies from her bottom desk drawer, taking one before politely sharing.

Mel took one and nibbled on it thoughtfully. She didn't like the idea people were paying such close attention to what she was doing. Perhaps that was yet another reason to head back to Chicago. There, no one noticed anything. You were completely alone despite being surrounded by hundreds of people. A grimace passed over her face. The thought wasn't as comforting as it was supposed to be.

Turning her attention back to Beth, she addressed the issue of the town's gossip. "Despite what everyone thinks they've seen, there's really nothing between Ryne and myself. As a matter of fact, once I'm done with him today, I'll probably be leaving."

"Really? That's too bad. I've enjoyed your company." Beth looked disappointed for a moment, but after a second or two smiled and started cajoling her. "If you'd stay longer, I'd be able to talk Josh into getting a new sofa with the extra rent money."

"With a request like that, how could I not?" She laughed, just as Beth had probably intended her to. "Don't worry; you might not be rid of me as fast as you think. I have to see what flights are available back to Chicago." She set down her coffee and pulled her chair into place in front of her computer. "Where's Josh today?" She asked idly while waiting for the internet to hook up.

"He's home, still complaining about his tooth, the big baby!" Beth shook her head. "I told him to stay away, because I didn't want to hear him whining all day after listening to him all night. He said if it quit hurting by noon, he'd do some work around the cabins, trimming bushes and doing a few repairs."

Mel nodded in acknowledgement of the information and went to her e-mail account. She'd check for any messages and then try to book a flight home.

"Will you be heading out to Ryne's when you're done here?" Beth finished her snack and put the box of cookies away.

"Actually, someone told me last night he was working at Miller's today, to make up for being away yesterday."

"I wonder why he was out of town." Beth's eye sparked with interest. "Maybe it's something worth reporting!"

"I have absolutely no idea, but let me get my interview out of the way before you start to question him." Mel answered distractedly while staring at the computer screen. "Now this is funny."

"What's that?" Beth scooted her chair over to take a peek.

"That website I applied to yesterday sent me a message. They're considering my status as a Lycan, once more research on my background is completed. I can expect to hear back from them in two to four weeks." She sat back in her chair feeling perplexed. "I never thought I'd get a reply."

Beth giggled. "So you might become a card carrying member of the Lycan community?

"Right." Mel rolled her eyes. "It has to be some kind of scam. They'll probably get back to me and try to sell me a membership or demand more money to complete the background search."

"You're probably right," Beth concurred. "After all, there's no such thing as Lycans."

Both women shook their heads at the utter ridiculousness of the idea and then turned back to more important matters. Beth tapped away on her keyboard, writing articles about local happenings while Mel checked out flight information. After a few searches, she discovered there was a flight out of Toronto with seats available Friday night and another on Saturday. She chose the Saturday one, thinking she'd like to spend part of the day in Toronto shopping at the Eaton's Centre, a large shopping mall in the city's core. If she had time, she might even see a show.

She hovered the cursor over the accept button, feeling some regret. Once she clicked on the icon, she was effectively saying goodbye to Stump River forever. There was little chance she'd ever return to see Lucy or Beth or Al or Ruth or Armand. When she thought about it, it was surprising how many people she'd come to know in such a short time. Back in Chicago, she didn't even know the name of the people who lived next door and they'd been there for months!

Her mind had purposely skirted away from thinking about Bryan and Daniel. She hadn't seen them often, yet in some ways she viewed them as the brothers she had never had. It had been fun hanging out with them last night. At least until Ryne appeared. Would she miss him? Firming her jaw, she gave an emphatic 'no'. The man wasn't to be trusted and the sooner she was away from him, the better.

Before she could change her mind, she clicked the 'accept' button and watched the screen flash her confirmed flight. The ticket would be waiting for her at the airport. For some reason that fact made her feel ill. Blinking away the prick of tears, she checked her watch and then shut down her computer.

It was time to find and confront Ryne. There was no point in putting it off. They'd parted badly and she really didn't want to see him, but it was like removing a bandage; fast and clean was the only way. Once she stated the interview had to be done today because she was leaving, he'd see she was no longer willing to play along with his little games. Oh, he'd probably protest and make excuses, but she wouldn't stand for it. Even if he was working, he could answer her questions while he pumped gas and changed tires. With her steno pad of questions firmly clutched in her hand, she bid farewell to Beth and headed out the door.

Chicago, Illinois, USA...

Aldrich leaned back in his leather chair and stared out his office window. His feet, encased in highly polished designer shoes, were propped up on his desk while the fingers of one hand idly twirled an engraved, gold-plated pen. His other hand held a receiver lightly to his ear as he listened to Greyson's instructions.

The view from his fifteenth storey window was impressive, though Aldrich hardly ever bothered to notice it. This type of location was part of the prestigious perks that came with working for Greyson, one of the wealthiest men in the country.

It was a far cry from where he had started his legal career; a small office in a rundown three storey walk-up. He'd been fresh out of school, in debt up to his ears and eager to make his mark on the world. Note the absence of the word 'idealistic'.

Aldrich smirked. He'd never been idealistic. Know where to be, who to talk to and when to look the other way; that was his motto and so far it had served him well. Hence, his job with Greyson Inc.

A few drops of rain fell on the glass, drawing his attention to the weather. The sky was grey and overcast, matching his mood perfectly. Greyson was being more difficult than ever and Aldrich was stretching his patience to the limit as he attempted to remain calm and unflappable. While he'd never openly admit it, he found the tycoon difficult to handle. He'd been working for the man for five years now and still never knew what to make of him.

Greyson was rich, powerful, moody and more than a little eccentric. Today, it was one of his eccentricities that was giving Aldrich a headache. Honestly, how the man had ever managed to amass a fortune was a mystery. He had no sense of the value of a dollar, squandering money on foolish projects, ignoring the safety of priceless art objects.

"Are you listening, Aldrich?" The voice barked down the line at him and Aldrich momentarily removed the receiver from his ear.

"Yes, sir. You were explaining you'll be incommunicado for five days." He didn't add it was a monthly ritual and there was no need for the phone call. Humouring clients was all part of the job.

"Good. Thought you'd dozed off in that cushy office I pay for."

"No, sir. I'm taking note of your instructions. You will be unavailable for the usual five days. The west wing of the house is sealed and all but a skeleton staff will be given a long weekend. No one is to enter the estate, except emergency personnel in the event of a fire or some other such tragedy. If that is the case, the Ryne Taylor photograph is to be saved first." He hesitated to speak what was on his mind, but given Greyson was on the other end of a phone line and not in the room, Aldrich decided to be bold. "Sir, the chances of a fire are negligible and, if such an event were to occur, other pieces of your collection are worth considerably more than that one picture."

"I don't care. They belong to me and like everything I own, I decide their fate."

"Of course, sir." Aldrich allowed himself the luxury of rolling his eyes. "Is there anything else, sir?"

"The girl, Melody, make sure she does her job. I'll expect an update on her progress the next time I call."

Aldrich bit his lip. He'd like to say 'Progress? What progress?' but knew better. Greyson believed she'd do the job to his satisfaction. It was best to let the man have his way. If Greene messed up and blew the assignment, well Aldrich would be able to whisper an 'I told you so' once his employer was out of earshot.

"And Aldrich? I'm holding you personally responsible for the success of this project."

"But..." Aldrich sat up straight, his feet hitting the floor and the chair squeaking in protest at the sudden movement. The injustice of the statement had him almost sputtering. It wasn't fair. He hadn't chosen the woman. If she failed, it wasn't his fault.

"Ha! Made you sweat, didn't I, Leon?"

Settling back in his seat, Aldrich sneered before answering, but his voice held no evidence of the fact. He hadn't come this far, without being able to exercise considerable self-control. "Another of your jokes, sir."

"Maybe. I'll let you think about it while I'm gone."

The phone went dead and Aldrich slowly set the receiver down. Greyson had to have been joking. There was no way he could be held accountable for that girl's incompetence, especially since Greyson himself had hired her, despite advice to the contrary.

Aldrich sat back in his chair and steepled his fingers. Greyson liked to play games with him, and this was, quite likely, one of them. Or so he hoped. The old codger was unpredictable.

Just in case, he'd better pay extra attention to Ms. Greene and her assignment. She couldn't be allowed to mar his impeccable record of service.

Chapter 27

Stump River, Ontario, Canada...

Ryne glanced at himself in the side-view mirror as he bent down to accept payment for the gas he'd pumped into the car. There was no sign his nose had been broken the previous night. No bruising or swelling, and the bridge was as straight as it had ever been. Thank goodness Lycans healed quickly.

Daniel had done a good job dealing with him last night. His packmate's calm and logical manner had been what his angry wolf had needed. He made a note to commend the boy. No, make that 'man'. Daniel was maturing and Ryne knew he needed to quit treating him as a kid, give him more responsibilities. As a matter of fact, both Bryan and Daniel were quite competent. The problem was, being a small pack, in a quiet town; there really wasn't a lot that needed doing and so they tended to slack off. Their occasional shifts at the lumber yard left them with a lot of free time. Maybe with the arrival of the new members...

He turned his attention back to the occupant of the car, Mrs. Swain, and accepted the money she handed him. She was eighty if she was a day and the personification of a sweet old lady, down to her silvery grey hair, bifocals and floral print dress. He always spent extra time chatting to her since he knew she lived alone.

"I heard all about you, you bad boy." She smiled up at him, her eyes twinkling with merriment behind her thick glasses.

"And what did you hear?" He played along, knowing full well what was coming since every customer so far had said the same thing.

"You were fighting over that new girl in town." She shook her head and tsked at him. "And here I thought you only had eyes for me."

"Mrs. Swain, they are rumours, nothing but vicious rumours. You know I'm waiting for you to turn sixteen so I can start courting you." He pressed a hand to his chest and tried to look besotted.

It must have worked for she giggled girlishly and patted his cheek before leaving. He watched her drive away, noting how she carefully looked both ways at the traffic light before sneaking through on the red with a slight squeal of her tires. What a little rebel, he chuckled to himself.

After depositing the money from the sale in the till, he returned to the service bay where he'd been changing tires. He'd only taken two steps into the work space when he froze. Over the smell of oil, tire rubber and exhaust, he detected something else drifting in through the open bay doors.

Melody.

Her scent was sweet and feminine with a hint of green apples. Turning, he saw her determinedly walking across the parking area towards him. Her jaw was set and tilted upward. In one hand she was tightly holding a steno pad, while the other seemed to have a death grip on the shoulder strap of her purse.

Damn! He'd been hoping to avoid this for a few more hours, though why he didn't know. It wasn't going to be pretty, no matter when it happened. Steeling himself for what must be done, he walked to the entrance and leaned against the door frame.

When she was a few feet away, she caught sight of him and stopped. "Ryne."

"Melody."

They stared across the open space, assessing each other as one might before entering a battle. What was she thinking? Her eyes were narrowed, her lips compressed. An aura of determination surrounded her. She'd definitely come here expecting to kick his ass.

"I'm not here to talk about yesterday. All I want is to finish this interview and then I'll leave you alone." She waved the steno pad at him while delivering her message in clipped tones, with no emotional undertones.

He mentally congratulated her on her self-control. Shoving his hands in his back pockets, he shrugged and set out to be as obnoxious as possible. "What interview?"

"The one you agreed to give me about your work."

"Yeah, well, I've changed my mind." Ryne let his gaze slide away and feigned interest in the truck parked across the street. He detected a change in her breathing pattern. How would she respond?

"You've changed your mind? Just like that? Can I ask why?"

"Ask away. I may or may not answer." He looked at her blandly.

"But we had an agreement. You said—"

"I said I had complete control and I'm exerting it. I've decided I don't want to be interviewed. I don't want or need the publicity and you're not paying me, so it's off. Sorry you wasted your time." He shoved away from the door frame and stood straight. "Now go home. I have work to do."

"But that's not fair! I've done nothing to warrant you cancelling our agreement. In fact, I've been very patient and spent a lot of time waiting for you, humouring you. I've never complained about all your teasing and innuendo. It's only fair you give me some of your time in return." He could tell she was close to losing control. Her breathing was rapid, the colour rising in her cheeks.

"Life's never fair, sweetheart. You were...moderately...entertaining, but now you're bordering on boring. It's time for you to leave."

"I am *not* leaving until I get my interview!" She stepped into his personal space, poking him in the chest with her finger.

He had to give her credit. Very few people were brave enough, or foolish enough, to do that. It was fortunate he had a soft spot for her. The last person to poke him in the chest like that had ended up with their hand in a cast.

He loomed over her, keeping his eyes narrowed, his expression cold. Even before he spoke, he saw how Melody responded to his aura; there was a faint tremor running over her and she had difficulty maintaining eye contact. Good. She was nervous and unsure of him. He pressed his advantage, delivering his message in icy, clipped tones.

"You're very lucky I have such good control over my temper. Most people wouldn't be walking away from an encounter like this." Casually, he reached forward and chucked her under the chin, causing her teeth to click together. "Now, run along, little girl, before my benevolence disappears and I take exception to your attitude." He heard her gulp and gave a minute nod of satisfaction. She was definitely getting the message. Feeling he had done his job, he turned and went back inside, completely ignoring her.

Even with his back turned, he was aware of her continued presence. He bent over to pick up a ratchet and glanced behind him. She stood there gaping at him, no doubt processing what had just happened. Out of the corner of his eye, he saw her snap her jaw shut then toss her hair back from her face before striding inside. Oh great, he muttered under his breath, now she's going to try and show she has a backbone. Why couldn't women run the other way when a wolf growled at them?

He kept working, resolved to ignore her, even when she stood directly behind him.

"Where did you grow up?"

Ryne didn't answer.

"What schools did you go to? Do you have any family? Do you see them often? What do they think of your work?"

Clenching his teeth, he yanked the rear wheel tire off the car he had up on the hoist and sent it rolling towards a pile destined for recycling. Turning, he grabbed a new tire, forcing Melody to step back in order to not get hit.

Appearing unfazed, Melody continued her barrage of questions, waiting only a few seconds after each before asking a new one or rephrasing an older one. Where had he lived previously? What were his favourite colours? Did he have a favourite artist whom he admired? Where had he sold his art? What was his first camera? Where had he taken most of his pictures? What was his favourite picture? Did he plan on another exhibit in the future?

Finally, Ryne had enough. He turned with a snarl and grabbed her upper arms. "I said there would be no interview." He accompanied each word with a little shake. Her hair swished back and forth as her head bobbed, the scent of her shampoo wafting around him. He steeled himself against its enticing effects. "Now get it through your stubborn head before I do something I'll regret." The last word was accompanied by a backwards shove and he released her arms. Without the support of his hands she stumbled and he restrained himself from reaching out to steady her, despite the fact his wolf was growling angrily at him.

Brushing her hair from her face, she glared at him, but stepped right back up to confront him once again.

"This interview is important to me." Her chin was stuck out, her face belligerent.

"And it isn't to me."

"There's a lot riding on it. Finishing my education—"

He snorted. "Do I look like I care?"

"If it's money you want, maybe I could work something out." Her tone changed. Ryne could see her mind racing and wondered what she'd come up with. From things she'd told him earlier, he assumed she had no cash reserves. He could use that against her right now.

"Forget it. You don't have enough money to cover what I'd want and if you think the sex we've had can be used as a down payment, forget it. You weren't that good. It wouldn't buy you five minutes of my time."

She gasped at the spitefulness of his statement and for a moment he thought she'd slap him. He had to hand it to her, his Melody was never predictable. Instead, she tried to kick him.

Ryne easily sidestepped the blow she aimed at his groin. In response, he grabbed her wrist and twisted her arm behind her back. Using it to keep her under control, he dragged her close so their bodies were pressed together. Pitching his voice as menacingly as possible, he growled a warning. "That wasn't funny, sweetheart. Little girls who play those types of games better be prepared for the consequences."

Before she could protest, he gripped the back of her head and delivered a punishing kiss. He ravaged her lips, ignoring her whimpers. There was no tenderness, no concern for her pleasure. She struggled against him, but he pulled her closer and ran his hand insultingly over her body. A tear trickled down her cheek; he tasted the saltiness but hardened his heart. Mercy didn't enter into this; others were depending on him to get rid of Melody.

Lives hung in the balance. Personal feelings had no place in the situation he was faced with.

When he ended the kiss, he hissed into her ear. "Now listen closely, Ms. Greene. There will be no interview. Not now. Not ever. No matter how many times you plead and beg and spread your legs for me. It's not going to happen. My suggestion is you go back to where you came from and forget you ever heard about me because if I see you around here again... Well, I'll let you finish the sentence."

Ryne allowed her to pull away fractionally, the threat hanging in the air between them. He could hear her heart pounding, her rapid breathing. There was an aura of hurt and fear and temper around her. It was exactly as he had planned, even though it tore at his soul.

She stared up at him, mouth compressed into a straight line, then spat in his face and pulled herself completely free. He made no move to grab her nor to wipe the spittle from his cheek.

"You bastard."

"And don't you forget it." He winked, blew her a kiss and walked away, nonchalantly grabbing a socket wrench and started to loosen the nuts on the next wheel he needed to change. His sensitive hearing conveyed the story unfolding behind him. Melody stood behind him, her breathing ragged. There was a hitch to it, as if she'd like to cry, but wouldn't allow herself the luxury. Finally, he heard her spin on her heel and stalk away muttering obscenities about him under her breath.

Once she was out of hearing range, he let the tool fall lifelessly to the ground. The sound of metal hitting cement echoed through the cavernous space of the garage. It was a cold, lonely sound and reminded him he stood alone in the dim and damp space. He ran his hands through his hair. That had been awful. Hurting her was the last thing he'd wanted to do, but there was no other way. She couldn't be here when the Loberos arrived. And the longer she stayed, the more his wolf got attached to her.

The beast inside him had been wily these past few days; first convincing him there was a logical reason to keep Melody around, then encouraging him to agree to the interview. Supposedly, he was to have been determining her motives. In actual fact he'd done only the barest minimum with regards to investigating. Instead, his wolf had led him into a crazy relationship with the woman, one that should never have even started.

He compressed his lips. It was over and done with now; he'd sent her on her way and hopefully she wasn't masochistic enough to return. So far, she'd given no indication she knew about Lycans. As long as it stayed that way, he could let her live. He had a few contacts in Chicago he'd use to keep loose tabs on her activities. If it looked like she was going to head back to Smythston or start investigating him again, well—his hands clenched into fists—that would have to be the end of her.

Mel walked with quick angry steps down the length of Stump River's main street. She wished it was longer because she was quite sure two blocks wouldn't be sufficient for her to have vented her anger or to get a handle on the sense of betrayal filling her soul.

How dare he cancel the interview?

How dare he say she was only *moderately* entertaining?

And as for spreading her legs! Could he have been any cruder? While they had never really exchanged tender words, she'd believed there were some gentler feelings growing between them. Now, after the way he'd just used her...

Blinking rapidly, she pushed back the tears. He wasn't worth ruining her mascara over! The man was a jerk, a bastard and a...a... She couldn't think of any words vile enough, but when she did, she'd add them to the list.

She was storming up the other side of the street now and Ruth's was right ahead. She'd better make her call to Aldrich and tell the miserable man she was heading home. At least she was angry enough there was nothing he could say that would upset her any more than she already was.

Pulling open the door with more force than necessary, she went to the pay phone and jabbed at the buttons as she dialled his number. It only rang twice before he picked up. Giving him no time to talk she launched into her speech.

"Mr. Aldrich, it's Mel Greene. I'm leaving Stump River and I'll be back in Chicago in a few days. I'll contact you then."

"Can I assume your trip has been successful and you've met your objective? That you've discovered the necessary information regarding Mr. Taylor?"

She gave a short, ironic chuckle. "Oh yeah. I've discovered lots about Ryne Taylor."

"Good. I'm both surprised and pleased to hear that. I'll see you in a few days."

She didn't bother to correct his assumption that what she'd discovered about Ryne was relevant to her assignment. "Right. Bye, Mr. Aldrich." She hung up and then wondered why she always felt the need to say 'bye' when she didn't even like the man. Damn her mother for instilling manners in her!

Turning abruptly, she walked right into Lucy who was arriving for her shift.

"Fancy seeing you here this early, Mel. You're going to throw my whole day off schedule."

"Sorry. My plans for the day took an unexpected turn and I had to make my phone call earlier than planned." She wandered over to her usual seat and plopped down, crossing her arms in front of her.

Lucy automatically set a cup in front of her and then headed towards the back to hang up her coat. She called a question over her shoulder. "I've been meaning to ask you, who do you call every day? Not that it's any of my business, I'm just wondering."

"It's a guy named Aldrich. He's sort of like my supervisor and I hate calling him. He's super critical and never happy about anything I tell him."

Ruth poked her head out of the kitchen, spied Mel and started wringing her hands. "Mel, what are you doing here? You're never early! Oh this messes up everything." She seemed agitated and kept peering into the kitchen behind her.

Taken aback, Mel apologized. "I'm sorry. Do you want me to go?"

"No, no need to do that." Ruth wiped her hands on her apron and took a deep breath.

"Are you sure? I could leave." She started to stand and Ruth rushed forward shaking her head.

"Don't do that dear, it's just..." She paused and then burst into speech. "Al and I planned on surprising you. I went on the internet and found a bunch of recipes and Al and I've been practising making those fancy coffees you're always talking about. We were all set to surprise you today. When you asked for one, I was going to be ready to hand one over."

"Oh, Ruth, that's so sweet of you." She stood and gave the woman a hug, wincing when her arm came in contact with Ruth's boney frame. "Where's Al, I want to thank him, too."

"Oh, he's out back arguing with our meat supplier; the hamburger has been too greasy lately. He'll be out shortly."

Mel sat back down, absentmindedly rubbing her arm.

Lucy returned and noticed the gesture. "Hey, how's your arm doing?"

"Sore." She extended the limb and was surprised to see it showed red around the edges of the bandage.

"That looks infected." Ruth shook her head. "I have some antibiotic cream in the back that will fix it right up. I'll go get it."

After Ruth had doctored the wound to her satisfaction, Al appeared and Mel thanked him for his efforts in learning how to make *fancy coffee*.

"Nothing's too good for my favourite girl." He rubbed his chin self-consciously, but then grinned sheepishly at her. "You liven things up around here. Ruth and I reckon we're in a rut."

"That's right." Ruth nodded, beaming. "We're going to try to expand our customers' horizons and make some special dinners every Saturday and Sunday. Maybe even fold the napkins all fancy like I see in the restaurants on my soap operas."

Al rolled his eyes at this comment, but said nothing, merely grunting he had to return to the kitchen to start work on the lunch menu. Ruth followed, after insisting Mel keep the antibiotic cream, just in case.

Mel watched them go. "I'm going to miss them."

"Miss them? Are you leaving?" Lucy looked up from the silverware she was wrapping in napkins.

"Yeah, it's time I headed back home."

"But, you've not finished your interview with Ryne, have you?"

"No. He changed his mind and isn't granting me one."

"Why that dirty bastard." Lucy glared across the street to where Ryne was backing a car out of the service bay.

"My sentiments exactly, but it will be nice to get back home." Mel tried to sound positive, but in truth the idea of her dumpy little apartment surrounded by concrete, pollution and too many people held little appeal.

"I'd like to go to Chicago some time. It must be pretty exciting." Lucy sounded wistful and on the spur of the moment Mel made an offer.

"Would you like to come back with me for a visit? You can stay with me and I can show you the sights."

Lucy's whole face lit up. "Do you mean that?"

"Sure, why not?" The more Mel thought about the idea, the better it seemed. She didn't really want to go back to Chicago, but if Lucy was with her, it wouldn't be so bad. "Can you get some time off? Maybe a week?"

"It shouldn't be a problem. I haven't taken a vacation in years. Let me go check with Ruth and Al and then I'll call Armand. Oh, I'm so excited!" Lucy hurried out back, grinning ear to ear.

With Lucy gone, Mel allowed herself a few minutes of doubt and self-pity. She was really in a pickle now. Once she was home in Chicago, Aldrich would want to know what she'd found out and when the article might be ready. He wouldn't be pleased to learn there was no article because Ryne had backed out. And then there was the whole issue of the cash advance. Last time the subject came up, Aldrich had basically said if she didn't produce, she'd have to return everything. All expenses would have to come out of her own pocket. Unfortunately, said pocket had nothing in it.

She caught herself chewing on her thumbnail, but was too worried to feel guilty about falling back into old habits. Staring across the street, she wondered if she dared ask Ryne one more time. Maybe if she begged and told him she really needed to earn the money this article would bring...

No. She couldn't do it. Not only would it be pointless, but her pride wouldn't allow her to grovel like that, not after the way he had treated her. There had to be another solution, but what?

There had to be another solution, but what?

Chapter 28

Lucy was ecstatic about being able to get some time off work and with such amazing ease. Mel obtained another ticket to Chicago, even though it did mean rebooking for Friday rather than Saturday. It was almost a ten-hour drive to Toronto, but by taking turns behind the wheel, they'd get there in plenty of time to catch their flight if they left by mid-afternoon.

While Lucy packed, Mel headed back to the Gazette to say her goodbyes to Beth. She offered to pay rent for the rest of the week, but Beth had refused, saying it wasn't fair for her to pay when she wouldn't be using the cabin. Mel didn't argue the point, since she was in serious doubt as to her finances. If Greyson started legal proceedings in an attempt to retrieve the entire advance, she didn't know how she was going to survive. Hopefully, she could get her waitressing jobs back, but all thoughts of finishing her education in the near future would have to be put on hold. On top of that, the rent on her apartment was only paid until the end of the month, after which she'd be searching for friends who had couches she could crash on.

She drove back to the cabin to do her own packing, spending much of the drive mulling over various scenarios for her future. None of them were very appealing. She'd known she was taking a gamble when she accepted this job, but it had seemed like such a perfect opportunity. Now, she was in a worse mess than ever.

Depressed, she parked the car in front of the cabin and climbed out. She'd miss this place; the peace and solitude, the fresh air, the sounds of the birds. There really wasn't anything about this experience she hadn't enjoyed. Well, except for her encounter with the wolves and that jerk, Ryne.

Thinking of him made her blood boil and she slammed her car door. The sound echoed through the quiet and was followed by the sound of someone calling her name. It was Josh. He was approaching from the rear of the cabin, his hand raised in greeting.

"Hi, Josh. Beth said you might be doing some work outside the cabins. I see she was right."

"Yep, too nice a day to be stuck inside so I thought I'd do some tidying up and start to get ready for the summer visitors." He cleared his throat. "Er...I found something under the bushes back there you might want to take care of."

"Really? What would that be?"

He handed her a rumpled bundle of men's clothing.

"Um...thanks?" She accepted the offering, thinking the clothes looked vaguely familiar but not sure why Josh thought she needed to 'take care of them'.

He cleared his throat. "I recognize the shirt as Ryne's. Apparently, you two must have been...you know, and he forgot to collect his stuff afterwards." He rubbed his neck and looked everywhere but at Mel. "I didn't think it was warm enough outside yet for that sort of thing, but you young folks are made of sterner stuff, I guess." He shuffled his feet and coughed again. "Anyway, I'll let you give those back to him. I'll just...um...go finish up around the other cabins." He headed on his way, leaving Mel staring at the clothes she was holding.

How had Ryne's clothes ended up under the bushes? Last time she'd seen that shirt on him, he'd been... She felt her jaw drop. He'd been wearing it on

Tuesday when the 'wolf by the river' fiasco had happened! He had stormed out of the cabin buck naked carrying his clothes and claiming he'd get dressed outside.

Surely, he hadn't walked home bare-assed in the middle of the night! Even up in northern Canada, there must be rules about that sort of thing. But what other explanation was there? His clothes were here. She hadn't seen a vehicle parked anywhere nor had she heard the sound of an engine. So he must have walked home. Naked. In near-freezing weather.

This confirmed she needed to get away from Stump River. Ryne wasn't only a bastard; he was some kind of perverted nudist-flasher, too!

Walking up to the cabin, she dumped the clothes on the floor by the door and went to do her packing. After the way Ryne had treated her, she wasn't about to do him any favours. The clothes could go in the garbage for all she cared.

It took surprisingly little time to gather her things. Giving the room a last glance, she spied the t-shirt she slept in poking out from underneath the pillow. As she picked it up, she recalled the sensual dream she'd had on her first night in the cabin. It had seemed so real. A smile began to curve her lips when a horrible thought occurred to her.

Oh no! Surely not! But... Could it have really happened? She hurried into the main room and stared at the pile of Ryne's clothes. If the man was willing to run home naked in the middle of the night, would he also be the type to creep into a bedroom?

The very idea spurred her to action. As fast as possible, she finished tidying the cabin and packing her car, now more anxious than ever to leave Stump River— and Ryne Taylor—far behind.

Ryne was thankful there was a rush on tires. It kept him busy all day and gave him a chance to work out his anger without damaging anyone or anything. His encounter with Melody had left him in turmoil as his head argued with his wolf over what had occurred. Hours of lifting tires and struggling with rusted bolts and nuts had taken some of the edge off his mood.

As he put away his tools and began to wash up, Ben wandered in with Harley at his heels. The dog immediately went over to Ryne and wagged his tail, fawning around his legs. Ryne scratched his ears and gave a low rumble of approval that had Harley sighing happily. The beast licked his hand before flopping down on the ground, obviously feeling all was right in his world now he had the Alpha's approval.

"See you got a lot of work done today." Ben had a stack of completed work orders in his hand. "I'd have thought fighting over that girl last night would have left you tired out, but if anything, you've worked faster than ever."

Biting back a sigh, Ryne explained the situation yet again. "I wasn't fighting over her. I was trying to talk to her and Watson took exception to the fact. He swung at me first."

"Uh huh." Ben nodded. "Whatever. Thing is, she seems to be a nice girl and you could do worse. She even likes Harley."

Harley lifted his head and thumped his tail at the sound of his name.

"Funny thing though," Ben continued with a puzzled frown on his face. "When I was talking to her yesterday afternoon, she told me this story about seeing Harley out in the woods and thinking he was a wolf. I guess she's never seen a real wolf before, because Harley doesn't look much like one, if you ask me. Anyway, I told her it couldn't have been him, since I took him to the vet on Tuesday for his rabies vaccine and then kept him inside for the rest of the day."

Ryne froze, his mind racing and connecting the dots even as Ben kept on speaking.

"She had a funny look on her face then. I guess she realized she must have really seen a wolf. You know, you could use that to your advantage, boy. Tell her there are wolves around, but you'll protect her. Not that you need help with women." Ben chuckled. "Anyway, I came back here to tell you to take tomorrow off. You got us caught up on all the pending jobs. I figure with that big house you're fixing up, you can always use some extra time to work on it."

"Uh, yeah. Sure. Thanks, Ben." Distractedly, he took his leave of the older man and loped out to his truck.

He drove home on autopilot, too busy thinking about what he'd discovered. Melody had mentioned something about him not even being honest about a dog. Damn. She knew it wasn't Harley she'd seen by the river and she knew he'd lied, but had she made the ultimate connection? Given how she'd been acting this morning, he thought not, but there was a sinking feeling in his stomach and his fingers clenched the steering wheel.

Realizing he was now in front of his house, he shut off the engine and went inside. The television was blaring as usual, making it easy for him to locate his packmates. Daniel was sitting in the corner, his head bobbing in time to whatever song he was listening to through his earphones while typing away on the computer. Bryan was lazing back on the sofa, his feet on the coffee table while he idly flicked from station to station. Some Lycan pack they made.

He walked up to Bryan and kicked his feet off the table, grabbed the remote and turned off the TV.

"Hey! I was watching that!" Bryan stood up and attempted to snatch the remote back.

"Pack meeting." Ryne spoke tersely and nudged Daniel.

The boy looked up and immediately unplugged from his music. "What's going on?"

Ryne leaned against the fireplace and surveyed his friends. "You know how I was away yesterday? I was meeting a family, the Loberos, and..." He paused for effect. "They're going to join our pack."

It took a minute for the news to set in, then Bryan and Daniel gave out whoops, leapt up and high-fived each other.

"Great! It's been too quiet around here." Bryan was grinning from ear to ear.

Daniel smiled. "Yeah, it'll be nice to have more members. I miss being part of a big group."

Ryne gave them a few minutes to enjoy the news all the while knowing he'd soon have to put a damper on things.

"So, how many are coming?" Daniel sat back down his eyes fixed on his Alpha.

"Four in total. Marco, his mate Olivia and their son, Angelo, as well as Marco's sister, Tessa."

"Ages? Jobs?" Bryan actually looked the part of a Beta at that moment, already trying to figure out how the new members would be assimilated into the pack.

Ryne was pleased to see a serious side in Bryan. When he'd taken the young man on as his Beta, it had been a question of necessity rather than a belief in Bryan's innate abilities, but he was showing signs of growing into the role. Look at how he'd handled the little incident at the bar, smoothing things over so no one was any the wiser.

Realizing he hadn't yet answered Bryan's question, Ryne shared what he knew and ended with a half mocking warning. "And Bryan? Give Tessa a break.

She's had a hard time and doesn't need you sniffing around her the minute she arrives."

Bryan actually looked offended. "Hey, I wouldn't do that to a pack member. She's family now."

Nodding, Ryne pushed away from the wall and began to pace the length of the room. "There's something else I have to tell you. It's about Melody. I mean, Ms. Greene." He shoved his hands in his back pockets and lifted his chin. "I've severed ties with her."

"What? You're kidding." Neither Bryan nor Daniel looked like they could quite believe what they'd heard.

"Yeah, especially after last night." Ryne rubbed his neck and sighed. "Uh...thanks for helping out by the way. You both did good. Real good. But it re-emphasized to me my wolf is getting too attached to her and it's dangerous to have her around. She's here to ask questions and I can't take the chance that someday she might fit the pieces together."

"The Keeping?" There was no smile on Bryan's face as he uttered the words.

"Exactly. We have new pack members joining us and I have a responsibility to them."

"Mel seems harmless enough," Daniel added quietly.

"That she does." Ryne stared out the window, a vision of Melody's big brown eyes and soft golden hair forming before him. He turned away from it and tightened his jaw. "But looks can be deceiving. A while back, I was talking to Kane and he said a reporter had been looking for me in Smythston, specifically mentioning the wolf photo. It was Mel."

The other two looked solemn, knowing the story behind the picture.

Bryan spoke first. "Why didn't you say something when she first came? All you said was to stay away. We figured it was a territorial jealousy thing your wolf had going."

Ryne shrugged. "In part it was, but mostly it was caution. I wasn't sure if she knew anything about Lycans or if she was simply a reporter with a bee in her bonnet. Either way, I decided to wait and see then make my decision." He turned to look out the window again. "I'm pretty sure she has no suspicions, but, as I said before, I'm done taking chances. This morning I sent her packing."

"Um...Ryne?" Daniel sounded worried. "There was an e-mail today from the Registry."

"About the Loberos?" Ryne turned to look at the boy.

"No. Someone from this area was going through the Lycan site and made an application for membership. They wanted to know if we were aware of anyone in the area who was a shifter."

Bryan frowned. "How would the Registry know it was from here?"

Daniel rolled his eyes. He was the pack computer geek. "The IP address. When someone gets an e-mail, you can usually get a general idea of where it came from by right-clicking on the sender. You go to view message source, find what IP address it's from and then do a search where it's located. There isn't a specific home address, but a general area appears. I didn't think much about it, when I read the e-mail this morning. I figured it was probably a hoax. You know, some kid playing around, but now, from what you've said about Mel, I'm not so sure."

A chill crept over him. Had Mel been searching for information about Lycans? Was it because of the slip-up he'd made over Harley? Or was it merely a coincidence as Daniel had said, some kid fooling around?

Bryan frowned and walked over to the book shelves. "That reminds me... The day after Mel slept over, I was straightening up in here and I saw the heritage books were just shoved back on the shelves." He pulled the books out and looked at Ryne. "I wondered why they weren't put back properly, since you're usually so careful with them."

"I haven't had time to look at them in weeks." Ryne strode across the room and plucked a book from Bryan's hand, checking the title. Lycanthropy. Raising the book to his nose, he took a sniff. A faint trace of Melody's scent remained. "I think we have a problem."

.

Chapter 29

Ryne pulled into the parking area in front of Melody's cabin and forced his jaws to relax. The drive over had been accomplished at record speed, but the urgency he felt left no time for traffic laws. He had to ascertain what she did or didn't know and deal with it swiftly. Curses had tumbled from his lips the entire length of the drive. His complacency, his arrogance, his lust. All three had combined and conspired against him, causing him to ignore his duties as Alpha. And now, because of him, the lives of his pack and Kane's could very well be at stake. But no more. He climbed out of the truck, slammed the door and strode up to the cabin.

He forced himself to knock rather than pound on the door. It would only increase Melody's reluctance to talk to him and, after his performance earlier in the day, he'd be lucky if she didn't slam the door in his face.

Not that it mattered. She'd talk to him, and tell him what he needed to know, whether she wanted to or not. At this point in time, he wasn't above using some strong interrogation techniques. If she was innocent, she'd add it to his already lengthy list of sins. But, if she knew more than she should...well, it didn't really matter then, did it?

There was no response to his knocking and he strained his ears to hear sounds of movement inside. Either she wasn't home, or she was sleeping. Checking over his shoulder to ensure no one was watching, he strategically applied force to the door and it popped open. Once inside, he listened again, but the small cabin was silent. He scanned the kitchen area, then quickly made his way to the bedroom, only to freeze in the doorway. The bed was stripped and the open closet door revealed empty hangers. Pulling open the dresser drawers, he swore. Melody had already packed and left.

A frustrated growl rose in his throat as he contemplated his next move. Her scent was easily detected, so she hadn't been gone too long. Would she stop in Stump River before she left? Possibly.

Gravel spewed from beneath his tires as he gunned the engine and headed to town. He had to find Melody before she left, discover what she knew and, if necessary, ensure she never had the chance to spread the information further. He parked behind Miller's Service Station and jogged across the road. He'd check the diner first, then the Gazette. Surely, between the two places, he'd find her or at least information on where she'd gone.

Pulling open the door, he stepped inside. The supper crowd was starting to wander in, the general din slowly rising as debates were held about the various menu selections while Al banged and clanged his pots and pans in the kitchen. Blocking out the noise, Ryne scanned the tables. Melody wasn't there and his fists tightened in frustration. Forcing a casual expression, he wandered up to the counter and sat down hoping Lucy was on duty. He hadn't talked to her much recently, his attention having shifted to Melody, but he was sure the waitress would be willing to chat and share some information with him.

"Hi there! Can I help you?" A cheery young voice spoke behind him and he swung around in surprise. He'd been so intent on looking for Lucy, he'd missed the presence of the other waitress. Pencil and order pad clutched in her hands, a young girl of about seventeen stood smiling at him expectantly.

"Yeah, I need to speak to Lucy."

"Sorry, but she's gone on vacation. I'm filling in for her. Do you want to see a menu?"

Gone? Lucy was always here or at the bar. He stared at the girl's name tag. Tabitha. She probably wouldn't know anything useful about Melody. "Is Ruth available?"

"Probably. I didn't do anything wrong, did I?" The girl shifted from one foot to the other. "This is my first time waitressing and—"

"No. Everything's fine." He pasted one of his most charming smiles on his face to reassure her. "I just need to ask Ruth a question."

"Oh. Okay." Tabitha grinned at him and scurried off into the kitchen.

Ruth appeared soon after, wiping her hands on a towel. "Oh! It's you, Ryne. I wondered who that girl was talking about. She was practically giddy about the hunk who wanted to talk to me." Ruth chuckled. "I should have known it was you or one of your friends. What can I do for you?"

Impatient over the time he'd already wasted, Ryne got right to the point. "I need to find Melody. Do you know where she is?"

"You just missed her. She and Lucy left around four-thirty."

"Left? For where?"

"Chicago. Mel was heading back home for some reason. She never did say why she was going so sudden like." Ruth frowned before continuing her train of thought. "Anyway, Lucy was going with her for an impromptu vacation. It'll do Lucy good to get away for a while, don't you think? That girl works way too hard. And she'll be a help for Mel, too, seeing as how the girl wasn't feeling good when she left."

"Melody was sick?" He wasn't sure why he cared. Her health wasn't his concern. All that mattered was how much she'd discovered about his people.

"No. She had a cut on her arm from the fight you were all in last night and I think it was infected. I had her put some salve on it but by the time they were ready to go, she was complaining of it aching and having a fever and chills. Al and I both tried to talk her into staying and going to the clinic but she was determined to leave. I suppose it was hard to get that last-minute seat for Lucy and then there was her boss to deal with too."

"Her boss?" Ryne's brain went on high alert. Melody had said she was here of her own accord because she was writing an article about him. Why hadn't he caught on to the deception?

"Yeah. Some guy named Aldrich, I think. I overheard her telling Lucy the man was really hard to please and I don't think she was exaggerating. You know, she reported to him every day she was here? It was like clockwork, she'd come in, place a call—it was always short—and then she'd sit down for some coffee and a chat." Ruth sighed. "We're going to miss her. She was a nice young thing, wasn't she? It's a real shame she had to leave so suddenly."

"Yeah. A shame." Ryne stood up and distractedly thanked the older woman before heading towards the door.

Smythston, Oregon, USA...

Kane gripped the phone tightly, vaguely acknowledging the cracking sound as the plastic casing began to break under the strength of his grasp. He'd had a sense of foreboding the minute he'd heard Ryne's voice.

The longer they talked, the worse it became. "You're sure she knows about Lycans?"

The sound of heavy sighing met his ear before Ryne spoke. "I'm almost certain. Everything points that way. The fact she was checking out the books was bad enough, but if she's actually trying to get into the website, she must have strong suspicions. And then I messed up by letting her see me as a wolf and trying to pawn it off as a dog. Damn! I knew better, I just..."

Kane knew social protocols would have him uttering platitudes, but right now he had none. His brother had effectively been playing Russian roulette with all their lives and if the man had been in the room with him right now, he'd probably be ripping his throat out. Instead, he had to be satisfied with firing accusing words at his brother. "Yeah. You should have known better. You were supposed to deal with her; make sure things never got this far. What the hell happened?"

In his mind, he could see Ryne running his hand through his hair in frustration. "I don't know. When I'm around Melody, my wolf starts to take over and I find myself doing things I know I shouldn't."

"Your wolf? Is it looking on her as a mate?" Kane frowned at this possible complication.

"Damned if I know. I'm not into this life-long mate thing. That's your area of expertise. And right now, quite frankly, it doesn't even matter. The Keeping outlines my course of action."

"One I seriously doubt you'll be able to uphold if your wolf is intent on claiming her. I'd better take over."

The snarl that echoed down the phone lines left Kane in no doubt as to Ryne's feelings on the matter. "You'll stay the hell away from her. This is *my* problem and I'll be the one to fix it." His tone softened." Besides, it isn't safe for you to get involved. She doesn't know who you are or that it's you in the damned picture. All she has is the knowledge Lycans do exist."

"And does she suspect you're one?"

There was a pause. "Possibly. At the very least, she's suspicious."

"So what do you propose to do, if she's already on her way back to Chicago?"

"I'm following her there. I'll find out what she knows and take the necessary steps."

"*If* your wolf lets you."

"It will. I'm in control."

"If that were the case, things wouldn't have gotten this far." Kane knew he was pushing, but he had to be sure Ryne was capable of carrying out his duty.

"That's a low blow."

"But the truth."

Silence followed, then quiet words. "Yeah. I fucked up."

"And?"

"It's not an issue anymore. The needs of the pack are more important."

Kane detected a certain steel-like tone in his brother's voice, but this was too important to leave to chance. A blunt warning never hurt. "Remember that or I *will* take care of it myself."

A low growl was his response followed by a pause and then, "I need some information from you."

"Such as?"

"Can Elise check the books at the Grey Goose and see how Melody signed in? I want her address in Chicago, her phone number, her credit card number and anything Elise can find. You never know what might prove helpful if Melody turns into a runner."

"I'll call you with the information as soon as we have it."

"Make sure you call me on my cell phone. I'm leaving for the airport in less than an hour. If I'm lucky I'll be able to get a stand-by seat to Chicago."

"All right." Kane hung up, not bothering to say goodbye, his anger and frustration roiling about in his gut. The decision to let Ryne deal with this on his own was debatable, yet Kane knew the more wolves involved the greater the danger of discovery. Inaction ate away at him as he played out various scenarios out in his head, none of them pretty. If Ryne's wolf was looking for a mate, his judgement could be impaired. Yet, Ryne was an Alpha, biologically programmed to protect his pack. The question was, which instinct would win out?

Narrowing his eyes, Kane considered the situation before pulling a heavy book from the shelves. Flipping through the yellowing pages of the Book of the Law, he found the passage he wanted.

The keeping of our secret is a wolf's primary duty. Threats of exposure must be swiftly eradicated. Should more than two outsiders learn of our existence, dispersal of the young will begin immediately. Remaining members will obliterate all evidence of the pack's existence. Humanity is a disease covering the earth, a force that cannot be fought. Better that a few should die to stop the scourge, than to risk the perishment of all.

Chapter 30

Chicago, Illinois, USA...

The young woman hummed to herself as she sat feeding documents into the paper shredder in an upscale law office. She was a temp and, as usual, no one left her any real important work to do. Filing, shredding, a bit of typing and answering the phone; it was pretty easy and that's the way she liked it. Working full-time wasn't on her agenda. Nope. She planned on finding a rich lawyer and settling down as soon as possible. Too bad this particular job didn't hold any matrimonial prospects. The lawyer she was temping for was a grumpy old man, at least fifty if he was a day. However, age and looks wouldn't matter if he was rich enough. She gave the office an assessing perusal, adding up the cost of the decor and factoring in the location. He might be a possibility. Unfortunately, he was in court and not scheduled back for several hours.

That left her plenty of time to do her work as well as wander the halls looking for eligible professionals. It was always a good policy to keep her options open.

She checked her appearance as it reflected in the window. Her blond hair was up in a respectable knot at her nape with a few tendrils falling about her face and her makeup appeared flawless. Giving a satisfied smile, she stood, thinking maybe she'd go for a walk and see who might be in the halls or gathered near the elevator.

The phone rang and she answered it, automatically falling into a smooth, professional mode. "Good morning. You've reached the law office of Leon Aldrich. Ms. Matthews speaking. How may I help you?"

"Put me through to Aldrich." A male voice barked the order at her.

"Mr. Aldrich is out. May I take a message?"

"No. You may not. Where's Ms. Sandercock?"

"She's away at a funeral. I'm filling in for her for a few days."

"Humph! When will Aldrich be back?"

Ms. Matthews opened her mouth to respond. "I—"

The caller cut her off. "And don't tell me *you can't say*. Of course you can say! You're not mute and you know damned well when he's coming back. It's written in his day-planner on his damned desk. Now get up, walk into his office and check."

"I...I'm sorry, sir..." Ms. Matthews quivered at the vitriol in the man's voice, but did her best to withstand it.

"No, you're not sorry. But you will be once I tell Aldrich you didn't follow my orders. Do you know who I am, girl? My name is Greyson. Anthony Greyson. I own the building you're sitting in. Hell, I probably own the apartment you live in, too. And I know I own Leon Aldrich. Now if you expect to ever work in this city again, you'll do as you're told. Now!"

Ms. Matthews jumped as if the man was actually in the room barking orders at her. Some instinct told her every word he had spoken was true. She scurried into Mr. Aldrich's office and checked the planner on his desk, then relayed the information to Mr. Greyson.

The man's tone of voice changed, becoming calmer, almost pleasant. "Good. I like the way you follow orders, girl. Now is there anything else written in his book from yesterday or for the next four days?"

"Mr. Greyson, I'm not sure...."

"Are you defying me, girl?" The dangerous edge was back in the man's voice.

Gripping the phone tighter, Ms. Matthews swallowed hard. "No, sir. Of course not. Just let me look... Okay, he has only one message on yesterday's date. It says 'Greene called. Returning. Next few days. Report."

"Ahh... That is good news. Unexpected, but good. All right. Now you may take a message for me. Tell Aldrich I will want Ms. Greene's complete report delivered to me in four days' time. Got that?"

Ms. Matthews scribbled the message down. "Yes, sir. You want Mr. Aldrich to deliver Ms. Greene's report."

"Excellent. Now what else does he have written down?"

She flipped through the next few pages of the planner. It was blank. "There's nothing there, sir. I believe I heard him mention something about going away for the weekend."

"While the cat's away. Thank you, Ms...er... What was your name?"

"Matthews, sir. Mary Matthews."

"Right. Thank you, Ms. Matthews. You've been most helpful. I like to keep close tabs on my employees. Tell me, which agency did Aldrich get you from?"

"Richardson's." She answered hesitantly, not sure where the conversation was going.

"I'll keep that in mind and recommend you to some of my other employees when they need a temp. I think, Ms. Matthews, you and I might work well together."

"Together, sir?"

"You heard me. I'll be in touch. Make sure Aldrich gets my message."

The man hung up without saying goodbye and Ms. Matthews slowly put the phone down. She wasn't sure, but something was telling her Mr. Greyson might want her to do some snooping for him. It didn't sound exactly on the up and up, but Greyson probably had lots of wealthy people working for him. Lots of wealthy, *eligible* people. A smile curved her lips as she considered the possibilities.

Aldrich walked into his office and flicked on the lights. It was six-thirty and he was tired. The damned judge hadn't wanted to call a recess for the weekend; making them stay until all evidence was presented and arguments given. Well, the man could spend his weekend deliberating legal points if it made him happy. All Aldrich wanted was a quiet weekend at his cottage by the lake.

Walking to his desk, he scanned the messages the temp had taken. Nothing important there, thank goodness, except... He paused over the very bottom slip of paper. Greyson had called and wanted the complete Greene report in four days. What the hell?

Why would Greyson think there was a complete report? As far as the man knew, Greene was in Stump River attempting to get information out of Taylor. His gaze fell on his day-planner. It showed yesterday's date and he knew it had been turned to today's date when he'd left that morning. Someone had been in his office.

He tightened his jaw. Either Greyson had stopped in for a visit—which was highly unlikely since the man was leaving today—or he'd phoned and bullied the temp into going through the planner. It wouldn't be the first time it had happened. Pacing the room, he considered his options. Greene had said she was returning, but there was no mention of a completed report. Hell, he'd be surprised if she had ten words down, but he couldn't tell Greyson that.

Greyson had hinted he'd be held responsible for the success of Greene's assignment. It might have been a joke, but with that crafty old coot, you never knew. Aldrich stared around his well-appointed office noting the leather furniture and expensive art on the wall. Then he considered his European sports car and the penthouse suite he'd inherited when Greyson's last lawyer no longer needed it. He shuddered, recalling how the former lawyer suddenly closed his practice and left town, leaving no forwarding address; at least that was the official story Greyson Inc. told anyone who asked. Aldrich had helped construct the tale, ensuring everything was nice and tidy.

Everyone involved in the *misunderstanding* had an alibi and there were no inquiries from the former lawyer's family or friends. Greyson preferred to hire employees with no outside ties; it smoothed over complications if things 'didn't work out'.

Yes, Aldrich knew only too well the fate of his predecessor. The gardener had been only too happy to re-landscape the backyard of the estate in preparation for the yearly charity dinner hosted by Greyson Inc., and never questioned the extra-large hole dug for the new evergreen. Nor had the gardener asked why said evergreen was planted overnight rather than during the day. Like most of Greyson's employees, he had known when to turn a blind eye to strange happenings.

Aldrich studied the message again recalling he'd never dared inquire why the lawyer's services had been...terminated. Perhaps he should have.

Damn! He crumpled the paper in his fist. There was too much at stake and he wasn't about to let a slip of a girl mess it up. He narrowed his eyes as he considered his next step.

The journey from Stump River was interesting. Mel took the first shift driving, getting them as far as Timmins before the throbbing in her arm forced her to abandon her role as chauffeur. Lucy, however, was only too happy to take over. It turned out she was a speed demon behind the wheel, weaving in and out of lanes, passing transports and viewing speed limits as helpful suggestions rather than rules. While not usually a nervous passenger, Mel was only too thankful the pain killer she'd taken made her drowsy, causing her to sleep on and off for most of the journey.

It was well past midnight when they arrived in Toronto. Realizing she was soon going to be short on funds, Mel had tentatively suggested they rest in the car at the airport rather than getting a room. Lucy agreed, viewing it as all part of the adventure. Tipping back the seats, they dozed until dawn then used the airport facilities to tidy up and prepare for their flight.

Mel tried not to draw attention to the fact she was feeling progressively worse in case the airline wouldn't allow her to fly. The problem was just the cut on her arm but would they listen to her explanation?

While Lucy browsed for magazines, Mel snuck another peak at the injury. It was hot to the touch and the redness was spreading even though there was no sign of infection. In fact, the cut was nearly healed, which was more than a little puzzling. To be truthful, her whole body felt different; tingling as if each individual cell was up to something. A dull headache had been her constant companion for the past two days as well, and she had the strangest feeling of paranoia; as if there was someone else in her head, privy to her thoughts.

She popped another pain killer and loosened her collar as a wave of heat came over her again. Wiping her brow with a trembling hand, she pasted a smile on her face when Lucy re-appeared with two coffees and several magazines.

"Here, this will make you feel better. It's one of those special blends you always talk about." Lucy sat down beside her, pressing a cup into Mel's hands.

She thanked her and took a sip, waiting for the familiar rush only a good cup of coffee could bring. The rush, unfortunately, was more of a fizzle and she sighed. Just her luck; the first cup of coffee back in civilization and it was a dud. Resignedly, she continued to drink the beverage, wondering if it was the fever that was making the coffee taste different or if the upscale coffee chain had managed to mess up one of her favourite drinks.

After what felt like an interminable time, their flight was called and boarding went smoothly, no one giving her more than a cursory glance as she settled into her seat. As the flight took off, she closed her eyes and idly listened to Lucy chattering away. The pain killers had taken effect and she was pleasantly fuzzy headed. It took her some time to realize Lucy had grown quiet. Opening her eyes, she noticed the other woman was frowning and nibbling on her lip.

"What's the matter?"

"Hmm? Oh, nothing." Lucy looked away.

"Come on, tell me. Are you feeling air sick? Because if you are—"

"No! It's just...I was wondering what he was up to."

"Ryne?" She sat up straighter. Why was Lucy thinking about Ryne? Hadn't she been assured there was nothing between them?

"Not Ryne. Armand."

"Armand?" Mel couldn't keep the surprise from her voice.

"Yeah. He was sort of upset I was leaving."

313

"I thought you said he was okay with you taking time off?"

"He was. It's just that when I went to leave, he...well...he kissed me."

"Oh." She absorbed the information. "And...?"

"Armand's never kissed me before." Lucy picked at an invisible piece of lint on her pant leg.

"You mean, you and he never...?"

Lucy made a wry face. "Nope. We never."

"But I thought you said you'd...you know"

"Almost everyone, but not Armand. I've teased him and ignored him and practically thrown myself at him, but he never responded. I'd actually wondered if he might be gay or celibate or something, but now, I don't know what to think."

Mel sat back and frowned. "Gee Lucy, I don't know what to tell you. Maybe he's had a secret crush on you all this time."

"Then why did he have to wait until I was leaving to do something about it?" Lucy folded her arms, her face a study of consternation.

"Maybe he needed the idea of you leaving to shake him up."

"I suppose it's a possibility."

Mel studied her friend's face. It appeared Lucy had a crush on the bearish man and she didn't know what to do about it. "So, how would you feel about it, if Armand has his eye on you?"

"I'm not sure. For years I've been saying I want out of Stump River so I can make a fresh start, but then again Armand is really good to me." She shrugged. "I just don't know."

"Then this week away might be the perfect time to get things in perspective."

"Yeah, maybe so." Lucy was silent for a moment, before turning the tables on her companion. "And how do you feel about leaving Ryne?"

"Ryne?" Mel snorted and turned away. "I don't want to ever see him again. He's nothing but a lying bastard." Something inside her quivered as she spoke the words, almost as if part of her was protesting the thought, which was ridiculous. After the way he'd treated her, the things he'd said, nothing could redeem him in her eyes.

"Ouch! Is all that anger over him backing out of the interview?"

"Yes. No. Some of it is and some of it is because of stuff he said." Mel took a quivering breath. "He said I was only moderately entertaining and I wasn't worth very much in bed."

"Ryne said that?" Lucy looked aghast. "I don't believe it."

"It's not the sort of thing I'd imagine."

"No. Of course not, but there must have been a reason. Ryne's not usually quite that rude. He isn't exactly what people would call refined, but he's a decent guy."

"Not with me, he isn't." Mel glowered at the back of the seat in front of her as Ryne's words echoed in her head.

"Well, I wasn't there, so I don't know exactly what happened, but I bet there's something else going on. Something we don't know about made him act that way."

Mel shook her head, unwilling to hear anything that might exonerate the man.

Lucy sighed and turned away. A silence fell between them and Mel became lost in thought over recent events. It kept her occupied for the remainder of the flight but by the time they landed in Chicago, she had no clear answers as to what demon had made Ryne act as he did. From the look on Lucy's face, the other woman hadn't been successful in her musings, either.

Suppressing a derisive snort, Mel stiffly rose from her seat and prepared to depart the plane. Wasn't this just fine and dandy. Here she and Lucy were ready for an exciting week together exploring Chicago, and instead of planning girlfriend fun, they'd spent the last few hours dwelling on the men they'd left several hundred miles away.

They survived the wait at Immigration and even found their luggage with minimal difficulty. Luck continued to be with them as they easily got a taxi-cab and headed to Mel's apartment. Lucy enjoyed the ride, exclaiming over the large buildings, multi-laned highways, and throngs of people. By the time the trip came to an end, even the taciturn driver was smiling over her enthusiasm. As they climbed out of the cab, Mel was uncomfortably aware her neighbourhood was going to be a let-down for her friend. The rundown buildings, weedy cracked sidewalks and the constant rumble from the nearby public transit was quite a change from Stump River. However, Lucy either didn't care or didn't notice, instead chattering about what she hoped to do during her visit.

After climbing the stairs—the elevator was out of order again—Mel unlocked her apartment door and pushed it open. Stale air wafted into their faces, only slightly more pleasant than the scent in the hallway, where the smell of boiled cabbage was predominant.

"Here we are, home sweet home." She ushered Lucy inside and shut the door, automatically chaining it, and turning the various locks.

"I don't think I've ever seen so many locks on a door. Do you use them all the time?" Lucy stared in amazement.

She nodded. "Yep. This isn't the safest of
neighbourhoods. The crime rate is high; theft, drugs,
assaults. You can't be too careful."

"But what about the people next door? What if
they want to pop in for a visit? All that locking and
unlocking must get tiring."

"Lucy, I don't even know the names of the people
next door." She paused and then qualified her answer.
"Well, I do know one person's name but only because I
hear the woman calling it out when they're…you know."

"You can hear that? Ew!" Lucy wrinkled her
nose.

Mel laughed. "Yeah. I agree. The walls are
pretty thin, but the rent's cheap." She flopped down on
the sofa and closed her eyes. Travelling was tiring at the
best of times and this infection, or whatever was wrong
with her, seemed to be draining all her energy. If she
didn't feel better by morning, she'd have to go to a clinic;
there went more money she didn't have.

"You look all done in, Mel. Why don't you go to
bed? I can take care of myself."

Forcing her eyes open, she tried to sound perky for
the sake of her guest. "No. I invited you to come with
me. Let me rest for a few minutes and then I'll head to
the corner store and get some groceries."

Lucy folded her arms. "Nonsense. You rest. I
can go out. It'll be my first adventure in Chicago."

It was a short-lived argument and soon Mel was
lying in bed while Lucy left to purchase food. The cool
sheets felt good against her hot skin and she began to
relax, enjoying the first bit of peace and quiet she'd
experienced in several days.

Her eyes drifted shut only to snap open when she
heard a voice beside her. Startled, she sat up and looked
around, but no one was there. Grumbling about noisy
neighbours, she glared at the adjoining walls. She

debated banging on the plastered surface but knew from experience it would do little good. Instead she flopped back down and put the pillow over her head, determined to get some rest. A moment later, the voice spoke again, the murmuring indistinguishable, yet definitely nearby. She stiffened, feeling the hairs rising on the back of her neck. There was definitely someone speaking, another presence close at hand. Slowly she removed the pillow from her face and glanced nervously about, trying to determine the source. It wasn't coming from the walls or the dead clock-radio beside her bed, yet there was no doubt she was hearing a voice. A shiver ran over her as she recalled the dubious stain on the carpet when she'd moved in. Had it been blood? Was her apartment haunted?

As soon as the idea popped into her head, she scoffed at her own foolishness. No, she wasn't going down that road again, not after what happened last time at Ryne's house. Taking a deep breath, she concentrated on the sound. It seemed to be...inside her head?

She tugged on her ear and gave her head a shake before listening again. There! It was definitely a voice! Furrowing her brow, she tried to decipher what was being said, but just as suddenly as it had appeared, the voice was gone. She swallowed and pushed her hair from her face with a shaking hand. Was she losing her mind? No. Of course not. She was overtired, that was all. Rest was what she needed.

Latching onto the idea like a lifeline, she plumped her pillows, wiggled into a comfortable position, closed her eyes and breathed deeply. Good. No voices resounded in her head. Her muscles relaxed and she sank into the softness of her mattress.

Sleep, glorious sleep. Everything was calm and quiet. She was on the edge...drifting away...

The phone rang and her eyes popped open. Damn.

Well, she wasn't getting up to answer it. Whoever was could leave a message. She rolled onto her side and firmly shut her eyes again. Unfortunately, as much as she tried to ignore it, her curiosity won and she strained to hear who was calling when the machine turned on.

A supercilious voice filled the room. "Ms. Greene? Pick up the phone."

It was Mr. Aldrich.

He huffed when she didn't comply. "I know you're home. You can pretend you aren't, but rest assured I have my sources...." He paused and then audibly sighed. "Fine. Play games if you wish, but I expect you at my office at ten o'clock tomorrow morning with a complete report. No excuses, unless you're prepared to face legal proceedings for the return of the funds advanced to you. And make no mistake; I have the papers here on my desk, ready to be filed. By the time I'm done with you, you won't have a penny left."

She groaned. How had he known she was home? Did he have spies at the airport? And how could she hand in a report, but there wasn't one? Mr. Ryne-pain-in-the-ass-Taylor had only given her the most meagre details about himself. All she really knew was how he took pictures. How in heaven's name was she supposed to write a report when the only information she had—

Her thoughts skittered to a halt as she considered a possible solution. Those pictures from Ryne's camera were still on her computer. While she'd never looked at them, she hadn't dumped the recycle bin, either. Maybe...

Dragging herself out of bed, she found her laptop and turned it on. If she studied the pictures carefully enough, she might be able to gather enough information to satisfy Aldrich, at least for a while. What Greyson would think of the report was another story since she'd never dealt with him in person, but she'd cross that bridge when she came to it.

Opening the picture file, she tried to ignore the guilt pricking her conscience. Ryne hadn't wanted her looking at these yet what choice did she have?

She glanced around her apartment. The furniture was old, the decorations cheap but it was all she had. The thought of losing everything she owned gave her a sinking feeling. What would it be like to start over, with absolutely nothing?

Surely, Ryne was over-reacting. Letting the world know a little about his life wasn't such a bad thing. Trying to convince herself she wasn't doing anything wrong, she leaned close to the screen and began to analyze the images.

At four in the morning, she finally clicked save then rubbed her gritty eyes and arched her back. The report, such as it was, was complete. She'd read it over again before printing, but didn't think there was much else she could add to it.

By examining the pictures on her laptop and noting their sequence, she'd been able to piece together a plausible background for Ryne. Much of it was supposition, but if the man didn't grant interviews, who would ever know? And there were some concrete facts. His work on cars and the restoration of the house were facts. He'd mentioned running and by the look of his lean muscled body—she suppressed the physical response the image invoked—he must be into fitness. The photography lessons he'd given her had provided insight into his techniques and even his street-crossing lessons with Harley showed a love of animals. She was actually rather impressed with herself over what she'd managed to piece together.

In some places, she had really stretched things. A picture of an older couple in front of a large house had her writing he had an extensive extended family and wanted a big family himself one day. After all, why would he have purchased that oversized monstrosity outside Stump River, if he was going to live there alone?

Their dinner at Armand's had allowed her to state he enjoyed life's simple pleasures; cold beer, time spent with friends and a good movie. Her more personal experiences with him and his sexual prowess, however, were definitely not included. Some things weren't meant to be shared.

The piece de resistance of the whole report was her deduction regarding where Ryne took his pictures. She knew Greyson was extremely interested in that point and felt he'd be pleased with her sleuthing. The background, clothing, numbering of the pictures and even the weather, led her to believe all were taken on the same day somewhere near Smythston, Oregon. Even more exciting was the fact that in one picture, she was sure she saw wolves in the distance. The image was fuzzy, but unmistakeably some form of canine. If Greyson was looking for where a certain wolf picture had originated, she was sure she'd found his answer.

Just to cover herself, she'd generalized that while Ryne worked mostly in the Oregon area, he never revealed exact locations. This, she said, was because of his great commitment to the environment and his desire to prevent people from disturbing the delicate balance of nature in the places he worked. It was sappy, but any person who claimed 'they didn't exist before photography' could very well say something like her final statement.

She stared at the picture that had wolves in the distance. Something niggled in her brain when she looked at it, as if there was something she should know or remember. Unfortunately, the harder she tried to bring the thought into focus, the more it faded away. With a sigh, she gave up and shut down the computer. She was too tired to think. Maybe after a couple hours sleep she'd be able to figure out what it was about the picture that called to her.

Yawning, Mel stood up, hoping the sketchy report would satisfy Aldrich and get him to leave her alone for a while. Heading towards the couch—she 'd told Lucy to sleep in her room—she shed her robe and lay down. As she tried to get comfortable on the lumpy, old couch, she bemusedly realized at some point during the night, her fever had broken. Thank heavens for small mercies.

Chapter 31

"Are you sure you'll be all right?" Lucy frowned with concern at Mel. "You don't look so good."

The two women were leaning against the kitchen counter sipping coffee and preparing to start their day. Mel, however reluctantly, had to head off to meet with Aldrich, while Lucy was going to spend the morning taking a city bus tour.

Rolling her eyes, Mel reassured her friend, yet again. "Honestly, I'm fine. The fever broke last night. My arm's not as sore. It's lack of sleep and nerves over this meeting that are making me look less than prime. I'll go see Aldrich and give him this report while you're on the tour. Then we'll meet back here for lunch and go shopping."

"Why don't you e-mail the report and come with me?"

She sighed. "I wish, but Aldrich hates e-mail. He wants face to face contact. I think he likes to watch people squirm." Noting Lucy's concerned expression, she added a light laugh. "Don't worry. I'll be fine."

"Well... If you're sure."

"Go." She made shooing motions with her hands. "You know you want to take the Chicago Gangster Tour and see where Al Capone hung out. If you don't leave now, you'll miss the bus."

It took some doing, but Mel finally had Lucy out of the apartment and on her way. Gathering her purse, the report on Ryne and a jacket, Mel left as well, though with considerably less excitement than Lucy had.

She really didn't want to see Aldrich and she really didn't want to give him the report. Even if Ryne was a jerk, she was betraying his trust.

Her mental debate lasted all the way to Aldrich's office and continued as she sat in the intimidating reception area, waiting to see him. At least, being a Saturday and outside usual business hours, the secretary was absent. Mel recalled the feeling of disapproval that had emanated from Ms. Sandercock, Aldrich's personal assistant. Sitting in her presence had been distinctly uncomfortable.

Shifting in her seat, Mel fiddled with the report; curling the corners with her fingers then trying to press them flat. An incredibly ugly clock ticked away on the wall, its sound accompanying the bland music that was piped in from hidden speakers. It was a far cry from sitting and waiting in The Broken Antler. At least there, Armand would be giving her beer to drink. Maybe that's what she needed right now. Some alcohol-induced bravado to get her through her encounter. An inelegant snort escaped her as she contemplated Aldrich's response should she stumble into his office tipsy and wiggling her ass. She doubted he'd be as amused as the patrons had been at the bar the other night.

She stifled a sigh and smoothed the wrinkled papers in her hand. The longer she waited the worse she felt about giving her findings to Aldrich. She crossed her legs and inhaled deeply before staring at the neatly typed pages once again.

A sound from Aldrich's office caught her attention. He must have finished whatever it was he'd been doing. She straightened in her chair and then on impulse folded the report and shoved it into the inside pocket of her jacket. The pages crinkled as she leaned back in the chair, trying to appear casual. She'd play it cool; feel Aldrich out as to his client's intentions with regards to Ryne and then she'd hand over the information...maybe.

The door to Aldrich's office swung open. She rose to her feet and gave the lawyer a tentative smile. "Good morning, Mr. Aldrich. I got your message and came over as you requested."

What might have been a smile, passed over the man's lips. "Of course you came; what other option did you have?"

Feeling it was a rhetorical question, she didn't answer, instead entering the lawyer's inner sanctum and sitting down in a low-slung chair in front of his desk; it forced her to look up at him, increasing his intimidation factor. She remembered the room from when she'd interviewed for the job; leather, wood and what was probably a beautiful view, if one wasn't so over-powered by the occupant of the office.

Damn, she was sweating again. Had the fever returned or did the lawyer just make her that nervous? Surreptitiously, she wiped her hands on her pant legs and waited for Aldrich to speak.

Unfortunately, he didn't. Instead, the annoying man sat there, casually leaning back in his leather chair, fingers steepled, staring at her blandly. His eyebrows raised in the faintest hint of inquiry. She licked her lips. What was he waiting for? Nervously, she shifted in her seat and refolded her hands, met his gaze then looked away. Why didn't he say something? Finally, unable to stand it any longer, she broke the silence between them.

"Well, I'm back." She immediately winced at the idiotic comment.

"So you are. A stellar comment, Ms. Greene. I can only hope your observations on Mr. Taylor are equally...profound."

"About that..."

Aldrich sat up straighter. "You do, of course have a report for me."

She could feel the pages poking her in the ribs, each jab like a prod to her conscience, reminding her their existence was her fault. "Um..."

"Yes?"

"I was wondering what exactly Mr. Greyson was going to do with the report?"

The lawyer's eyebrows shot up. "That is really none of your business. Mr. Greyson did not hire you to delve into his personal motivation."

"It's just that Ryne—Mr. Taylor—was reluctant to share much about himself. He likes his privacy."

"Artists, authors, movie stars; they're public persons. A certain amount of celebrity is part of their job description. Some degree of privacy must be sacrificed if they wish the public to buy into their product. I'm sure Mr. Taylor knew this when he began his career. Now he must 'suck it up' as I believe you young people are fond of saying."

"I know celebrities have to—"

"Ms. Greene. I do not have the time, or the inclination, to debate the issue. Kindly hand over the report and let's be done with it. I have other appointments today."

"No."

"No?"

"No. I...I want to think about this some more."

"You do have a report, don't you?"

"Yes! Of course! It's just—"

"If you've been paid to write a report, Ms. Greene, then you have a legal obligation to hand over said report. If you choose not to, you may not like the steps I will be forced to take in order to gain ownership for my client." Aldrich stood up and rounded the desk.

His tone was no longer bland and boring, nor was his face impassive. A nastiness had crept into it, making Mel feel nervous and bringing with it a wave of nausea. Her head started to spin and her skin prickled all over.

Swallowing hard, she stood and backed around behind the chair she'd been sitting in, gripping its back to keep her balance. The papers in her pocket seemed to crinkle with betraying loudness as she moved and she instinctively clutched her hand over them. Aldrich's gaze zeroed in on the gesture and he stalked closer, eyes narrowed and his tone threatening.

"You will hand over those papers or live to regret it, Ms. Greene. The power wielded by Greyson Incorporated is not something you should take lightly."

An unexpected flash of anger sparked inside her, the feeling of sickness being pushed aside by a force that was ready to snarl at this person who dared threaten her. Speaking with much greater conviction than she felt—or at least than she thought she felt—she threw back her shoulders and raised her chin. "Back off. I'll give it to you when I'm good and ready and not a minute sooner." Then she whirled around and stalked out of the office, catching a vague impression of Aldrich's shocked face before slamming the door shut.

The noise of the terminal washed over Ryne as he strode across the concourse, a small tote containing the bare essentials slung over his shoulder. His gaze was set on the exit, his expression a deadly scowl that had the swirling mass of humanity quickly stepping out of his way. Not that he noticed; his mind was occupied with far more important things.

After speaking with Kane, he'd had Daniel search the airlines for a last-minute flight to Chicago, then drove like a maniac to Toronto only to arrive too late for the Friday flight. Thankfully, there'd been a seat available on

Saturday and he was now where he needed to be, which was in Chicago on Melody's trail.

As much as he hated abandoning his new pack members, he needed to deal with this situation quickly or there could very well be no pack to worry about. Bryan and Daniel were capable of carrying out their duty in his absence. His instructions had been specific for each of the possible scenarios that might evolve. At best, he'd be home in forty-eight hours happily helping the Loberos get settled. If the worst-case scenario came to pass... Well, the evening news would tell that tale; sensational stories of murder and mass suicide always made the headlines.

The bright sun made him squint as he stepped outside and settled into the long line of people waiting to catch a taxi-cab. He could push his way to the front—a warning growl and a hard stare would keep anyone from protesting—but he was trying to keep a low a profile. And so he joined the line with barely suppressed impatience and spent the time reviewing his plans while arguing with his inner wolf over their wisdom.

Despite what he'd told Kane, he had doubts about his ability to deal with Melody dispassionately. Inexplicably, his wolf had started to bond with her, ignoring all reason. Melody was human. There was no cause for his wolf to respond to her; it never had to any of the other human females he'd bedded. Why did it have to become difficult now, when he needed to be at his most ruthless?

"Hey, do you want a cab or not? We don't have all day here!"

A disgruntled voice broke into his reverie and Ryne realized he was finally at the front of the line. Climbing in the back of the waiting vehicle, he gave the driver the address Kane had texted to him and then sat brooding over what he might have to do. He didn't know Chicago all that well and it would make things much more difficult. There were people everywhere and he imagined most were just waiting to be witnesses and report any strange goings-on, hoping for a few minutes of fame on the local news.

He'd have to lure Melody out of her apartment to a remote location. If he questioned her in her home, she might become suspicious. Actually, given how they'd parted, she might not want to talk to him at all. Had he known he would need her cooperation, he might not have been so harsh.

The cab pulled up in front of an apartment building and Ryne stepped out onto the sidewalk. He paid the driver then surveyed Melody's home. To say it was rundown was being too generous and the neighbourhood... A grimace of distaste passed over his face as the smell of exhaust and garbage bins wafted past. How could she stand to live in such an environment?

He walked up the steps and entered the building. Of course, there was no security at the entrance and the yellowing 'out of order' sign on the elevator told him it hadn't been working for quite some time. Taking the stairs, he easily climbed the five flights then, with studied casualness, strolled the length of the hallway, scanning the numbers on the doors until he came to Melody's. Sounds came at him from all side but her apartment, however, was silent.

A glance up and down the hall revealed no prying eyes, so he grabbed the knob and rammed the door jamb with his shoulder. Not surprisingly, the wood quickly gave way and he entered her home.

Melody's scent surrounded him the minute he stepped inside. He paused and closed his eyes, inhaling deeply. A low rumble emitted from his chest as the delicious smell filled his nostrils and nourished his spirit.

The female! Where is she? His wolf stirred with excitement.

He peeked in the bedroom and bathroom, noting Lucy had been there at one point, her scattered clothing, as well as her scent, betraying her presence. Back in the kitchen, a few papers were on the counter and he flipped through them. Junk mail, bills, nothing of importance, but...ah ha! On a nearby table, Melody's laptop was open and still on. He sat down in front of the machine and checked the start menu for recent activity.

His name leapt off the screen, as did a certain picture file, which he knew he'd deleted. That little bitch! She'd managed to get more copies of his pictures. He opened the file with his name on it and scanned the document, his expression growing ever grimmer as he realized how much she'd managed to piece together. By the time he reached the final paragraphs, he was ready to hurl the machine across the room.

It was all there in black and white. She knew he'd taken the pictures in Oregon.

As the extent of the implications set in, Ryne felt the colour drain from his face. How many connections and assumptions had her agile brain come up with? If she knew about Oregon, did she know about Kane? Did she know the wolf in the picture was actually a Lycan? And was she, at this moment, telling her boss, Aldrich, that not only was Ryne Taylor a Lycan, but that a whole pack resided in Smythston? His mind filled with images; hordes of scientists and TV crews, men with tranquillizers and guns, gawkers and protestors, all descending on Kane's pack.

They'd surround the territory; breach the perimeter, possibly question why there was no resistance. The invaders would approach the deathly quiet houses, cautiously entering, only to find bodies. Dead bodies. Strewn about the house. In the bedrooms. In the kitchen. In the games room where the pack used to gather. Cold lifeless bodies that would stare with unseeing eyes at the invaders who had unknowingly precipitated the massacre.

All identifying papers would have been destroyed. Kane would see to that. The nameless corpses would be studied to no avail and then buried in unmarked graves, their identities forever lost amid the swirl of rumours that would arise. Words such as cult, brainwashing and mass suicide would be bandied about. Pictures and stories would be plastered in newspapers and magazines, across TV and computer screens around the world.

Ryne's mind focused on one particular image; Kane and Elise lying dead in each other's arms, their hands on the small mound that would have been their first born.

He shook his head. Surely Kane wouldn't allow Elise to stay; he'd send her away. Yet would she go? Not likely. She was devoted to her mate and wouldn't abandon him.

Rage filled him. This was all Melody's fault and he'd make sure she would pay. Pay for each life lost, for each pup left orphaned. When his wolf howled in protest, he ruthlessly crushed it. There was no excuse, no explanation that would spare Ms. Greene from his vengeance.

Knowing what he must do, he took out his phone then stared at it, an icy cold replacing his fury. He watched with detachment as he dialled the familiar number and brought the receiver up to his ear. His lips barely responded to his command to speak, to utter the words no Alpha ever wanted to say.

"Kane? Start the dispersal."

.

Chapter 32

After speaking with Kane, Ryne searched Melody's computer, ruthlessly deleting information. When he came upon Aldrich's address and the name Greyson Inc., he made note of it before erasing the rest of the relevant files. Melody was probably with her co-conspirator at this very moment and, with any luck he'd catch them together. Filled with ruthless determination, he pushed away from the computer, wiping his prints from the keys before exiting her apartment. In a similar manner, he cleaned the door handle, just in case. His prints weren't on file anywhere, but you could never be too careful.

Should anyone have cared, it was a reasonably pleasant day for early spring. The sun was shining, pollution levels were low and the noise—for a large city at least—was moderate. A gentle breeze was even drifting down the street. As he exited the apartment building, an all too familiar scent had him stepping back into the shadows of the doorway and searching the sidewalk. Melody was approaching.

Confronting her on the street was too public so he moved inside, curbing his impatience and watching her progress through the glass doorway. There was something off about her appearance, though he couldn't put his finger on it. She was moving differently and he was sure he detected slight shivers wracking her body.

His wolf whined in concern but he ignored the beast, instead backing farther into a corner close to the stairwell. Once she was completely inside, he'd have her.

The outer door opened. A sliver of bright sunlight fell across the dull terrazzo floor causing her profile to be perfectly silhouetted. He could see the curve of her cheekbone, the fullness of her lips, her cute nose.

Yes! We are together again! His wolf slipped through his defences once again and rumbled in approval at her proximity.

"Melody." He stepped out of the shadows.

She started and stared at him in shock. "Ryne! What are you doing here?" Her voice sounded raspy, but he didn't have the time to wonder why; she was already backing towards the door.

He moved quickly, grabbing her arm and dragging her towards the stairs before she could reach the doorway. She gave a cry of pain and struggled against him.

"Let me go!" She tried to kick him, but he was prepared for the move by now and pulled her flush against him, wrapping one arm around her. She wriggled in an attempt to free herself and he heard her inhaling in preparation for a scream. He clamped a hand over her mouth and manoeuvred so she was pressed between him and the wall. Her struggles had her body rubbing against his and unexpectedly he felt himself becoming aroused. Without meaning to, he nuzzled against her, inhaling deeply. Her scent was heavenly, but…something was different.

Frowning, he sniffed again, trying to place what it was only to give a muffled cry of pain. She'd bitten him! Jerking his hand away he opened his mouth to rebuke her, but she spoke first.

"What they hell are you doing here? And why are you sniffing me? What are you, some kind of a dog?" Melody was pressing hard against his chest. She was breathing rapidly, heat radiating from her, yet at the same time she was shivering, her voice quavering as she spoke.

Grabbing her upper arms, Ryne held her away from him, studying her curiously, his earlier anger set aside by the new information coming at him from his senses. Her skin was pale, her eyes glassy and unfocused. If he didn't know better, he'd say she was...

With a sudden cry of pain, she stiffened and then went limp in his arms.

He reacted instinctively, scooping her up and running up the stairs to her apartment. Shouldering the door open, he laid her down on the couch and then stared at her nonplussed. What was going on? She was unconscious and convulsing. He sniffed again and swore. Damn if she didn't smell almost like a Lycan, but how could that be?

Not knowing what else to do, he dialled the number for Kane's nurse practitioner, Nadia.

"Nadia? Ryne here. I have a question for you."

The woman was a no-nonsense sort who revelled in the knowledge she could make even the fiercest Lycan put its tail between its legs. She answered in clipped, impatient tones. "Ryne, I don't have time for your nonsense. Kane's put everyone on high alert and I'm too busy—"

"Too bad." Ryne wasn't in the mood for her attitude and had no compunction about throwing his authority around. "Listen to these stats. Female. About twenty-five years old. Unconscious. Giving off heat like a blast furnace. Slight convulsions. Eyes were glassy and unfocused before she collapsed, and she was in pain."

"Ryne, I don't—"

"And she smells like a wolf."

His last statement stopped the woman's protests. "Twenty-five, you say? Rather old for undergoing her first change. What's her family background?"

"How the hell should I know?" He ran his free hand through his hair. "Nadia, up until five minutes ago,

I thought she was a pure-blooded human, but for some reason her scent's changed since I last saw her and now it's distinctly Lycan."

The woman snorted. "Obviously, she *wasn't* fully human. There must be some recessive Lycan genes in her background and something triggered them. Did you bite her during sex?"

"No! I didn't bite her."

"Was she having sex with another Lycan?"

He thought of Bryan and Daniel, but knew they hadn't been near her. Hell, if they had, he'd rip their throats out. "No. Just me."

"Well, something happened. It would take a combination of at least two bodily fluids and sometimes three to activate latent genes." She listed them off. "You'd need semen, saliva and or blood; are you sure you didn't nip each other by accident?"

Thinking back to their encounter at the Broken Antler, Ryne replayed the scene. He'd dragged her into Armand's office. She'd been drunk, almost playful at first before they'd started to argue. When Melody had tried to leave, his wolf had taken over. He'd pulled her back and they'd struggled before... A groan escaped his lips when he remembered he hadn't used protection.

"We had sex and I didn't use a condom, but I'm sure I didn't bite her."

"What about in the period following? Could there have been an accidental blood exchange in, oh, say...the next twelve hours? As long as there were traces of semen in her body, a blood exchange could trigger her recessive genes even without saliva.

Accident? The word had him swearing under his breath as he thought about the bar fight. He recalled falling and landing on top of Melody. His nose had gushed blood everywhere and later on, hadn't he noticed Melody with a bloody cloth on her arm? Was it possible his blood had seeped into her wound? Picking up her arm, he pushed her sleeve out of the way. A faint scar marred the creamy surface of her forearm. When he sniffed the area, he had his answer. Damn!

"Nadia, the mystery is solved. I know how it happened, now what the hell do I do about it?"

"It sounds like her body is trying to adapt to the cellular and chemical changes it's experiencing. That's tough on anyone, but since it's the full moon tonight, her body is also trying to undergo its first transformation and she's not ready for it."

He tightened his grip on the phone. "So what's going to happen?"

"She'll have bad spells like this, interspersed with periods when she feels relatively fine, but in the end she'll either live or die, depending on how much her body can handle. There's nothing you can really do about it. If anyone were to ask before attempting this type of thing, medical advice would strongly discourage any genetic changes during a full moon. It's way too risky."

"Yeah, well, this wasn't exactly planned." He pinched the bridge of his nose. "So I just watch her and twiddle my thumbs? That's the best advice you can give?" He stared down at Melody's pale face, hating feeling helpless.

"Pretty much. Keep her calm. Cool cloths for the fever. Aspirin not Tylenol. That stuff's going to be deadly to her from now on."

"How long before I know if she's going to make it?"

"It depends on the individual and how many generations back the connection is. Best guess is between two to five days from the initial introduction of the triggering agents."

He did the math. The fight had been Wednesday night. It was now Saturday morning. About two and half days. He sighed heavily. "All right. Thanks, Nadia."

Nadia's voice softened. "I hope it goes well for your friend. Does she have anything to do with the alert Kane has placed us under?"

"Yeah. Sort of." He ended the call without further explanation and started to pace the room. Shit! Now what was he supposed to do? Melody was turning into one of his kind, but how would she react to the news? He knew of instances when those recently changed embraced their new life while others refused to accept it, eventually going rogue and having to be terminated for the good of the pack. What category would Melody fall into? And did it really matter? She'd already betrayed them.

He sat down beside her and brushed his fingers over her soft lips, tracing her brow and marvelling at her long lashes.

Perfect. She's perfect for us. His wolf murmured.

He ran the back of his hand over her cheek. The skin was hot to the touch. Yes, she might be perfect for his wolf, but what about the pack? He had to think of them first. She was the source of their current predicament.

His earlier rage surfaced. He'd told her there was to be no interview yet she'd expressly gone against his orders. Defying an Alpha, betraying the pack. Curling his fingers around her slender neck, he considered his options. It wouldn't take much to end all this, a quick twist and...

He could feel her pulse fluttering against his fingers. His own heart was beating heavily, his pulse drumming in his ears, blocking out all other sounds. He licked his lips and stared at her lovely face one more time before bringing the image of Kane's pack to mind. The good of the pack took precedence; he knew that fact as well as he knew his own name. One last time, he caressed her soft skin with his thumb and then watched with detachment as his fingers started to tighten...

No! He couldn't do it! Pulling back his hand, his shoulders slumped in defeat. Hell, what kind of a weakling Alpha was he? The safety of his pack came first.

But she is our female!

The argument bounced back and forth between him and his wolf.

There has to be another solution. The pack could run, hide...

No. If the humans found nothing, they would keep searching; rumours would grow, rewards would be offered. He and Kane had discussed it in detail. Only by finding something, would the searchers truly believe the supposed 'lead' was a hoax.

Kidnap her; carry her off.

And hold her captive for the rest of her life?

Eventually she would come to accept her fate.

But what if she ever escaped?

She'd be under around-the-clock supervision.

And what about her boss, Aldrich?

The door suddenly opened and he was forced to abandon his conflicted thoughts. Jumping to his feet, he turned to face Lucy.

"Ryne, what are you doing here?"

"Hi, Lucy. I...um..."

She walked up to him and kissed his cheek, before moving to take her coat off. "Never mind. I know the truth."

"You do?" He stiffened, assuming the worst.

"Of course. You're sorry for your fight with Mel and came here to make up."

"Uh... Right. That's it." He latched onto the lifeline she'd unknowingly handed him. "I'm here to make things right."

Lucy nodded, glancing at Melody lying on the sofa, her face quickly changing from a happy grin to real concern. "Oh, is she sick again?"

"Yeah. She fainted coming into the building and I carried her up here. She has a fever. I was just going to give her an aspirin."

"I'll get some from the medicine cabinet." Lucy turned to go.

"No. I already checked. There isn't any. Um...why don't you sit with her and I'll go to the store." He felt the need to get away for a few minutes and think things through. Lucy's arrival had just thrown another curve into this mess.

"Sure. I'll take care of her while you're gone. Don't worry."

He nodded, gave Melody a lingering look and took his leave.

Lucy bustled about the small apartment her morning out having somehow added an extra level of brightness to her usually upbeat personality. She eased Mel's jacket off and hung it up, then got cold cloths to bathe her face, all the while thinking about Ryne's unexpected appearance. It was so sweet that he'd come all this way to see Mel. Whatever argument they'd had couldn't have been all that important. They'd be able to work out their differences.

Grinning, she tried to picture Ryne down on his knees apologizing, but then shook her head. No, it wouldn't happen. The man was too arrogant, but his heart was in the right place. He and Mel would work things out and make a fine couple when all was said and done.

Noises were coming from next door and Lucy grimaced, recognizing the sounds. Someone was getting lucky. It made her think of Armand and how she'd yet to share a bed with him. Was there a future for her in Stump River with the bartender? She furrowed her brow and wandered to the window considering the question. Should she finally make the move she'd always talked about and live in a big city like this?

Staring down at the street, she watched the traffic going past, people hurrying along the sidewalks never even acknowledging the other pedestrians. A train rattled by and the whole apartment shook. If she left Stump River, would her new home be this impersonal? Yet wasn't that what she wanted? To make a new start where no one knew her or her reputation?

She thought of the stop she'd made on her way home from the Gangster tour. There'd been a big cathedral and she'd been drawn in by the architecture, even boldly entering when she saw the door was open. It had been cavernous and cool, the arched ceiling reaching towards the heavens leaving her feeling small and alone. Her steps echoed on the tile floor as she took in the ornate carvings and stained glass. When a voice spoke behind her, she'd almost jumped out of her skin!

"Are you here for confession, my dear? Or perhaps some quiet reflection before Mass starts at the top of the hour?" An elderly priest had asked.

"Er...." She'd looked around nervously. Her mother had taken her to church once or twice as a child but...

"Remember, whatever you need can be found if you look in the right place." He'd glanced upwards and then walked to the rear of the building, entering what appeared to be a small closet flanked by similar structures on either side, their doorways covered with velvet drapes.

She'd looked upwards but only saw a pipe organ and some painted murals on the ceiling. They were nice paintings though—much better than Armand's—and the images seemed to be looking down on her with kindly faces. Of course, the priest hadn't been referring to the ceiling, even she knew that, but it had made her realize she didn't belong here.

As quickly and quietly as possible, she'd made her way towards the door, her intention being to sneak out but for some reason she'd paused and looked to where the priest had disappeared. Giving a shrug, she'd figured why not give it a try. She'd come to Chicago for new experiences, right?

Now she decided that perhaps it had been a sign, a first step in starting a new life here in Chicago. A big city, a new job, Mel introducing her to new friends. Maybe they could share this apartment, at least until she was on her feet. It might be exciting.

Her musings were interrupted when a long black vehicle pulled up at the curb. It looked out of place in the neighbourhood with its shiny chrome and tinted black windows that screamed of wealth and power. In fact, it reminded her of something a crime boss might drive, and she wondered who the occupants were here to visit.

The phone rang beside her and she answered, idly watching the vehicle below.

"Hello?"

"Ms. Greene?"

"No, this is her friend, Lucy Chalmers. Can I help you?"

"Kindly put Ms. Greene on the phone."

"I'm sorry; she's not well right now. Can I take a message?" Lucy glanced over at her friend who was moving about restlessly and muttering in her sleep.

"Tell her to quit playing games with me, Ms. Chalmers, if that's really your name."

"What do you mean, if that's really my name? Why would I make up a name just to answer the phone?" Geez talk about a weirdo.

"Never mind. I know what Greene is up to. If she thinks holding out will get her even more money, she's sadly mistaken. Either she hands over whatever information she has in the next two minutes, or I'm coming up to get it."

"Coming up? Where are you?" She had a sinking feeling she already knew the answer.

"I'm parked right in front of the building. As a matter of fact, I can even see you standing at the window."

She gave a squeak of surprise and jumped towards the middle of the room. How dare this person act like a Peeping Tom! She prepared to give the man a piece of her mind, but then thought better of it, having heard all about gangsters and crime lords on her tour that morning.

"Listen, Mel's really sick. And I don't know anything about a report. Why don't you come back tomorrow? She'll likely be feeling better by then, and you can talk all about it." She used her sweetest, most cajoling voice.

"Nice try, but it won't work. You have two minutes." The phone went dead.

She dropped the phone and spun around not knowing what to do. Oh dear Lord, what has she stumbled into? She'd wanted some excitement, but this was taking things too far. She dared a peek out the window, looking up and down the street for Ryne, thinking he might know what to do, but of course there was no sign of him. Typical man, never there when you needed him! Of course, what did she expect, when he hadn't even fixed her faucet like he'd promised! She firmed her jaw, she'd have to defend herself and Mel as best as she could.

Glancing about the small apartment for some form of weapon, she finally found a large carving knife and a heavy frying pan. She was pretty sure she'd never have the guts to use the knife so left it in favour of the latter. Testing the weight of the pan in her hand, she took a defensive position by the door.

Minutes passed before she heard footsteps approaching down the hall. Flexing her fingers, she checked her grip on the frying pan and braced herself for what might come. The steps paused outside; she took a deep breath and held it as she watched the handle slowly turn. Letting out the breath and taking another to steady her nerves, she waited for the door to open slowly. Instead, it swung inward with enough force to make her jump. Taking no time to think, she swung the frying pan with all her might towards the newcomer. Unfortunately, her aim was off and she missed her target, hitting the wall with a resounding clunk.

Before she could comprehend what was happening, something hard hit her across the head and she fell to the ground stunned.

After that, everything was a kaleidoscope of pain, sounds and blurred images, as she drifted in and out of consciousness. She had the impression of something warm and sticky running down her face and pooling about her cheek where it pressed against the floor. Some instinct for self-preservation kept her from moving or making any noise during those times she was awake. Vaguely she heard a man's voice talking as if on the phone.

"Aldrich here. I'll be at the Greyson estate in an hour ... That's right. I'm inspecting the state of the property and I don't want to be disturbed ... Greyson's incommunicado, but if you insist that I contact him the fallout will be on your head ... Yes, I knew you'd see it my way. Have the gates open. Remember, no one is to be outside."

The call ended and through her lashes, she watched feet walking towards the sofa. Someone grunted, the sofa squeaked. An arm dangled near the ground... Mel? Was someone moving her? But why? And where to? The man's voice, hadn't he said the Greyson estate? The feet shuffled by her. The door shut and the apartment was quiet now.

Lucy forced her eyes open and stared at the tiled floor in front of her. How long ago did she see those feet? Had she passed out again? The pool of blood spreading out around her head was much bigger than she remembered. She needed to tell Ryne. He'd save Mel. A hint of laughter escaped her lips as she slowly moved her hand, dipping her finger in the blood. How cliché. This was like in the gangster movies; she was leaving a message written in blood. G – R – E –Y – S...

She tried to focus, but her eyes were drifting shut despite her desperate attempts to stay awake. Darkness was creeping in again. Tired...so tired. It felt good to quit struggling, to drift away where there was no pain, where no one knew about her past. Hmm... There was a pinprick of light ahead, flickering warmly, beckoning to her. It reminded her of the muraled ceiling in the church. Should she go? It might be nice for a change...

Chapter 33

Ryne trudged up the stairs to Melody's apartment, his thoughts dark and heavy with indecision, regret, and foreboding. It was more than the usual unease caused by a full moon. Young Lycans, in their first year of transformation found the effects impossible to resist, but mature wolves, such as himself, were much more controlled. If circumstances allowed, a wild and raucous celebration of the celestial event was an entertaining way to let off pent up energy. But not this month; at least not for him nor the members of his pack or Kane's. Circumstances could hardly be less conducive for a celebration.

His head throbbed dully and he was thankful for the bottle of aspirin clutched in his hand; he'd almost forgotten to get it, having spent the last half hour aimlessly walking around the neighbourhood, lost in thought. He'd almost done it; almost carried out the Keeping. It was the right thing to do, yet he doubted he'd be able to live with himself afterwards. What he needed was real proof she was turning on them. Possibly she hadn't shared her information with this Aldrich person. He hung onto that faint hope with both hands. If she hadn't told anyone and she was now a Lycan herself, then there might still be hope that this could work out.

The initial steps he'd have to take were easily determined. First, he'd send Lucy off on some complicated errand to ensure she didn't return too soon. Once she was out of the way, he'd wake up Melody, using whatever means necessary, so he could grill her about what she knew and who she'd told.

Tracking down her boss, Aldrich, would be next on his list. He'd have to cross-check what Melody said to ensure she'd been truthful. At this point Ryne knew he couldn't afford to trust her word, too much was at stake. So he'd find Aldrich... Damn, that was his first stumbling block. How was he supposed to track down Aldrich while at the same time keeping Melody under observation?

The cold, logical part of him said to drag her along, regardless of her condition, but not only did his wolf howl in protest at the idea, it wouldn't be easily accomplished. Even in a neighbourhood as seedy as this, a cabbie would question someone carrying an unconscious woman about. If it wasn't for Lucy, he could leave Melody by herself and hope her condition didn't worsen while he was gone, but Lucy was a factor. He couldn't keep her occupied forever and what if Melody transformed in the other woman's presence? Or took a turn for the worse and Lucy called 911? The complications that would involve brought another knot of pain to his already throbbing head.

There was no easy answer and he didn't have the luxury of time. Not only was Kane waiting for his call, but the longer he took figuring out this mess, the farther the information could be spreading.

Continuing to ponder the problem, he approached Melody's apartment, only to come to a sudden halt. Something was wrong. The smell of fresh blood filled the air and an aura of evil oozed down the hallway, as palpable as a living thing.

Cautiously, he traversed the remaining distance to Melody's door, then cocked his head and listened. His keen hearing caught the barely perceptible sound of breathing inside. Slowly he reached out and nudged open the door while testing the air for subtle clues that existed under the scent of blood. The acridness of fear lingered as did the unmistakeable odour of another male. Possessiveness flared inside him and he fought to keep it from clouding his judgement.

Lazily, the door swung open about a foot, squeaking on the partially broken hinges that were evidence of his earlier break-in.

"Hello?"

There was no response.

Muscles tensed and ready to respond, he quickly pushed the door open wider and stepped inside. The door responded to his shove until the presence of something unexpectedly stopped its inward motion. As it bounced back towards him, Ryne turned to see what was impeding its movement. There was nothing at eye level and his gaze immediately dropped to the ground.

There was a heartbeat of silence, then a savage growl erupted from his throat at the sight before him.

"Lucy!"

The woman was lying in a crumpled heap surrounded by a pool of blood. He dropped to his knees to check for a pulse. Pressing trembling fingers to her throat, he detected the faintest hint of a throb. It was weak, but offered some hope.

Grabbing the phone, he dialled 911 while visually searching the apartment for signs of Melody. When the operator came on the line, he rattled off the needed information, hanging up without answering the superfluous questions peppered at him. He had no time to talk.

A swift circuit of the apartment confirmed what he already suspected; Melody was gone.

"Damn! I shouldn't have left." Muttering self-retributions, he returned to kneel at Lucy's side, feeling more ineffectual than he had ever felt before. He was

Alpha, his job was to protect, to nurture and defend, yet despite his desperate wish to do something for his dying friend, he was helpless. As his hands hovered uselessly over her body, he noted a partial message written on the floor; Greys. What could that mean?

He stared unseeing across the room. Greys... The word niggled at his memory, but why? His gaze lighted on Melody's laptop. Greys...Greyson? The name was in one of the files he'd found. Shit! Whoever had attacked Lucy must have something to do with that damned report Melody had written.

A change in Lucy's breathing caught his attention; it had been shallow before but now it was uneven. His heart thumped heavily as he stared at her pale face and blood-soaked blond hair. With trembling fingers, he brushed her cheek, leaning forward and softly calling her name. There was no response and he swore vilely.

It wasn't fair she was hurt and possibly dying. This wasn't her problem. She'd never done anything mean or hurtful. Lucy was warm and giving to a fault, always happy... The backs of his eyes pricked and he blinked rapidly as he recalled her teasing, the way she'd sashay across the room with a tray of drinks in her hand and a smart comment on her lips. Compressing his lips, he wished he could do something for her; that he could stay and hold her hand, but the lives of so many hung in the balance. He needed to find the truth on the off-chance he could halt the Keeping before Kane took the final steps.

Reluctantly, he rose to his feet, moving to the sofa and sniffing where the smell of the unknown male lingered. A scent and a probable name; they were meagre clues. In a city this size the scent would be impossible to track and the name Greyson meant nothing to him. What the hell was he supposed to do now?

The sound of approaching sirens filled the apartment and he knew he had to leave quickly or risk being caught at the scene of the crime. He felt like a cold-blooded bastard leaving Lucy alone, but time was of the essence and his presence would do nothing to help her. After scanning the room one last time, he grabbed the laptop in case there was pertinent information still stored there.

He crouched beside Lucy's body. She was breathing, though barely. "I'm sorry, Lucy. I'm so sorry. You didn't deserve this." He pressed a brief kiss to her cheek and then slipped out of the apartment and down the back stairs.

Melody's scent and that of the unknown male were inextricably blended, so Ryne could only assume she and the man were together. Whether or not she'd gone willingly he didn't know, but right now it was a moot point. The trail disappeared at street level, lost in the myriad of other smells that filled the city's air. Working on his only other clue, he looked up Greyson Inc. Of course, the phone call got him nothing but a recorded message asking what extension he wanted. Taking a stab in the dark, he chose public relations.

The woman he spoke with gave him a nice overview of the company; Greyson Inc. was involved in a wide variety of industries both at home and abroad. It was public-minded, hosted several charitable events and the owner was Anthony Greyson. Mr. Greyson was an extremely private person who never granted personal interviews.

As he hung up, Ryne smirked. It wasn't much, but at least he had a full name to work with. The question remained, what should he do with it? Should he try to find Greyson or try to locate this Aldrich person who was supposedly Melody's boss. And how were the two men connected? A man of Greyson's public stature wouldn't be personally involved in abducting Melody from her apartment so was Aldrich his flunky?

He stared at his surroundings, trying to determine his next step. He was on a busy corner with traffic whizzing past him. Music blared out of open car windows, snatches of conversations barely audible as masses of humanity surged across busy streets. Some were power walking, their minds probably intent on making a deadline while others stopped at a trendy coffee house. He narrowed his eyes.

At one point, Melody had told him how she liked to sit in coffee houses, sipping her favourite brew and surfing the net. Giving a half smile, he decided to use that glimpse of big city life to his benefit. It was time to call in the reserves and spread the work out.

In less than half an hour, Ryne was settled anonymously in the back corner of an upscale coffee shop, exchanging information with Daniel over Melody's laptop. The boy was only too pleased to have a reason to attempt hacking into the Greyson Inc. website. While Daniel did his part, Ryne used the address for Aldrich that he'd copied down earlier to obtain a phone number for the man's office. A phone call there might reveal something useful.

Aldrich wasn't in, but his paralegal was. Using his sexiest voice and some well-placed flattery, he charmed the woman into sharing several interesting pieces of information. Apparently, Aldrich had been scheduled to meet with Melody and had unexpectedly left shortly afterwards. Since then, the lawyer had called in to cancel the rest of the day's appointments. Too coincidental, Ryne decided.

The computer chimed; Daniel had information for him. He bent over the laptop and they began to compare notes, piecing together a plausible theory. Aldrich was

Greyson's lawyer, his name appearing in several court documents as a legal representative. His duties also appeared to include carrying out a variety of odd jobs for the wealthy man. Greyson was an art connoisseur, with a special interest in wolves. Connecting the dots, they concluded Greyson had Ryne's photo and knew—or at least strongly suspected—it wasn't an ordinary wolf. Melody had been hired through Aldrich to do the leg work. But did Melody know why? Right now, Ryne didn't really care. Finding her was more important; she was the key to plugging the information leak.

Aldrich drove to the back of the Greyson estate, keeping a watchful eye out that none of the employees were wandering the grounds or peeking out windows. No one should be about. When Greyson was absent—or incommunicado as he liked to call it—most of the employees were given an extended holiday. Still, Aldrich believed in caution and so he made his way along the twisting driveway at a leisurely speed more suited to checking the general condition of the estate, which was the story he was using if anyone dared question his presence. The unconscious woman on the floor in the back was covered with a light blanket, so prying eyes would have no clear idea as to what he was transporting.

The far back corner of the expansive grounds contained a seldom used shed that had once housed garden tools. Several years back, Aldrich had suggested a newer building be constructed in a more convenient location. The gardener had happily moved to the newer building and no one noticed or seemed to care the old abandoned shed was repaired rather than being torn down. Doors and windows were reinforced and the walls were strengthened from the inside to form an impenetrable structure. While vines and long grass grew around the building, almost hiding it from sight, the interior was fitted with a small generator and wireless communications, all cleverly concealed by old potting tables, benches and tool hooks. The rough wooden floor hid a trapdoor leading to a secondary underground safe room and then to an escape route through the sewers that emptied into a drainage ditch near the edge of the nearby woods. As he'd explained to Greyson, one should always be prepared for the unexpected and a conveniently located hideaway might be useful at some point…such as today.

Ms. Greene had to be kept somewhere. He wasn't stupid enough to take her back to his office or even to his own home; he wanted no link between the two of them. Snatching the woman had been impulsive on his part, but the presence of her feisty friend had thrown him off. Why hadn't the woman cowered and cried in the corner? If she hadn't swung at him when he wasn't expecting it, he wouldn't be in this mess.

No one would expect it to look at him but he knew how to handle himself in a street fight. He'd been born on the proverbial wrong side of the tracks but he was also smart; smart enough to know he'd end up dead if he didn't get out of the hell-hole he grew up in. So he'd studied, got a scholarship and a degree, and then carefully buried his past with a name change and a few forged documents. His present persona was staid, pompous and gave no indication of ever having known what it was like to claw one's way up out of the gutter. He liked the image and intended to keep it.

Unfortunately, he now had to do some quick work to ensure no stain of wrongdoing touched him. The frying pan wielding woman wasn't going to make it. He knew what that much blood meant. It had forced him to scoop up the Greene woman, rather than brow-beating her where she lay. Leaving the scene of the crime before anyone noticed his presence, had taken precedence.

So here he was, thankful Greyson was away and he had a nice safe place to stow this uncooperative person. He was sure he'd be able to get the report from her and have it ready for Greyson's return. She wouldn't hold out against persuasion for long and, once he had the report, she would leave town the same way the former lawyer had. It was regrettable, but in the grand scheme of things, she was expendable.

Parking the car, he double-checked no one was around before carrying the unconscious woman to the shed-turned-safe-room. She murmured as he moved her, lashes fluttering and muscles twitching. Good, she was waking up. He could begin to question her about the report and its contents.

Not for the first time, did he wonder why Greyson was so interested in wolves. It went beyond a mere hobby, more like an obsession and lately he'd latched onto Taylor and the wolf picture he'd taken. Aldrich had spent more than a little time trying to determine his employer's motivation. As yet, he'd been unsuccessful. Perhaps, something in Ms. Greene's report would provide some illumination. He didn't like not knowing what drove the people around him.

He set the woman on one of the low-slung benches. There was no need to use the hidden room below. Once he had the outer door shut, he proceeded to gently slap her cheek.

"Come now, Ms. Greene. Enough of this. You need to wake up and hand over the information on Mr. Taylor."

"Hmm?" Her eyes partially opened and she stared at him blearily before closing them again. "G'way...tired."

"No, Ms. Greene, I will not go away. Not until you cooperate." He grabbed her shoulders and forced her into a sitting position. She opened her eyes completely and frowned at him.

"Mr. Aldrich? What's going on? Where am I?" She rubbed her eyes and looked around the room.

Satisfied she'd stay upright, he released her and stepped back, assuming his usual pose of powerful arrogance.

"Where you are is of no concern. Why you are here should be obvious. You didn't think you could defy Anthony Greyson and not suffer the consequences, did you?"

"Consequences?"

"Yes. Consequences. It was decided you represented too great a flight risk and measures needed to be taken to prevent any such action."

"A flight risk? I'm not some criminal out on bail, you know."

He kept his face bland while inwardly rolling his eyes. Even ill, the woman was feisty. Why couldn't things ever be easy? His weekend away was being wasted arguing with a chit of a girl. "Yes. A flight risk. Your background shows in the past you've frequently moved about the country. We can't have you leaving without fulfilling your obligations first."

"I wasn't planning on leaving. My friend is with me. We're spending the week sightseeing and shopping." She rubbed her head and furrowed her brow. "She'll be wondering where I am. I was supposed to meet her at my apartment for lunch."

"Your friend is not my concern; the report is. Now—"

She interrupted. "Wait! I remember leaving your office. I was walking into the apartment building and someone called my name. It was Ryne. He's here in Chicago!" She looked around as if expecting to see him lurking in the corner.

"Taylor is in town? Now that's interesting news."
Aldrich pulled at his lower lip, puzzling over this latest bit
of information. Maybe he could use it to his advantage.
Mr. Greyson wanted information on Taylor, but would he
be even more pleased to have the man himself? He'd
have to consider that point.

Chapter 34

Smythston, Oregon, USA...

Kane paced the length of his office. Ever since receiving Ryne's call, he'd been on the phone informing other packs to expect an influx of refugees. That had been the easy part. Now he had to decide who lived...and who died. His mind skittered away from the unpalatable point; for the moment he'd concentrate on those who would be sent out first. Of course, the pups would be spared, the expectant and nursing mothers too. Young families, strong males. Each group would need a leader, someone they could turn to during the difficult times ahead as they tried to assimilate into a new pack, but who did he choose?

A few had already stepped forward, volunteering to stay behind. Helen had been one of the first; she was the wife of the late Alpha and, as she'd said, her life was empty without her mate. Kane understood and agreed, but the others... John, his Beta, said he'd remain, but Kane had refused. The man had a mate and a young son. Besides, John was a good leader; he could easily handle being in charge of a group.

The door slammed open behind him and he turned, ready to growl at the unannounced intruder. Instead, his growl turned to a greeting. Elise stood framed in the doorway, the sunlight streaming behind her, casting her in an angelic glow. It was how he saw her; his angel, his mate. She was gentle softness, the comfort he turned to, understanding, giving...

"What the *hell* are you thinking, Kane? I won't do it!" Her uncharacteristic venom shocked him.

"Elise, I'm busy. I don't have time right now."

"Then you can damn well make time. We need to discuss this. You can't just order me to leave!"

It was then he noticed the piece of paper in her hand. She'd been out when he'd gone to tell her to pack for the dispersal. He tightened his jaw. "You're pregnant. Of course you're leaving."

"And I don't get any say in this?"

He was tired, stressed; he didn't need an argument. He stared out the window. "I'm Alpha. You'll do as I say."

"No. I won't go."

A rebuke was ready on his lips when he turned to look at her and noticed the watery shimmer of her eyes. He stepped towards her. "Elise—"

"I won't go, Kane. I won't leave you." She had folded her arms tightly around herself, but her chin was lifted in a sign of defiance.

He walked over to her and gathered her close, resting his chin on top of her head. "Elise, you have to go. Think of our child."

"Growing up in a strange pack, without a father?"

"At least he'll be alive."

"But what kind of life will it be? Another Alpha's son won't be easily accepted. He'll be viewed as an interloper, a potential threat. The others will be wary of him."

Kane rubbed his hand over the slight curve of her waist. "As they should be. My son will be an Alpha one day. He'll lead his own pack. But only if he's given the chance to grow up." He leaned back and touched Elise's chin, forcing her to look at him. "It's your duty to ensure our child survives."

She bit her lip. "I don't want to lose you."

"And you might not. This could turn out to be nothing, but we can't take the chance."

She ran her hands over his chest and he closed his eyes, revelling in the exquisite sensations she could create with the simplest touch. How he'd miss this.

"Kane, can I at least stay until the final call comes? It will be torture, being away from you, not knowing what's happening." Her voice trembled as she spoke and she tightened her fingers on his shirt until they were clutching the material.

He groaned as he opened his eyes and saw tears beginning to slowly drip down her cheeks. He cupped her face, trailing his lips over the damp surface. "Shh, don't cry." How desperately he wanted to tell her everything would be all right, that there was no need for tears, but it would be a lie. His heart ached just as hers did; the very idea of being separated from her eating away at the core of his being. He pressed his mouth to hers, offering his comfort and his love, all the while hoping against hope Ryne was making progress.

Chicago, Illinois, USA...

It was a stab in the dark, but something had told Ryne to head to Greyson's estate if he wanted to find Melody and her boss. The city was too big to search, so following his instincts seemed as good a course of action as any. He informed Bryan of his plans and reaffirmed the protocols to follow should he fail to check back in. Daniel was to continue to search for information on Greyson and Aldrich; the packs needed to know everything they could about the men they were up against.

Satisfied he'd done all he could, Ryne hailed a taxi and gave the address for Greyson's estate.

As he sat in the back, he stared unseeingly out the window. The driver wove in and out of traffic, the vehicle swaying from side to side or jerking forward when brakes were suddenly applied; shouts of annoyance and coarsely worded threats were tossed between drivers. Lost in thought, he let it all wash over him.

His wolf desperately needed to find Melody; to know she was safe. The thought of her alone, going through the change with no warning, no one to comfort or explain, ate away at his gut. Would her body and her mind accept what was happening or would she fight against the inevitable? What if she refused to accept it? Or if the effects of the full moon forced her body to transform before it was ready? Nadia said not everyone survived.

Yet, did it matter? If she knew of the secret, if she'd already spread the word, then she was as good as dead anyway. Wasn't it better to die from a rejected transformation than from his hand? Could he actually look her in the eye and deliver a fatal blow?

He was Alpha. He knew his duty and yet... Images of Melody danced before him. Her big, brown eyes and long lashes, the way she'd lift her chin and narrow her eyes before delivering some acerbic comment. Her quirky humour, her knack for getting into trouble. The wonder in her eyes as he pointed out the intricacies of nature. The way she looked under him, lost in the throes of passion.

He tightened his lips. The throes of passion; there hadn't been enough of that. Twice he'd taken her; both times had been hurried, unexpected. How he longed to have the chance for a slow drawn-out mating. A chance to explore every inch of her body, to taste her, to have her crying out for the relief only he could give. He'd sink his teeth into her...

No. A blood-bond was out of the question. He didn't mate; he had sex. Mating implied something permanent and he couldn't see a city-dwelling, coffee swilling reporter settling down in Stump River. Not that he planned on asking her to, of course.

He shifted in his seat knowing he was lying to himself. The fear that had gripped him since finding Lucy was more than just fear of the Keeping. It was fear for Melody, for her well-being. Admitting the truth to himself was probably a mistake though; it would only make things harder in the end.

Sighing heavily, he noted his surroundings. They'd left the city centre some time ago. Houses were spread farther apart and situated on expansive lawns. He checked a road sign as they drove past; almost there. A wooded area was coming up to the right. It seemed as good a place as any. He signalled for the driver to pull over.

"This isn't the address you wanted." The driver glanced back at him through the rear-view mirror. "Greyson estate is five miles up the road. I've driven past it before, but never gone through the gates. Apparently, it's real showy. You know the guy?"

Ryne grunted in a non-committal way and handed over some money, choosing to ignore the man's question.

"Right. None of my business. I'm just paid to drive." The man tucked the money away and shrugged. Once Ryne was out of the vehicle, he drove off without a backward glance.

Ryne stepped into the woods and, hidden from view, changed into his wolf form.

His padded feet made minimal noise as he ran through the small grouping of trees that constituted a 'woods' in city terms. By Stump River standards it was barely worth mentioning, but nonetheless, he was thankful for the cover it provided. Daniel's research showed the Greyson estate was walled on three sides; the fourth was comprised of this long narrow strip of trees. Some type of alarm or motion sensor was likely installed along the perimeter, but his animal form should be able to slip through undetected.

The trees were beginning to thin when his nose picked up a familiar scent. Melody was near. Slowing his pace, he pinpointed the exact direction from which the scent was coming, an abandoned shed almost invisible due to being covered in vines and surrounded by overgrown shrubbery. She wasn't alone though. The stench of the male he'd scented in her apartment was also present. A low growl rumbled up from his chest.

We will exact our revenge now; revenge for Lucy, for Melody. His wolf moved into hunting mode, stealthily approaching the small building, carefully gliding from shadow to shadow. His muscles were tensed and ready for action. Every sense was alert, searching for signs of movement, listening for clues as to what might be happening inside.

At first, the voices were indistinct. One was lower pitched; obviously the hated unknown male. The other was softer, hesitant, confused. Melody! At least she was awake. The knowledge provided some small degree of comfort.

He returned to his human form and, pressing his body against the wall, carefully peeked inside through a dirty window. Melody was sitting on a bench facing an elegantly dressed man. Ryne focused on the conversation, trying to determine what was going on.

"Come now, Ms. Greene. Your scruples are going to get you in trouble. Life isn't simply black or white. Situations such as this are so ambiguous. I totally understand how you might feel some form of misplaced loyalty to Mr. Taylor, but think about it. He reneged on your agreement, forcing you into this untenable circumstance. There is no obligation on your part to uphold any verbal agreement you had with him. We can easily avoid further unpleasantness, if you'd simply be reasonable." The man—whether it was Aldrich, Greyson or some other player Ryne had yet to encounter—was negligently leaning against a table.

Ryne noted the whiteness of Melody's knuckles as she held onto the edge of the bench. He surmised she was still feeling ill, still fighting the effects of the approaching full moon and the genetic changes taking place inside her. He wished he was beside her, offering comfort, explaining the strange feelings and thoughts that were no doubt going through her. He watched as she shook her head before speaking.

"This doesn't make any sense to me. Ryne Taylor is a photographer. No one goes to these lengths to get a report on a guy who takes pictures."

"As I've told you before, it isn't your place to ask questions." The man lifted his chin and stared down his nose at her, as if daring her to make another query.

"Sorry. Asking questions is part of my job. There's something strange about this. All along I thought it was eccentricity, but now, you've basically kidnapped me."

"Kidnapped? That could be considered slanderous, Ms. Greene. You have no proof you've been kidnapped. For the past several hours, you've been delirious with fever. This is merely a safe place to stay until your condition can be properly assessed. Who knows? You might be contagious with some strange disease you picked up in the wilds of Stump River. You don't want to risk infecting an unsuspecting public now, do you?"

Melody looked around. "A safe place? In a garden shed? Come on, Mr. Aldrich. Do you really expect me to believe that?"

From his position outside, Ryne nodded, noting the name Melody had used. So this was the mysterious Aldrich she had called every day. She definitely didn't appear to be in league with him at this point.

Back inside the building, Aldrich shrugged. "It was convenient."

Ryne weighed his options. He could easily slip into the shed in his wolf form and attack the man, who he now knew was Aldrich. The problem was, he wasn't sure what he was dealing with. From what she'd said, Melody didn't know what she'd stumbled into, unless she was lying; at this distance, he couldn't tell for sure. Aldrich appeared to know the real story; he just needed the report to confirm his facts. And then there was the mysterious and wealthy Mr. Greyson. Ryne knew in his gut the supposed art collector had it all figured out. The question was, how to get to him?

A sound from inside drew his attention. Melody was groaning and clutching her stomach. His wolf leapt inside him, and before he realized what he was doing, he was rounding the corner and pushing open the door of the shed. The sound of his arrival drew the attention of the other two.

"Ryne!" Melody looked up, pain etched on her face.

"Mr. Taylor? How kind of you to stop by." Damn, but Aldrich was fast. Ryne chastised himself as he saw the gun now pointed at his chest. In the brief second he'd used to look at Melody, the other man had drawn the weapon. Shit! His wolf's attachment to Melody was going to be his downfall, he just knew it.

Adopting his most annoyingly arrogant manner, Ryne leaned against the door frame and sneered. "Yeah. This looked like such a nice little place; I just had to see inside." He kept a bland expression on his face as he tried to ignore the gun. All too well, he remembered the burning pain of the last bullet wound he'd sustained. At this close a range, the shot could be lethal and he'd be unable to help Melody. Best not to irritate Aldrich too much.

"That was an ineffectual attempt at humour, Mr. Taylor."

"Yeah? Well, what did you expect? I'm a photographer, not a comedian." He shrugged and looked casually around the room, slowly shifting closer to Melody under the guise of checking out the atmosphere of the shed. "You know this place could use some fixing up. A few of my pictures on the wall could go a long way towards improving the atmosphere of this room."

"Ah, yes. A photographer. I wonder how an *ordinary* photographer managed to follow me here. I was very careful." Aldrich narrowed his eyes, seeming to consider this new turn of events.

Ryne watched as the man ran his finger back and forth over the trigger of the gun, giving an imperceptible sigh of relief when the movement eventually stopped and the lawyer shrugged.

"At this point, how you found this place is irrelevant. Though I will figure it out eventually; we can't have any loose ends now, can we?" What might have been a smile flickered over the man's face. "Your wolf picture has been a source of fascination for my client, Mr. Greyson. Would you care to speculate why?"

"Not really." Ryne watched as Aldrich's finger flexed on the trigger again. The man was not quite as calm as he would have others believe.

"Mr. Taylor—"

A sudden scream from Melody cut him off. Both men turned to stare as she crumpled to the ground, her face twisted as if she were in agony. The air around her shimmered like heat rising from hot pavement. Her form wavered in and out of focus and for a brief moment a wolf appeared in her place before shifting out of focus and returning to that of a young woman.

"Melody!" Heedless of the gun-wielding man, Ryne rushed across the room and gathered her shivering body in his arms. Beads of sweat trickled down her face as she panted, barely conscious, while spasms wracked her body. Instinctively, she curled into a ball, wrapping her arms around her middle. He could only imagine the pain she was experiencing as her ill-prepared body tried to readjust to its changing form.

"What...?" Aldrich blinked, then his lips twisted into a self-satisfied smile. "Well, well, well. Now, this does make things interesting doesn't it?" He rubbed his chin. "Might I speculate, Mr. Taylor, the issue at hand is not so much photographing wolves as it is...*were*wolves?"

"I have no idea what you're talking about." Ryne smoothed his hand over Melody's trembling form, resisting the automatic urge to correct the man's terminology from werewolf to Lycan. "There are no such things as werewolves."

"Mr. Taylor, I am neither blind, stupid, nor subject to hallucinations. As a matter of fact, something of this sort was actually one of my theories when considering Mr. Greyson's avid interest in wolves, but I passed it off as too fantastical for serious consideration. I now see I need to revise my thinking."

Ryne gave no outward reaction to Aldrich's words, instead slowly easing Melody to the floor. If Aldrich was busy speculating, then maybe he could...

"Ah, ah, ah! I know how your mind is working, Mr. Taylor. Lunging for this gun would be a serious mistake, especially since we have so much to discuss." The man leaned back against the old potting table. "Now, let me see if I can figure this out. You took a picture of a werewolf and Mr. Greyson somehow realized this. Did you know your subject wasn't what it appeared to be?"

Ryne quirked his brow and snorted derisively. "I'm a nature photographer, not some guy into Hollywood special effects, or an eccentric old man on the edge of senility."

"Mr. Greyson will be seriously offended when he hears of your disrespect." Aldrich mocked.

"I'm trembling with fear."

"And so you should be. My employer is not a man to be taken lightly. But I digress." Aldrich gave a tight smile before continuing. "Mr. Greyson is immensely curious as to where you took that picture. Now, I can see why. If we find the location, our chances of capturing a real live werewolf increase astronomically. The money that would be paid for such a specimen is mind-boggling."

Ryne forced himself to not flinch or tighten his fists, despite the fury raging inside him. The man was talking as if his people were little more than animals to be bought and sold.

"One thing has me puzzled though, is how Ms. Greene fits into all of this. She's obviously some form of werewolf herself. Why didn't Mr. Greyson use her? He chose her specifically for the job, so he must have had some knowledge of her background." Aldrich stared at Melody with a furrowed brow. When he continued, he seemed to be talking to himself. "This requires further analysis before I make my next move. It's no longer an issue of obtaining a report to keep Mr. Greyson happy. It's a question of whether or not I tell him about what I've discovered. Working for Mr. Greyson has opened a number of doors for me, but he also likes to believe he has me on a leash. With Ms. Greene under my control, I'll be able to break free." He focused his attention on Ryne. "Tell me, does she do this changing thing often? Is it under control?"

Clenching his jaw, Ryne made no reply.

"Nothing to say? Don't you know the answers? Or possibly, you're in shock yourself." Aldrich paused and snapped his fingers, his eyes widening as if he suddenly came upon an amazing discovery. "That's it, isn't it? You didn't know your girlfriend was an animal. I must say, you seem very calm about the fact." A speculative look came over the man's face. "Tell me, did you have sex with her?"

A growl threatened to escape Ryne's chest as Aldrich's gaze slowly went over Melody as if stripping her naked. How he wanted to wipe the leering expression off the lawyer's face. Only the knowledge that any reaction on his part might further endanger the packs, kept him from reacting.

"Tell me, Taylor, what's it really like...fucking a bitch?"

Anger roiled in Ryne's stomach and he barely held his tongue. He knew the man was trying to get a rise out of him in the hopes he'd reveal something in the heat of anger.

Aldrich stepped closer and laughed when Ryne automatically shifted so he was in front of Melody. "Don't worry. I have no plans for her yet. Though it might be an interesting experience."

The civilized veneer slipped from the man's face and he now reminded Ryne of some of the more unsavoury people his stepfather had associated with; thugs and petty criminals, 'friends' who would stab you in the back if the price were right. It would appear there might be more to Aldrich than met the eye. Ryne stored the information away; it paid to know your enemy.

Aldrich played with the trigger of the gun again, seeming to relish having someone under his power. His dark eyes narrowed as if gauging the response to his comments, looking for a reaction, a sign of fear.

Ryne wasn't about to give the man the satisfaction and forcibly relaxed his muscles, assuming a careless pose. His forearm rested on his bent knee and he blinked at the man slowly, conveying the attitude he was unimpressed with the other man's posturing and rhetoric. "Are you through? This is really getting tedious."

For a moment Aldrich's face began to flush at the insult and Ryne cursed himself for not keeping his mouth shut. Then the man's expression cleared and the smooth cultivated tones of the successful lawyer reappeared. "I see you're going to be difficult. Luckily time is on my side. Mr. Greyson won't be back for a while, so I'll be able to leave you two here to think things over. Possibly when I return, you'll be feeling more cooperative. Hand over your cell phone." He waited with his hand extended and the gun at the ready. When Ryne finally complied, Aldrich nodded and left, bolting the door behind him.

.

Chapter 35

"Aldrich! Is that you? Dammit man, what the hell are you doing on my property?" The voice of Anthony Greyson boomed across the lawn, startling the lawyer who had just exited the supposedly abandoned hut at the rear of the estate. To give the lawyer his due, he composed himself quickly but Greyson had the satisfaction of knowing he'd caught the man off guard. His amusement faded though, as he pondered what possible excuse Aldrich might have for being where he shouldn't be.

"Mr. Greyson, sir! I'm surprised to see you. I thought you'd be gone for a few more days."

"I never said I was gone. Merely that I was incommunicado. There's a difference, Leon. As a lawyer, you should know that."

"I do, sir. It's just the reports stated—"

"I know all about your 'eyes and ears' that report my movements to you. But they only see and hear what I wish. I left, and as soon as they reported me gone, I returned." The older man rocked back on his heels, secretly enjoying the flabbergasted look passing over the other man's face before it disappeared behind a carefully schooled expression. Greyson loved playing mind games with those around him; people thought they could pull the wool over his eyes, that he was an old man in his dotage. Ha! He was sharper now than he'd ever been.

"I beg your pardon, sir. I never meant—"

"Don't start boot-licking now, Aldrich. You watch me. I watch you. Neither of us got where we are today without hedging our bets. It's smart business, even if it is damned impertinent of you."

Aldrich nodded, but Greyson noted how the man's eyes were assessing him. It appeared Leon might be getting too comfortable in his role, maybe even considering usurping his master. Definitely time to consider a little shake up. He gave the lawyer a steely look. "Remember I sign the paycheck you're so fond of, and no matter what you think you know about me, I know even more about you. If I wanted to make you squirm like a worm on a hook, I could."

The lawyer didn't even so much as blink, but Greyson was sure Aldrich's busy mind was wondering exactly how much his employer really knew about certain past indiscretions. Good, let him sweat. People got too damned complacent; they needed to be kept on their toes.

"A worm on a hook, sir? Not a pretty picture. I'll certainly do my best to avoid inciting such a circumstance."

Greyson guffawed before turning serious. "Your attempts at humour are pathetic, but even so, you amuse me. Now, why are you here? I believe my orders were quite specific. All non-essential staff were to be off the estate for five days. Last time I looked, you weren't essential to the running of this place. Explain yourself."

"I was checking on the state of the safe room. Ensuring it was up to date and in running order in case you ever need it, Mr. Greyson."

"Humph." He narrowed his eyes and stared at the man he sometimes called friend. In his life, friend and foe were often two sides of the same coin. Which side was Aldrich right now? He glanced towards the hut. Did his peripheral vision catch Aldrich nervously twitching his fingers or was it merely a shadow from the leafy branches overhead? Hmm... "All right. It's a good enough reason. Damned efficient of you. But next time I say to stay away, I mean it."

Aldrich bobbed his head. "Will you be incommunicado for a few more days, sir?"

Greyson stared past the lawyer towards the main house. He might be getting old but his eyesight was keen enough to pick out the window in the upper right-hand corner of the west wing. There was a flicker of movement there—a flash of white—but it was enough to let him know he needed to get moving. He drew his gaze back to the lawyer. "That's right. No contact. And don't you dare let on to anyone I'm here. You won't like the consequences, if I discover this information has become public knowledge. Now clear out."

"Of course, sir. I do, however, need to make a few adjustments to some of the equipment in the safe room. It will cause less suspicion if I do it now, while almost everyone is away."

He studied the lawyer. Something was off, but what? Movement in the upper window of the main house drew his attention again. Damn! There was no time for this. "All right. But I want you gone by sunset. Understood?"

"Perfectly." Aldrich nodded serenely as he pulled open the car door. "I'll go get what I need and return in about an hour. You'll never even know I was here."

"Make sure of it." Greyson watched Aldrich get in his car and drive away at a sedate pace. Once the car was out of sight, he turned and studied the small camouflaged hut that housed his secret safe room. Leon was checking the equipment and would be back to fix it. Uh-huh. He rubbed his chin, weighing his options before heading back to the house at a brisk pace. Aldrich might be up to something but it would have to take a back seat to the more pressing matters awaiting him at the main house.

Ryne stepped back from the door, where he'd been eavesdropping on the conversation outside. The walls appeared to be reinforced and if it hadn't been for his keener than normal hearing, he'd never have been able to make out what had been said by the men standing some several feet away. It would seem Aldrich might be planning on double-crossing Greyson, since no mention of Melody or himself had been made. A falling out among the enemy could work to his advantage.

He turned to check on Melody. She was resting, her eyes closed, exhausted from the stress and pain of a partial transformation. If she'd been a full-blooded Lycan, the first change would have been slightly uncomfortable but not painful. In fact, once one got used to it, transforming was actually a pleasant feeling of release, rather like a small orgasm. Unfortunately, Melody's body wasn't ready for the experience. Some cells were changing, others weren't. She likely felt as if she was being torn in two.

Not knowing what else to do, he began circling the room, hating the feeling of being trapped. His wolf required space and freedom; confinement went against his very nature. Testing the window, the door and the walls, he began looking for any weakness in the structure. Using his elbow, he tried to shatter the glass in the window but it had to be some form of bullet proof or shock resistant substance since it didn't even crack. Similarly, the door and walls resisted his attempts to break them down; the only thing he managed to do was bend the door handle out of shape and give himself a sore shoulder. A frustrated growl rumbled up from his chest. Yep, this was definitely a safe room and, while it was designed to keep people out, it also served to keep people in.

He rubbed his aching joint and sat down on the floor next to Melody, brushing her hair from her forehead.

Her breathing was even; the sleep was natural rather than the unconscious state she'd been in when he left her apartment. How many hours ago was that? He glanced at his watch, having lost track of time. Okay, he had an hour before needing to check in with Bryan. It was cutting it close, but there was still time so that was one positive. Unfortunately, after that everything else went straight to hell.

Kane was waiting for his call. His brother would be anxious, not wanting to disperse the pack but not willing to risk their safety by waiting too long. Ryne ground his teeth and cursed Aldrich for taking his phone. The dispersal was one thing; if it happened, the members could be called back, but how long would Kane wait before issuing the order to destroy the remaining pack? A knot formed in Ryne's gut as he contemplated what would happen if he didn't make that call in the next few hours.

Leaning his head against the wall, he inhaled deeply and forced himself to be calm and logical as he puzzled over who knew what and the implications of each piece of knowledge. How many people did he need to find and silence? Together Aldrich, Greyson and Melody each had possession of a plethora of truths, half-truths and misconceptions. Out of the three, Melody knew the most; she just wasn't aware of it yet. In a way, it made her the most dangerous to the safety of his kind. How she reacted when the pieces of the puzzle fell together would determine her fate.

Beside him, Melody stirred and pressed closer to him. The simple gesture made his heart beat faster. In her sleep she trusted him, but how she would feel once she was awake might be a different story. When she'd first seen him at her apartment building, she hadn't been pleased, no doubt still feeling the sting of their parting words. And, even though she called out his name when he had charged into this room, it was probably due more to surprise than any actual joy at his presence.

Loathe to disturb her, but knowing they had an hour at best before Aldrich returned, he gently shook her awake. He needed to figure out if she was really an innocent in all of this, explain about the transformation, formulate a plan to get out of here in one piece and then deal with those who knew more than they should.

"Melody? You have to wake up. We need to talk."

"Hmm? Ryne?" She blinked at him, her brow slowly furrowing as awareness returned.

He could tell by the expression on her face the moment she realized where she was.

Pushing herself upright, she brushed her hair from her face and looked around at her surroundings. "What the hell is going on? Why are you here? And why am I here?"

He helped her sit up, steadying her until she found her balance. "It's complicated."

"Complicated?" She glowered at him. "And, why do I suspect the complications are mostly your fault?"

Her tone of voice irritated him and he snapped back at her. "Strictly speaking, your presence is what started everything."

"Me? I didn't do anything!"

"You kept insisting on interviewing me."

"So? It's a perfectly reasonable request!"

"Which I chose to decline. You should have just gone away." He chose to take a hard line with her. If he pushed enough, he might get to the truth behind her presence in Stump River and Smythston.

"Gone away! After chasing you half way across the continent? I don't think so! There was too much money involved."

He pounced on her statement. "So now we have your real motive. You said the interview was for a course you were taking. That you were interested in my art. But that's not the whole truth, is it? You're in this with Aldrich!"

Melody huffed and looked away.

He pressed his advantage. "I'm right, aren't I? That's why you won't look at me. You lied about the interview. What's the real reason you were trying to find me?" He grabbed her shoulders, forcing her to face him.

She compressed her lips before sighing and giving in. "All right. I'll tell you, especially since it appears Aldrich was lying to me or has gone off his rocker or something."

He settled back, keeping his eyes carefully trained on her so he could gauge the truth of what she said.

"This rich guy named Greyson wants information on you. I was never told exactly why; they hinted it might be for an article in an art magazine and he was this big collector who liked your work. Anyway, Aldrich was in charge of interviewing people for the job and managed to get hold of my name. I was surprised I was hired because he didn't seem to like me, and I'm still a student. But for whatever reason, I was offered the job. It paid a small fortune; enough I could quit working and go back to school full time, so I took the assignment."

Ryne narrowed his eyes. It sounded too simple. "If that's the case, why didn't you tell me?"

"Because secrecy was one of the conditions of the job." She shook her head. "I know, I know; it sounds suspicious, and I did wonder, but the money was too good to pass up. And then, when you didn't want an interview, Aldrich said Greyson would sue me for the return of all the money, even what I'd already spent tracking you down." Melody rubbed her hands up and down her arms as she stared about the small room. "It was just an interview with a nature photographer, for heaven's sake. I figured it was easy money." She snorted inelegantly. "Now look at the mess I'm in!"

"Yeah." He rubbed the back of his neck. "In normal circumstances, an interview with a nature photographer would be a simple job." She was speaking the truth so at least part of his concerns had been dealt with. Now came the hard part; breaking the news to her about Lycans.

Melody fixed her eyes on him, a speculative look on her face. "But you're not a simple photographer, are you Ryne?

"Not exactly."

"Then what? Do you smuggle drugs in the picture frames? Are you in debt to the mob? Wanted for murder? Robbing a bank?"

"No. Nothing illegal."

"Then what?"

"Well..." He tried to think of any easy way to tell her, but knew they didn't have time to beat around the bush. "I'm a Lycan."

She blinked at him then gave a distinctly un-amused laugh. "Right and so am I. And when there's a full moon, I get all furry and start howling." She rolled her eyes. "Come on, Ryne. Give me a break. I feel like crap and I'm not in the mood for stupid stories."

"I'm not joking. I really am a Lycan and so are you. Well, technically you're only partially a Lycan since you're still undergoing cellular changes, but eventually you will be."

She got a funny look on her face and then began to ease away from him. "You actually believe those books I saw in your house, don't you? And I bet you're a card-carrying member of that Lycan website I came across, too."

"We don't really carry cards, but yes, my name's on the registry."

She threw her hands up in the air. "Oh, this is just great. I'm locked in a room with a wannabe wolf-boy and some psycho lawyer is trying to 'persuade' me to hand over a report about said wolf-boy. It's like the whole world has gone insane."

"Stop with the wolf-boy crap and get rid of the attitude." His patience wearing thin. It had never been one of his strong points, and Melody's mocking was stretching it to the limits. "This situation is serious. A lot of lives are at stake, not just ours, and we don't have much time before fucking Aldrich returns. There are Lycans. I'm one. You are becoming one and Aldrich wants the report so he can find other packs and do who knows what to them."

His tone of voice caught her attention and she sobered. "You really believe this stuff, don't you?"

"Not only do I believe it, I live it, every day. And soon you will, too." He saw her open her mouth to comment but headed her off with stern words. "Let's cut to the chase. I'll do a little demo. You will not scream or pass out or do anything else clichéd. You will sit, watch and then we'll discuss the situation in a calm, rational manner. Got it?"

She nodded and he couldn't help but allow a fleeting smile at the way she shut up and listened when he went into Alpha mode. Damn, that made for a nice change.

Stepping back, he brought forth his wolf. Around him, the air seemed to shimmer, his vision temporarily blurred, then just as quickly, it cleared and he was looking up at Melody's gaping face. He couldn't help but give a delighted yip and wag of his tail at being able to rub her face in her disbelief. However, the situation was too serious to spend time on such childish actions. Quickly, he transformed back and sat back down.

"Wow."

He raised his eyebrows at her bland response and waited expectantly for further comment. When none came, he frowned. "That's it? Just 'wow'? No questions? No 'how'd you do that?' No one sees their first Lycan transformation and just accepts it!"

"Oh, I have questions. Lots and lots of questions. Like, what kind of drug did you or Aldrich slip me? And why? I mean, sure you might have this fantasy life thing about Lycans but why do you have to drag me into it?"

He growled in frustration. "You weren't drugged. You really did see me change into a wolf and as for why I'm dragging you into this...well...you're becoming a Lycan, too."

"Right." She snorted. Her disbelief irritated him no end.

"Think about it! You've been inexplicably ill for the past few days—"

"It's not inexplicable. It's from the cut on my arm."

"The cut was part of it, but didn't you notice how quickly it healed? And haven't you wondered why, if the cut is gone, your arm continues to be sensitive? And what about the fevers that come and go? Or what about this? Have you been hearing voices in your head?"

That one got to her. She paled at the mention of voices. So her wolf had been awakening and trying to make itself known and she probably thought she was losing her mind. Little wonder she was in denial right now.

The thought of her distress softened his attitude towards her. He inched closer and spoke softly. "It was an accident. A freaky accident that mixed my blood with yours and awakened some hidden Lycan genes in your system."

"I don't have Lycan genes!"

The anger in her tone let him know he might be getting through to her. "I beg to differ. Somewhere in your family tree there must be a Lycan; maybe a parent or a grandparent."

Melody started to speak but then paused, her brow wrinkling. Good, at least she wasn't totally rejecting the idea.

He pressed his advantage. "The genes might have stayed dormant for your entire life and you would have shown only trace characteristics if you hadn't become involved with me."

"Trace characteristics?" She spoke distractedly and Ryne wasn't really sure how much she was taking in, or if she was in shock and operating on autopilot. He suspected the latter. Whichever it was, he didn't have time to waste and ploughed onward delivering even more information.

"Trace characteristics include better than normal eyesight, acute hearing and sensitivity to smells. A strong immune system. I bet you were hardly ever sick as a child and never visited the doctor." He watched carefully and caught her slight flinch. "There's also a tendency to instinctively submit to alpha personalities even when you don't want to. Did you know you tilt your head to the side exposing your throat when I'm upset with you?"

She gave a short laugh, shook her head and rubbed her temples with her fingers. "This is so weird. I can't believe I'm having this conversation. I am awake, aren't I? It's not another dream, is it? Because sometimes I have these really real dreams. There was this one about wolves and then the wolf became a man and..." She stopped and blushed.

Ryne knew exactly what dream she was talking about and tried hard to keep a straight face. He didn't feel this was the time for confessions of that nature. "We're awake. It's not a dream. You haven't been drugged. Now listen while I explain..."

Chapter 36

"Cassandra! I told you to stay away from the windows. It's still light out and the sunshine could bring on another migraine." Greyson stood in the doorway, looking at the young woman who occupied the upper room in the west wing of his mansion. Her dark hair was pulled back in a long braid, revealing the paleness of her skin and the dark shadows under her eyes. He tried to not let his worry show.

"I'm sorry, Uncle. It's just such a sunny day, I thought it would be nice to go outside." She obediently moved back and let the heavy velvet curtains fall shut.

Greyson stepped into the room and gently took her by the elbow, leading her back to bed. "In a few more days, when the danger of another migraine has passed, you can go outside. Did you take your medication? I'm surprised to see you awake."

She looked up at him with a tentative smile. "I forgot."

He cupped her cheek, noting the stark difference between his gnarled hand and her soft youthful skin. She was such a beauty, just like her mother. "You know what the doctor said. Prevention is the key. It's a monthly treatment; five days of pills and then you're fine for the rest of the month."

Cassandra reached out and squeezed his hand before stepping away. "I know. It's just...maybe I should see another doctor."

"Doctor Friedrich is the finest physician money can buy. You know what he told you. Every girl's body is different. This is how you react to the monthly changes you experience."

"All right, Uncle! Stop, please stop." Her face was flushed with embarrassment. "I'll take the darn pill. Anything to keep from having this conversation again."

"Cassandra, I've known you since you were a baby."

"But I'm not a baby anymore. And my bodily functions aren't a subject I wish to discuss with you."

Greyson chuckled. "Of course. At seventeen, you're so very, very old."

"Almost eighteen."

"I stand corrected." He kept his voice even, resisting the urge to chuckle. Ah, the young. Always wishing to be older.

"Old enough to want some privacy in certain areas." She folded her arms and pouted.

"And you shall have it, once you take your pill and get back into bed." Greyson kept his voice gentle, but firm. For a moment, she stared at him defiantly and he noted how the green in her eyes darkened when she was upset. Seconds ticked by before she looked away, sighing.

"One of these days..." She muttered under her breath and she went to the bedside table, swallowing the disputed medication.

He nodded in satisfaction. "I'll be back to check on you later. Rest, like you're supposed to."

"That's all I can do when I'm on these pills. They make me so sleepy and I have the strangest dreams."

"An unfortunate side effect, but worth the benefits achieved."

Cassandra stuck her tongue out at him, but quickly changing the childish reaction to a grin, she hopped into bed and picked up a book.

Greyson closed the door and rested his palm on the handle while shaking his head. She was a minx, but the light of his life. Who would have thought a crusty old man such as himself would have been blessed with the care of one such as her? He smiled reminiscently, thinking of the joy she'd brought him over the years.

At first, he'd been unsure of how to handle the tot, but with the help of a few trusted employees, he'd muddled through. He made sure Cassandra had the finest of everything; clothing, private tutors, individualized lessons for sports and art, vacations around the world. And all along, he'd managed to keep her out of the public eye. Only a few hand-picked employees interacted with her; she always travelled separately from him. It had worked perfectly until two years ago. Then, as she approached adulthood, he found he needed to have a closer hand in her supervision. Unfortunately, even this situation wouldn't work for much longer and then what?

He wanted her to remain an innocent, naive little girl as long as possible, but she was tugging at the reins, becoming headstrong, questioning. Even taking her medication was becoming a source of friction. He grimaced. The nurse should have been watching her more closely. Who knows what could happen if Cassandra missed a dose?

Letting go of the handle, he strode down the hallway in search of the nurse. He'd have to remind the woman if she didn't carry out her duties any better than this, then she might have to be...dismissed.

Cassandra listened to her uncle's retreating footsteps and then grinned. She reached into her mouth and pulled the hated pill out from its location between her cheek and gum. There was a nasty taste in her mouth since it had partially dissolved. Rats! Her plans to make it through the cycle un-medicated were going sadly awry.

The nurse her uncle hired never left the room until at least half an hour after each pill was taken. Obviously, the woman was suspicious and wanted to ensure that even if her charge did manage to keep from swallowing the pill, it would dissolve in her mouth. It was only by surreptitiously resetting the clocks and accidentally breaking the woman's watch, that Cassie had managed to get her out of the room, the nurse believing there was an hour before medication time. She'd planned on flushing the pill down the toilet and then claiming she'd taken it on her own when the nurse returned. Unfortunately, her uncle had appeared first and Cassie had never been able to lie to the man. Well, at least she wouldn't be quite as muzzy headed as usual.

Not for the first time did she wonder about the mysterious migraines everyone insisted she had. Honestly, she couldn't recall being sick the first time it happened, but apparently she had been, for suddenly her uncle had her meeting with a doctor who talked in medical babble, gave her a few cursory pokes and prods and then issued instructions for monthly treatments.

She didn't have many friends and there was really no one to talk to about the situation, but her research on the internet led her to believe something wasn't normal. She'd started her monthly cycles quite late for modern females, around her sixteenth birthday. And strangely enough, they only occurred every three months, with only minor spotting in between. Migraines could accompany menstruation, but the medications she took made her almost comatose, too groggy to do anything and strangely unaware of what was going on around her.

Dr. Friedrich, in her estimation, wasn't much of a doctor either. He hadn't really examined her. Not that she wanted him to—the man gave her the creeps—but looking in her eyes and ears and poking her stomach through her clothing really couldn't give him much of an idea as to her internal functions.

Cassie knew her uncle loved her and spared no expense when it came to her care, but something wasn't right and she was determined to figure out what it was. Her first step was supposed to be going without her medication, but so far that wasn't working. At least she'd managed to avoid most of this dose. Hopefully, she'd be able to figure out a way to miss the next one, too.

Cocking her head to the side, she listened carefully. Good. No one was coming. She climbed out of bed and made her way to the window. Carefully easing the curtain aside, she took a peek. What was happening at the small hut near the back of the property? Earlier in the day, a car had been there and her uncle's lawyer had carried something inside. Then her uncle had talked to Mr. Aldrich for a while and the man had left, leaving the bundle behind. Her curiosity was piqued and she longed to sneak out and see what was going on.

She chuckled, thinking about how her spying abilities had served her in the past. Uncle tried to keep her sheltered from the world and his life, but she knew more than he suspected. For example, she knew about Mr. Aldrich even though Mr. Aldrich knew nothing of her. She'd spied on several of their meetings, not really understanding what was going on, but enjoying the trick she was playing on them. As of late, her spying wasn't so much a game as a desire for knowledge. There was a mystery surrounding her very existence and she was determined to find out what it was.

Melody had listened in stunned disbelief as Ryne spouted information about werewolves...er...Lycans. The whole idea of mixing body fluids and genetic heritage was preposterous. Her father, whoever and wherever he might be, wasn't a Lycan. Her mother and grandparents weren't either. Nor was she turning into one. Yet, Ryne sounded so sincere and there was the weird hallucination she'd just had where he'd changed into a wolf.

The whole situation made her head spin, and if he said another word on the topic, she was sure she'd scream. She leaned her head back against the wall. "Ryne, stop it. Please. I can't take any more of this."

Immediately he stopped the pacing around the room he'd been doing while lecturing her. Sitting beside her, he felt her forehead. "You're getting fevered again."

"Yeah. This infection or flu or whatever—"

"I already told you what it is. Your body is undergoing changes at the cellular level." He sounded almost angry with her for not believing his tall tale.

She licked her lips, suddenly too tired to argue. "Sure. Whatever. I hurt. My head is swimming. Even my vision is blurring."

Ryne suddenly gripped her shoulders and made her sit up straight. "Blurred vision? Any tingling?"

"A bit. My hands and feet."

"It's a sign you're about to transform. Fight it! Don't give in. It's too dangerous for you to shift yet. Your body isn't ready."

"Fight it? Fight what? And how?"

"It's a full moon tonight. Like I was telling you, the moon has an effect on us. The younger you are, or the closer you are to your first change, the greater the pull. You have to hold off as long as possible until your body is able to handle it."

"And how do you propose I do that?" She bit her lip as sensations cascaded over her. It was strange, like someone was pouring sand all over her, bringing to awareness nerve endings she'd never realized existed.

"Concentrate on being human. Think about your body as it is in a human state; how it feels and moves.

Don't focus on the tingling, it will only quicken the transformation."

As soon as Ryne said to not think about it, her traitorous mind began to concentrate on nothing else. The strange feelings slowly began to build inside her. Her limbs began to tremble.

"Melody!" Ryne gave her a shake. "I said don't think about it!"

"I'm trying, but I need a distraction! When you say don't think about something, I can't help but think about it."

"Fine." He made a rumbling sound and the next thing Mel knew, she was in his arms, his lips locked on hers. At first, she stiffened in surprise, but then as he slid his tongue over hers, she began to relax, kissing him in return. The sensations had been crawling up her arms and legs faded from awareness as Ryne caressed her back.

Mmm, it felt so good to have his warm, hard body pressed close, to have his mouth on hers, his arms holding her tight. She inhaled the scent of him, the taste of him, the rumbling sound in his chest. She popped her eyes open. Rumbling, growling. The wolf by the river. The paw prints around her cabin!

She pulled her mouth from his and pushed him away. "You're a wolf!"

"That's what I've been telling you." He moved to pull her close again, but she braced her hands on his chest.

"No. I mean you really are a wolf; a furry, four legged, howling-at-the-moon wolf!"

"So?"

"I saw you. At the river. And those were your paw prints around my cabin. And...you snuck into my cabin one night, didn't you?" When he looked away, she shrieked and hit him. "Pervert!"

Ryne winced and covered his ears. "Hey! No screaming. My ears are sensitive."

"You molested me in my sleep." She smacked him again and he caught her hands holding them to his chest.

"No. I stopped by to check on you because you'd hit your head. I didn't like the idea of you being by yourself, but when I arrived, you were having a bad dream so I slipped inside to comfort you."

"Comfort! Is that what you call it?" She struggled against him, glaring. "I could have you arrested!"

"It was one kiss!"

"And that makes it okay? You are such an ass! I can't believe I ever had a dream about you!"

"About me? So I was the star in your dream?" The corner of his mouth twitched and he looked entirely too pleased with himself.

Damn! Why had she said that?

Ryne zoomed in and planted a kiss on her lips. "Next time it won't be a dream."

But back in Stump River you said—"

"Shh..." He laid his finger over her lips. "I said lots of stupid stuff, trying to get you to go away so you wouldn't get caught up in the Keeping."

The statement quickly sobered her mood as she recalled parts of his earlier lecture. She shifted away from him. "Is it really that serious? You have to kill people if they find out your secret?"

He nodded.

"So...what about me? I know about Lycans now. Are you going to kill me?"

"We *do* let a select few know of our existence, if it benefits the whole pack. And we screen those people very carefully."

She gulped. "Do I qualify?"

"In normal circumstances, probably not. But since you're transforming into one of us—"

She started to protest there was absolutely no way she was becoming a Lycan, but then stopped. If he believed she was transforming, then she was safe. She pasted a smile on her face. "So I'm immune to the law."

"Unless you refuse to accept your transformation and start telling everyone or go rogue, letting others see you changing, things like that."

"Nope. Not me. I promise to keep mum." She put her hand up as if making an oath and then mimed zipping her lips. Even if she told people, who would believe her? "So, what happens if Aldrich and Greyson tell other people?"

"If it appears the secret has been spread to others, the pack that has been discovered enters into something akin to a suicide pact."

She shuddered as the import of what was going on finally sunk in. "I've endangered your whole family by interviewing you, haven't I?"

Ryne stood up and began to pace again. "I started it by taking that photo of Kane in his wolf form and then not guarding the picture closely enough. When Greyson bought it, he must have examined it closely and discovered certain anomalies between Kane's wolf form and that of a real wolf."

"But Greyson must have suspected Lycans existed before then. Most people don't look at a picture of a wolf and say 'Hey, there's something different about this one. It must be Lycan.' Normal people don't think that way."

"Apparently Greyson does because it's the only reason I can think of for him to be searching for me. My pictures are good, but not that good. Not good enough to spend thousands of dollars on finding me just for an interview."

She stared at the floor, thinking before speaking. "Aldrich was very insistent Greyson wanted to know where you took your pictures." She looked up at Ryne. "He must want to find more Lycans!"

He nodded grimly. "That's what I'm thinking, too. And if we can't stop him, my brother and his whole pack will self-destruct rather than let Greyson find them."

Chapter 37

Smythston, Oregon, USA...

Kane drummed his fingers on his desk, checked his watch, then stared at the phone, willing it to ring. Why hadn't Ryne called yet? Something was wrong, he knew it. Had Ryne been unable to find the girl? Or had she already told others of her discovery and arranged for Ryne to be captured? Ryne had an affection for the girl, even if he was unwilling to admit it. But did the girl return those feelings or was she playing him for a dupe? Had she lured him into a trap where he was, even now, fighting to escape and warn the others of impending doom?

His expression became stony. He was Alpha. It was his job to ensure the safety of his pack. Waiting would only heighten the danger. Picking up the phone, he punched in the needed numbers and waited impatiently for his Beta to answer.

"John? Ryne missed his check-in. We're not waiting any longer. Contact the group leaders and have them gather those assigned to them ... No ... No exceptions. I want everyone on the dispersal lists packed and out of here within the hour ... Yeah ... We'll hold on as long as possible back here. I won't make the final decision lightly ... Yes, I'll break the news to Elise and make sure she's in front of the house waiting for the van ... Yeah, good luck to you, too."

He hung up the phone, contemplating what he'd say to his mate. She didn't want to leave, but there was no way he was endangering her life and that of his unborn child by letting her stay, despite her pleas. But how do you begin to convince someone to leave you behind to face almost certain death? And how did you bid that person farewell, when you knew it would be forever?

For a moment he gave his emotions free rein. Surprisingly enough, it was anger that came to the fore. Anger at Melody Greene for her snooping. Anger at Ryne for not dealing with her swiftly and ruthlessly. Anger he'd never see his child or hold Elise again.

His breathing hitched. It was like a knife, cutting into his very soul. How would his death affect her? Would she know when he died? Feel an aching emptiness in her heart? If there was a way to spare her that pain, he would take it; but as his life force seeped away, would he be strong enough to maintain a shield between their minds? He hoped so.

With a heavy heart, he exited the office and went in search of his mate.

Chicago, Illinois, USA…

Greyson eased himself into his favourite chair and sighed. He seldom allowed himself the luxury of feeling tired, but his concern over Cassandra was slowly wearing away at him. The girl was beginning to ask questions and he wasn't sure how he would answer them. For so long he'd shielded her from the truth; once she learned of it, would she accept it? Perhaps he should have told her years ago, but the danger had been too real and she'd been too young to be trusted not to tell someone.

Reaching into his pocket, he withdrew a key and unlocked the drawer in the table to his right. He eased it open and lifted out an envelope and a picture from within. The envelope was his Last Will and Testament and left everything to Cassandra. He'd written it himself using sufficient legal mumbo jumbo to make it legal and unbreakable. Only a few people knew this copy existed. Another sealed version was at Aldrich's office, but even the lawyer didn't know its true contents. Greyson had never told the lawyer about the girl, and if he had his way, her existence was going to be kept a secret as long as possible. His life and business associates would not be allowed to taint her as long as he was alive. He put the will back in the drawer and focused on the picture. His gnarled fingers trembled as he traced the features of the woman in the photograph.

"Ah Luisa, you'd be proud of the girl. She looks just like you and has your fighting spirit, too." He cleared his throat as emotion overcame him. "I wish you were here to see her, to guide her. You left her in my care and I've done my best, but now... I'm not sure what to do anymore."

He stared intently at the picture as memories unfolded. It had been eighteen years ago in Spain...

~~~

He usually didn't walk home, preferring the luxury of his limousine, but he'd wanted time by himself to dwell on his most recent success. Taking over the small Spanish import-export business gave him another toe-hold in the country. It was part of his master plan to get his hands on the parent company; a large conglomerate with connections in several European nations. If done carefully enough, with little fanfare, no one would realize he had a controlling interest in the voting stock until it was too late.

The streets were mostly deserted which wasn't surprising given the late hour. His driver was tailing him, a respectful two blocks away, ready to pick him up when he tired of his solitary stroll. Noise drifted out of small establishments as people laughed and sang, enjoying friendship and frivolity. What a waste of time. So what if it's New Year's Eve? Transactions needed to be completed, fortunes built; commerce waited for no one. True, commerce made a cold friend, but if he needed companionship, he could find it. The flash of diamonds and a bottle of champagne would have women clamouring to hang on his arms, should he so desire.

Shoving his hands in his pockets, he hunched his shoulders against the cool wind and walked on. A scuffling sound from an alley caught his attention and he turned to stare into the murky depths. Nothing moved, and he turned to go when a soft cry sounded. He wasn't one to get involved, so he had no idea what inspired him to walk down the alleyway.

His steps echoed off the pavement; the stench of garbage causing him to curl his lip. He searched the shadows and then he saw it. A face, pale and battered, blood smeared across the cheek, one eye swollen shut, the other filled with fear. It was a young girl and she shrank back as he approached.

He scanned the area, suspicious this could be a set up. What better way to distract a wealthy victim, than to present him with a helpless female and then attack when he was otherwise occupied. However, there were no signs of movement, no sounds except the girl's laboured breathing.

Murmuring reassurances in Spanish, he crouched beside her to assess the damage. Her arm hung limply at her side and her leg was twisted grotesquely, both obviously broken. He considered himself a hard man, but when he observed the girl protectively clutch her good arm around the swelling at her waist, even he was moved. What kind of bastard would beat up a pregnant woman?

"Who did this to you?" His voice was harsher than he intended and she cringed. With effort, he forced himself to speak in a gentler tone. "Who hurt you? I'll call the police and ensure the villains are dealt with."

Panic flared in her eyes. "No! No police! Please, tell no one. Just help me up." She struggled to move and he firmly held her in place.

"Don't be ridiculous, girl. Your leg's broken. You can't move."

She raised her chin. "Yes, I can. I got myself this far—"

"Then you're a fool. You've probably damaged your leg irreparably and will limp when it heals."

"I might be a fool, but I'm also a survivor. I will live for the sake of this little one." She rubbed her stomach and glared at him defiantly.

Damn, she was a fighter. He liked that. "Fine. You want to live for the child. Well then, give it a chance. Let me help you." Holding out his hand, he kept his gaze steady as he stared into her liquid brown eyes. The girl hesitated and then placed her hand in his. As his fingers closed around her fine bones, he knew he was lost. In a matter of minutes, the girl had done what others had spent years trying to do. She'd slipped past his protective shield and made him remember he did have a heart.

Things happened quickly after that. He called for his car to be brought around and they drove to his house. She refused a hospital and barely agreed to have a private physician look at her. Amazingly enough, the doctor stated she was bruised, but otherwise fine. He declared the man a fool, whipping back the covers—much to the girl's embarrassment—and demanding he look at her broken leg. The doctor raised his eyebrows and Greyson managed to muffle a cry of surprise when he realized the broken leg was no longer broken.

For probably the first and only time in his life, he'd gaped like a fish, only the silent plea in the girl's eyes keeping him from commenting on the startling phenomenon. The leg had been broken, he knew it. And her arm was fine, too! As he stared at her face, he noted even the cuts and bruises seemed less severe, some barely noticeably.

Once the physician had left, he demanded an explanation. Shouts, tears, even threats ensued before she finally crumpled under the force of his personality and explained.

At first he refused to believe her story, but the more she spoke, the more it made sense. Her name was Luisa and she was a Lycan, or shape-shifter. She'd been promised to her pack's Beta, but fell in love with another. When it was discovered she was with child, her lover had been killed and she was severely beaten for her transgression. Knowing her child would be taken from her and her own future would be nothing but misery, she'd run away.

"I shouldn't be telling you this. But," she explained. "They would kill me anyway, in the end. You don't betray the ruling family as I did and live long afterwards." She moved to get out of bed. "Thank you for giving me a place to rest. Unfortunately, my presence endangers you and your household. I'd better leave before they track me here."

Greyson scoffed. "You'll stay in bed until I decide you're well enough to get up. And I have half a dozen armed bodyguards, so your Lycan friends don't worry me."

"You should be worried. Two of Pablo's enforcers could take out all your bodyguards in seconds. The threat they represent is not to be dismissed."

He could tell her fear was real. Well, his business was done anyway. "Fine. Then we'll leave as soon as my private jet is ready."

"Leave? For where?"

"America, of course."

"There's no 'of course' about it! I barely know you. I'm not travelling halfway around the world with a man I just met." She folded her arms and glared at him.

"And what's the alternative? By your own admission, it isn't safe for you here. How far will you have to run before you're out of the reach of this Pablo you so fear?"

Luisa was silent before reluctantly acquiescing. A few hours later, they were in the Greyson Inc. jet, heading to the States and leaving the danger behind, or so he'd thought.

The next year had been the happiest he'd ever known. Luisa was his constant companion, and the child she eventually bore was like his own. Baby Cassandra, named after his mother, was his delight and if at times Luisa seemed distant, he put it down to being tired, knowing the newborn was a great deal of work.

Cassandra was four months old when Luisa came to him with her plan. She wanted to go back to Spain to see her family. Lycans, she explained, were social creatures. While she loved him, she also missed her family and wanted them to know about the baby. He doubted the safety of this course of action and they argued bitterly before he finally gave in, though not without taking every possible precaution.

They would stay in Portugal near the border and she would cross over, quickly visit her parents and then return. It would be a quick, secretive meeting. Greyson wanted to go with her, but she insisted he stay behind to watch Cassie. He argued for her to take bodyguards, but she would only agree to one person, following at a distance, so as to not draw attention to herself.

~~~

"I never should have let you go," he whispered to the smiling woman in the photo. "I knew something would happen. How those murderous bastards got wind of your presence, I'll never know." Greyson swallowed hard and pushed aside the memory of finding her broken body dumped in a ditch alongside that of the lone bodyguard. They'd both been mauled to death.

He'd wanted revenge, but fear for Cassandra had him fleeing the area instead. If they ever found the baby...

A light tap on the door had him hurriedly putting the picture away and straightening in his chair. "Come!"

Franklin, his butler, entered the room. The man was one of the few persons Greyson trusted implicitly. They'd been together for years. "I'm sorry to disturb you, sir. Cook is wondering how many for dinner."

"Just myself, Franklin. She can send a light meal up to Cassandra's room, but she might not be awake enough to eat it."

"Very well, sir. And how is Miss Cassandra this month?" Franklin had been with him even before Luisa and Cassandra entered his life. He knew the whole sordid tale.

"The medication is working. No sign of a change yet."

A smile spread across the butler's usually passive face. "I'm glad to hear it, sir. I'm not sure what we'd do if she ever did transform." The man hesitated and then spoke again. "Have you had any news about finding a pack here in the States?"

"I'm on the trail of one. It looks promising."

Franklin fidgeted nervously. "Begging your pardon, sir. But how do you know an American pack would be willing to accept her?"

Greyson tried to hide his concern by clearing his throat. "I don't. That's why I've sent someone else in ahead of time. To test the waters, so to speak and see if they're receptive or not."

The butler nodded. "That would be Ms. Greene."

"Correct. Their reception of her will let me know if it's safe to have Cassie approach or not."

"But what of Ms. Greene?"

"If she safely makes contact, all the better for her. If she doesn't, well...collateral damage does occur. It's regrettable, but the woman isn't my primary concern. Cassandra is."

Franklin nodded again. "True. I'll tell cook about dinner." He gave a slight bow and left.

Rubbing his chin, Greyson considered the situation. Given what Luisa had told him and the cold facts of how she'd been treated by her own kind, he was reluctant to introduce Cassandra to other Lycans. Unfortunately, he also recalled all he'd seen during his time with Luisa and the information she'd shared with him about transforming with the moon, blood-bonds, fertility cycles. He couldn't let Cassandra flounder through life scared and uninformed. She needed the support and guidance of her own kind. The potent sedative Dr. Freidrich—a well-paid actor—prescribed was doing the job for now, but the girl was questioning the monthly treatment.

Yes, finding a pack to accept her was the best solution. He wouldn't live forever and she couldn't be left alone. Wolves needed a pack. And so, he'd spent the last seventeen years looking, for one, his efforts unsuccessful until he'd purchased the Taylor picture.

Now he knew there was a pack out there. The question remained, where?

Melody Greene was his hope. Aldrich scoffed at his choice, but after viewing secretly taped footage of her, Greyson knew she was the one. He'd watched the videos of her, fascinated by the subtle signs she was showing, signs he would have passed over if he hadn't watched Cassie growing up. The way she lifted her head slightly and sniffed the air, the way she cocked her head to listen. Greene didn't know it, but she had a Lycan someplace in her background.

It was an unexpected turn of good fortune, finding Ms. Greene. Greyson reasoned if she found a pack and was accepted by them, it would follow they'd accept Cassandra too. Once he knew their location, he'd establish Cassandra in a house in the area—with secret body guards strategically living around her of course—and then wait and watch for them to sense her.

Mel joined Ryne in pacing across the small room. The strange feelings inside her had subsided again; she refused to dwell on their meaning since she had a sneaking suspicion they meant a certain arrogant Lycan was right and she was on the verge of transforming into one of the beasts. Instead, she'd concentrate on how to get out of this room before Aldrich returned.

"So, what are we going to do?"

Ryne ran his fingers through his hair. "I don't know. I can't break us out of here."

"I thought Lycans had all these superhuman powers and stuff."

"We do have keener senses and are relatively stronger and faster than humans, but there are limits. Bullet proof walls being one of them."

"Oh." She was sort of disappointed in that one. If she was going to be a Lycan—which she wasn't, she reminded herself—she'd hoped for a few more benefits than just being able to smell things really well. Where was the advantage in that? She suppressed a shudder as she imagined being keenly aware of the scent of public washrooms, garbage and the cabbage her neighbours were so fond of cooking. Ugh!

Giving her head a little shake, she looked around for a sink. suddenly realizing she was thirsty. Strangely enough, there didn't appear to be one. "Hey, Ryne?"

"Yeah?" He was examining the door hinges.

"You said you overheard Mr. Aldrich calling this a safe room, right?"

He grunted in acknowledgment.

"And if this is a safe room, people are planning on being holed up here for a while, correct?"

"That's usually what they're constructed for. What are you getting at?" He turned and looked at her.

"So shouldn't there be supplies? Food? Water? Communications? Maybe even a bathroom?"

He frowned and stared around the room. "You're right. There should be. But there isn't."

"You know, it was always rumoured the gangsters had secret rooms and hidden escape tunnels. Maybe Greyson has one in this place." She got up and began pushing the bench aside, stamping the floor with her foot, listening for a change in sound that might indicate a tunnel.

Ryne joined in the search, checking out the centre area of the room, then moving aside a table. She was near the window when her stomping produced a hollow, drum like sound. They both looked at each other and grinned.

She dropped to her knees and Ryne rushed over to help her, both running their fingers over the floor, searching for a seam or finger hold. Soon they were pulling back a section of floorboard.

"You were right!" Ryne lifted the heavy wooden panel to reveal a tunnel leading to somewhere under the shed. He lay flat on his stomach and peered into the darkness. "It looks like there's a room down here. I'll go and check it out. You wait here."

She nodded in agreement. Usually she'd balk at being left behind, but it was dark and there were cobwebs. Just this once, she'd let Ryne have the fun.

Soon, his voice echoed up at her. "It's a short tunnel with a room at the end and I think there's a way out through the sewer."

The sewer? She wrinkled her nose, picturing creepy crawly things and filth. "I'm not so sure about that, Ryne. There are probably rats down there."

"Ah, come on!" His voice held a teasing quality. "You're a big bad wolf now. You're not going to let little rodents best you."

"I'm not a wolf!"

Ryne appeared at the entrance to the tunnel. "You'll have to face the fact sooner or later."

She folded her arms and gave him a mutinous stare.

"Fine. We'll leave it for now." He held out his hand. "Come on, Melody. I'm big and bad enough for both of us. No rat in its right mind would bother me."

Reluctantly, she sat down and dangled her feet into the hole. "Whoever said rats are in their right mind?"

Chapter 38

Aldrich drove at a sedate pace, passing through the massive gates that marked the entrance of the Greyson estate and making his way to the safe room at the back of the property as if time was of no importance. Rushing would only draw attention to himself and he didn't want that. One reckless move and the opportunity that had fallen into his lap would be gone.

He'd returned to his apartment to gather the small tool box he used to maintain his various listening devices and surveillance cameras. Having told Greyson he was adjusting the equipment, he wouldn't put it past the man to check up on him.

Greyson was a suspicious bastard, but then he wouldn't have gotten where he was any other way. It was a cut-throat world and Aldrich had a grudging respect for his employer in that regard. On the other hand, the man was cold-hearted, arrogant and likely to turn on you the minute you let your guard down. At present he was in Greyson's good graces, but it was a tenuous position at best. Greyson made a bad enemy, so Aldrich had sucked up, kowtowed and carried out every task the man had set before him.

But not anymore. Melody Greene was going to be his ticket out. She was a werewolf and if Greyson was interested in werewolves then there had to be a profit in it. Money was the only language Greyson understood. It was even rumoured his heart was a bank vault. Well if that was the case, Leon Aldrich was about to make a personal withdrawal. He'd take the girl and tuck her away in his cottage. Once she was secured, he could start putting out feelers among his old contacts, people who would know where he could get the greatest profit from her sale. Private collectors, scientists. Who knew where there might be a market for such a specimen?

Alternatively, he could keep her. Put her on display, charge admission, perhaps even rent her out. Briefly he'd considered the idea but then decided against it. A quick turnover would be the easiest way. The money would be his safe guard out should Greyson blame him when Ms. Greene never returned with a report.

A less clever person would try to disappear along with Ms. Greene, but Aldrich knew if he suddenly quit, Greyson would be suspicious. It was better to stay around for a few months and then hand in a carefully worded resignation before slipping away to enjoy the fruits of his labour.

Aldrich smiled as he parked the car, noting it was about an hour until sunset. Greyson wanted him gone by then and he would be. He'd planned everything down to the last detail; had all the angles covered. Get rid of Taylor, collect the woman and be on his way.

Tool box in one hand, he stepped out of the car and casually glanced around. Excellent. No one was in sight.

He walked to the shed, set the tool box down and pulled out the key. One final glance around and then he took a deep breath and unlocked the door. The snick of the tumblers sounded louder than normal, his hearing intently focused on any betraying sounds coming from inside the shed. He suspected they would try to attack the minute he entered the room. Flexing his fingers on the weapon he'd drawn from his pocket, he took another deep breath, turned the handle, and then in a rush shoved the door open.

Muscles tensed, he braced himself for an attack except...it didn't happen. His gaze quickly skimmed the room, suspecting an ambush until the sweep of his eyes came to an abrupt halt at a gaping hole in the floor. Dropping his arm to his side, the gun dangled uselessly from his fingers. They'd found the escape tunnel.

This wasn't part of his plan and, for an uncharacteristic moment, he let his fury get the better of him, slamming his fist into the wall and kicking the table. Then exerting the self-control he'd cultivated all his life, he pocketed the gun and considered his options while rubbing his sore knuckles. They hadn't won yet. There were always alternatives if one was just clever enough and persistent enough to find them.

He widened his eyes as a possibility occurred to him. The route through the sewers was convoluted, involving crawling through sludge and pulling open a series of grates. There were also a few dead ends if one took the wrong turn. However, the above ground route to the culvert where the sewer ended could be traversed in a more direct and far shorter route.

Smirking, Aldrich exited and locked the door before taking off through the woods to the drainage ditch where his werewolf would be emerging.

Cassandra rolled over in bed, cautious to not make any sounds that would indicate she was awake. She eyed the crack of light beneath the door connecting her bedroom to the sitting room. The faint sound of voices let her know the nurse was engrossed in her favourite television show. In the week the woman had been employed by her uncle, she hadn't varied in her routine, always watching the latest craze in reality shows at this time. Since the program lasted an hour, Cassandra calculated she had plenty of time to sneak out, check the small hut at the back of the property and be back in bed without anyone noticing her absence.

While it remained light outside, her room was dark due to the heavy curtains on the windows. This would work to her advantage should anyone peek inside to check on her. Climbing out of bed, she arranged her pillows to mimic the shape of a body. Then she drew the covers over them and stood back to admire the effect. It was a juvenile trick, but since everyone insisted on treating her as a child, she had no other recourse.

After giving the covers a final twitch, she hurriedly pulled on jeans and a t-shirt, slid her feet into her running shoes and peered out the window.

The trees cast long shadows in the late afternoon light, everything appearing as it usually did except for the vehicle parked on the gravel near the hut. It was Mr. Aldrich's car. And he was exiting the hut and heading off through the woods. Now that was peculiar. Perhaps she'd follow him first rather than checking out the hut. Casting a final glance at the sitting room door, ensuring the nurse was still engrossed in her TV show, she exited her room and stealthily crept down the hallway.

There was an old dumb-waiter at the end of the hall. No one ever used it, its existence almost forgotten. It was a fact she'd used to her advantage several times. Despite its age, the miniature elevator worked smoothly due to her application of baby oil to the pulleys and gears. With practiced ease, she climbed in and lowered herself to the main floor, just inside the kitchen pantry. Holding her breath, she listened as she heard Franklin speaking to Cook.

"Mr. Greyson will be eating by himself tonight."

"And Miss Cassandra?"

"He said you could send a light meal up to her room, though he doubts she'll be eating much."

"Poor dear, plagued with such dreadful headaches."

"Indeed. Oh, and don't forget to send something up to the new nurse."

Cassie heard the cook tsking in what sounded like disapproval.

"Some nurse. She's here because she thinks it's a cushy job. Hardly good enough for our young miss."

"I believe Mr. Greyson might be inclined to agree with you. I overheard him chastising her half an hour ago. Apparently, Miss Cassandra changed all the clocks on her and the woman didn't even notice." Franklin spoke in a conspiratorial tone and Cassie clapped a hand over her mouth to stifle a giggle. For all his supposed dignity, the man loved a good gossip and was nothing but a teddy bear inside.

Cook laughed. "Serves her right. You have to be on your toes around our little miss. She's a sneaky one."

With that the two servants could be heard walking away.

Cassandra opened the door a crack and peeked out. Seeing the coast was clear, she jumped down, landing lightly on the balls of her feet. After closing the door of the dumb waiter, she headed towards the rear exit.

Knowing exactly where all the sensors and security cameras were, she began the careful process of avoiding each device as she made her way towards the woods where Mr. Aldrich had disappeared from sight. It was the long way around and would give him a considerable head start, but it couldn't be helped if she wanted to avoid detection.

Greyson put down the financial reports he was trying to read and rubbed the back of his neck. He always had a strange feeling there when something was wrong. His mother had said it was the fairies trying to warn him of danger. At the time, he'd scoffed; his mother's old Irish tales had meant nothing to him. Yet, over the years, he'd learned to trust that tingling feeling. It had kept him from bad business deals and at least one attempt on his life. The last time he had ignored the sensation, his beloved Luisa had died.

Pushing back his chair, he stood and concentrated on the feeling. On occasion, he'd get some indication as to where the trouble might be coming from, but usually it was just a sense of unease that made him extra alert to those around him and their possible motives.

Nothing, he thought, was happening tonight. No business deals. No guests. Perhaps he should check on Cassandra. Maybe the little minx was up to something. As he climbed the stairs, a horrifying possibility crossed his mind. Had she only pretended to take her pill earlier on? Was she on the verge of transforming?

He quickened his pace. The nurse was with her, but had no idea as to the girl's true condition. He wasn't about to trust such sensitive information to a temporary employee, and all the nurses were temporary. If he kept one around too long, they might become suspicious of the medication.

He gave the briefest knock on Cassie's door before pushing it open, without waiting for a response. A sigh of relief escaped him when he saw she was in her bed. About to leave, he noticed the window curtain had been pulled aside but hadn't he watched the girl close it? Pivoting on his heel, he studied the bed again, then stalked over. The lump was too large, too uniform. He yanked back the covers and found a row of strategically arranged pillows.

"Damn that girl!" He exploded, contemplating what he'd do when he finally got his hands on her. Didn't she realize the danger she was putting herself in? He threw the covers to the ground.

On the off chance she was in her suite, Greyson barged into the sitting room, surprising the nurse who was biting her thumb and hugging a pillow as she watched TV.

"Where's Cassandra?" The barked question had the nurse jumping to her feet.

"In her room, resting. Just like always, sir."

"Like hell she is!" Grabbing the woman's arm, Greyson dragged her into Cassie's room and shoved her towards the bed. "Look. Pillows! Dammit woman, when did you last check on her?"

"N-n-not too long ago." The nurse stammered, nervously twisting her hands together.

"Well, it's been long enough for her to slip out on you!" Greyson fumed as he tried to figure out where his young ward might have gone. Remembering the crooked curtain, he strode to the window and looked out. Cassie had been staring at something earlier today, but what? He studied the view and realized the small safe house was visible from this window. Had she seen him and Aldrich talking earlier on? If so... He rubbed his chin. Aldrich's car was back. Could Cassie have gone to investigate? It was worth checking.

Turning he saw the useless nurse hovering near the bed. "You're fired. I want you out of here in less than an hour. Understood?"

The woman nodded, then burst into tears and ran from the room.

As Greyson hurried down the stairs, he considered calling the sole security guard that had remained on duty to help in the search for Cassandra but what if she had transformed into a wolf? No, it was too dangerous to get the guard involved. It was better he looked himself. She'd listen to him, no matter what form she was in.

Mel was sure it was hours since she and Ryne had begun crawling on their hands and knees through the sewer pipe. Her knees were complaining from the unaccustomed use and her palms were screaming for mercy as tiny nicks and cuts abraded their surface. The bottom of the pipe was covered in a sludgy substance that hid rocks, twigs and other sharp bits of debris. It also made disgusting sucking sounds each time they moved as if it was trying to keep them from escaping its slimy clutches. Ryne insisted it wasn't a sanitary sewer, but rather one used to collect runoff from rain water. She dearly hoped he was right, but had her doubts given the stench permeating the air.

At least they were no longer commando crawling on their bellies like they had been initially. After making their way through a series of mesh gates, the pipe had widened to a more comfortable height. Finally off her belly and able to open her mouth without fear of ingesting the disgusting muck that splashed in her face, she made her feelings known.

"Ryne, if we ever get out of this pipe, I'm never listening to another idea of yours again."

"I didn't hear you come up with a better one." He paused in his crawling and looked at her over his shoulder. The lighting was almost nil, but she managed to make out his filth-splattered face.

"If you'd listened to me, we wouldn't have turned left at the last junction."

"So I made a wrong turn. With the fumes down here, I can't scent which direction fresh air is coming in from."

"But I said we should have gone right. If you'd listened to me we wouldn't be crawling backwards out of a dead end. We might have even been out of here."

"It was only a short detour and besides, Lycans usually have an impeccable sense of direction."

"Yeah, if they know where they're heading in the first place. We have no idea where this tunnel might be taking us."

"So, in other words, you think you could do a better job leading us?"

"It probably couldn't be any worse."

"Fine. When we get back to the junction you're in charge."

"Oh." She hadn't really expected him to agree, but wasn't about to back down from the challenge. She kept crawling in reverse until they reached the relatively roomier 'T' where the tunnel branched off. Wiggling herself around, she headed to the right and Ryne followed behind. He was soon muttering under his breath.

"Now what are you complaining about?" She peeked under her arm to look at him.

"Your feet are splashing this muck up into my face."

She smiled knowing he probably couldn't see. "Oh. So sorry. It's not like I had to put up with it when our positions were reversed."

Ryne grunted, but kept quiet after that.

They crawled along in silence for a while. She mulled over the idea of turning into a Lycan, not totally convinced, but realizing perhaps, just in case, she should try to be open to the idea. It surprised her she hadn't freaked out more when Ryne changed in front of her, but she supposed the clues had been there all along. Her subconscious must have been processing and accepting them for quite a while so when she was told, it wasn't too big of a leap to acknowledge Lycans existed. As for turning into a Lycan herself, if she did actually have those genes within her, then there was no use crying and complaining about it. It was a done deal.

She was, if nothing else, practical and decided she'd make the best of the situation. In a way, it was sort of sexy, the idea of shifting shapes. Would her strength increase to a level similar to Ryne's? Or would being a Lycan with mixed blood create certain limitations? Hopefully, it would tone her muscles and increase her metabolism so she could eat as much as she wanted without any adverse effects. She grinned at the idea of being able to add whipped cream to her cafe mochas and not feel even the slightest twinge of guilt.

Lost in that happy thought, she suddenly let out a shriek as something cold and slimy grabbed at her ankle.

"Shh! Are you trying to let everybody within a ten-mile radius know where we are?"

She looked back realizing it was Ryne's hand grabbing her lower leg, not some sewer monster. "What?" Frowning in irritation, she jerked her leg away.

"We're getting near the end of the tunnel."

She peered ahead, but saw no sign of light. "How do you know?"

"The air's different."

She sniffed. It still stunk to her. "Are you sure?"

"Yep. It's fresher which means an exit is coming up."

She considered gloating that she was the one to lead them to the exit, but Ryne continued speaking, and the opportunity passed.

"When we get out, I have to find a phone fast. It must be past my check-in and Kane will be worried sick. I don't want him doing anything rash."

She furrowed her brow, trying to recall all Ryne had told her. "He's your brother, right?"

"Uh-huh. And if I don't contact him soon, he's going to assume the worst. He's probably already dispersed most of the pack. I have to tell him to hold off on phase two. There's still a chance I can fix this mess."

"Phase two? That's where they all..." She hesitated to speak the words. "Take poison?"

She could almost make out Ryne's grim expression. "Yes. The pack self-destructs so when outsiders come looking for a bunch of Lycans, they'll only find dead bodies."

"But wouldn't autopsies show they weren't human?"

"No. When a Lycan dies, within minutes the trace elements of magick that make us what we are disappear."

They were both silent for a moment then Ryne sighed heavily. "Anyway, as we near the entrance, be as quiet as possible in case anyone is around."

She nodded and resumed crawling as quickly as possible, all too aware of the deadline they were operating under.

Smythston, Oregon, USA...

Helen wrapped her arm around Kane's waist as the last of the vans drove out of sight. She patted the Alpha on his back, offering what little comfort she could. He'd just watched most of his pack leave, including his mate and unborn child. The feeling of loss must be incredible, even worse than when her Zack had died. For weeks she'd been inconsolable, the aching void within making her wish she, too, were dead. But at least she'd had her daughters and the rest of the pack. For Kane, however, he was on the verge of losing everything. It was an Alpha's worst nightmare. Sworn to protect his pack, the feeling of failure would be overwhelming.

"Kane?"

"Hmm?" His gaze didn't leave the driveway, despite the fact it was now empty.

"Do you want me to go around and hand out the vials?" It was a grim job, handing your friends a packet of death, but she'd do it, to spare him. Kane had been good to her and she owed him. When she'd found herself widowed and no longer Alpha female, Kane could have insisted she leave, but he hadn't. Instead he'd let her stay in the pack house and keep many of her previous duties. The familiarity had been a great comfort to her until she'd found her feet again.

"No, I'll do it. It's my job." He finally looked at her. "You know, Helen, I keep thinking if I stay here and look hard enough, I'll still be able to see them; that they won't really be gone."

Helen gave him a one-armed hug. "I know. When we buried Zach, you had to drag me from the cemetery. As long as I stood there, he seemed near. By walking away, I had to admit we were separated forever."

Kane looked down the road once more. "Helen?"

"Hmm?"

"Do you believe in an afterlife?"

"I think so. I can't believe a love as strong as mine and Zach's can just disappear. I like to think it somehow lives on and we'll be together again."

"I hope you're right, Helen. I hope you're right."

Chapter 39

Chicago, Illinois, USA...

Ryne watched the darkness of the tunnel slowly dissipate as the entrance approached. The sun hadn't set yet. Melody gave a tiny squeal of excitement and crawled even faster, the movement of her feet kicking the filthy water into his face more than ever. He slowed his pace, dropping farther behind her to avoid the splashing sludge.

When she reached the end of the tunnel, a relieved sigh echoed back towards him. Ryne smiled watching her climb out, while thinking she really had been a trooper throughout their underground journey.

He could see her legs as she stood at the tunnel's entrance. She lifted one foot as if to step away, but then stopped mid-stride. He paused, sensing all was not well though unsure what it might be. The answer came soon enough as he heard Aldrich's self-satisfied voice.

"Well, well, well. What do we have here? Why, it's my runaway werewolf. Very naughty of you to try to escape me. Where's Taylor? Hiding in the tunnel behind you?"

"No! Um, I mean he was behind me for a while, but..." Ryne could almost hear Melody's mind sorting through various scenarios that might explain his absence. Keeping his ears tuned to what was going on outside, he slowly began to move deeper back into the pipe.

"Speak up girl? Where is he?"

"He started to follow me, but he's scared of small dark tunnels and rats so he went back."

Ryne bit back an oath. He was not afraid of the dark! He scowled while admitting it was quick thinking on her part.

"You won't mind if I check out your story, will you?" There was definitely doubt in Aldrich's voice.

Ryne heard footsteps approaching and scooted even farther back into the pipe. A sliver of light played off the walls, but didn't reach where he was. Aldrich had a small flashlight with him; the keychain type that wasn't very powerful.

"See? I told you he was too chicken to follow me." Ryne could picture the smug look on Melody's face.

Aldrich's laugh was tinged with derision. "I should have known. Those artsy types are usually nothing but insipid weaklings. Never mind, I locked the door of the safe house so he can't get out that way. I'll finish him off later."

Melody spoke again. "Listen, Mr. Aldrich, I don't have your stupid report with me, but if you let me go back home, I can print a copy for you."

"Even if I wanted the report, it wouldn't be a wise move. I imagine the area is cordoned off as a crime scene by now."

"Crime scene? What do you mean?"

"Didn't I tell you? Your friend surprised me when I went to your apartment. Unfortunately for her, I have very quick reflexes. When I left, she was next to dead, lying in a pool of her own blood."

"No!" The pain in Mel's voice was undeniable.

Ryne had to steel himself not to rush out and comfort her. He hadn't told her about the waitress, wanting to spare her the grief for as long as possible. Damn Aldrich! The fucking bastard sounded almost happy to share the news with Melody. Maybe it was even a strategy on his part, delivering bad news to unnerve her so she'd be too shocked to think. Soundlessly, Ryne moved closer to the entrance again, trying to assess where Melody was in relation to the lawyer. The man probably had some kind of weapon, so rushing out might be dangerous. Melody could get hurt and, in her newly transforming state, she probably didn't have sufficient healing abilities to deal with any kind of serious wound.

"So you see we can't go back to your apartment. However, the report is of no importance to me now. That was Mr. Greyson's project. Mine is quite different. You, my dear, are what I'm after."

"Me? Why?" From his new location, Ryne could just make out Melody's shocked profile.

"Aldrich!" Another voice entered the mix. It sounded winded, as if the person had been hurrying. Ryne had to restrain himself from poking his head out to see who had arrived.

"Mr. Greyson, sir. I wasn't expecting you."

"Dammit, Aldrich! Have you gone mad? I gave you orders no one was to be here and now I find you traipsing all over my property! I've killed people for less and you damned well know it. Now what are you up to? And that's Ms. Greene isn't it? Why the hell is she in the middle of the woods with you?"

"I—" It seemed Aldrich was about to explain when Greyson interrupted him.

"Don't give me any of your bull crap, Leon. I'll deal with you later." Greyson's tone softened when he spoke next. "Ms. Greene, I'm happy to finally meet you in person. I take it you have my report on Taylor?"

"Not really, Mr. Greyson. You see—"

This time it was Aldrich who interrupted. "Both of you shut up. Greyson, stay where you are. She's mine. I don't know what your plans were for her, but she's going to make me a very rich man."

Unused to such disrespect, Greyson blew up at the lawyer. "How dare you speak to me like that? I can have you terminated and planted under a tree, just like your predecessor. Put the damned gun away and watch your impudence. And what do you mean rich? You told me she was basically penniless!"

There was a certain quality of delight in Aldrich's voice. "So you really don't know? Curious. Who would have believed a coincidence like this would occur? She's a werewolf, you old fool. The first damned werewolf ever captured."

Ryne chanced a brief glance outside. Aldrich hadn't put the gun away, though it was partially lowered as he glowered at Greyson. Greyson was staring at Melody with what could only be described as excited interest. "Really? She's a full werewolf?" He swung his head back to look at Aldrich. "How do you know?"

"I saw her start to change." The man was so self-satisfied Ryne had to grit his teeth.

Greyson sounded urgent, almost desperate, as he addressed Melody. "Ms. Greene, I have to talk to you! I knew you had at least some wolf in your background, but I never suspected this. There are things I need to know, things you have to tell me!"

The sound of a gun being cocked had Ryne tense.

Aldrich issued a warning. "Lay off, Greyson. She's mine. Any information she has belongs to me."

Melody began to move out of Ryne's field of vision. He frowned, but then realized she was walking away from the drainage pipe in a slow circle. A smile spread across Ryne's face. Without their knowing it, Melody was manoeuvring Aldrich and Greyson so their backs were to him! It would make it much easier for him to take Aldrich by surprise. His smile faded however, as he noted the quavery sound of her voice.

"Listen, I don't know what the hell either of you are babbling about. For the last time, I'm not a werewolf! I'm a reporter—a student reporter at that!"

Ryne compressed his lips in concern. The stress of finding out about Lucy and of having a gun pointed at her was starting to show. Could it trigger a transformation as her inner wolf fought to rise up to meet the present danger?

It was also getting later; he could feel the pull of the full moon himself and knew Melody would soon be helpless in the face of its power. A glance outside showed the lengthening shadows cast by the surrounding trees. The encroaching nightfall would provide him with some cover. Seeing the others were focused on Melody, he silently slipped out of his hiding place, to the relative safety of a nearby bush.

Melody flicked a glance in his direction before concentrating on her adversaries again. However, it was enough for their eyes to meet and convey a message. She was ready for whatever course of action he took. Shifting into his wolf form, Ryne crouched, muscles tense and ready to strike.

Greyson ignored Aldrich's threats. He looked beseechingly at Melody. "Ms. Greene. Please. I promise I won't tell anyone about you. I...I know about the Keeping; how you protect your secrecy by eliminating those who have stumbled upon your existence. If you feel you need to take my life, so be it, but first hear me out. I need information about your people, not for myself or monetary gain, but for my ward, Cassandra. She's one of you, though she doesn't know it yet."

Aldrich blinked. "Your ward? What ward? Who—?"

Ryne chose that moment to leap out and tackle Aldrich. Greyson shouted. The lawyer's gun went off and a scream echoed through the night.

Stump River, Ontario, Canada...

Bryan stared at his cards, supposedly concentrating on his poker strategy. In reality, he didn't even see the cards before him; it was the image of the clock that floated in front of his eyes. It was well past the scheduled check-in time but Ryne hadn't called. The phone was working, there were no text messages, no e-mails. Where the hell was their Alpha?

Kane was wondering the same thing. Just half an hour ago he'd had a blistering conversation with the other pack's Alpha. It was understandable Kane was on edge; having a vial of liquid death in front of you while you waited for the call to drink it, would be enough to sour anyone's mood.

Ryne would call. Soon. Bryan kept the thought foremost in his mind, despite the weight in his stomach that increased with each passing minute. What could be keeping him? Surely, Mel wouldn't have turned on him. Not Mel.

"Are you in or out?" Marco's voice brought him out of his reverie. That morning, he'd invited Marco and his family to check out Stump River, thinking it would help to fill the time. Olivia and Tessa hadn't come; the baby was fussing and Tessa was too nervous. Marco, however, had welcomed a chance to see his new home and, having had the grand tour, was now keeping them company as they awaited Ryne's call.

"Out." Bryan folded his cards and threw them down on the table.

Marco reached out and flipped them over. It was a full house. "Is this how you play poker in Canada?"

"Sorry." Bryan roughly pushed his chair back. "I can't concentrate. I keep waiting for the damned phone to ring."

"As do we all." Marco gathered the cards and began stacking the chips. "Have patience. He will call."

"But what if he doesn't?" Daniel looked up from the computer game he was playing. His face reflected his worry.

Bryan studied his friend, noting the anxiety in his voice, how his muscles were tensed. Daniel was as worried as he was but... Damn! He was Beta, and while Ryne was gone, he needed to take responsibility for the safety and well-being of the pack. That included putting on a brave face, even when he didn't really feel it. Lifting his chin, he straightened and spoke in a firm, confident voice. "Marco is right. I'm just being a nervous old woman. Of course Ryne is fine. He's survived worse scrapes than this. By now he's talked to Mel, found out there was nothing to worry about and they're reconnecting, if you know what I mean." He ended the comment by wiggling his eyebrows and giving a knowing look.

"Reconnecting?" Marco frowned over the word, then grinned. "Ah! *Ryne y Mel estan haciendo el amor.*"

Daniel visibly relaxed and gave a brief chuckle. "If that means they're having sex then, yeah."

"Our Alpha is—how you say—a ladies' man?"

"Something like that." Bryan smiled realizing Marco was trying to lighten the mood as well. He sat down again and tried to keep the conversation going. "So, what was your old Alpha like?"

Marco snorted. "He is a bastard and not fit to rule."

Bryan leaned back, propping his feet on the table and folding his arms behind his head. "A real nice guy, then."

Marco looked confused but then seemed to grasp the sarcasm of the statement. "Yes. A real nice guy. He allows no discussion or debate; pack meetings are never held unless he is issuing orders and anyone who disagrees, disappears without a trace."

"He kills them?" Daniel set down his computer game and leaned forward, intrigued by the tale.

"There are no bodies, but everyone knows." Marco narrowed his eyes, his voice bitter.

"And no one tries to stop him?" Bryan found it hard to believe in this day and age, a pack would put up with such treatment.

"Many have tried and have died in the attempt. Most of my pack have learned through experience to endure the misery and live in hope for the day he finally grows old and weak. A few, such as myself, have dared to leave, but it is dangerous."

Daniel frowned and studied Marco intently. "You left for Tessa, right?"

"Yes. For her and for my son. It is no way to live. I wanted better for them."

Bryan frowned. "I'm surprised he's that powerful, at such a young age."

"Who said he is young?" Marco queried. "Pablo turned forty-five this year. He's been Alpha for almost eighteen years now."

"Forty-five? And he was after Tessa? No wonder you wanted to leave." Daniel shook his head in disgust. "Why doesn't he have a mate already?"

"He's had three, but they were all, supposedly, accident prone. I was not willing to risk Tessa having a similar *accident*." Marco clenched his fist and a muscle in his jaw throbbed.

Bryan got up and clapped a hand on Marco's shoulder in a gesture of support. "I'd have left too, man." He wandered to the window and stared outside. "You'll find things are different here. Ryne is a great Alpha and he's real easy to get along with."

"And even if you mess up, he doesn't stay angry for long." Daniel chimed in.

Marco nodded. "I look forward to getting to know him better when he gets back."

Right, Bryan thought as he surreptitiously checked the time and then looked at the phone. When he gets back.

Chicago, Illinois, USA...

Cassie ran as fast as she could towards her uncle's house. Her heart was pounding so loudly she couldn't hear anything but its thump. Frantically, she kept looking behind her while trying not to stumble over the exposed tree roots criss-crossing the ground.

She'd been hiding behind the trees, eavesdropping on the confrontation taking place between her uncle, Mr. Aldrich and the woman. The conversation hadn't made much sense, but she'd listened intently when her uncle began claiming she was like the woman, the one they said was a werewolf. It had seemed ridiculous and she even questioned her own hearing until she saw a man crawl out of the culvert and turn into a wolf! The wolf had attacked Mr. Aldrich and as the lawyer fell to the ground, his gun went off.

It had been like a scene from a horror movie. The wolf snarling; its teeth gleaming. A surprised cry coming from her uncle and then... Oh no! The flash of light and noise as the gun discharged. Her uncle falling. The image of a bullet hole, like a third eye in his forehead, drops of blood spattered on his face as he dropped to the ground. Her knees grew weak at the memory and she paused, clutching a tree for support while trying to gather her strength and force her panicked mind into some form of order.

427

She hadn't known what to do. Naturally, she'd screamed. Who wouldn't? And then, as she'd stood transfixed by the unfolding events, the wolf had actually looked up at her! Its eyes were strangely intelligent as if it were noting what she looked like and planning her fate. That one fact had leaped out at her, even though the look had been fleeting. In that instant she recalled her uncle saying werewolves killed those who discovered their secrets. Mr. Aldrich had found out, and the wolf was attacking him. And she'd just watched the man change into a wolf, so now she knew the secret, too. Of course, she'd be next in line!

Pushing off from the tree, she ran to the house as fast as possible. She entered through the front door; all thoughts of stealth forgotten. Time was of the essence now. She had to get away. Quickly she entered her uncle's office and yanked open the drawer where she knew he always kept some spare money. She grabbed a handful of bills before rushing upstairs. In her room she threw open drawers and closets, grabbed a gym bag and began randomly throwing clothing into it. In the bathroom, she swept the contents of the vanity in on top of her clothes, grabbed her purse and thundered down the stairs.

Franklin must have heard her for he appeared in the front foyer, looking concerned. "Miss Cassie! What's wrong?"

"Franklin, Uncle is—" Her voice caught on a sob and she was unable to get the word out. Even as Franklin stepped towards her, she was reaching for a set of keys from the hall table. "I'm sorry. I can't stay. He saw me."

"Who miss? Who saw you? And where is Mr. Greyson?" Franklin peered behind her as if trying to find his employer. When the man in question didn't appear, he walked towards Cassandra, his arms held out in front of him. "Why don't you calm down and let me help you?

Cassie shook her head and backed away, tears streaming down her face. The man had been her confidant for years, but this was too dangerous. She couldn't tell him, couldn't endanger him. "Franklin, I'm sorry!" She spun around and ran out the front door to the converted carriage house where the cars were kept.

Behind her, she could hear Franklin calling her name, but she didn't stop to answer. Yanking open the door to the garage, she pressed the remote control that opened the large external doors, then hurried to her car. Throwing her bag in first, she slid into the seat and started the engine. Impatiently, she waited for the garage doors to open, her fingers flexing nervously on the steering wheel. Come on, come on, she muttered under her breath. Her peripheral vision caught sight of Franklin hurrying towards her. Damn! Silently she asked for forgiveness, then slammed her foot onto the accelerator, the roof of her car scraping against the partially opened doorway as it shot forward. Without a backward glance, she sped away.

Ryne saw the young girl and quickly took note of her appearance before swinging his attention back to the man beneath him. Aldrich was struggling for breath, his throat partially ripped open, blood spilling onto the ground. Ready to finish the deed, a cry from Melody had Ryne once again looking away from his victim.

Melody was curled into a ball, her body shaking uncontrollably, her face contorted in pain. Abandoning the dying man beneath him, he changed forms and rushed to her side. Pulling her into his arms, he murmured words of encouragement.

"Fight it, Melody. Don't give in. Think about being human. About driving your car, using your computer, drinking that damned coffee you love so much." He rocked her back and forth praying she could maintain her form. Looking around, he realized sunset was only minutes away. The time of the full moon was almost upon them. Nadia's words rang through his mind. 'In the end she'll either live or die, depending on how much her body can handle.'

Hoping if he took her somewhere dark, away from the moon's effects, it might give her a fighting chance, he picked her up and eyed the pipe they'd crawled through, but shook his head. It was too small for him to carry Melody and she was in no fit state to crawl. He glanced around desperately, searching for a solution, then spied Aldrich's key chain on the ground; the little flashlight was cutting a small beam across the ground.

At least the man had proven useful for something. Snatching up the keys, Ryne gave the lawyer one last glance before turning away. He'd come back to deal with the bastard once Melody was safe.

Holding her close, he ran through the woods uncaring of the low hanging branches clutching at his hair and ripping his skin like the talons of some evil creature. All that mattered was Melody's laboured breathing and the rapidly setting sun.

He knew the pull of the moon only too well. The need clawing inside you, fighting to get out; wild thoughts invading your mind as the wolf became dominant, fighting to take over the human side. It was an irresistible feeling that had the person reaching and striving for release. It took inner strength and discipline to resist the ancient instincts.

Yet Melody wasn't ready; only part of her body had undergone the genetic changes needed. Could anyone live when their bone structure shifted to that of a wolf, while all their internal organs were still human? Brain signals would be speeding up her human heart to that of an animal, but how would it react to the strain? He wouldn't be able to bear it if she died. She was exasperating and smart mouthed, quirky and headstrong, but he loved every inch of her. He pressed a kiss to the top of her head. She had to make it. She had to!

A blood red stain was beginning to flood the sky by the time he arrived at the safe house where Aldrich had left his car. Setting Melody gently inside the vehicle, he buckled her in, jumped into the driver's seat and sped away. Glancing in the rear-view mirror, he noted the large house in the background was ablaze with lights and there were at least two figures running in front of it. His jaw clenched and he tightened his grip on the steering wheel. Where had the young girl gone? Who had she told? Beside him, Melody gave another pained cry and he refocused on driving. She needed him right now; the rest he'd figure out later.

If he remembered correctly from the taxi ride to the estate earlier, there was a shopping mall with an underground parking garage a few miles away. The lowest level should provide a sufficient shield.

As he drove, he glanced at the speedometer. The needle crept ever higher, trees and sign posts flashing by as he ignored the posted speed limits. His heart pounded heavily, while Nadia's dreaded words played over and over in his head; 'lives or dies', 'too risky', 'how much can her body handle'. The phrases swirled in his mind.

Negotiating a sharp turn, something thumped against his hip. Glancing down he spied the cell phone Aldrich had taken from him earlier. A quick look at the clock on the dashboard had him swearing. Shit, his agreed upon check-in time was past! He prayed Kane had held off, that he hadn't made any rash decisions!

Ryne fumbled with the phone, speed dialling his brother's number.

"Damn you, Ryne! Where the hell have you been?" Kane's voice roared in Ryne's ear.

Relief washed over him. If Kane was alive and angry, then the rest of them were safe too! "I don't have time to explain. Just hold off. Don't do anything, just hold off!" Melody whimpered beside him and he looked at her, causing the car to swerve. "I'll call you later!" He shouted the words over his brother's swearing and threw the phone down, concentrating on driving.

Shooting glances sideways, he noticed the air around Melody kept shimmering. Hell! Her change was getting closer. "Hang on, Melody, we're almost there. Just a few more minutes, babe. Focus on me, on the sound of my voice."

Ryne babbled away. Teasing her, apologizing for the mess she was in, for how he'd treated her. He told her he loved her, that everything would be all right. Bribes spilled from his lips; offerings of coffee and chocolate, giving her free rein in decorating the house in Stump River.

She was quieter now, her breathing shallow, her face pale. Beads of sweat formed on her forehead. How could such a string of unlikely circumstances ever have happened? He never had unprotected sex. And then the fight, his broken nose, her cut arm. The chances of those events occurring in the correct order and time frame were a million to one, and yet they had.

What had Nadia said? If anyone were to ask before attempting this type of thing, medical advice would strongly discourage any genetic changes during a full moon. It's way too risky.

Yeah. Easy for her to say. He hadn't planned this, though. It was as if the fates had conspired against him. Or maybe it was his own fault and not the fates. He'd been too cocky. He'd teased her, keeping her in Stump River with promises of an interview he knew damned well he'd never give. He should have kept his hands off her, sent her away. But his sexy bad-ass persona had become so ingrained over the years, he hadn't been able to control it when he'd most needed to.

If she died, the fault was his, no one else's. His eyes stung and he dashed his hand across them, trying to clear his vision.

'Lives or dies...dies...dies.' He shook his head, trying to dislodge the heart-stopping thought as icy fear encased him.

Chapter 40

Smythston, Oregon, USA…

Kane threw the phone onto his desk, not even trying to hold back the growl that rose from his chest.

"What's wrong? That was Ryne, wasn't it?" Helen's face was pale and there was a noticeable tremor in her hands as she pushed her hair back from her face. Like all the remaining pack members, her nerves were strung as taut as a fiddle string. She sat in a wing-back chair near the window, having chosen to spend her final hours with her Alpha.

"Yeah, it was Ryne."

"He didn't say—" She didn't finish the question, but Kane knew exactly what she meant. It was the question on everyone's mind. Was today the day they died?

"No. He said to hold off."

"Thank goodness." Her shoulders slumped and she leaned her head back, closing her eyes.

"He didn't say it was over, Helen. He said to hold off."

"No explanation why?" She straightened, her expression curious.

"No. And then he hung up on me!" Kane stood up and began to prowl around the room. "I don't know what it means. Is the crisis over? Has he eliminated the threat or is there still a chance—?" He compressed his lips and ran his hands through his hair. "Dammit. I'm tired of sitting here on edge waiting for news. I have men and women all over our territory waiting for my orders. I can feel their fear, their mental pain, and I don't know what to say."

"But at least it wasn't bad news." Helen clasped her hands. "If he said to hold off then there's still a chance everything will work out. It's a positive thing."

He growled, but conceded the point. "You're right. Sorry. My nerves are shot."

"And I'm sure Ryne's are too. This hasn't been easy for him, Kane, knowing it was his picture that caused all this. He must feel horribly guilty. And if that girl—Melody—is possibly his mate, then he's been fighting every instinct he has."

"Yeah. I know." He sighed heavily and sat down again. "Patience isn't always my strong suit."

"Consider this training for when you're a father. Then you'll need all the patience in the world."

He gave the briefest of chuckles, before picking up a picture of Elise he had taken just days ago. She was wearing a loose white dress and her arms cradled the slight swell of her belly. He gently ran his finger over the picture, then set it aside. Picking up the vial of deadly poison that all the remaining pack had been issued, he twirled the blood coloured liquid within, watching as it flowed and shifted. "Yeah. Someday when I'm a father."

Chicago, Illinois, USA…

The shopping mall loomed ahead and Ryne forced himself to slow down, entering the driveway at a reasonable pace. His fingers drummed on the steering wheel as he waited in a long line of cars. Finally, it was his turn at the gate. He collected his ticket and headed for the basement level. As the cool darkness of the cement structure closed around them, he listened intently for any change in Melody's breathing. Was it deeper? More natural? He hoped so.

It was a multi-storey garage with a steep, winding ramp leading from level to level. Ryne concentrated on manoeuvring the twisting incline with as much speed as possible. The air grew progressively cooler as they descended and artificial lighting glowed overhead.

Finally reaching the lowest level, he drove to a poorly lit corner and parked behind a pillar, thankful Aldrich's black car would be relatively unnoticed in the gloom. He didn't want anyone coming by to see what was going on.

Turning off the engine, he twisted in his seat and checked Melody. Her eyes were shut, her dark lashes fanned out over the pale shadowed skin below. She was more stable and when he touched her hand there was certain solidity; no shimmers distorting the air around her. Her muscles weren't spasming. Slowly he unclenched his jaw. His plan seemed to be working.

Brushing his hand over her cheek, he noted her skin was cool to the touch and her breathing was deep and even. No doubt exhausted from the strain, she'd fallen asleep. He pressed a tender kiss on her forehead and then leaned his head back and thanked the gods she'd managed to hold on.

It had been touch and go, but tonight was probably the worst. By tomorrow the moon would already be waning. With Melody one day farther into her change and the lunar effects ebbing, it should be easier for her to withstand the transformation.

Closing his eyes, he ran through all the things he needed to do. Calling Kane, of course, was paramount. The whole pack was waiting his report. He wished he could give them a definitive answer, but the truth was he needed to check Melody didn't have another copy of that report stashed away. Then he had to retrieve her laptop from the public locker where he'd stashed it. And then there was Aldrich. The man had been near death when he'd scooped up Melody and left. Surely no one would have arrived in time to save the bastard.

He gave a dark laugh recalling the last time he had thought a villain was dead, only to have her crawl away when they weren't looking. Not this time. No assuming. He wanted to see a dead body before he told Kane things were one hundred percent safe.

Wearily, he picked up the cell phone to call Kane back. He imagined the other man was ready to rip a strip off him; after all, no one dared hang up on Kane Sinclair! About to dial, he caught sight of himself in the rear-view mirror and froze. His face was streaked with mud and his hair stood up on end. And, he didn't have any clothes on! His frantic form-shift to save Melody had caused him to miss a step. Giving a brief chuckle, he dialled Kane's number and braced himself for the coming onslaught.

Somewhere in the USA...

Cassie wearily got off the bus, dragging her small bag of possessions behind her. She ached from the stiff uncomfortable seats and, not for the first time, thought wistfully of the luxury vehicle she'd abandoned hours ago. Arching her back, she forced herself to forget the car. There was no time for regret; more pressing matters needed to be dealt with such as—she paused and surveyed her surroundings—where she was. It was a bus station in a small town, but where exactly? All she knew was it wasn't near her uncle's estate where he... She couldn't bring herself to finish the thought.

It was the middle of the night and the town was mostly in darkness. An old motel across the street had a vacancy sign, so she crossed the road and entered the dingy front office. The clerk looked at her askance, no doubt wondering what illegal substance she was taking, then continued on with his phone call. As she waited for him to finish, she looked outside, catching sight of her own reflection in the darkened window; her eyes over-dilated and her face pale, framed by long unkempt hair. Shivers swept over her body as if she needed the next hit of her drug.

When the man finished his call, she explained what she needed and handed him a handful of bills. The clerk slid the key card over to her and she took it, giving a brief nod of thanks.

"I don't want no trouble, you hear? This is a clean, family motel." As he spoke, the clerk spat a wad of tobacco juice into a can on the counter.

Sure. A family motel. Cassie glanced around, noting the open can of beer on the man's desk, the porno flick playing on TV and filthy, torn linoleum floor before looking back at him. "I won't cause any trouble." She exited the office and wrapped her arms around herself in a futile attempt to quell the shakes wracking her body.

"Damned druggies." She heard the man mutter before the door swung shut.

As she crossed the parking lot and made her way to her room, she laughed. It wasn't an illegal substance that was responsible for her present appearance. It was the damned migraine pills. She hadn't wanted to take them, but as the night advanced, the strangest feelings came over her; a tingling sensation in her arms and legs, a tension coiling inside her that made her shift restlessly as she drove. Fearful of being alone and sick while on the run from the terror she'd left behind, she'd finally pulled over and taken one of the pills. Unfortunately, a few miles later the pill had started to take effect and she'd been forced to abandon her car, realizing she was in no condition to drive. Too scared to stay where she was, she'd found a bus station and taken the first available bus to...well...wherever she was now.

At the moment, she was too tired to care. Fumbling with the key card, she opened the door and went inside. A bed dominated the room and she stumbled towards it, desperately wanting to lie down and let the pills work their magic. For over a year, she'd hated the fuzzy, floating numbness the pills invoked. Now she craved it and the deep dreamless sleep that followed. It would help her forget. Dropping her small bag of possessions on the floor beside the bed, she lay down, her eyes half shut.

The room was rundown, but appeared clean and a faint antiseptic smell lingered in the air. Shifting, she managed to snag the blanket folded at the foot of the bed and wrapped it around herself.

Slowly she relaxed, her limbs feeling heavy. She'd been fighting the need to sleep for hours, not daring to do more than rest on the bus. Fear had forced her to keep watch, constantly checking if the bus was being followed and examining each new passenger that boarded. Of course, the werewolf man had never appeared, but she knew he wouldn't forget about her. If the bus driver hadn't finally told her it was the end of the road, she would have stayed on; constant movement made her feel safer.

Well, she was in the middle of nowhere. If she didn't even know where she was, then how could he? There was a flaw in her logic, but she couldn't focus enough to decide what it was. Drifting in and out of consciousness, bits and pieces of the night's events played out in her mind, but it was as if she was detached, watching a movie where she didn't really care about any of the characters.

It had been so weird seeing that man change into a wolf. There'd been a shimmering, wavering change in the air and then the man was gone and a wolf had stood in his place. A massive, black creature with large white teeth. Then it snarled and leapt forward, so quickly it had been just a blur.

Her uncle had shouted in surprise and then the sound of a gun firing had filled the air. Her mind skittered away from the image of her uncle lying dead and instead focused on the wolf. The man inside the beast was still present. She knew it. Even though gore had dripped from its jaws. A whimper escaped her at the thought of those large teeth piercing her skin and ripping her flesh.

She curled into a tighter ball. The floaty feeling was leaving already. Fear poured into her; fear and a crawling sensation as if her very skin was alive and had a mind of its own. The need for...something...was filling her and she shifted restlessly on the bed. Her head was starting to spin; she could actually hear the blood thrumming through her veins.

Thinking the first pill must have worn off and a migraine was looming, she sat up and pulled her bag onto the bed beside her. Her fingers shook as she fumbled to find and open the medicine bottle. The cap came off and she spilled most of the tablets on the bed. Damn and double damn—she didn't want to waste any of them; who knew when she'd be able to get the prescription refilled. The hated medication was now her friend.

Managing to pick one up, she swallowed it, almost gagging as she forced the pill down without water. A lamp was on the table by the bed and she reached to turn it on, but paused. Light made the symptoms worse, she'd been told. A sliver of moonlight was peeking in through a crack in the curtains and she used it to help her see the pills strewn over the bed. When all the tablets were accounted for and back in their bottle, she lay back down and tried to hold back the tears filling her eyes. She wished she were home, but it was too dangerous now. Her uncle was gone; the wolf was after her. Her skin prickled again and she curled up in a ball once more, rubbing her hands over her arms in an attempt to ease the sensation.

What had her yoga instructor told her? Think of a happy place? She furrowed her brow. Where would she rather be right now? An amusement park? A museum? Vegas? She chuckled at the random thought, but then latched onto the idea. She'd seen pictures of the place before. Bright lights, large crowds; crowds she could get lost in, where no werewolf would ever find her.

The image clarified in her mind. Gambling machines, showgirls, the hot desert, tourists. The patch of moonlight that splashed across her room became a spotlight, guiding people to their hotel, beckoning them to heed its call. A strange feeling came over her. Her whole body vibrated and it felt like her head was going to explode. She clenched her fingers around the strap of her bag, her muscles tightened and then the air seemed to shimmer.

Back in Chicago…

It was morning. Mel reclined in her seat as Ryne slowly drove the car out of the parking garage. They'd talked on and off throughout the night and she had finally accepted the truth of what he'd been telling her. She really was becoming a Lycan. There'd been anger and tears; Ryne had even apologized for his own part in the situation. Eventually she'd come to a numb acceptance of the fact she was no longer Melody Greene, waitress and journalism student. Now she was Melody Greene, secret Lycan.

From what she could gather from Ryne's 'crash course on wolves', they were social creatures and lived in packs. There was an Alpha who kept everyone in line and made the important decisions, though pack meetings were held to discuss options. Full moons were a time to party and, if you were new to the whole Lycan thing like she was, you had no control and transformed once a month. Older wolves could fight the effects if they wished, though most didn't.

It gave her a headache, trying to figure out how she'd manage. She'd have to lock herself up every month so no one would discover her secret, which would really play havoc with her job and her studies. Then there was going into heat once a season. Ryne had enjoyed explaining that one to her. Just the thought of being turned on for a whole week had her cheeks warming.

"I know what you're thinking." Ryne leaned over to whisper in her ear, his tone teasing. He grabbed her hand as he steered the vehicle with the other.

His touch was comforting, so she didn't pull away, even though his comment made her bristle. Deciding to put him in his place, she commented on his current apparel. "Actually, I was thinking how cute you look in those clothes. Short plaid golf pants are so you!" His expression made her laugh. "You should be thankful Mr. Aldrich had a suitcase of clothes in the back and all those wet wipes. Otherwise we'd both still be filthy."

Ryne grunted and she wisely kept silent for a while, watching the scenery. Eventually, Ryne spoke again.

"What are you really thinking about?"

"I'm trying to figure out how I'll manage being a Lycan in Chicago."

"In Chicago?" He looked surprised.

"Where else would I be?"

"Back in Stump River, with me." Ryne stated the fact as if it were a foregone conclusion.

"With you?"

"Yeah."

"Says who?"

"Says me!"

"And what if I don't want to go?" She pulled her hand away and crossed her arms over her chest, turning to stare out the window. Ryne didn't respond and she checked on him out of the corner of her eye. He was gripping the steering wheel hard enough his knuckles were turning white and a muscle ticked in his jaw. She looked away and they drove in silence. Finally, he sighed and spoke in a low voice.

"Why? Why don't you want to go back? Is it too quiet? You don't like my house? The lack of a coffee shop?"

She shrugged and picked at the material of the seatbelt.

"Is it me?"

His voice sounded uncertain and when she looked his way, there was a general air of hurt about him.

"Well..."

"Melody, I apologized for what I said in Stump River. I didn't mean any of it. It was all because of the Keeping. You were asking questions and I couldn't provide any answers. If you found out and then told someone else..." He sighed. "Your life was at stake. Your life and the lives of my brother's entire pack. I couldn't take the chance."

"Why didn't you trust me?"

"It's almost bred into us. The need to hide, to not let outsiders in, to be suspicious of human motives. Our people were persecuted for millennia, almost hunted to extinction. Centuries of distrust are hard to ignore. Even when a human is your friend, you tend to hold back."

"I suppose. I guess I've forgiven you, though you didn't need to be quite so mean."

He chuckled. "You're stubborn, Melody. If I didn't come down on you hard, you'd have kept hanging around, trying to worm your damn interview out of me."

A guilty smile curved on her lips. He knew her so well.

"So you'll forgive me and come back?" He sounded hopeful, but Mel wanted more.

"Why do you want me back?"

He shrugged. "You're a Lycan now. You need a pack to help you. Going it on your own is tricky. Most lone wolves don't survive."

"So, my returning is totally for my own good." She raised her eyebrows, questioning his reasoning.

"Sure. You need a home. My pack needs more members. You like Bryan and Daniel. Oh, and did I tell you about the Loberos? They're joining us, too. There's Marco, his mate Olivia, their son—he's just a baby—and Marco's sister, Tessa. You'll get along great with them and Olivia is about your age, I think."

"Uh-huh." She stared out the window and fought to swallow past the lump in her throat. He wasn't saying anything about caring for her, loving her. She'd been so sure last night, when she'd been almost delirious and fighting not to shift, that he'd said he loved her, but there was no mention of it now.

She felt him flicking glances her way; sensed his worry, but had no inclination to talk any more. Ryne was arrogant, rude and domineering. He was also clever and witty, courageous and strong, good-looking, sexy and, when she'd really needed it, he'd been gentle and tender. Damn, she hated to admit it, even to herself, but she loved the man. But if he wanted her to be a part of his life, he'd have to do better than he had so far at expressing his feelings. If she gave in to him now, it would set a precedent for the rest of their time together.

Instead, she focused on herself, pondering where her Lycan genetics might have come from. It could be her father or maybe somewhere in her mother's background. Likely it was a mystery she'd never solve, especially since they had to keep their existence a secret. She could hardly walk up to her mother and say 'Hey, are there any Lycans in our background?'

Of course, knowing how off-beat her mother was, the woman would probably dive into the whole concept with both feet. Thinking of all the trouble her mother might inadvertently stir up, she shuddered. Yep, asking her mother would definitely not be a good idea. They didn't need another round of this whole Keeping business and, in the end, it didn't really matter where the genes came from. She was a Lycan now.

During the night, she'd confessed to Ryne she'd applied to Lycan Link as a joke and hadn't believed it when they said they'd research her background to see if she qualified. He explained how it worked; that on the surface the site was for fans of the paranormal but its purpose was to locate wayward Lycans such as herself. The real Lycan Link existed beneath layers of security, completely hidden from human view. She'd given a wry laugh thinking of how she and Beth had said she'd become a card carrying Lycan. Little did she know it would come true!

They arrived back at her apartment building and Ryne pulled into a convenient parking spot. He turned off the engine and stared straight ahead. Silence reigned.

She pasted a fake smile on her face. "Well, I'm home."

He cleared his throat and turned to look at her. "It doesn't have to be. Your home, that is. You could live in Stump River. With me. I... I really want you to." When she didn't answer, he shifted closer and gently took her chin, turning her to face him. He stared intently at her, his gaze moving over her features before returning to her eyes, seeming to be searching for something. Finally, he gave a half smile and leaned closer, brushing his lips over hers. "Melody, I love you and want you to stay with me. Please say you'll come back to Stump River."

She smiled against his lips. "Took you long enough to say it." She kissed him back.

"I told you last night." He had the faintest of pouts on his face.

"But I wasn't sure if you had really said it, or if it was all part of the whole transformation thing. I was having some pretty weird thoughts."

He wiggled his eyebrows at her. "Wanna share?"

She flushed. "Maybe later." She had a feeling her wolf was going to be a lusty creature and somehow Ryne knew it.

He kissed her again, gently at first and then with increasing passion. She returned the kiss with equal ardour, burying her fingers in his thick, silky hair, relishing the feel of his stubbly skin gently abrading hers. It was only when a group of teens walked by, hooting encouragement, that they pulled apart. Ryne glared at them through the windshield and the young hooligans immediately fell silent, backing away and then turning almost as one to run down the street.

She chuckled softly. "I wish I could do that."

"I'll teach you." He brushed the hair from her face and then moved back to his own seat. They sat in companionable silence for a moment before he looked at her regretfully. "So...what about your apartment?"

She pursed her lips and exhaled slowly, staring up at the window of her apartment unit. From what she'd been told, this was where Lucy had been...injured. Her mind shied away from using a more final term, as a faint hope fluttered within her. Perhaps...

Ryne cleared his throat and asked softly, "Do you want to go in, or should I—?"

"No, I need to do this. Lucy's my friend, too." She drew a shuddering breath and squared her shoulders. "I'll go in. I imagine the police will have started an investigation and there'll be questions to answer. What should we tell them?"

"Don't worry. I'll take care of it. As a Lycan, you get lots of practice creating plausible half-truths to cover things up." Ryne gently squeezed her hand and then opened the car door.

The time in the apartment wasn't pleasant. It was cordoned off and a police officer was on guard. Ryne did most of the talking, the lies rolling off his tongue with no hesitation. By the time he was done, even Mel half-believed the tale. The police officer allowed them in so Mel could check if anything was missing; the police were operating under the assumption Lucy had walked in during an attempted burglary.

A chalk line showed where Lucy had fallen, in case the blood stains on the floor hadn't been sufficient indication. Her breath hitched as she stared at the spot before forcing herself to look away and blink rapidly, holding back the tears that threatened to fall.

The apartment units surrounding hers were unusually quiet, almost as if everyone knew of the tragedy and were paying their respects. As she walked into the living room, her footsteps echoed in the silence. Bits of dust floated on a sunbeam that had managed to work its way through a crack in the curtains, its brightness a stark contrast to the general air of gloom pervading the space.

As she looked around at the shabby furnishings, she realized there wasn't much she would want to keep.

A few personal papers, some photographs, a teddy bear from her childhood but that was all. She forced herself to think dispassionately, making calm, logical plans. Call the phone company, contact the landlord. It wouldn't take much time to box up her things and have them shipped to Stump River.

While Ryne talked to the officer, she walked around the rooms, trailing her fingers over the back of a chair, adjusting a crooked picture on the wall. This place represented her past; a person she no longer was. It hadn't been much of a life, but it had been hers. She'd been free to come and go as she wished. There'd been no need to hide, no secrets to keep from friends. Sure, things had been tight but it had all been so normal. A part of her mourned the loss.

Eventually, she made her way back to the spot where Lucy had been struck down. Grief and guilt warred within her. If she hadn't offered to take Lucy to Chicago, the woman would still be here, possibly planning a future with Armand.

She blinked back tears, thinking of the printed report sitting in the pocket of the coat she now had casually slung over her arm. Ryne had asked her to retrieve it so they could destroy the final piece of evidence. If she hadn't taken the job interviewing Ryne, then Greyson would be alive and that young girl wouldn't be completely alone in the world. Even the slime ball, Aldrich, would still be around. Whoever would have thought trying to interview a photographer could have led to such an end?

She said as much to Ryne as they left her apartment. He shushed her, claiming if she wanted to lay blame, it was his fault.

"If I hadn't taken that picture, Greyson wouldn't have gone looking for me. Sometimes the simplest of things can cause a landslide. What's important is everything you did was done with the best of intentions."

"I suppose so." She gave a heavy sigh. "Ryne?"

"Yeah?"

"Can you give me a hug?"

"Sure." He slipped his arm around her shoulders and gave her a gentle squeeze as they exited the building.

"We'll need to contact Lucy's family."

"That would be me."

"You? You're her family? But you two—"

"No. I mean she didn't really have any family. I'll take care of things."

"Oh." Something Lucy had said on the flight to Chicago came to mind. "You might want to talk to Armand. Apparently, just before she left, he indicated he was interested in her."

"Damn!" Ryne shook his head. "I always wondered about that, but the man was afraid to make his move."

"Why?"

"Lucy and I were casual so it didn't matter she wasn't aware of my true self, that I was a Lycan, I mean. But Armand, he was always afraid to get close in case it did come to mean something."

"I don't understand."

"I suppose I can tell you. Remember, now that you're one of us, you're bound by the Keeping. You can't tell anyone." Ryne waited until she nodded and even made a 'cross your heart' gesture.

"Armand is a bear."

"A bear?"

"Uh-huh."

"He didn't seem surly to me; actually, quite the opposite." She frowned and then brightened. "Oh, you mean he looks like a bear; big and hairy."

"No. I mean he *is* a bear. A shifter or were-bear, though he hates the fact it rhymes."

She leaned back and stared at Ryne in disbelief. "A were-bear? Exactly how many other shifter creatures are out there?"

"Almost any creature you can think of, though it's mostly larger predatory animals. Tigers, panthers, lions. I think the non-predators died out pretty early, not being able to defend themselves." Ryne reached over and ruffled her hair. "So you won't have to worry about were-rats in the sewers."

She cast a dirty look his way before climbing into the car. "Hey, what are we going to do about Aldrich's car? We can't keep driving around in it."

"Don't worry. I'll take care of it. I've had experience with this type of situation."

"Oh, really? Exactly what type of experience? Grand theft auto?"

Ryne merely smirked and started the car, leaving her to wonder exactly what else might be hidden in his background.

Chapter 41

It had taken a week before the police wrapped up the investigation into what had transpired at the apartment. It was deemed a random act of violence, the perpetrator likely looking for something to steal and Lucy had unfortunately surprised him. It grated Aldrich would never be blamed for the crime, but involving him would result in too many questions and it wouldn't change anything.

With that settled, they'd returned to Stump River with Lucy's casket. Everyone mourned the loss of the friendly waitress, especially Armand. The twinkle was gone from his eye and he literally shuffled about The Broken Antler. After the memorial service, he disappeared for a week and Mel wondered if he had shifted into his bear form and was wandering the woods. Were his emotions any less intense when he was an animal? Or was he scratching trees and ripping open logs, trying to work the grief out of his system? Whatever the case, he eventually returned looking haggard, but seeming to have found some inner peace.

Beth and Josh ran a long article in the paper, featuring quotes from the various citizens and random pictures of Lucy at several town functions as well as a full colour picture on the front page. It was nice to have the picture, giving them a last look at the young woman they were all fond of. The service had a closed casket, Ryne having stated Lucy was always proud of her appearance and wouldn't appreciate people gawking at her. Mel agreed it was best this way.

Ruth declared Lucy was a hero who had been trying to protect Mel's apartment and everyone else in town concurred. It wasn't the complete truth, but Mel knew the hero part was correct. While she'd never know exactly what happened that fateful day, she suspected Lucy had been trying to defend her.

Life in Stump River slowly fell back into its usual rhythm, though there were a few changes. Ruth's seemed quieter; The Broken Antler more subdued. On the positive side, the Loberos moved to town and caused quite a stir of speculation. And Ryne had some business to finish off with regard to the Keeping.

Ryne sat down with Bryan and talked to Kane. They were trying to tie up all the loose ends.

"We have to take care of Aldrich. He knows too much." Kane's voice was firm as it came over the speaker phone.

"Agreed." Ryne rubbed his chin thoughtfully. "I tried to get into the hospital several different times last week, but security around him was too tight. Greyson—the guy he shot—was a multi-millionaire and there's a big investigation going on. Since the police already knew what I looked like from seeing me at Melody's apartment, I didn't dare get too close." He growled in frustration. "Too bad the butler went looking for Greyson as soon as he did. If he'd waited longer, Aldrich might have been dead before the old man found him. At least the bastard won't be saying anything right away. The report Daniel hacked from the hospital's computer states Aldrich has been unconscious for almost a week with severe damage to his windpipe and vocal cords."

Bryan chuckled. "Too bad Mel couldn't have held off until you finished him off." Ryne flashed him a dirty look and he quickly qualified his answer. "Not that it's her fault in any way, of course."

454

"Right." Ryne glared at Bryan once more before continuing. "He'll probably keep the story to himself since without proof, people will think he's crazy, but we can't take any chances."

Kane agreed. "I'll contact a pack I know in the area. Maybe they can find a way to get someone through the security net. We'll have to try to get them to burglarize the estate as well. I want the picture back before it can cause any more trouble."

"And we'll deal with the girl." Ryne suggested.

"Sounds good to me." Kane could be heard pacing in his office.

"Anxious, Kane?" Ryne teased.

His brother growled in response. "You know damned well I am. Elise is still away and I need her back here with me. The sooner we get Aldrich taken care of, the sooner I can allow the dispersal groups to return home. Until such time, let's just say it's best to give me a wide berth."

Ryne chuckled. "You could always go visit her and *relieve* some of that tension."

The sound of pacing ceased. "You might be on to something, Ryne."

Ryne and Bryan exchanged glances, but kept their laughter in check. Both were aware of how devoted Kane was to his mate and knew the forced separation was hard for him to deal with.

Once the conversation was over, Ryne sighed heavily and rubbed his face with his hands. "The young girl, Cassandra, she's just a kid and likely scared spitless over seeing her uncle murdered, let alone watching me transform and attack Aldrich."

"You said Greyson apparently raised the girl since she was an infant and knew all along she was a Lycan? I wonder where he found her and how he knew what she was?" Bryan got up and started to pace the room.

"I've been thinking about that, too. He said he was looking for a pack for her to join."

"But she doesn't know any of this?" Bryan queried. "Hard to believe if she's about seventeen, like you said."

"I only got a glimpse of her, but I'd say she was around that age and from the look on her face, I'd say she was in shock. I think she must have been eavesdropping. You know, I thought I scented another Lycan, but I was too caught up in what was going down to have time to check it out."

"But how could she not know she's a shifter? She should have gone through her first change."

"Greyson must have hidden it from her somehow; maybe he drugged her each month." Ryne shrugged. "Now she's out there on her own and who knows what might happen? We need to find her and bring her in before an outsider figures out what she is."

Bryan had been staring out the window, but turned as Ryne stopped speaking. "Ryne, I'd like to find her. I've always been a pretty good tracker."

Ryne gave him a crooked grin. "I was wondering how long it would take for you to ask. You can go. Tomorrow. Mel's going to have her first transformation tonight and it would be nice if her whole pack was here to support her."

"Tonight? But it's not a full moon."

"Nadia said given Mel's recent genetic changes and several partial transformations, it would be best to try her first full one without the added stress of a full moon."

"Have you told her *everything*?" Bryan had an evil glint in his eye.

"Well, not the clothing part. I think she might be pissed off when she realizes she's the only one in the pack who won't be able to magick her clothes on and off."

"Oh, I'd love to hear that conversation."

Ryne stood, intent on heading towards his room where Mel was rearranging the closets to hold her things. "Who knows? If she's mad enough, you might. Be listening for a loud scream of fury in about ten minutes."

Mel awoke slowly from one of the best sleeps she could ever recall having. Smiling contentedly, she stretched, pleased to realize her muscles weren't protesting. Last night she'd transformed into a wolf. It had been strange, but exhilarating at the same time.

She'd shifted with Ryne in the woods, just the two of them, even though it was tradition for the whole pack to be present. Given her half-human background she'd been told she would probably lack some of the abilities the others possessed; specifically, she probably wouldn't be able to magick her clothes back on. The news hadn't sat well with her, and Ryne—with a little persuasion on her part—had made some readjustments to the usual ceremonies to accommodate her.

As they gathered in the woods at full dark, Bryan had teased her to no end over the fact she'd be naked.

"Aw, come on, Mel. Don't be standoffish." He pleaded.

"I will not waltz around in the woods buck naked in front of you and Daniel and the whole Lobero family."

"We won't mind." Bryan had laughed before dodging the punch she aimed at him.

"It's not just me. Our Alpha made the final decision." She tried not to sound too smug about the fact she'd been able to convince Ryne to see things her way. It had only taken a few carefully chosen words to have Ryne seething with jealousy.

"That's right. It's my decision as Alpha." Ryne slid into place behind her and wrapped his arms around her waist, nuzzling her neck. "No one sees her naked except me." He looked up and growled at Bryan who paled and backed away.

"Uh, sure, Ryne. Whatever you say. We'll just...uh...wait over there." He gestured vaguely to the north.

"Make sure it's really far *over there* where you can't *accidentally* peek." She warned.

Bryan winked, shot a nervous glance at Ryne, who was still growling lightly and then walked away calling for the others to follow him.

The change had come amazingly easy to her, however the coordination needed to walk on all fours had been difficult to master, let alone running and dealing with the amplified sensations coming at her from all sides. She did more than a few face plants before managing to walk far enough to greet her packmates who had already transformed and were patiently waiting for her some distance away.

She'd soon adjusted, however and enjoyed her first night running through the forest. In fact, she'd been reluctant to return home and Ryne eventually had to pull rank, nipping her heels so she'd follow him!

Now it was the morning. Ryne was sleeping peacefully in bed beside her but she was still keyed up from the experience. Mischievously, she leaned over him to nibble at his ear.

Ryne murmured and shifted slightly before settling into sleep again. She snickered to herself and kissed his jaw while her fingers traced patterns down his well-defined torso, slowly lowering the blanket covering him. He jerked awake.

"Melody!" His voice husky with sleep.

"'Morning." She kissed him enthusiastically not stopping until he gripped her shoulders and eased her away.

"I didn't know I was getting involved with such a lusty woman."

"I tried to keep it a secret so you wouldn't run away." She murmured trailing butterfly kisses down the cord of his neck to his collarbone.

"I never run from a challenge." With a growl, he began to tickle her.

"Hey, no fair!"

"Who says I play fair?"

Ryne smiled down at Melody. Tired from their game, she lay at his side, her face flushed, her expression relaxed and happy. His gaze drifting over the form of the beautiful woman who had barged into his life and turned his world upside down. He loved her. How her brain worked, her curiosity, her stubbornness, her courage. He hadn't known he'd needed her, had been waiting his whole life for her to appear and complete him.

"Melody, remember when I told you about blood-bonding?" He brushed his thumb over her lower lip.

She nodded. "Lycans become connected with their mates, forming an almost telepathic bond."

"It's permanent, for life, until one of the pair dies." He drew in a deep breath.

"Like a marriage, but with no chance of divorce."

"Right." He paused and licked his lips. "Would you... Would you blood-bond with me?"

Her eyes widened. "Are you proposing?"

His mouth twisted into a lopsided grin. "Yeah. I guess I am."

"I thought you'd never ask." She gave squeal of delight and launched herself at him knocking him over.

"So, is that a yes?"

She hit him playfully. "Of course, you big dummy."

"Are you sure?" He looked at her intently, his expression serious. "It's forever, you know."

"I'm sure." She reached out to cup his face, tracing his cheek bone with her thumb. "I want to be with you for the rest of my life."

"Same here," he whispered as he leaned down kissed her reverently. "Shall we do it now?"

"Really? Here? Right now?" She looked around nervously.

"Well, I don't know where else we'd do it. I guess we could go outside..." He teased her and then kissed the tip of her nose.

She rolled her eyes at him before questioning him further. "I'd have to bite you?"

"And I'd bite you. Then we'd drink a bit of each other's blood. Just a few drops and just this once. It's not like we're vampires having a feast."

She grimaced at the idea, then nodded. "Okay. So, how do we start?"

He grinned. "We have great sex and then, part-way through, our canines lengthen and we bite each other."

"Oh. Okay." She took a deep breath and then smiled at him tremulously. "I guess I'm ready then."

"Good."

He leaned forward to kiss her again, pausing just inches away. Her breath was soft puffs against his mouth. Her big, brown eyes looked at him so trustingly, so full of...love. A lump formed in his throat and, ridiculously, he had to blink a few times, his eyes pricking with emotion. She was his woman. His mate.

Closing the gap between them, he sank into the embrace, knowing he'd finally found his other half.

Sometime later, Mel lay sprawled on the bed. Ryne's head rested between her breasts, his leg wrapped over hers.

"Hey," she whispered to him.

Hey yourself. His voice echoed in her head and she gave a start before giggling. So this was the mental bond he talked about. Pretty cool.

"Yeah it is, isn't it?" He murmured against her still heated flesh. "Apparently, it's always strongest after sex."

"Well, I guess our bond will be pretty strong then, since I plan on having lots and lots of sex with you."

"Really? I like how you think." And with that he flipped her over so he was on top and her arms were pinned over her head.

"Ryne!" She giggled and tugged at her arms, but he didn't let go.

"You know, barely a month ago I was at the Broken Antler on my birthday thinking I'd never find a woman to put up with me."

"And then I appeared."

"I couldn't decide what to do with you. I was such an idiot."

"You won't get any argument from me."

He glared down at her, his gaze eventually softening as he took in her form.

"Ryne?"

"Yeah?"

"If you don't touch me soon, I'm going to scream."

He chuckled. "Well, you're going to be screaming sooner or later, anyway."

"You sound pretty confident, Taylor."

"I am, Melody. Indeed, I am." He gave her a devilish grin and then proceeded to prove to her exactly how right he was!

Epilogue

Back in Chicago...

Leon Aldrich lay in a hospital bed, his eyelids half open. A ventilator pumped air through the breathing tube in his newly repaired throat. The pain medication made him groggy and the room kept going in and out of focus. In his hand he held a crumpled copy of Greyson's will. He couldn't believe he never knew about Cassandra Greyson and that she'd inherit everything. Hazily he thought that, if he'd been able bodied, he would have changed the will in his favour, searching the estate for the other two copies of the will Greyson had mentioned.

Since he couldn't do that, he needed to find the girl. But how?

The sound of the door opening caught his attention and he slowly shifted his eyes to observe the newcomer. It was a nurse.

"Hello, Mr. Aldrich. And how are we today?" She chatted as she checked the ventilator and peered at his bandages. "Nasty wounds. I must say I've never heard of a wild dog attack in Chicago."

Aldrich tried to speak.

"No, no, no. You can't try to talk. Your throat can't stand the strain. If you need something, press the call button and use this whiteboard." She held the objects up for him to see and then placed them on the tray in front of him.

He blinked twice. It had been his main means of communicating until today. Two for yes. Three for no.

The nurse smiled and applied cream to his dry chapped lips. "You must be exhausted after that police interview. It was so brave of you to step between Mr. Greyson and the attacking dog."

Aldrich blinked twice again. That was the story he'd painstakingly communicated.

Straightening his covers, the nurse continued. "I heard the police talking as they left. They agree it was an unfortunate accident; the dog jumped at you just as you fired the gun and the bullet hit Mr. Greyson by mistake. You're so lucky the beast ran off before it killed you."

Two more blinks.

She squeezed his hand. "Your secretary is here to see you. She's such a sweet thing. When I said I needed to check your bandages and medication, she told me she'd go downstairs for a few minutes and browse the gift shop until I was done. I'm sure she'll be back soon." With a final pat to his hand, the woman left.

If nothing else, the woman's chatter had helped clear his thinking. He found it easier to concentrate on the problem of Cassandra Greyson. She stood in the way of him getting his hands on Greyson's money. As long as she was missing, the estate would be tied up. It would give him time to heal, but once she was found, then what? She wasn't yet eighteen. Possibly, he could have himself appointed her guardian, worm his way into her confidence. But how to contact her? A gleam entered his eye as he noticed a newspaper lying on the chair by his bed. Slowly, he grabbed the white board and began to write.

By the time he was finished, he was wet with sweat from the exertion, but a satisfied look covered his face. He ran the message over in his mind. 'Place a personal ad in all major papers around U.S.A. It should read 'Cassandra, please come home. You're in grave danger from the wild ones. Only I can protect you. – A.'

He frowned then added one more line.

There was a light rap on the door and Ms. Matthews walked in. He assessed the temporary secretary carefully, knowing she was the person who had caved to Greyson's demands she snoop in his appointment book. She wasn't exactly trustworthy. Damn Ms. Sandercock for being away! At least Ms. Matthews seemed biddable enough. And she had brought him Greyson's will. Not really having any other choice, he made his decision.

"Hello, Mr. Aldrich." Ms. Matthews set a magazine down on his bed table. "I brought you something to read, in case you're bored. Is there anything I can do for you?"

He gestured at the white board and she picked it up.

When she was finished reading, she gave him a puzzled look. "This is the girl mentioned in the will?"

He blinked twice.

"All right. I'll have a personal ad put in the papers for you and get some extra guards posted outside this room, though I can't think why. The police were here all week..." Her voice trailed off as she copied the message down on a sheet of paper. "Oh, by the way, Ms. Sandercock called, and she's taking an extended leave. Some family business about the relative who passed away. Richardson's Temp Agency is willing to give me the position until she returns, if it's all right with you."

He blinked yes, knowing he really had no other choice. It wasn't like he was able to interview for the position.

"I was hoping you'd agree. You seem like such a nice man." She stepped closer and brushed his hair back from his forehead, letting her hand trail slowly down his arm. "If you need anything, anything at all, just ask. And

465

feel free to call me by my first name. It's Mary, though some people use my nickname, Marla." She smiled widely and stepped away. "I'll go place this ad for you now. See you tomorrow."

Stupid girl, he thought as she left the room, vaguely noting she had the slightest limp. If she thinks I'll fall for that act she's a fool. I know her kind only too well.

~**Fin**~

A Message from Nicky

Hi!

Thank you for reading The Keeping. I hope you enjoyed the story. If you did, please consider leaving some feedback at a book review site, or email me; I love hearing from my readers!

I'd never intended to write a book about Ryne but when he finally appeared on the pages near the end of The Mating, I knew he had a story to tell! And of course, now that this book is done, I'm thinking about poor Bryan. He didn't get Elise, he didn't get Melody... There has to be someone out there for him? But who?

If you are interested, check out the next book in the Law of the Lycan series!

~ Nicky

Connect with Nicky Charles

Email me at
nicky.charles@live.ca

Visit my website:
http://www.nickycharles.com

Follow me on Facebook:
https://www.facebook.com/NickyCharles/

Books by Nicky Charles

Forever In Time

The Law of the Lycans series
The Mating
The Keeping
The Finding
Bonded
Betrayed: Days of the Rogue
Betrayed: Book 2 – The Road to Redemption
For the Good of All
Deceit can be Deadly
Kane: I am Alpha
Veil of Lies

Hearts & Halos
(Written with Jan Gordon)
In The Cards
Untried Heart